PROMISES...

To "Ma Bev"
...the best daycare provider in Atlanta. Thank you for taking the time to take a look at my work. I appreciate the support!

B.C. M[illegible]

PROMISES...

...sometimes they're better off broken

B.C. Meekins

A JayMay Publication

iUniverse, Inc.
New York Lincoln Shanghai

PROMISES…
…sometimes they're better off broken

iUniverse books may be ordered through booksellers or by contacting:

iUniverse
2021 Pine Lake Road, Suite 100
Lincoln, NE 68512
www.iuniverse.com
1-800-Authors (1-800-288-4677)

ISBN-13: 978-0-595-41853-4 (pbk)
ISBN-13: 978-0-595-67946-1 (cloth)
ISBN-13: 978-0-595-86198-9 (ebk)
ISBN-10: 0-595-41853-8 (pbk)
ISBN-10: 0-595-67946-3 (cloth)
ISBN-10: 0-595-86198-9 (ebk)

Printed in the United States of America

Acknowledgements & Thank you's

First and foremost, my savior Jesus Christ for giving me the gift of entertaining others with my words. My parents who are my heroes. My wife and kids who all this is for. Also, thank you to everyone that helped in this long process. There are so many of you to name. I'll try not to leave anyone out even though I know I will. Let's just start from the beginning. Tasha (my first fan), Tameka (because I know I'd hear about it if I didn't), Quan (even though I never heard if you ever finished it, lol)…my ACS people. Thank you for being the very first unofficial book club. The ones that were asking for chapters faster than I could write them. My ADP people…() the ones that bought up my first run of books. My unofficial editors, Tonaka, Ruby and my big bro Dwayne. My homegirl Tori for gracing my cover with her beautiful eyes. It's time to come up girl! A special thank you to Mrs. Diane Diederich for the cover background work. A wonderful photographer with amazing work. Just a huge THANK YOU to everyone that has encouraged me through the years as I finished my work. I wouldn't have been able to keep my focus without you and thank you all sooooo much for the praise and encouragement. I wanted to keep this as short and sweet as possible so for now I'll just say another big THANK YOU ALL and let it be done. Stay in touch with me through my website, www.bcmeekins.com and check for upcoming book releases. For you Myspacers, check me out at www.myspace.com/snoopdodub. Leave me a message, comment, complaint, praise or just shout out. It's whatever. I always want to hear from you guys. Also, check out my homegirl Tonaka Gary's poem at the back of the book. You can find her on Myspace too just go to my page and she's under my friend's list. If you like what you read, hit her up and let her know it. All us writers need a lil' praise every now and then. Well that's it for now. Just

stay posted and if you keep readin' em, I'll keep writin' em. Keep your eyes open and I'll give you something to look at.
Bless!

Lasaia: (pronounced la-sie-ya),
variation of the name Glasyia.
Meaning: The most beautiful seductive evil

That Night

Her hair brushed across his face. An orgasm began to build. She felt it, he knew it. Her arms had given way to ecstasy and she went limp on top of him, shaking. It was the third orgasm she had ever experienced. All given to her by him. This was the first time their bodies had met in this way, the first time her body had met any man in this way. She had heard stories of the pains a woman went through her first time but there was none. Her body accepted him and nothing but pleasure resonated through her frame. She screamed his name over and over. It was pleasure but her calls were more of a beckoning, her calling him to her.

Two becoming one.

Completing her in some way.

Teddy Pendergrass was on the radio demanding that some woman *Turn off the Lights*, as the scene unfolded. It was the same song that had filled the air the night they had tried this as teenagers. In a way they both felt like they were back in her bedroom 10 years ago.

They both wanted it.

They both needed it.

But, at this point, it was forbidden.

That probably made the encounter that much more intense. Marcus and Lasaia had been friends since they were 10 years old and now they were finally acting on the feelings that they both felt so many years before.

He flipped her over, got on top.

Dove inside of her over and over, making her body arch as her screams made their impressions on the walls around them.

Poetry couldn't depict the level of passion that flowed between them.

He was hers, she his.

Nothing else mattered.
Not then.

He was gentle with her.
He knew she was a novice.
Pleasure made its home on her face.
He pulled out after making her body vibrate one more time.
Plunged his face between her legs causing her to suck in as much oxygen as her lungs could hold. She gripped the back of his head like she was riding some kind of erotic bicycle.
Handlebars.
She needed something to hold onto while she road this rollercoaster of passion.
He flicked his tongue in and out of her and across her clitoris making her jerk back and forth like she was possessed by some kind of erotic demon. She hadn't felt anything like this before.
He inched backward until he found the edge of the bed and went to his knees on the floor, pulling Lasaia along with him the entire way. After a few more courses in the class of Licker-ature Marcus worked his way back up her body.
Face to face.
Eye to eye.
Mouth to mouth.
Her kisses her like butterfly wings.
Soft.
Beautiful.
"You've done this before." She whispered, with a giggle.
He smiled, kissed her again.
Entered her again.
Another deep inhalation.
Not many words had been said between them in the last 40 minutes. Just moans and groans of a passion that should not have been. Maybe 10 years ago, not now.
He grabbed her arms and wrapped them around his neck, gripped her thighs and rose to his feet, still inside her. Lasaia's head flew back as he went deeper. Her screams echoed in the huge bedroom as he lifted her up and down onto him, slamming her body against his.
It was like he was marking his territory but she was already his.
More than he knew.

She had waited 10 years for this moment and would have waited 10 more if she had to. To her, he was always the only man for her.

He walked her over to the sofa that was across the room and laid her down.

"Turn around." He said as he towered over her.

She gave him a flirtatious smile and did as she was told.

He knelt down and entered her from behind.

Lasaia threw her face into the cushion, trying to suppress the screams as she stroked in and out of her again.

Every part of her body tingled with each stroke.

"You ready for me to come?" Marcus said as if he would have been able to stop it if she said no.

"Yes baby, come inside me," she yelled as he continued to thrust. "I want to feel you come inside me."

Their simultaneous orgasm pushed through their bodies like an electric wave. He fell over on top of her, weak from the pleasure...still inside her. He could feel her internal muscles contracting against him, quivering. She shook under him, uncontrollably. After taking a few minutes of recoup time, Marcus picked up Lasaia's limp body and carried her to the bed. She was barely conscious. Passion had taken her to another plateau. This was their first time, her first time. No regrets on her end, on his...many.

It was forbidden.

Marcus was married, had been for 7 years. Two kids, girls. Would he want someone doing this to either of his daughters? What would his wife say, or worse do? None of that would matter for the next few minutes. He had no idea what he had gotten himself into. As he stood there looking at his affair the day they had found each other again ran through his mind.

One

"I don't like this Marcus."

"Come on baby, are we going to go through this again?" Marcus said shaking his head. He knew how paranoid his wife could get over the smallest thing.

"It's just two days; I'll be back Monday night."

"What if something happens to me or…or the girls, then what?"

"You're reaching now." Marcus said, still packing his bag.

Sherise crossed her arms as a silent sign of defiance and just looked at him. He could feel her heat vision burning a hole in his back. He knew she had that one raised eyebrow look as if she was thinking, *I'm what?* Before she could unleash a verbal attack, he stopped his progress and looked up at her.

"Baby, it's only 2 days and a football game. My brother just moved to Atlanta and I haven't seen him in 2 years. He has tickets to the Falcons and I've never been to the Dome before. It's only 6 hours away."

He almost had her calm then she slipped on a face that he knew all too well.

"You know how I feel about you hanging out with you brother."

Marcus zipped up his bag and let what his wife said register for a few seconds. A puzzled look visited his face.

"You can't be serious. Don't tell me you're going back ten years to find a reason to stop me from hanging out with my brother this weekend."

Her face changed quickly.

She realized how silly she was being.

"Well, he did convince you to cheat on me."

Marcus just looked at her, shook his head, and laughed.

"Baby that was 10 years, a marriage, and two kids ago. We were a couple for what, three weeks?"

He wrapped his arms around her.

"And he didn't 'convince' me. It was my mistake, all mine. It was the first time, the only time. Ok?"

She rested her head on his shoulder and settled into his soul.

"I still don't like it. I have a bad feeling about you going." She said, her head pressed against his chest.

He smiled and said, "You have a bad feeling about me going to the mail box."

She giggled and threw her arms around his neck and gave him a kiss.

"Ok, ok you're right. I want you to have a good time. We'll be fine. Go see your brother, have fun...good wholesome, married man fun."

They both smiled and shared a laugh as he threw a few more items into his bag. He gave her a silent nod of compliance and they walked out of the bedroom into the hall of their beautiful Mediterranean home. Hand in hand they walked along the open walkway overlooking the immaculate foyer. Cream-colored walls lined with pictures and paintings of their happy family greeted them as they reach the top of the cherry oak railed staircase.

They quickly shuffled down the steps and into the large family room where they found two of the most beautiful little girls God ever created.

"Girls, daddy's about to go." Sherise called out to them.

Lasaia looked up from her coloring book with her big beautiful brown eyes and immediately jumped up and ran to her daddy's side, her little green and orange hair balls bouncing with every step. He dropped his bag and scooped her into his arms.

"Do it dad, do it!!" she said grabbing onto her father's shoulders.

Marcus rolled his eyes pretending he didn't want to, then started spinning around and around in the large doorway. Lasaia began to laugh uncontrollably. She loved when her daddy did that. Sherise looked at the two of them and smiled.

"Are you going to be back for my birthday daddy?"

"Honey, I will be back on Monday. You're birthday isn't for another 3 weeks."

She let out a giggle as he put her down. She had been waiting on her 6th birthday like it was the last great thing on her life's "To Do" list. He knelt down and gave her a big kiss and a hug.

"Wait, I gotta get you something." Lasaia said darting off toward her coloring book on the floor.

She carefully ripped out the page she was working on and in almost a second flat she was back at her daddy's feet.

"Here Daddy, I made this for you." She said as she handed him a page with red ducks, a green fox, and blue grass...none of it all the way inside the lines.

"Oh sweetie, it's beautiful." Sherise said looking over her husband's shoulder. Her eyes beamed up at her mother and a bright smile skipped across her little lips.

"Yeah baby girl. This is amazing." Marcus said making her smile grow even bigger.

"You be good for your mom while I'm gone, ok?"

"Ok Daddy, and make sure you look for me a good birthday present."

"Ok little lady." Marcus said with a chuckle.

Lasaia darted back to her coloring book as Marcus folded up her picture and put it in his wallet. He looked over to another little person who didn't even seem to notice that he was in the room. He walked over and stood behind his two-year-old second born child. She stared at the television completely engulfed in *Sesame Street*. She just sat there rocking side to side as Elmo, Big Bird and Grover chanted out the letters of the alphabet.

"Angela?" He said softly, breaking her trance.

She tilted her head back, almost falling backwards but catching herself with her hands. A big, but not full-toothed, grin appeared on her face as she realized her daddy was standing there. She climbed to her feet and raised her hands signaling him to pick her up.

"You be good for your momma too, ok little bit?" Marcus said holding her in his arms.

The little one nodded her head and said, "K'".

He sat her down and she returned to her video as if nothing happened.

Marcus walked back to his wife and grabbed his bag. As they made it to the front door and Marcus grabbed the knob they heard the words, "You be good Daddy," run up behind them.

They just looked at each other and laughed.

"That's definitely your daughter." Marcus said opening the door.

"I like the way she thinks." Sherise said following him out.

They walked down their attractive walkway lined with cobblestone and Chinese lamps. The yard was perfectly manicured and a perfect compliment to the 5 bedroom 4 ½ bath house. They walked over to his pearl white Cadillac Escalade and he opened the door. Her shiny black Lexus GS500 sat in the garage still shining as if it had just come off the show room floor. There was no shortness of success in this family. He, the vice president of marketing for *Streamline* advertising, one of the most reputable advertising agencies in the southeastern United States. She, a hair salon owner known all throughout the city of Jacksonville. *Sherise's* was a local town favorite loved by all. If you needed a wrap, flip, weave, cut, shave, updo, downdo, Scooby-Doo, manicure, pedicure, all your cures…*Sherise's* was where you wanted to go

Marcus threw his bag in the passenger seat of his truck and turned back to her. She looked like she missed him already. Discontent was written all over her lovely face as he climbed into his truck. He gave her a kiss through the window, looked into her eyes and said, "Two days, that's it."

"I know, I know. I want you to go. Have fun. Be good daddy." she said not really meaning her words.

"Ooo girl, you know I like it when you call me daddy."

She laughed.

Their lips met again

Another sultry kiss.

An are-you-sure-you-wanna-leave-this-for-two-days kiss.

"I love you."

"I love you too."

She turned to walk back into the house. Marcus, being the playful person he was, couldn't leave without making her smile. He waited until she got a few more steps up the driveway and yelled out.

"I hate to see you go, but I love to watch you walk away."

She turned her head and laughed at him.

"Get outta here."

That's what he was waiting on. He loved every piece of his wife, from the tips of her toenails to the roots of her hair. He couldn't leave with the thought of her being upset riding shotgun. He smiled at a job well done as he pulled out of the driveway and onto the street. All he could think about was in the next few hours he would be with his brother.

Sherise walked back into the house and closed the door. She yelled out, "Who wants a snack," as she passed the family room. "I do, I do!!" could be heard echoing behind her as she entered the kitchen. She giggled and opened the door to the refrigerator. While she was cutting up some fresh fruit for the kids to snack on she happened to glance over at the breakfast table. Marcus's directions sat in the middle like they were a centerpiece.

"Great." She said in a disappointed whisper.

She walked over to the phone and dialed Marcus's cell phone number.

⚘ ⚘ ⚘

Marcus had his music blasting. Outkast was apologizing to *Ms. Jackson* for hurting her daughter as he bobbed his head to the beat. The music was so loud that he couldn't hear his phone ring and his voicemail picked up. Sherise left him a message.

A few minutes later Marcus pulled onto the interstate and turned the knob on the radio, quieting the music. He heard a chirp come from his overnight bag next to him. He reached over and unzipped the bag while trying to keep his eyes on the road. He fumbled around for a second or two and finally got his phone.

"Missed call?" he said to himself.

He dialed home.

"Hello?"

"More bad feelings?" he chuckled

"No, but guess what you forgot."

"What?"

"Some directions to a certain brother's house."

"What? Aw, damnit." Marcus said, looking around his car realizing she was right.

"You gonna come get them?"

"Nah, I'm on the interstate now. I'll…I'll just call him when I get close and have him talk me in."

"Ok, well I'm getting the girls a snack. Drive careful and call me when you get there."

"Ok baby, I will. Bye."

"Bye."

Marcus continued on his way to Atlanta, excited about the thought of seeing little his brother, Alonzo. He hadn't seen Alonzo since he walked across that stage at Florida A & M University's graduation 2 years ago. Alonzo was a business major and had recently opened his own nightclub. *Cloud 9* was the biggest, soon to be the hottest nightclub in Atlanta, Georgia. At least, if you asked Alonzo that's what he would tell you. But, he must have been doing something right. He kept a packed house, full of people spending big bucks, ever since the doors opened. It was the newest spot to see celebrities and local big timers. Politicians, judges, businessmen and businesswomen. People who pretty much ran the city. On any given night you were sure to see at least a handful of influential people getting their grove on, or their grove back. "Zo", as he liked to be called, was always sending his brother pictures of himself with different celebrities. He probably owed a lot of his success to the "Angels", his club promotion team. They brought in the big acts and were always at the club circulating through the crowd making sure all the people were happy…mostly the men, considering all of the "Angels" were women. The "Angels" were six of the most beautiful women to ever set foot on God's green earth. Zo constantly sent his brother pictures of them too. Marcus always had to delete those emails fairly quickly though. Sherise might have a few things to say about him getting pictures of other women. Zo always did know how to get people to party.

"Cloud 9" was an upscale, classy establishment that catered to a more sophisticated and older crowd. You could still catch a hip-hop vibe but it was more of a place where grown folks went to get their party. A place where you didn't have to worry about being caught in the middle of two groups of young knuckleheads fighting over sides of town that neither of them owned property on. Even though he was only 25 years old himself, he knew which crowd spent the most money. Alonzo was never a fool. He was known for always having some kind of scheme going…even back when they were kids in Albany, Ga. He was never involved in anything illegal, like drugs or robbery, but Alonzo knew how to keep his pockets filled. He was the little boy in middle school sold candy to other students in the halls between classes. He was the young man in high school that got ticket stubs from people at football games, and then sold them through the chain link fence to people for half price. He always had some kind of hustle. In college, he was the guy on campus that could hook anybody up with anything. You need a cell phone, calling card, a book for a class that's sold out, backstage passes to the homecoming concert, anything? Alonzo was your man. So this nightclub thing was right up his alley. Ruthie and Daniel Downing's kids had done well for themselves.

"Atlanta 20 miles…" Marcus whispered, exhausted from the trip.

He wasn't a road trip kind of guy and making the trip alone didn't make it any easier.

"Let me call this fool and see what he's doing." Marcus thought as he reached for his phone.

He flipped it open and dialed the number. All he heard was three quick beeps.

"What? I know damn well I ain't roaming." Marcus said to himself.

He tried again and got the same result. He looked at his phone and saw he had no signal. "Perfect." He whispered, frustrated.

Marcus figured he would just wait until he got a little closer to town and try again.

❧ ❧ ❧

As Marcus approached downtown Atlanta he grabbed his phone again. "Still no signal, what the hell is this?" Marcus really got frustrated. He saw an exit headed east and took it. He knew his brother lived somewhere in Decatur, and knew Decatur was East, but had no idea how to get there. He drove for what seemed like forever. Maybe it was fatigue, but it seemed like everything was starting to look the same.

"I know I've seen this already." He said to himself.

Marcus decided to take the next exit and ask for directions. He exited the highway, pulled into a Waffle House parking lot and parked his truck. He checked his watch.

"Damn, 7:30?" He said to himself.

He left at one o'clock and should have been at his brother's house by now. He knew Sherise was probably going out of her mind by now. He rushed into the restaurant and up to the counter. The waitress kept writing on the little pad in her hand and said, "What can I get cha'?"

"I don't need anything, but can I use your phone?"

She continued to scribble on her pad and still didn't make eye contact.

"Can't let you use the phone. It's against company policy."

Marcus tried to be polite but the stress of the road, the phone not working and the fact that he was lost was too much.

"Ma'am, I just got off the road from Florida. I don't know where I am and don't know how to get where I'm going. Can I please just use your phone to call my brother so he can tell me how to get to his house?"

The lady finally stopped writing on her pad and looked at him.

"Please, it will only take a second." He said practically begging with the lady.

She motioned for him to come around the counter and over to the phone in the corner by the table busing area. Marcus picked up the phone and dialed his brother's number. All he got was a message that said, "Your call can not be completed as dialed." He tried again and got the same result.

"Just not my night," Marcus whispered to himself. He walked back over to the lady and said, "Thanks for the phone. Can I get a cup of coffee?"

Marcus decided to sit, rest and try to come up with a way to get to his brother's house some how. He took a seat in a corner booth facing the large glass window. He stared out into the dark parking lot as one of the waitresses brought him a hot cup of coffee.

About halfway through his coffee, a brand new Jaguar pulled into the parking lot. The door popped open and out stepped a pair of the most beautiful legs Marcus had ever seen. The woman stepped from the car and closed the door. She had long silky black hair with highlights that seemed to be in every right place. She had on a tight, black, very form-fitting skirt and a half shirt with a low cut neckline that showed off her cleavage. She had lips so full it looked like it would take a whole paper towel to blot them...breasts so perfect she made Barbie dolls jealous...and an ass so big and round it looked like you could fit about three or four drinks on it comfortably. She had a small waist and a face so beautiful it made her body look average. Marcus couldn't take his eyes off of the beautiful creature.

"Helloooo ATL," he thought to himself.

He quickly reminded himself that he was married.

Marcus tried to play off his stare as she walked through the restaurant entrance. He started to sip his coffee over and over. The lady walked in and went to the register. The waitress said something to her and she had a seat at the counter. Marcus couldn't fight the urge to look again. He turned his head slowly, looking out the corner of his eye at first. She wasn't looking. Marcus turned his head to try and get a better look. Just as he turned his head and got a good look, the woman turned her head toward him and their eyes met. Marcus quickly turned back to his coffee feeling very high school-ish. The woman saw his adolescent act and just smiled and giggled a little.

Marcus took a look at his watch again. It was five minutes to eight now. He really needed to get going and find a working phone so he could call his brother. He took one big gulp of his coffee and didn't realize how hot it was until it singed all of the taste buds off of his tongue. He tried to stop from spitting it all over the couple in front of him and swallowed it down. It blazed a fiery trail down his throat and he felt his stomach heat up as it splashed down. Marcus slammed his fist down on the table trying to keep from screaming like a little girl in front of that room full of strangers. The vibration from the strike caused his cup and saucer to fall off the table onto the floor with a shattering crash. All eyes in the restaurant turned toward Marcus. He tried to play it off by coughing a little but it didn't work. Just a few seconds of stares and everything went back to normal.

"Are you alright sweetie?" one of the waitresses said as she walked over with a broom to sweep up the glass.

"I'm fine, I'm fine thank you. Look, I'm sorry. I broke your mug; please put it on my ticket."

The woman declined.

"You ain't the first and won't be the last, sugah." She said followed by a chuckle. Marcus didn't realize it but the woman he was watching before was now watching him. He settled his bill with the lady, thanked her again and before he turned to leave he heard the cook shout out a familiar name.

"Lasaia! Order for Lasaia Lewis!"

The woman Marcus couldn't keep his eyes off of stood to her feet and walked to the counter.

She paid for her order as Marcus just stood there in the middle of the restaurant in shock. His hands began to sweat and his pulse raced. The woman got her order and walked out the door without missing a step. Marcus, still frozen in time, snapped back to reality and darted out the door and chased her down.

"Excuse me, excuse me miss?" he said walking quickly behind the woman.

She looked back and slowed her gait.

"Yes?" she said in a sexy voice.

"Your name's Lasaia Lewis?"

"Do I know you?" she asked taking a closer look at him.

They both stared at each other for a few seconds in silence like they were trying to figure each other out.

"Are you from Albany?" He asked.

She looked a little closer at him and covered her mouth in shock.

She gasped and said, "Marcus?"

"Yeah."

She set her things on the trunk of her car and threw her arms around his neck and screamed.

"Oh my God, I can't believe you're here, what are you doing here?" she asked with tears forming in her eyes.

"I'm here to visit Alonzo, he just moved here like four months ago."

"What? Oh my God! I can't believe it…Where are you now?"

So many questions came to her at once that she stuttered to try and get them all out. Both of them were so excited they could barely speak.

"I live in Jacksonville now."

It had been almost 10 years since the two of them last saw each other. Lasaia had lived next door to Marcus and Alonzo back in Albany. She moved in when Marcus was about 7 years old. For the first couple of years she never really stepped outside of the house all that often. Marcus would see her in the halls at school, around lunch, sometimes a football or basketball game but that was about it. They never really talked at first. Not until he was about 10 years old. That was when they had their first real conversation.

♣ ♣ ♣

It was a cool fall night and Marcus's family was finishing up their dinner. His mother asked him to take the trash out back and he did as he was told. They kept the big trashcans next to the shed in the back yard. As soon as he stepped outside he heard his neighbors fighting as usual. All he could think was, "There they go again." It seemed like they fought every day and night since they had moved in 3 years earlier. They fought so much that people in the neighborhood had even gotten used to it. Marcus took the bags out and dumped them in the large containers, but before he could turn and go back he heard some noises coming out of their shed. He slowly tiptoed over to the metal doors and tried to peek through the crack. The closer he got, the clearer the sound became.

Marcus figured it was a neighbor's cat that got into the shed and couldn't get out. Peoples' cats where always getting into stuff and getting stuck around the neighborhood. Marcus couldn't see anything but darkness through the crack so he stuck his little skinny fingers in between the two metal doors and pulled them apart. There inside was a pretty little girl with a ripped shirt and a bruise on her shoulder. She was balled up in the corner crying into her hands. Marcus could barely make her out with only a little bit of moonlight shining in on her. She hadn't even heard Marcus outside and continued to cry. After he took his first step, she looked up. Tears were falling from her eyes so fast she looked like a fountain. He recognized her face right away. It was his neighbor. "Lasaia?" He said, as he got closer. "What's wrong?"

He sat down next to her and put his arm around her shoulder. In the past 3 years, he probably hadn't said much more then a combined total of 13 words to her. Tonight, he would beat that record.

Marcus was young but he was nobody's fool. He saw the bruise on her arm, heard the fighting in the background on that quiet night and saw tears flowing freely from her eyes. He knew what was up.

"You ok?" he asked.

She gave a silent nod between sobs. She had stopped crying by now. She just wiped her eyes and sniffed.

"You want me to tell my dad and mom?"

She just sat there with her head on his shoulder.

"Stay here; I'll go get my dad." He said getting up to his feet.

Before he could step one foot out of the shed she yelled out, "Nooo…wait."

He stopped.

"You can't tell them. You can't tell nobody. It'll just get worse if you tell." She said.

Marcus went back and sat down next to her.

"How long have they been doing this to you?" Marcus asked.

"No 'they'…HIM! I hate him. He ain't my real daddy noway. I hate him so much."

"How long?"

"I don't know, long as I can remember."

"What you gonna do?"

"Nothing I can do, my mom gets it worse than I do. I told her we should run away. She told me she tried that a few times, even before I was born and even when I was a baby. He always found us and she always let him come back. I guess she just stopped trying."

"You ever run away?"

"Nah, ain't got nowhere to run to. Plus, I can't leave my mom to face him alone."

"Why does he do that?"

"Drugs…alcohol…When he gets on that stuff he loses it."

"I think we should tell somebody."

"No, no, no. Please, I'm fine, see?"

Lasaia jumped up and stretched.

Marcus could see that it was still hard for her to move the arm with the bruise on it.

"You sure?" He asked

"Yeah, I'm ok. Sorry for hiding in your shed, alright? It was the only place I could find."

"No problem."

"Hey, do me a favor?"

"What?"

"Promise me you won't tell nobody about this."

"Why?"
"Just promise."
"Ok, I won't tell nobody."
"No you gotta promise."
"Ok. I *promise.* I won't tell nobody."
"Ok, thanks."

Lasaia darted out of the shed, into her backyard and around to her window on the back of her house. Marcus just watched from the open shed doorway. In less then a second she was up and in the window and out of sight. Looked like this was not the first time she had done that. Marcus was stunned at the whole idea of what he just experienced. His father always told him that his word was his bond and a man could have everything taken from him but he had to give up his word. He never told anyone about the conversation he had with Lasaia that night in his parents shed.

Marcus walked back into the house and slowly strolled across the kitchen floor as if everything was fine. His mother was washing the dinner dishes and said, "Boy…what was you doin' out there all that time?"
She sounded concerned and angry at the same time.
Marcus quickly remembered his promise and came up with an alibi.
"Miss Johnson's um…cat was stuck in the shed and I had to get it out." He said trying not to sound guilty.
His mom just looked at him and said. "Oh, well gon' in there and take ya' bath, It's almost time for bed. It's 8:15…"

Two

8:15. Marcus looked down at his watch and back up at the woman he had chased out of the diner. It was hard to believe that this was that little girl crying in my shed 19 or so years ago. Neither of them could hold back the fact that they were so happy to see each other again.

"Marcus, I hate to run but I came to get this for a friend. You have to give me your number or something so I can call you."

The excitement of the moment made Marcus forget that he had no clue where he was. He pulled out his palm pilot and showed her his brother's address.

"Do you know where this street is?" He asked.

He explained how he had been riding down I-285 for over an hour and still couldn't find his way.

"That's because 285 is just a big circle around the city." She said laughing.

"Oh that's funny huh?" He said trying to be serious and laughing right along with her.

She took out a pen and wrote him some directions on the back of one of her Waffle House napkins. As she was writing Marcus pulled out one of his business cards and handed it to her when she finished.

"Oooo Vice President of marketing huh? My little Marcus is a big man now huh?" she said.

He laughed.

"I got something for you too." She said flirtatiously.

She went to the driver's side door and opened it. She bent over the seat and reached for something on the dashboard. Marcus couldn't help himself. He remembered his wife but he had to sneak a peek at the *new and improved* Lasaia.

Poets were known for the many words they used to describe the minutest details. Too bad Marcus wasn't a poet.

The only word that popped in his head was, *Daaaammmnn!*

He couldn't get over how fine she had gotten over the years.

The rest of her perfect body reappeared as Marcus averted his eyes just as she spun around to face him. She walked back over to him and handed him a business card.

"Intrigue Modeling Agency? Owner: Lasaia Lewis. Wow, you own a modeling agency?" Marcus asked.

"Yep, you like?" She asked with a giggle.

"Very nice…Well look I'm not going to hold you up. I know you have things to do, but it was great seeing you again."

"Well, why don't you call me tomorrow and we can hook up or something. We have a lot of catching up to do."

"Ok, I'll do that."

"Promise?" She asked moving closer to him.

"Guaranteed or your money back." Marcus said trying to keep a cool head while this beautiful woman stood less than an inch away from him. She gave him a big hug and a kiss on the cheek.

"Ok well I will wait for your call." She said while she grabbed her stuff off of the trunk and headed for her door.

"Bye bye." She said before getting in the car.

Marcus managed to barely get out a goodbye before she closed her door and started the engine. She backed out of the space, gave him a quick wave and pulled off into the night.

Marcus stood in his spot next to her space for a few seconds before turning toward the diner. Every male eye in the restaurant was focused on him like his name was Goldie, from *The Mack.* They didn't know the two of them went back farther than candy necklaces. Two brothers were giving him the thumbs up at a job well done and one guy was getting chewed out by the woman sitting across the table. Marcus just walked to his truck and got in.

Marcus followed the directions, and even though they weren't perfect they did get him in the general area. He was able to find his way to his brother's street and found the house. Marcus pulled into the driveway and parked his truck in Alonzo's grass. He sat back in the seat and thought about what had happened.

It was 8:45. Marcus jumped back into reality. He gathered his things and rushed to the front door. Alonzo's house was a little more modest than his but it was nice. Nothing flashy. Alonzo was never in one place long enough to pick a "dream home." It was just a quaint little 3 bed 2 ½ bath split-level home. The grass in the front yard was almost a foot high. He probably hadn't cut it since he moved in. A small backyard with a fence could be seen as he walked up. Alonzo probably had a Rottweiler or two back there. His candy blue Suburban was parked in the driveway. Marcus remembered that truck from the pictures his brother had sent him. Alonzo had every feature available on that vehicle. TV's, Playstation2, spinning rims, and a sound system so loud that you can hear him coming from at least ½ a mile away. Alonzo might not have the best looking house, but if you saw him in the streets somewhere you swear he lived in a mansion or was a rap star or something. Hood rich was his middle name and ghetto fabulous, his first.

Marcus rang the doorbell and heard it echo through the house. After a few seconds, he heard footsteps toward him. That sound was followed by the click of the lock and the door opening. His brother just smiled and shook his head as he opened the glass storms door.

"Ooooooooo," was the first word out of Alonzo's mouth before he started laughing. He used to do that back when they were kids whenever Marcus was about to get in trouble.

"Man, it's about damn time. Your ole lady been callin' here like every ten minutes talking about, 'Is he there yet…Is he there yet?'"

Alonzo continued to laugh as he moved to the side to let is big brother in. They gave each other a quick pound followed by a hug and Marcus followed Alonzo. They walked though the front hallway towards the living room.

"Man that was one crazy ass ride. I left the directions on the table at the house and then tried to call you on the cell when I got in town and couldn't get a signal. I rode around lost for about an hour, then almost had to bribe the lady at the Waffle House just to let me use the phone…then finally got her to let me use the phone and I dialed your number and got an error message." Marcus said giving him the highlights.

"Oh you have to dial the area code round here. Can't just dial the seven digits and get through."

"Now you tell me. Don't do me much good now though."

Alonzo just laughed.

They continued to walk through the house toward the living room. Marcus heard the TV getting louder as they got closer.

"Have a seat man, I'll be right back. You want a beer?" Alonzo asked as he pointed into the room.

"Yeah whatever you got."

Marcus walked into the living room and dropped his bag in the corner. He turned around to see a fine brown skin female seated on the couch with her legs crossed.

Damn do they breed fine ass woman in ATL?, Marcus thought to himself.

She was just sitting there looking up at him as he turned. Marcus quickly reverted back to his gentleman side.

"Hey, how you doing? I'm Marcus." He said walking over to shake the young woman's hand. She stood up and pulled down her skirt, hiding her goodies. She offered him her hand and said, "Hi, I'm Lisa."

Alonzo walked into the room.

"Here man." He said handing Marcus a cold beer and they all had a seat.

"Lisa this is Marcus, Marcus…Lisa." Alonzo said barely introducing the two.

"Yeah we just met." She said.

The three of them sat there for a second engaging in a little small talk.

After about 20 seconds the phone rang. "Twenty bucks says that's your wife." Alonzo said as he jumped up to get the phone. Marcus just sat back in the recliner and closed his eyes.

"Hello…nah nah he's here now, just walked in the door…aight…aight hold up."

Marcus heard the one-sided conversation and knew who it was. Alonzo handed him the phone and sat down picking at his brother to his female friend.

"Hey baby." Marcus said sounding exhausted.

"Uh huh, I'm just being paranoid huh?" She said.

"Ha, ha. Man, that was a crazy ride. Wait until I tell you all the stuff I went through when I got to Atlanta."

"Like what?"

"It's a long story but I will tell you tomorrow. Oh and I have a surprise too. You will never guess who I ran into on my way here."

"Who?"

"I told you I'll tell you tomorrow. How are the girls?"

"You can't just say something like that and change the subject. The girls are fine. Angela is sleep and Lasaia is taking her bath right now. She's about to get in the bed too. Those two really know how to work my nerves. Tell me!"

Marcus laughed and said "Nope…na…since you want to make fun of me you gonna have to wait until tomorrow to find out."

"Ooooh that's real messed up. You know I'm too nosey for that…Well I'm glad you made it up there ok."

Marcus heard a loud, "Mooommmieee," in Sherise's background.

"Lawd, what this girl done got into?" Sherise said.

Marcus chuckled

"You ok?" Sherise yelled to her.

Marcus tried to hear what was going on. He heard a muffled reply.

"Yeaaa, I dun a to el."

"What happened?" Marcus asked trying to figure out his daughter's problem.

"She says she doesn't have a towel. I'm gonna go tend to *your* daughter and get her ready for bed. You want me to call back?"

"Nah, I'm bout to get some rest, that ride beat me up."

"Ok, well call me tomorrow morning, and I want to know what happened."

"Alright babe."

"Love you"

"Love you too"

"Goodnight"

"Nite"

Marcus hung up the phone and placed it down on the coffee table. He looked at his watch and sat back in the comfortable leather recliner again. He took a deep breath. The kind of breath you take when you finally complete a long, arduous task.

"9:07, It took me 8 damn hours to make a 6 hour trip. Next time you move, move somewhere a brotha can find you." Marcus said joking.

"Don't get mad at me because you left your direction, that's your fault. Shouldn't have been moving so fast. Where you been all this time anyway?" Alonzo asked.

"Man, I don't even know. I was at Waffle House a few exits up from this one. I got onto 285 and started riding East, then that shit said 285 North, then West, then South and then East again. I passed the airport, and 75/85 like twice. I'm in there driving like, 'What the fuck???'"

Alonzo and Lisa both burst out laughing as Marcus continued with his story. "Then I take this exit and pull up into Waffle House and just about had to strong arm rob the place just to use the phone."

Alonzo, still laughing from before, said, "Aaaah man, you know 285 just goes around the city right?"

"Yeah genius, I do now. See, this is the kind of stuff you need to tell people who have never been here before but thanks, seriously, thanks for the update." Marcus said.

He was glad to see his little brother again, even though he was joking on him. "Ok, ok, ok...So how did you find your way here then?" Alonzo asked.

"I'm getting to that part...So, I'm sitting in Waffle House trying to figure out how to get to your house right?

Alonzo interrupted again.

"Why ain't you just ask somebody in the Waffle House?"

"Man didn't I just tell you I had to just about bribe the lady to use the phone. If she get that 'iffy' about a phone that ain't even hers...you know I didn't want to ask for no directions. Anyway, I'm sitting in Waffle House drinking some coffee and thinking right? I look out the window and this tight ass Jag' pulls into the parking lot. The door opens and this fine ass woman steps out, I'm talking finer then cat hair sliced twice type fine. She comes in the Waffle House and I'm just sitting there peeking out the corner of my eye." Marcus reenacted the night's events just as they happened. He told them about how he broke the mug and then chased the woman out of the diner.

"And you won't guess who it was." Marcus said waiting for Alonzo to guess.

"Some video hoe?" Alonzo said shrugging his shoulders.

Lisa slapped him across the arm for his statement and Alonzo looked at her confused.

"Lasaia!" Marcus said, sitting back in the chair like he was gloating.

"Lasaia...Lasaia," Alonzo said over and over, almost in a whisper, "Lasaia? Your daughter?"

"Yeah," Marcus said with sarcasm written all over his face, "Yeah I saw my 5 year old drivin' a Jag in a Waffle House parking lot in Atlanta. No ya' dumb mutha...Lasaia...from back in the day, in Albany. I swear for somebody with a degree you slower than a constipated turtle." Marcus said.

"Ooooh, whaaa...damn where you see her at?" Alonzo asked.

"I just told...Waffle House fool. How the hell you graduate. Ok, let me break it down. I ran into Lasaia, from back in the day, our neighbor, not my daughter, at Waffle House. She's the one who gave me directions to your house, and that's how I got here." Marcus said finishing his story.

Lisa just sat back and laughed as the two brothers went back and forth. She could tell that they had always been like this.

"Man, I ain't seen her since…since yall's graduation. How she doin'?" Alonzo asked.

"She must be doing damn good. She drivin' a brand new Jaguar and owns a modeling agency."

"Modeling agency?"

"Yeah, she gave me her card and everything." Marcus said while digging through his pocket for the card.

He passed it to Alonzo.

"Intrigue modeling? Where do I know this name? Oh, these are the people that some of the 'Angels' go through for modeling gigs and shit. I ain't know Lasaia owned the company. That's wild." Alonzo handed the card back to Marcus.

"Aight shawty, let's ride." Alonzo said standing to his feet.

"Ride? Ride where?" Marcus asked.

"Cloud 9 playa, gotta make a stop by the money maker." Alonzo said while helping Lisa to her feet.

"Man I'm tired. I just got off the road. My six hour drive just…"

Alonzo stopped him before he got his rant started.

"Don't even try it. You were supposed to be here two hours ago. You drove away your rest time. Anyway, I already told everybody my big brother was coming through with me tonight. We'll only be there like 20 minutes, I promise. I want you to meet my people. Come on man."

Alonzo and Lisa walked through the house headed for the front door. Marcus took a breath and let out a low moan.

"Come on nigga." Alonzo yelled from the other end of the house.

Marcus climbed to his feet and caught up to the two of them.

The trio climbed into Alonzo's truck and a few seconds later were on the street headed for the club. Alonzo pumped up the music and they rode through the streets of Decatur. About fifteen minutes later, they pulled into the parking lot of Alonzo's club…

Cloud 9

It looked pretty much like every other club from the outside. It was a grey-bricked building about the size of a mini warehouse. Nothing special about the outside appearance. The two things that brought out its look were the red carpet out front and the rain guard like the ones found at ritzy hotels in New York City.

The huge neon 'Cloud 9' sign woke up as the small group approached the front door. Alonzo handed his keys to the valet and the young man took them as if he had been standing in that spot waiting for Alonzo all night.

"Usual spot boss?" He asked.

"Yeah." Alonzo said passing the guy and shaking his hand.

"What's up boss?" said the gigantic bouncer standing at the entrance to the club. His voice was so deep it seemed like it made the glass double doors vibrate. He was dressed in an expensive looking black and navy pin striped suit, which was perfectly pressed in every seam. He was clean but if worse came to worse he looked like he could break out of it like *The Hulk* and handle whatever the situation at hand was.

"What's going on Ricky?" Alonzo said as the giant opened the door for them.

"Nothing much, just the usuals." He replied.

"This is my older brother I was telling yall about." Alonzo said pointing at Marcus.

Marcus offered his hand to the giant, reluctantly. It looked like a light shake from him could dislocate a shoulder easily. They shook hands and Alonzo said, "You be safe tonight man."

The three of them walked through the door and into the front area of the club.

The lobby looked like a smaller version of a lobby from a five-star hotel. From the mini palm trees, to the large mirrors on every wall. A small fountain of a man and woman intertwined in each other was in the middle of the room and a chest high counter where you would go to pay for your entrance into the club was to the right. Alonzo even had fog machines that were set up to keep a thin layer of smoke on the floor so it was like you were walking on a cloud. Marcus was impressed with his little brother already and he hadn't even made it inside the club yet. There were three women behind the counter in front of them.

"Hey Zo." They all seemed to say in unison.

"What up yall?" Alonzo replied.

These three women did nothing all night but take money.

"This is my brother I told yall I was bringing through tonight."

Marcus greeted the three pretty young women with a smile and a short wave and the small party moved on.

"See yall later." Alonzo said before turning to walk into the club.

Now, there were three ways to party in 'Cloud 9'. You could just pay the cover, which let you on the main level of the club with the dance floor and bar and the usual club atmosphere. You could go for the V.I.P. treatment, which allowed you to go upstairs and mingle with some of Atlanta's celebrity elite. Or, you could get the V.I.P. Deluxe. This allowed you to be upstairs with the elite as well but you also got several other special options. You got four free bottles of any liquor of your choosing, and a corner of the club would be roped off so only the people you wanted to come around you would be allowed in. Each V.I.P. Deluxe area had its own bouncer that stood guard out front and allowed only people on your list, or people you gave "Permission To Enter" passes to, access to your V.I.P. section. These were passes that you could carry with you around the club and give to people should you want them to come to your V.I.P. section. You also got your own waitress who would get drinks for you and your party should you make it through your four bottles. There were two more bars on either side of the upstairs V.I.P. section so that people didn't have to go downstairs for drinks. Since there are only four of these V.I.P. deluxe sections available, they were usually booked weeks in advance and mostly only by the big names of ATL. But, for the small price of five hundred dollars you could be treated with the highest level of class 'Cloud 9' had to offer.

Alonzo's club was about as high tech as a nightclub could get. There were security cameras throughout the facility and customers even had the ability to instant message their requests to the DJ from terminals in a few locations around the bars. Alonzo really made his club a place you could relax and have fun.

Alonzo, Lisa, and Marcus walked through the club lobby and through another set of glass sliding doors with the words "CLOUD NINE" engraved in cursive in the glass. The inside of the club was a big open space with a stage at one end. The floor right in front of the stage was a huge wood paneled area which was the dance floor. There were two other wood paneled dance floors on opposite sides of the club for people to use. There were tables with chairs all over the place and even some vinyl couches and love seats for people to get comfortable. There was a huge rectangle shaped bar in the middle of the room, lined with bar stools and about six flat screen TV's hung from the sides. People could go to the bar and sit and have a drink or they could have the waitress bring their drinks to their table.

The DJ booth was to the right of the stage but the DJ hadn't come in to work yet so there was no music playing. 'Cloud 9' had all the usual club amenities. There were strobe lights, fog machines, bubble machines, and even confetti droppers for certain holidays and parties like New Years Eve.

As they passed through the doors there were two flights of steps to the immediate right and left. Those led to the V.I.P. section. V.I.P. was just an extended balcony of sorts that over looked the lower level. The only part of the club that V.I.P. didn't cover was the stage, so it lined the club in a "U" of sorts. To prevent anyone from getting too drunk and falling over the rail or getting in a fight and getting thrown over, Alonzo installed a series of thick glass windows that lined up with the floors of the upper level. It was strong enough to handle a load but was not really designed for people to stand on. Alonzo had fog machines installed in the sides of that too so he could make it look like there was a big floating cloud in V.I.P.

Alonzo and Marcus walked through the club as Lisa walked off to talk to a friend of hers at the bar. Alonzo introduced his brother to everyone he passed as they made their way behind the DJ booth. Marcus had no idea where they were going. Alonzo looked like he was headed straight for a dead end until he reached out and pressed on the jet black wall. A door seemed to magically swing open as he pressed and walked through. It didn't even look like there was a door back there.

"Come on man." Alonzo said looking back at his brother.

Marcus just chuckled to himself and followed his brother through the secret door.

Behind the wall was a hall which led to different offices and things for the employees. Offices, break room, restrooms…things like that. Marcus was becoming more impressed with his brother by the minute. This club had everything. Even a shower in both bathrooms. Why? That was anybody's guess…but maybe it would be needed for some reason. The two brothers walked into Alonzo's office and had a seat.

"Damn baby bro, you doin' the damn thing ain't you?"

Alonzo just smiled and sat down in his chair.

"I do what I can." Alonzo said in a humble tone. "I just wanna hollah at the Angels before we dip so I can tell them the game plan for this coming week. We about to take over for real bruh." Alonzo said.

He reached over and grabbed a miniature Falcons football from the corner of this desk and tossed it at Marcus, "You ready for the game this Sunday?"

"Most definitely." Marcus said.

"I mean it's just a pre-season game but we got some good seats so it should be straight." Alonzo said.

"I don't care if it's a game between the kids of the players; I just want to go to the Dome." Marcus said.

Alonzo laughed and then there was a knock on the door.

"Come on." Alonzo yelled out.

In stepped all six of the infamous Angels. These women were incredible. Marcus remembered them from the pictures but those images on his computer hadn't done them justice. They were in no way short of perfection. They weren't just all looks either. These women had brains and beauty. They were partly responsible for the success of the club and Alonzo knew it. He paid them well and that was exactly how they did their job. Fate must have brought the 7 of them together. It couldn't have been a coincidence. Their names were **A**ngie, **N**eecee, **G**ina, **E**rica, **L**achelle, and **S**tacy. The first letter in each of their names spelled out A.N.G.E.L.S. Alonzo went down the lineup as they each walked over toward the desk.

"Yo man, if you want, you can go get a drink or something at the bar. We gonna just be in here talking 'bidness for a minute, then we'll ride." Alonzo said as the girls took a seat.

Marcus left his little brother to his business and strolled back out into the club.

The DJ was in the booth getting the sound system warmed up. The music came through the speakers so clear and distortion free that it wasn't hard to tell that this system was quality. Marcus sat at the bar and took in the whole scene around him. He was really impressed at his little brother's vision. It really looked like a place you could have a good time. It had a comfortable feel to it and that's what was needed in a club. The bartender walked over to Marcus and asked, "What can I getcha' brotha'?"

"Just a beer will be fine."

The bartender gave him a bottle.

"What's the damage?" Marcus asked pointing at the beer with his wallet in his hand.

The bartender started to laugh.

"You think I'm gonna charge my boss' brother?"

"You know who I am?" Marcus asked the man.

"Man everybody that works here know you, your brother talks about you all the time. Whenever we have a meeting he always tells us about something you or your ole man taught him. He really looks up to you."

The bartender told Marcus to enjoy his drink and if he needed anything to just flag him down. Marcus turned around on his stool and smiled. He had no idea he had that type of affect on his little brother.

Marcus sat on the stool bobbing this head to the music and enjoying a few more drinks. About 40 minutes passed and the club heads began to file in a few at a time. It was still early for the club scene but the dance floors were even beginning to get some use. Lisa walked up on Marcus and had a seat on the stool next to him.

"Hey." She said tapping him on the shoulder.

"What's up?" Marcus said taking a sip of his beer.

"You like?" She asked referring to the club.

"This is nice. I like it. I'm not really a club person but I could chill in a place like this."

"Yeah it's cool. Your brother really knows how to throw a party." She said.

A little more time passed and the club really started to fill up. Alonzo's twenty minutes had turned into about an hour and a half. The dance floors were beginning to pack in and the DJ was cutting up some hits on the turntables. Marcus looked all around the club and saw nothing but fine women everywhere. It was like there was a group of judges outside that only let in the house wreckers. He had not been one place in ATL yet that he hadn't seen beautiful women. Lisa started bouncing on her bar stool to the music. A sexy woman in a skintight cat suit walked up to the two of them.

"Heeeey Lisa girl." She said.

"What's up Tracy?" Lisa said slapping her five.

"Girl it is gettin' thick in here," her eyes roamed over to Marcus and got stuck, "and who is *this*?"

"Marcus." He said extending his hand.

She put her hand in his and he raised it to his mouth and kissed it.

"Mmh…a man with some class…I like that." She said giving him a flirtatious stare.

Lisa reached her hand out and started rubbing Marcus's chest.

"No no girl…this one is taken." Lisa said breaking her connection.

"That's too bad…too too bad." Tracy said, her eyes never leaving his. "I'll holla at you girl, you already got your prey for the night. I'm still on the hunt."

She gave Marcus a quick wink and walked off. Marcus eyes were glued to her backside like if he looked away a bomb would go off, and far be it for him to risk the lives of others.

"Uh uun, you need to stop." Lisa said laughing at him.

"What?"

"Your wife is gonna beat you up, that's what."

"Anyway, I'm a man. We can't help it. It's like yall and yall mood swings. It's hormonal."

"Hormonal? Really?"

"Yeah hormonal…see, testosterone is a hormone just like estrogen, estrogen causes yall to act crazy and testosterone causes us to act crazy. I mean it's all about self-control. If you have self-control, you're cool. I can look all day long, as long as I don't touch. I'm straight. Marriage is like a diet. When you on a diet, you can still go in McDonald's. You just can't order anything. You have to be able to control the testosterone."

"Ok, well when your wife beats the testosterone outta you, don't say I didn't warn you." She said with another laugh.

Lisa couldn't control the juke bone in her body any longer and looked over at Marcus. "You wanna dance?" She asked. Marcus threw his hands up as if to say, *Sure why not*. They quickly stepped over to the dance floor and started to dance. The club got more and more packed by the minute and even V.I.P. was filling up. Marcus and Lisa stayed on the dance floor for a long time just dancing and having a good time laughing at each other. They had a dance contest between the two of them and even got some folks to participate in the infamous *Soul Train* line. Alonzo came out of nowhere and grabbed his brother by the shoulder.

"Couldn't fight that *Cloud 9* feelin', huh?" He said in Marcus's ear.

Lisa grabbed her man and pulled him on the dance floor and started grinding all over him. Alonzo looked surprised at first but just threw his hands on her hips and went with the flow. Marcus just grinned at how his little brother had stolen his dance partner and headed back to the bar.

He grabbed a seat and ordered another drink. Even though it was a different bartender, she knew who he was too and refused to accept his money. Tracy reappeared out of nowhere and stopped right in front of Marcus. It was almost like she materialized out of thin air.

"I see you lost your date," she whispered in Marcus's ear as she looked at Lisa and Alonzo on the dance floor, "You need a new one?" Marcus was flattered by the advance but decided it would be best to tell her the truth.

"She's not really my date. That's my brother's girl. She was just saying that because I'm married." Tracy looked disappointed but still kept her confidence up.

"Well tell your wife she is a lucky woman…and maybe I'll see you next lifetime." She said with another wink as she walked off. Marcus just smiled and turned back to his drink.

Alonzo was finally able to get Lisa off the dance floor and back to the bar. She may have stopped dancing but she was still all over him, kissing him on his neck…a sexual vampire.

"You ready to go bruh, the Angels got the run of the show for the rest of the night." Alonzo said.

"I'm ready when you ready." Marcus said.

The three of them walked out the club and into the lobby. It was 1:15 a.m. according to the huge glass mirror clock on the wall behind the three women they saw earlier. There were still so many people trying to get in that all three of the women were busy taking money and handing out passes. The trio walked through the crowd and out the front door.

"Don't hurt nobody out here tonight Ricky." Alonzo said to the doorman as he handed his ticket to the valet parking attendant. Ricky just laughed at Alonzo and said, "I won't, unless they make me."

They both got a laugh out of that. Lisa was still stuck to Alonzo's neck like she had been bitten by a snake and his neck contained the antidote. A few seconds later the valet pulled Alonzo's Suburban up to the curve in front of them and jumped out. That was an all-eyes-on-me moment for Alonzo. Money in his pocket, a beautiful woman pretty much throwing herself at him and a ride that had even the big-timers in the line jealous.

He loved it. The three of them climbed into the truck and started on their short journey home.

Fifteen minutes in the opposite direction and they were pulling back into Alonzo's driveway. The three of them staggered into the house like they were about to pass out. Alonzo showed his brother to his bathroom and bedroom and gave him some linen for a shower. Marcus grabbed his bag from the living room and opened it on his bed. He pulled out some shorts and a t-shirt to wear to bed and headed for the shower. That was one of the best showers he had ever felt in his life. It was like he was washing all the pains of the day away.

Marcus passed by his brother's room as he left the bathroom. He grinned as he heard a few moans and groans coming from the room. He knew what was happening on the other side of the door. He chuckled and shook his head while he walked to his room. He threw his dirty clothes in a corner and jumped on the bed. He relaxed and let his body sink into the mattress. He stared at the ceiling and thought about all the crazy things that went on that day…especially the fact that he ran into Lasaia. He replayed that meeting over and over in his mind, until he rolled over and put an end to a long day.

Three

Marcus slipped out of reality and made his way to dreamland. He dreamt of himself as a kid. After his run in with Lasaia that night in the shed he seemed to see her more often. He didn't know if it was the fact that he was looking for her more often, or if she was looking for him but he didn't mind. She would speak to him at school now and even wait for him some days after school so they could walk home together. The two of them started to become pretty good friends. Marcus was someone she could talk to after she would get into it with her stepfather. He constantly begged her to let him tell someone but Lasaia would always remind him that he promised not to so he never did.

One Sunday afternoon, Marcus and Alonzo were out in front of their house playing basketball. Lasaia saw them from just inside her screen door and stepped out onto her porch. She watched the two of them for a minute then kicked her meekness to the curb and started on her way over to them. Marcus saw her coming and tried to play off his excitement the way most young boys did, by ignoring her. She walked over and sat in the grass across the driveway from where they were playing. Marcus saw his chance to show off for someone and started using his size to dominate his younger brother. After several fake outs and made shots, Alonzo finally stole the ball from his big brother. He did a cross over that caused Marcus's ankles to buckle and he fell down to his knees. With his brother down and his chance to score in front of him, Alonzo went for the shot.

SWISH

Alonzo threw his arms up in triumph. The score was well in Marcus's favor but at that point, it didn't even matter. All that was heard was an, "Ooooh" from the single audience member followed by a giggle. Marcus got up off the ground and grabbed the basketball from beneath the basket, lodged it under his arm and looked over at Lasaia. She looked surprised as if she couldn't believe she actually had the nerve to make that noise. All she could do was display a little nervous smile and stay silent. Marcus walked over to her and said, "What you 'ooooh'in' about?" with an embarrassed tone in his voice.

She just looked up at him and said, "You just got schooled by your little brother," with a little more confidence.

"You think you can do better?" He said while bouncing the ball in front of her.

"I can do better then that." She said standing to her feet.

"Bring it on then." He said as he bounced the ball to her.

Lasaia caught the ball and at that moment realized that she has no idea what to do with it. She understood how the game was played but she had no idea how to dribble or shoot or anything. Until Marcus became her friend, outside activities were not even in her vocabulary.

Before they could get their game going three of Marcus's friends came riding up on their bikes. "Sup yall?" One of the boys asked putting his kickstand down.

"Sup Calvin?" Marcus replied.

Lasaia slipped back onto the grass with the basketball and breathed a sigh of relief.

"What yall up to?" Calvin asked walking over to them.

"Nothing man, just shooting some ball. What yall doin'?"

Calvin looked over at Lasaia sitting on the grass holding his friend's ball. Marcus never understood why but Calvin found pleasure in picking on Lasaia. Even before she would talk to them he would always start rumors about her in school and tell people she was dirty and all kinds of things that he had no proof about. Marcus never understood how someone could not like another person they didn't know anything about. He was constantly protecting Lasaia from this him.

The miniature bully walked over to Lasaia sitting on the ground and said, "What you know bout b-ball?" Before Lasaia could react, he reached down and grabbed the ball from her hands and started bouncing it, never taking his eyes off hers. She just looked up at him and didn't say a word. She didn't know what to say. She never had the option of defending herself. All she knew was submission. Marcus walked over and took the ball from Calvin and threw it to his little brother.

"She know enough. She just beat me in one on one." Marcus said breaking Calvin's staring contest with Lasaia. Calvin looked at the two of them and started laughing.

"Yeah right. Whatever man, yall wanna come wit' us?"

"Come wit' yall where?"

"We goin' over to the old Carter place. Mikey was over by there the other day and he said he heard something moving around in there."

"Ain't that were that guy got killed?" Lasaia asked nervously.

Calvin saw his opportunity to get under her skin.

"Yeah his wife went crazy in there and stabbed him in his sleep like twenty times. Then shot herself in the head. I heard at night you can still hear them in there fightin'. We goin' over there now." Calvin said trying to scare the already frightened Lasaia.

Lasaia's heart moved up into her throat. She just sat there looking at Calvin with fear in her eyes.

Marcus stepped in between them.

"Nah man, we ain't goin' over there"

"What?? You scared? That's cool, I wouldn't want you to start crying in front of your girlfriend." Calvin said walking back over to his bike.

"Scared? I ain't scared of nothing." Marcus said, "Probably ain't nothing in there but a buncha bums anyway."

Marcus hated to be called a chicken.

"Well come on then. Show me there ain't nothing in there." Calvin said egging Marcus on.

Marcus walked over and got his bike from in front of the house.

"I wanna go, I wanna go!!" Alonzo said excited about going anywhere with the bigger kids.

"No, you stay here."

"Aw, come on."

"No, Zo".

"Aww Man, yall don't never let me go nowhere." Alonzo said pouting as he grabbed the ball and headed for the front door.

Lasaia climbed to her feet and slowly started to walk toward her house hoping no one would pay her any attention and they would go on their merry little way. No such luck.

"Where you goin'?" Marcus said as he passed her with his bike.

He kept his voice down so the other boys wouldn't hear.

"I don't know about this Marcus." She said looking like she was about to burst into tears.
"Come on, ain't nothin' in there. Plus they gonna think I'm a punk if we don't go. Do it for me."
Lasaia was scared out of her mind and it took everything she had not to break down and run home crying. It was getting darker and darker every few minutes and that didn't help her in making a decision. She didn't want to go, but she didn't want to take a chance at upsetting the one person who had actually paid her some attention in the last few years. Lasaia looked into Marcus's eyes. Tears had started building a home in her eyes.
"Promise me you won't leave me in there." She said, her voice wavering.
"I promise."
"Yall comin' or what?" Calvin said sitting on his bike looking at the two of them. Lasaia finally gave in and jumped on the seat of Marcus's bike and held on to his waist.

The five of them rode off down the street and a few minutes later were standing in front of an old two-story condemned building. Half of the windows were boarded up and the other half was broken. Old torn pieces police tape were still flapping in the breeze from a few places around the property. The yard looked like it hadn't been cut since years before the house was empty. The small party hiked through the grass and onto the porch. The closer they got the more scared they became.
"Open the door." Calvin said to one of the other boys.
"You open it." He answered, nervously.
The two of them went back and forth for a minute and Marcus finally walked over to the door and turned the knob it.
"Yall some punks" He said as he pushed his way inside. The door was barely on the hinges from where the police had kicked it in and scrapped across the floor as it opened. The five of them walked inside the decaying house. Even though they were only about 3 years old when the house was abandoned it seemed like the house hadn't been used in decades. There were spider webs in every corner of each room and the setting sun cast an eerie shadow through the windows. They all walked around in silence, each of them taking baby steps trying to wait and see who would be the first hero. Lasaia clung to Marcus's arm like vice grips. The wooden floors made an unearthly creaking sound with every step they took as they made their way to the kitchen. All of their hearts were beating so hard it seemed like they could hear the sound coming from their chests. The

sun finally disappeared for its daily rest, and darkness stepped in for the evening shift.

The small party filed into the kitchen one at a time. They were all still in awe and hadn't said a single word since they had come through the front door. Every window in the kitchen had been broken and the moisture from the rain over the years had mildewed and destroyed the countertops and floor. The smell of the room was horrible and all they heard were crickets chirping through the broken glass. The refrigerator door was cracked open and Calvin tried to be the brave one and walked over and opened it. Everyone's eyes were on his as he pulled against the door. Without warning, a rat squealed as it fell from inside the door and ran across his feet and into a hole in the wall. Calvin jumped back and screamed like a five-year-old girl. Everybody started laughing at him, even Lasaia's fear left her long enough for her to get in a giggle. Calvin looked around at his friends laughing at him and began to get embarrassed. He picked who he thought was the weakest of the group and started thinking of a way to get the focus off of him. Of course, Lasaia is his target.

"That's funny to you?" He asked as he stepped in front of her.

"Yeah, you sounded…you sounded like a little girl." She said, still laughing.

She had no idea what Calvin had up his sleeve.

"You think you're braver than me or something?"

"Yeah, I'm braver than you if you let a little mouse scare you."

All of the boys started to instigate the interaction.

"Oooooo", "I wouldn't take dat", was heard in the background.

Calvin started to get upset. First, a mouse embarrassed him; now a *girl*, of all people, was making fun of him. Calvin grabbed her by the arm and pulled her out of the kitchen. Marcus and the other boys looked at each other and followed them out.

He dragged her to the bottom of the staircase and the other boys filed in behind them. They all stood there looking up at the almost pitch black staircase. The only light at the top of the stairs came from a room with a broken window allowing the moon to shine in. Calvin let her arm go and pointed up the steps.

"If you so brave, I dare you to go up to their bedroom."

Lasaia was frozen.

She looked back at Marcus as the tears began to moisten her eyes. Marcus just nodded to try and get her to go through with it. He wanted her to show these boys that she could do anything they could and more. None of the others would have dared to take that challenge, except for probably Marcus. She slowly reached for the rail and started on her journey up the stairs. Every step made its own distinctive eerie sound.

After what seemed like forever, she finally made it to the top of the stairs and rounded the corner. Darkness surrounded her. The only evidence the others had that she was up there was the sound of her footsteps and her shadow fluttering back and forth in the moonlight on the wall. The boys didn't say a word and just gazed as her shadow danced at the top of the steps. All they heard was her slow footsteps walking across the ceiling.

All of a sudden they heard her scream and her footsteps flew across the ceiling and over to the wall. The vibration from her running caused the front door hinges to give way and the door fell to the floor behind them with a loud crash. Calvin and the other two boys screamed and ran out the front door into the yard. In their minds, the ghost had gotten Lasaia and they didn't want to be its next victim. Lasaia heard the boys downstairs and ran to the room where the moon was shining in. She looked through the broken window and saw them screaming as they jumped on their bikes and road away. She was so scared that she didn't realize that Marcus was not with them. Her heart started beating harder and harder with every second that passed.

Marcus was still standing at the bottom of the staircase waiting for her to reappear

"Come on, come on, come on." He whispered to himself hoping Lasaia would come down the steps at any second. He was too scared to yell to her for fear of upsetting the ghosts. Even though he would have never admitted to it, Marcus was just as scared as the other boys. The only thing that kept him there was his promise that he wouldn't leave her.

By now, Lasaia was sitting on the floor under the window crying her eyes out. The tears flowed from her eyes so fast that she couldn't stop them. Marcus could faintly hear her slobs from the bottom of the staircase. She thought she was all alone in the haunted house and was petrified with fear. She couldn't move. All she could do was sit there and cry uncontrollably.

Marcus finally worked up the courage to take the first step. Every step made the same creaking noise as when Lasaia had climbed them a few minutes earlier. The sounds made her even more scared. She thought she was alone in the house so the only thing that could have been making them, in her mind, was the ghost. It had run off the others and now it was on its way up the stairs to get her. Marcus made it to the top of the steps and rounded the corner just as she had done. It was so dark he could barely see the floor in front of him. He heard her sniffles and followed the sound to the room she was in. He walked through the door and Lasaia looked up and saw his outline coming toward her. She covered her eyes and let out a loud scream that scared him back into the hallway. After he got over the shock, he walked back into the room and said, "Lasaia, it's me." She took her hands away from her face and looked up at him. She could barely contain her relief. She jumped to her feet and ran across the room toward him. She threw her arms around his neck and put her head on his shoulder.

"I thought you left me." She said between sobs.

"I told you I wasn't gonna leave you in here," He said. "You alright?"

She lifted her head from his shoulder and told him that the reason she ran was because something brushed up against her in the hall. Marcus told her how Calvin and the other boys ran out the house screaming like they were being chased by the Boogey Man. Lasaia laughed and that laughter calmed her down enough to actually be able to move again.

"Come on, let's get outta here." Marcus said as he grabbed her by the hand and led her into the hall. They cautiously walked out of the room, down the steps and out the front door. Marcus climbed onto his bike and Lasaia jumped on the seat and they rode home.

They pulled into Marcus's yard and jumped off. Lasaia just looked at Marcus for a second and gave him another big hug.

"Thank you." She said before running toward her house.

She disappeared through the screen door and Marcus just stood there watching.

"Marcus!" A voice shouted from inside the house.

* * *

"Marcus! Man, get up."

Marcus jumped out of his sleep and sat up in his brother's guest bed. His dream was over. It was morning already. He heard his brother calling him from the other side of the door.

"Yeah?" Marcus yelled from the bed.

"You want some breakfast man?" Alonzo asked through the door.

"Yeah sure, what time is it?" Marcus asked still disoriented.

"It's eleven o'clock."

"Aight, I'll be out in a minute."

Marcus fell back on the pillow and rubbed his eyes. After a few minutes he got himself together, opened the door to his room and walked down the hall. He could smell breakfast cooking in the kitchen. He walked to the living room and had a seat. Alonzo came into the room from the kitchen and sat in the recliner.

"Ain't been out in a while huh?" Alonzo said joking with his brother.

"Not like that," He answered said with a smile, "Man that's a nice spot you got though. How you hook all that up?"

"Aww man, let me tell you. Most of it was money I saved when I was living in Tallahassee eatin' Pop Tarts and cheese for dinner. Some from investors, people I had to pretty much beg for money. A lot of the equipment I got on a hook up from some cats in Alabama that lost their club because folks just weren't comin' through and they ain't know how to promote. And the rest was a loan that I actually got from the bank. To make a long story short, I already paid back everybody I owe and we just gettin' started. If this keeps up, I'll be able to retire in a few years. I made ten thousand dollars the first week we opened."

"Food's ready." Lisa yelled from the kitchen.

The two brothers got up from their seats and went into the kitchen. Lisa was turning off the stove as they walked in. She had set the table and had everything waiting for the two of them. Alonzo didn't know what he had in that woman. She had prepared a huge feast for the three of them. They all grabbed a plate and dove in.

While they ate Marcus brought up his dream.

"Man you will never guess what I dreamed about."

"What's that?" Alonzo asked.

"You remember that time we went to the old Carter place down the street from our house?"

"Man, yall ain't let me go. You told me to stay home, as always. Yall ain't never let me go nowhere." Alonzo said laughing

"Oh yeah, well I had a dream about that last night."

"Did you dream about that ass whoopin' you got for coming home after dark?" Alonzo and Lisa laughed.

"Nah, I ain't make it that far." Marcus chuckled.

"What's the Carter place?" Lisa asked.

"Just some place back home folks used to say was haunted by the ghost of this lady that killed her husband. One day Marcus and his boys decided they were gonna play all big and bad and went inside. It was a run down old shack that just sat there basically. For some reason folks seemed to be scared of it like there was really a ghost inside. Nobody would even buy the property and it took the city damn near 20 years to finally knock it down." Alonzo told her.

"So why don't you buy the land and build mama and daddy a new house? That lot is at least 3 times as big as the plot they got now." Marcus asked.

"Hell nah. Shit, it's a ghost in there. The hells wrong wit' you?" Alonzo said. They all laughed.

"Yeah, pops laid it down on you that night. But that was nothing compared to what your girl got." Alonzo said finishing off his food and getting up from the table to put his dishes in the sink.

Marcus had forgotten about the bruises he saw on Lasaia's body the next day at school. She never talked to him about them and as they healed they were slowly forgotten.

"What happened?" Lisa asked.

"The girl next door to us went with them and she ended up being late getting home with Marcus. Her step dad used to beat her and her mom's ass, seemed like every other day. So, she got a big dose of it that night." Alonzo said remembering like it was yesterday.

"That's messed up." Lisa said feeling even more sorry for this girl she had never met. "And that's the girl you ran into last night?" She asked.

"Yeah that's her." Marcus said.

Lisa and Marcus finished their food and cleared the table.

Marcus walked into the kitchen with the dishes and started to run some dishwater.

"Whoa whoa whoa, what you doin'?" Alonzo asked.

"I was just gonna wash these dishes and…"

Alonzo cut him off.

"Man you a guest in my house." Alonzo took the dishrag from Marcus.

"Only residents do dishes here." Alonzo said putting the dishrag in Lisa's hand as he tried to walk off.

She grabbed him by the back of his shirt.

"Uun uuun, nice try." Lisa said pulling him back into the kitchen.

Alonzo was just joking with her, but Lisa didn't think it was all that funny. Marcus took this opportunity to call his wife like he said he would.

He walked back to his room and grabbed his cell phone. "No signal…? What is up with this phone?" He said to himself. Marcus walked back into the kitchen and asked Alonzo for his phone so he can call his wife.

"Use the cell phone man. Got free weekends on that. It's in the room on my dresser."

Marcus grabbed the phone from his brother's room and dialed his house. As the phone rang he, walked back into his room and sat on the bed.

"Hello?" Said the angelic voice on the other end of the phone.

"Hey baby"

"Heeeeey"

"What you doing?"

"Nothing just hanging around. Lasaia's little friend Melissa from next door came over to play, so the two of them are in her room and Angela is following me around everywhere, getting into everything.

"Sounds like you're having all the fun." He said chuckling.

"Yeah right. Now...tell me."

"Tell you what?"

"Tell me what I had to wait until today to hear."

Marcus let out a quick laugh.

"You been waitin' all night for this, huh?"

Sherise let out a low grunt to let him know her patience was wearing thin.

"You know I have. I told you, I'm too nosey to be put on hold like that. I wanna know. Who did you see?"

"Ok, ok let me tell you the story. After I got lost last night I ended up at a Waffle House...So I'm sitting there and this woman walks in..."

"Mmh hmm" She said cutting in.

"Anyway, it wasn't even like that. Ok, so she came in and sat down. I'm in my booth finishing my coffee and the chef called out her order and you won't believe who it was."

"Who?"

"Lasaia Lewis"

Sherise took a few seconds to think about who he was taking about and then took a deep, shocked breath.

"The girl who lived next to you as a kid. The one you dated in high school?"

"Yeah her. I was just sitting there and she walked in. I didn't even recognize her until the cook called her name."

"Wow, how is she doing?"

"She must be doing pretty good. She was driving a Jaguar and owns her own modeling agency."

"Wow, that's great. So are you gonna see her again before you leave? Does she live in Atlanta?"

Sherise seemed to be more excited about Marcus's encounter then he was.

"I was gonna call her later today, but I doubt I'll see her again before I leave. I'm sure she has things going on. Far as I know she lives here though. She had a

Fulton county tag on her car and the address on her business card is in Atlanta."

"Well you guys should catch up. See how she's doing. Tell her I said hi."

Marcus was silent.

He didn't really know if his nerves would allow him to see her again.

Sherise broke the silence.

"Well baby, I'm gonna put this little girl in her bed for a nap because she is as sleepy as she wanna be."

"Ok baby, I'll call and talk to you later." Marcus said hanging up the phone.

He got up from the bed and returned his brother's phone to his charger. He walked back to the living room, had a seat on the sofa and grabbed the remote. Alonzo and Lisa finished with the dishes and came and had a seat with him.

"Man what you gettin' into today?" Marcus asked

"Nothing much. We about to get dressed and check out this car show at this park in Atlanta. Go check the scene, probably do a lil' club promotion. You down old man?" Alonzo asked.

"Whatever. Yeah I'm down. What time we leaving?"

"We can dip soon as you get ready. They said it started at eleven but you know CP time. It will probably just be gettin' started when we get out there." Alonzo said.

The three of them sat there for a few more minutes talking and then decided to start getting ready for their day out. After about 15 minutes Marcus and Alonzo met in the living room. Lisa was taking her time making sure she was perfect before she left. It wasn't long before Alonzo lost his patience.

"Come on girl, This ain't no fashion show!" Alonzo yelled down the hall.

A muffled, "I'm comin'!" could be heard from behind the closed bathroom door. "Women," Alonzo said walking back into the room with his brother, "they know they can take forever."

Marcus just threw his hands up knowing exactly what Alonzo meant. He had three women at the house so he was used to waiting.

About five minutes later Lisa emerged from the bathroom and came down the hall. She was dressed in some baby blue terry cloth daisy dukes with a matching top with the word "Perfect" across her chest. She did her hair and makeup and looked like a completely different person. Alonzo was in shock as if he had never seen his girlfriend look that good before.

"Damn, who are you? Where Lisa at?" Alonzo said looking down the hall behind her.

"Anyway, you tryin' to be funny?" She said laughing, feeling a little flattered.

"You look good baby. At least you took your time for a reason." Alonzo said kissing her on the cheek.

"Well let's go." He said headed for the front door.

The three of them filed out to the truck and got in. They drove down I-20 headed for downtown Atlanta. It took them about twenty minutes to get to the park, but when they got there, the scene was amazing. There were all types of different cars and people everywhere. It seemed like there was at least one of every type of car in the park that day. Everything from a vintage 1952 Cadillac Fleetwood to a tricked out 2006 Escalade. The paint jobs stole the show for most of the cars and trucks. It was clear that some of these cars cost more then the people that owned them made in a couple years. There was a sea of hoods and trunks as far as the eye could see.

And the women?

Marcus had found yet another place in Atlanta full of drop dead gorgeous women, most of them grabbing more attention than the cars around them.

Alonzo rode through the park for a few minutes and across the path from a friend of his whose truck was in one of the many competitions.

"What up playa?" Alonzo said jumping out of the truck and walking over to the group.

"Mr. Zo, what da' deal folk?" Jamari, the owner of the truck, said.

Marcus and Lisa slowly walked up behind the fast moving and excited Alonzo.

"What's up lil' lady?" Jamari said to Lisa as she took her place next to her man.

"Hey Juice." Lisa said.

Juice was Jamari's name on the street and the name tattooed all over his truck.

"I'm bout to go get me some water or something, it's hot as hell out here." Lisa said as she wiped her brow.

"Aight baby, we gon' be right here." Alonzo said giving her a kiss on the cheek.

Lisa walked off and dragged the eyes of every man standing in the group with her.

"What yall looking at?" Alonzo asked turning around to see a group of men looking at his woman.

All of them turned their heads as if they had no idea what he was talking about and pretended to hold a conversation. All of them except Jamari.

"You know I can't help it my nigga," Jamari said laughing, "I keep telling you about picking the fine ones."

Alonzo laughed it off and introduced his brother to Jamari.

"Yo Juice, this my big brother Marcus...Marcus this is Juice, my homeboy from FAMU. This the fool who used to hook me up with all kinds of ass back in the day. Now I gotta give him my old women's pager numbers so he can get some play."

"Aaaww whateva' nigga. Whas' up bruh."

Jamari and Marcus gave each other a pound and they all started to talk about the car show going on around them.

A few minutes later Lisa found a vendor but the line was longer than a ghetto girl's weave. She stood there with her arms crossed waiting for what seemed like forever. She swore they had to fill out an application to get a bottle of water as long as she had to wait. She stood there, getting hotter and hotter, and angrier and angrier, with every degree that the temperature went up. Even though she barely had on any clothes, she felt like she was about to burst into flames if she didn't get some water soon. She finally got to the front of the line and achieved her goal, an ice-cold bottle of water. It was a dollar fifty for the same 20 ounce bottle you could get at a gas station for a dollar. It was clear the hustlers were out today. As she cracked the top and began enjoying her liquid savior, she felt a light tug at her elbow.

"How you doing beautiful?" The voice said in her ear.

She turned around and was face to face with a gold toothed, pint sized, over dressed wannabe player.

"Fine." She said pulling her arm from him before turning to walk off. She was trying to be polite and not tell the man to leave her the hell alone but he just wasn't taking the hint.

"Where you going so fast angel. I just wanna holla at you for a second." He said grabbing her by the arm again. Lisa turned around and gave him a get-your-hands-off-me look.

Before she could get a word out she heard a familiar voice call out from behind her.

"Whas ya bumba clat problem mon. Cancha see dee woman na fi wan fuck wit chu."

The man saw his competitor and intimidation rested on his face.

He backed up.

"My bad folk…didn't know she was taken."

He turned and walked away without another word.

Lisa still hadn't worked up the courage to turn around and face the voice that she had been trying to escape from.

"Wassa matter likkle one? Ya nah wan see me?" The voice said as it got closer to her ear.

Lisa quickly jumped forward and turned around as if the voice was burning a hole into the side of her neck.

"What are you doing here?" She said in an excited whisper, barely able to breathe.

"Come now, ya gon make ya old man tink ya don't luv em nah more." The man said, stepping toward her.

His name was Richard.

He was a Caribbean born Atlanta resident who Lisa had dated before Alonzo came along. Richard would repeatedly cheat on her and take her for granted. He never gave her the respect she knew she deserved so as any respectable women would, she went searching for someone that would treat her right. That's when she found Alonzo and hadn't looked back since. Not long after she had made up her mind to leave Richard, he went to prison and was there for about a year. Alonzo knew nothing about him and Lisa had planned on keeping it that way, but she always knew in the back of her mind that Richard would find her. He was always the jealous and possessive type. Anytime another man would look her way, Richard would either end up fighting or almost fighting. He was quick tempered and Lisa knew as soon as he found out she had someone new he would start some trouble. She had recently heard that he was back on the street and knew she needed to handle the situation soon but didn't know it would be today.

"Look Richard, I can't deal with you right now. It's over between us." She said nervously.

"Ova…whacha mean ova. Nah. Cyan be ova til me say so." He said grabbing her arm. Lisa snatched her arm back and started to back up. She was always scared of Richard. He always seemed like he would do anything at any given time, and it didn't matter who set him off, he would just explode at the smallest thing.

"I…I…I gotta go." Lisa said slowly backing away before she turned and walked off. She couldn't believe that this was happening to her right now.

Richard didn't follow her, just watched as she left and smiled devilishly. He knew that he would see her again, soon.

Lisa's heart was beating feverishly as she climbed into the passenger seat of Alonzo's truck. She just needed a minute to think. She couldn't tell Alonzo she wanted to leave. She knew that would lead to a round of 20 questions. Her only hope was that Richard would leave things alone for now until she could come up with a way to bring everything up to Alonzo. She just wanted to hide. If he hadn't seen her get in the truck, she could just hide there until it was time to go. Alonzo hadn't seen his woman disappear into the truck but Marcus had. He didn't know Lisa that well but he knew she looked scared and tapped his brother on the shoulder and pointed at the truck. Alonzo saw Lisa sitting in the truck and looked at his brother. Marcus just shrugged his shoulders having no idea what could possibly have been bothering her.

She only went to get water.

What could have possibly happened in that short 15 minutes while she was separated from them?

Alonzo left the group and walked over to his truck to see what was bothering his woman. He stood by driver's side window and looked in at her. She didn't acknowledge him. Just stared out the windshield as if she was concentrating on something.

"What's wrong babe?" Alonzo asked.

"Nothing, I'm fine. I'm…I'm just cramping, that's all." Lisa said trying to give a reason for her sudden attack of anti-social behavior. Alonzo had a feeling that this was more then just a menstrual cycle thing and tried to get her to open up to him.

"Come on baby, I know you better then that. What's wrong, what happened?"

She looked up at him as a tear rolled down her cheek. She didn't want him to see that.

She really did love Alonzo and hated the fact that she had kept this from him for so long. She knew she had to face the fact that the past needed to come out but she didn't want it to be like this. But, she knew he deserved to know.

"Come here." He said opening the door, holding his hand out for her to get out of the truck.

She just stood there like a little child about to get a spanking while he wrapped his arms around her. She felt ashamed of herself for keeping this from him for so long, but didn't know how he would react. Standing there in his arms, she was able to block everything else out and her mountain became an anthill. That was one of the things she loved about Alonzo. All he had to do was take her in his arms and she felt safe…as if nothing could touch her.

The moment didn't last long as a tear dropped from her cheek and landed on his arm. He slowly loosened his grip and looked into her eyes. She looked disappointed that the moment ended, like a kid in line for their favorite amusement park ride but it broke down right before their turn. She couldn't even look him in the eyes. She just looked down at his shirt hoping he wouldn't ask any more questions and just hold her again.

"Baby, what is it?" Alonzo asked again.

He had never seen her shut down like that before, especially to the point where she wouldn't even talk to him. She finally worked up the courage to just say what she knew she had to say.

She took a deep breath.

"I have something I need to tell you. Before we…" Lisa was cut off by a voice from behind Alonzo. She was so upset she hadn't even seen him walk up.

"Wha' gwan?" Richard said walking up to the two of them accompanied by a dreadloc'd duo. Lisa's eyes grew huge on her face and Alonzo could almost see the fear circulating through her body. He turned around and was face to face with three men he had never seen before. After looking at how Lisa was avoiding eye contact with this man and making his own assumptions, he figured that this person had to be at the root of her mood. He immediately flipped the aggression switch.

"Something I can help you with, bruh?" Alonzo said sizing up his opponent.

Lisa quickly stepped between the two of them.

"Ricky! No! Not now. Don't…"

As she stumbled to get her words out Richard cut in.

"Don't wha'? Ah…me see. Dis muss be da new man, 'eh?"

Richard looked beyond Lisa at Alonzo.

"You can go now bredren. Ya services, dem no longa required."

Alonzo was already mad, that statement just pushed him over the edge. He stood there for a few seconds then Lisa turned to him with tears in her eyes.

That was the final straw.

He couldn't stand to see his woman cry and this guy was the one that was causing it all, which was making it worse. She started to walk to Alonzo as he took a step up to confront this pest. She could see the rage in his eyes and knew there was very little her small body could do to restrain him.

By this time, Marcus happened to look up at his brother and noticed the new company that was with them. He watched the events as they progressed for a few seconds and noticed his brother didn't look too happy. He tapped Jamari on the shoulder and motioned for him to check out the scene. Jamari stood to his feet and watched as the two men exchanged a few words.

"Da hell is this?" Jamari said not really liking the way things were looking. He was pretty sure this wasn't a social call. His outburst attracted the attention of the other three guys that were with him. The five of them stood and watched like kids seeing a lion for the first time.

Then it happened.

Richard stepped up to Alonzo and said something that obviously wasn't appropriate for the situation and all they saw was Alonzo draw back and punch Richard in his eye.

"Oh shit!" Jamari said as the five of them dropped what they were doing and darted around hit truck.

By that time, Richard's partners had already jumped on Alonzo and had him down to the ground. Lisa was jumping around frantically screaming for them to get off of him. Richard was recovering from his blow and was about to get a few licks in when Jamari came out of no where and tackled him in a fashion that would rival Monday night football. The two of them fell to the ground and Jamari began beating him like Lisa was his woman. Marcus and the other three men grabbed the guys holding Alonzo down and they immediately let him go. Lisa ran over to check Alonzo out and make sure he was ok. Marcus stopped fighting and went over to check on his brother. He helped Alonzo to his feet and turned to see Jamari and his friends taking the Jamaicans to the cleaners.

The two of them tried to break up the fight. After a few seconds Marcus was able to pull Jamari off of Richard and Alonzo got the other guys to stop beating on his friends. The nine of them stood facing each other six on one side, three on the other. Lisa stood separated from both groups. Her nerves were shot by now and she could barely contain her hysteria. A small crowd had gathered as a result of the fight and attention in the area was slowly shifting from the cars to the altercation.

"Dawg, I don't know who the fuck you are, but this shit ain't over." Alonzo said stepping forward from the group.

Marcus put his hand on Alonzo's shoulder to let him know that this was not the time or place and to keep it cool. Richard accepted his challenge and stepped forward on his side.

"Ya dun kno' me?" Richard said followed by a diabolical chuckle. "Ask ya gyal who I am?"

Alonzo looked over at Lisa confused. Her eyes and face were covered with tears and she was so scared she was shaking. She couldn't even get back half of the nerve she had to tell him now in front of everyone and she panicked. She ran to Alonzo's truck sobbing. Alonzo turned back to Richard with even more anger in his heart. He knew the man in front of him was some how responsible, but he didn't know how. Richard just looked at Alonzo with a smug look on his face and started to laugh. Alonzo took his arrogant attitude as an insult and jumped at him. Jamari and Marcus saw it coming and grabbed him before he could do anything. Richard just looked at Alonzo and kept laughing. Just as Jamari and Marcus got Alonzo settled, a police car pulled up along side the group. *Werr Wert*

The officers chirped their siren as they pulled to a stop. This thinned out the crowd that up until now was slowly growing. Two officers stepped out and walked over to the group with a cocky swagger to their step.

"What's the problem here fellas?" One of the officers said as he stopped in between the two groups.

"Nothin' man, we cool." Jamari said.

"You cool?" The officer said turning to Richard and his crew.

"Yea mon, every ting arigh'."

Richard and Alonzo stared each other down the whole time, never flinching. The scene resembled the beginning of a heavyweight championship fight. They just stood there and tried to intimidate one another.

"Alright then, let's break it up." The officer said waiting for the two groups to disburse. Richard and his friends turned and walked away while Jamari, Marcus and Alonzo headed over to Alonzo's truck. The other three men headed back to Jamari's truck replaying the whole fight blow for blow. To them it was just another opportunity for bragging rights, but to Alonzo it was much more serious.

"You good folk?" Jamari asked as they got to the truck door. Alonzo looked in the truck to see Lisa in the passenger side with her face in her hands.

"It's all good cousin, 'preciate the look bruh." Alonzo said extending his fist to Jamari. Jamari quickly drops his on top of Alonzo's and they gave each other a pound.

"You know I gotcha back brotha. So what's up? Yall 'bout to ride huh?" Jamari asked.

"Yeah man, I gotta get to the bottom of this shit." Alonzo told him.

"I feel you, I feel you...well man, I'll holla at you...Yall be easy." Jamari said giving a pound to Marcus as he took a step over to Alonzo's open window. Lisa's position hadn't changed since she got into the truck. Jamari stuck his head through the window a little and said, "Don't sweat it lil' sis, it'll be aight." She didn't respond and Jamari didn't expect her to.

"Aight man, I'll get up with yall boys." Jamari said to the two brothers as he walked back to his truck.

The two brothers climbed into the truck and pulled onto the path leading out of the park. Lisa had quieted down a little now, but still had her face in her hands. As they were pulling out of the park she lifted her face and just stared off into space out of the window. Her makeup was ruined. Lisa didn't wear much makeup, but the little bit she did have on was smeared all over her face and hands. Alonzo reached across her and into the glove compartment and handed her a few of the napkins he had collected in.

"Thank you." She whispered in a low meek tone. She began wiping her face and hands removing the smeared makeup and tears. Her sobs had almost stopped and she was finally able to compose herself. She just needed to get away from that scene.

When they got on the highway to go home Alonzo couldn't hold it in any longer.

"You wanna tell me what the hell all that was about?" Alonzo asked.

Of course she didn't but knew it was time to get it out in the open.

Four

"Do we have to talk about this now?" Lisa asked still sounding a little rattled.

"Yeah we do. When I get in a fight, I like to know why." He said sounding upset.

He knew Lisa knew the guy, but he wasn't sure what happened between them, or if it was still happening. To Alonzo it wasn't the fact that she was with the guy. He just wanted to know if she was with both of them at the same time. His mind jumped from scenario to scenario trying to figure out when and where she would have had time to see him. He had pretty much already made up in his mind who the guy was and he wasn't just a guy that worked with Lisa's sister that had a crush on her or some silly shit like that. In his mind the guy was somebody she was cheating on him with that had finally gotten tired of being the *other* man. Lisa just sat in the passenger seat and stared out the window hoping Alonzo would accept her silence as acknowledgement that she wasn't in the mood.

He didn't.

Alonzo pulled off the highway into the streets of Decatur. It had been silent in the car for a while and Alonzo finally asked the question that had been plaguing his mind.

"So you fuckin' him or something?" He asked.

The whole mood in the truck changed.

Even the air smelled different.

Marcus just sat back in his seat, tilted his head back, and closed his eyes. He thought his brother knew better then that. To accuse a woman, especially a black woman, of anything like that without proof was the quickest way to start an argument. Even though he had his eyes closed, Marcus could feel the look Lisa was giving his little brother. She let his question marinate in her brain for a second. She couldn't believe that he would actually have the nerve to ask her that.

"Oh, so I'm a hoe now?" She asked, forgetting her tears and jumping on the defensive.

"I ain't calling you a hoe. I asked if you was fuckin' him."

"You know what, I don't have time for this! Take me home!"

"Nah fuck dat, I'm out here fightin' ova you and shit. I at least deserve to know what it was all about. So, was you fuckin' him or not?"

"Ok, you wanna know? Ok. Yes Alonzo. Yes I was fuckin' him, about 2 years ago. He's my ex boyfriend. But he was no good and never gave a damn about my feelings, or me, or anything so I left. For about a month he always followed me around and stalked me and shit. He would start fights with any guy that he saw trying to talk to me. Two months after I broke it off he went to jail behind some drugs or something, I don't know. Two weeks later I ran into this nice guy at the gas station who asked me out. I was single and he was cute so I said yes. But since then I have been with him I haven't looked at another guy in that way. So in answer to your question, Yes I *was* fucking him."

Alonzo was silent and just stared at the road in front of him.

Once again his quick temper and attitude had perfectly placed his toes on his tongue. He tried to lighten the mood and changed his tone.

"Well, why didn't you tell me about him earlier?"

"You wanna know about the guy I dated in 10th grade too? You never asked me about any of my ex's."

"I ain't know I had to ask you about the crazy cats in your past." He said joking.

"Oh anyway, like you ain't never messed with no crazy women." Lisa said, her tone a little lighter as well.

"What…name one?" He said challenging her.

"Keisha, you told me she used to sit in front of your dorm in college for like 2 hours until you got outta class just so she could see you."

Alonzo laughed thinking about the moment.

"Tabitha, that girl that broke into your dorm room and spray painted the word, 'Whore' on your wall when she found out you were talking to Keisha. And oh…what's the girl's name. The one that walked from her job, past her own damn house, to your apartment when you had a car and refused to come get her."

Alonzo cut off the list. "Aight, aight, aight, Ok so maybe one or two."

Lisa laughed.

"They may have been crazy but they weren't violent." He said trying to make things sound better.

He reached over and placed his hand on top of hers and a grin made its home on her lips. He pulled her hand to his mouth and kissed it.

"I'm sorry baby." Alonzo said, still holding her hand.

"I'm sorry too." Lisa said.

Her tears were gone.

The mood in the truck lightened up and even Marcus came back from his neutral corner. They finally made it to Alonzo's house and he pulled into the driveway. Marcus noticed a car in the yard next to his truck.

"How your car get here?" Alonzo asked.

"Oh damn, I forgot…I was supposed to go with my mom and sister to the mall today."

They got out of the truck and Lisa walked over to her car as Marcus and Alonzo headed for the front door. She pulled a note from under the windshield wiper and opened it. Alonzo and Marcus stopped at the front door and looked back at her as she burst out laughing.

"What's it say?" Alonzo asked.

"Nothing, my sister just cussing me out because I wasn't here when they came. They must have drove both cars over here and left mine." She said walking over to them.

"I'm gonna go to my mom's house and see what they bought. I'll be back before you go to work tonight."

"Aight babe." Alonzo said giving her a kiss on the cheek.

Lisa walked back to her car and got in. She pulled out of the driveway as they walked into the house and shut the door.

"You're going to the club again tonight?" Marcus asked.

"Yeah man, got a lot of paper work to do. Orders to make, payroll, gotta check the expenses, and get with the A.N.G.E.L.S. to see how things went last night, shit like that. You can come through if you want."

"Nah, last night was enough for me."

Alonzo laughed at his brother and said, "Man you too young to be getting old. Well, I guess you can chill here. Not really too much to do but watch TV. We probably won't be back until about 4."

"That's cool, I'll be straight. Probably just have a few beers and watch some ESPN or something."

"You know what you need to do? You need to call your girl and tell her to come over here."

"Who?"

"Who", Alonzo said mocking his brother, "Lasaia fool".

"Oh, nah…I don't know about that. She probably got plans for tonight anyway."

"You sound just like you did back in the day when you was trying to ask her out. Might as well call and see."

"Nah, I'm just gonna chill."

"Alright, suit yourself. I'm bout to get out these dirty ass clothes and grab a nap before I head out. It's gonna be a long night." Alonzo got almost half way down the hall and turned around.

"Oh. 'preciate you getting my back like that today man."

"Aw man, you know that ain't nothin'. Gotta watch out for my lil' brother." Alonzo laughed and turned back down the hall.

"Alright man, I check you in a few hours." Alonzo said disappearing into his room.

"Alright." Marcus said heading for the living room.

He sat on the couch, grabbed the remote, turned on the 62' television and flipped through a few channels. Alonzo's comment replayed in his mind over and over again. Maybe he should call Lasaia and see how things were going. After all, it had been almost ten years, excluding last night's encounter, since they last spoke face to face. He wrestled with the thought for about fifteen minutes before he realized how ridiculous he was being.

I have a wife and kids and I haven't talked to her in almost a decade. What could happen, he thought to himself. He tried to convince himself that it was ok to call her. He battled it out for about ten more minutes before finally walking to his room to get the number. He grabbed the phone off of the end table as he walked back over to the couch. Marcus stared at the phone like it was some foreign device, still fighting an internal battle. Why was it so hard to just pick up the phone and dial her number? He didn't know then but that conversation was a fork in the road of his life. He took a deep breath, pressed the talk button and dialed Lasaia's number.

With every ring his heart began to beat a little faster. After four rings there was a click and her answering machine message started. Her voice was even sexier over the phone. Marcus was somewhat relieved to get the machine instead of Lasaia. He left a brief message just to say hi and gave her Alonzo's phone number so she could call if she wasn't doing anything. He made every attempt not to give any indication of the level of uneasiness he was feeling. He hung up the phone with a certain degree of relief.

He had done it.
No one could say that he hadn't attempted to contact her. He sat on the couch for a few more minutes watching TV.

It was about three o'clock in the afternoon and the house was completely silent. Marcus was used to miniature people running around the house at this time and his wife calling him to do some task that she could have done herself. This was just silence. He sat back on the cushion of the soft couch. His eyes began to get heavier and heavier with every second that passed. Either he didn't get enough sleep the night before or the day's events had drained him because ESPN slowly began to fade and Marcus drifted off to sleep.

About three hours later Marcus was brought out of his slumber by a muffled ringing noise. He opened his eyes and looked around, disoriented. He had pushed the phone down in between the sofa cushions during his nap and all that could be heard was a low stifled ring. It was enough to wake him up but he had no idea where it was coming from. He looked around and tried to follow the sound. By the time he was in full use of his senses, Alonzo's answering machine started up. After Alonzo's hood-style greeting ended Marcus heard that same sexy voice come out of the speaker. It was Lasaia calling him back. Her message was short and to the point. She had just gotten in from an unusually long Saturday meeting. She wasn't doing anything for the rest of the day and if he wanted to call her she would love to hear from him. She left her numbers, in case he had somehow lost them in the last few hours, and ended the call. Marcus's heart rate began to rise again. Everything was fine when she was busy, now what should he do?
Call her back?
Act like he didn't get the message and just not call?
Call her and tell her something came up?
Or, call her back and take his chances at embarrassing the hell out of himself?
Marcus regressed.
He was 17 again.
Feeling that same nervous feeling in his stomach.
He took a minute to calm down and picked up the phone. He slowly dialed her number and waited through two grueling rings. Then he heard a click and a sexy voice entered the telephone line.
"Hello?" The voice said.

"Hello."

"Yes?"

"May I speak with Lasaia Lewis please?"

"This is she."

"Oh, hey…this is Marcus."

"Oh heeeeeey, I was wondering who this was on my caller ID"

"Yeah, it was me."

"Oh, don't be calling over here sounding like a bill collector, using my whole name and stuff," She said with a laugh, "I just tried to call you."

"Yeah, I couldn't find the phone in time."

"Oh, so you finally made it to your brother's house huh?"

"Yeah, yeah…I just got here." Marcus said laughing.

"Oh anyway, my directions weren't that bad."

They both laughed and Marcus's butterflies fluttered away.

"So what's up?" Lasaia asked like they were back in Albany ten years ago.

"Nothing much, I was just calling to see how you was doing."

"Oh I'm fine. Just hanging out at home now. It has been a loooooong week and I'm just trying to unwind. You know what. I had a dream about you last night."

A smile sprinted across Marcus's face.

"Really, I had a dream about you too."

What were the odds of that?

"Really! What did you dream about?" She asked.

"You remember that time when ole' big head Calvin came over my house talking bout going to the haunted Carter place?"

"Oh yeah. You told him I had beat you in basketball." She said with a giggle. "I always thought you were cool for that."

Marcus couldn't believe that she remembered something that specific.

"Yeah, he was always picking on you. We almost got into a couple fights because of him talking bout you."

"Aww how sweet. My little night in shining armor." She said, "Yeah of course I remember that day. I thought I was gonna need therapy for sure after that. I remember I let him dare me into going upstairs or something and when I got up there something rubbed up against my arm and I screamed and took off."

They both laughed at something that had their hearts about to jump out of their chests when they were kids.

"Then all I saw was yall running out the front door and I was so scared I just sat there on the floor under the window and cried. Then you came in the room and scared the hell outta me."

Marcus laughed.
"I was coming to get you. I told you that I wasn't gonna leave you in there and I wasn't."
"You were always a charming little man. I hope that translated over to the adult Marcus."
There was a moment of silence.
"So what did you dream about?" Marcus asked.
"Oh, ok…You remember that time in middle school when I was doing real bad in chemistry and you were helping me. I had a dream about that time when you were suppose to help me study for my test."
"Oh yeah, I remember that." Marcus said laughing as he thought about it.

Lasaia started to tell the story of a Thursday afternoon in their neighborhood. She had just gotten home from school and ran straight up to her room. Marcus had been helping her all week to get ready for this test and she wasn't going to let him down. They had slowly become good friends over the last couple of years and even hung out on a regular basis. It had gotten to the point where it was strange for you to see one for very long without the other popping up a few minutes later. People would always tease them and talk about how they were in love and were girlfriend and boyfriend, but they knew the truth. They were just two friends that really had a lot to share with each other.

On this particular afternoon Lasaia ended up in her room with a book on her bed and a pencil in hand. Usually her room was the place where she could escape the mental and physical abuse her stepfather passed out on a regular basis, but today it was an institution of learning. She just sat there studying and every so often she would check outside to see if Marcus was home yet. He had promised to help her with her studying so she could do well on her test the next day, but he was nowhere to be seen. The afternoon went on and on and still no Marcus. She knew he had basketball practice but he was usually home by eight o'clock at the latest. She had been trying to study all afternoon but her worrying kept her from concentrating. Marcus had promised, and he had always done what he said he would.

Around nine 9:30 she finally gave up. She had learned a little bit of information from the chapters but nothing compared to how she grasped it when he was around. She just seemed to be a better person with him there. Lasaia closed her book and put all her things away. She was always good about being neat. She would always put everything in its place. She couldn't stand to see something in her room that was not where it was supposed to be. Her room was the only aspect of her life that she had complete control over. She got up and went to take a shower. Her mom and step dad were already asleep. Probably drunk or high for all she knew. She didn't really care any more. All she wanted to do was make it to 18 and she was free. She figured if her mom wasn't smart enough to get away from him then she would be the smart one and get out by herself. She took her shower, brushed her teeth, and did all of the other things in her nightly routine to prepare for bed.

She walked to the living room window and looked out one more time. Still no Marcus in sight. She looked at the clock on the wall. It was 10:04. She wasn't sleepy but trying to continue to study by herself was useless. She figured there was no way his parents would let him out to help her now even if he did come home. This was the first time he had told her he would do something and didn't follow through on it. He had finally not made his words a reality. She knew it was only a matter of time before it happened. No one was perfect.

Lasaia walked back to her room and turned off her light and jumped into bed. Her heart felt strangely heavy. She wasn't just sad that he didn't come help her study. It was more so the fact that it had been several hours and she hadn't seen her friend. She wanted to see him more than study with him. She didn't know what this feeling was, but it hurt and she didn't like it at all. She closed her eyes and tried to get some sleep.

After about a half hour, she was brought out of her sleep by a light tapping noise. She woke up and looked around the dark room.

The noise stopped.

As she was about to lay her head on her pillow again the noise rushed into the room again, this time louder. It was coming from the window facing her back yard. The window she had used many times to escape through when she was younger. Her eyes were a little blurry from her short nap but she got up anyway and walked toward the window. All she could see was a shadowy figure through the glass. The closer she got, the clearer the figure became.

It was Marcus.

She unlocked the window and lifted it up.

"Marcus what are you doing?" She said with a confused look on her face.

"I'm here to help you study." He said looking around to make sure no one had seen him sneaking around in the dark.

He had his chemistry book and notebook in hand, so she could see that he was serious.

"It's 10:30 at night, where you been?"

"Can we talk about this inside? I don't want nobody to see me out here and call my folks."

She extended her hand to get his books and moved out of the way so he could climb through the window. Marcus still had his basketball jersey on. He had pulled in right after she got in the bed and was just waiting for his chance to sneak out and here he was. Lasaia couldn't help but smile at the fact that he would take such a big risk just to keep his word to her. His parents would have killed him if they knew he had snuck out the house. This meant more to her then he knew.

"Get your books." He said taking his things from her before walking over to her bed.

She just stood there and looked at him as he opened his book and sat down. She really admired him as her friend and as a person. Before he caught her smitten gaze she rushed over to her books and picked them up and rushed back over to him.

The two of them studied for a couple hours and Lasaia soaked up everything that Marcus went over with her. She had read the same pages a few hours earlier and nothing stuck. With him there, she felt like she could learn anything. A little after one o'clock in the morning they finished the chapter and did the practice test at the end. Lasaia aced the test and Marcus looked at her and said, "I think you're ready." His seal of approval gave her the final boost of confidence that she needed. She looked up at him and smiled at his comment. He started to get his things together and headed for the window.

"I'll see you tomorrow." Marcus said inside a yawn.

She was sad that the time had gone by so quick.

"Hey." She said as he got one leg out of the window.

He stopped and looked back at her.

"Thanks…for…"

Lasaia was never all that good at expressing herself.

He just smiled and said, "No problem. You just better pass that test."

She nodded her head as he jumped out the window. She walked over to the window and saw Marcus fleeing through the darkness in their backyard. She lost site of him around an oak tree and closed her window to get in the bed again.

He had done it again.

He hadn't let her down.
Even after she had lost faith he still came through on his promise. She got in the bed actually feeling good about her life instead of wishing it was different.

❖ ❖ ❖

The two of them laughed about the situation over the phone.
"See and I got a 98 on my test too." Lasaia said.
"Would have been a 100 if you would have remembered that the mitochondria is the energy provider of the cell." Marcus said laughing.
"I'm real upset that you still remember that." Lasaia said laughing. "Anyway, we made a great team back then."
There was a moment of silence on the phone as Marcus thought back to how much fun the two of them had as kids. She broke the silence with the question Marcus was secretly hoping to hear.
"So, what you doing tonight?"
"Nothing just chilling at Alonzo's. He gotta go handle some business at his club tonight, so I'm just gonna be hanging out here."
"His club? As in he owns a club?"
"Yeah, he owns *Cloud 9* out here in Decatur. We went through there last night. It's a pretty cool spot."
"I've heard about that club. Some of my models are always talking about that place."
"Yeah, I showed him your card and he did say something about some of the girls at the club getting modeling jobs through you guys."
"That's a shame that we have been separated by like two or three people and didn't run into each other."
"Yeah, that's wild. So, he's headed out that way tonight. You don't have a date tonight? That's a shock. I figured a single successful business woman like yourself would have men taking numbers to get the chance to take you out."
"Anyway, you know I was never the going out type. Give me a couch and a TV and I'm good to go."
"Well it just so happens that there is a couch and a sizeable TV over here." Marcus tried to hint at her coming over and hanging out with him.
Lasaia had no problem catching the hint.
"Really? Hmmm…Well I do have some more things that I have been avoiding doing but need to do today. How's…uummm let's say 8:30?"
"That's cool. I'm not going anywhere."

"Ok well I need directions to get there"
Marcus realized that he had no idea how to get her from her house to his.
"Well I have no clue how to get you here. I don't even know where you are." Marcus said.
"Oh, I forgot you're a tourist." She said with a giggle. "Well just give me the address and I will look it up on the Internet."
Marcus gave her the address and she copied it down.
"Well let me go ahead and handle a few things and I'll see you around 8:30 'ish."
"Ok, miss lady. I'll see you then."
"Ok, Bye bye."
"Bye"

Marcus hung up the phone and a smile sprinted across his lips again. He was actually going to get a chance to see his old friend tonight. He had really missed her over the years. Lasaia and Marcus had really grown inseparable from middle school through high school. After all, he did name is first-born daughter after her. That's one of the biggest signs of affection you can give someone. For some reason after they graduated things didn't work out. Marcus didn't even think about that, he was just happy to get the chance to see her again.

After a quick jog down memory lane Marcus flashed back into reality and looked around the living room. The room was a mess. Magazines all over the place, beer bottles from the night before, the floor needed a vacuuming and for some reason there were a few t-shirts lying around. Marcus figured if he was planning on entertaining he needed to at least make the room presentable. He washed dishes, rearranged the magazines, vacuumed, fluffed pillows and even lit some incense that he found in a kitchen drawer. You would have thought the people from *Better Homes & Gardens* were stopping through for a photo shoot.

A couple minutes after eight o'clock Alonzo came into the living room and saw his brother's hard work. He hardly ever saw his house as clean as it was, unless Lisa got a cleaning bug and straightened things up.
"Damn, were you that bored man?" He said looking around at his spotless living room.
"Nah man just took your advice." Marcus said.
Alonzo looks confused.
"I told you to clean up?" He asked like amnesia had set in on him.

"Nah, you told me to call Lasaia and I did. She's gonna be here in a few minutes."

"Oooh, ok ok. True true, I told you you needed to call her." Alonzo said as he walked around admiring the newly cleaned room.

"You gonna change clothes, right?" Alonzo asked looking at Marcus.

Marcus looked down at his clothes and realized he had on the same outfit he had on all day. He was so caught up in cleaning that he didn't even think about how he looked. Marcus told his brother to answer the door if she came as he hurried off to take a quick shower. He shuffled down the hall to his room and picked out an outfit to wear. He hurried to the bathroom and jumped into the shower before the water even had a chance to warm up.

Alonzo had a seat on the couch and started watching television. About ten minutes later the doorbell rang. As he opened the door he saw the goddess Venus herself standing on his doorstep.

Words escaped him.

All he could do was stare at her.

Lasaia stood there looking at him through the storm door smiling, waiting for him to say something. She had on a tight black dress that looked like it was just a thin piece of cloth that wrapped around her body from her underarms to her thighs. Her gorgeous shoulders were exposed and the dress showed off every curve on her body. The hem was so high it looked like she would show off all of her business if she sat down without crossing her legs. Alonzo was moving in slow motion as he pushed the storm door open.

"Um, hi…Alonzo?" She said.

Her words snapped him back into reality.

"Lasaia? What's up girl?" He said letting her in and giving her a hug.

He knew he was staring and tried to play it off.

"You look different as a grown man," Lasaia said with a laugh, "I didn't even recognize you. Thought I had the wrong house for a minute."

"You look different ya'self. A lot different." He said trying to keep his inner dog on a leash.

Alonzo couldn't believe that this was the same girl that he lived next to as a kid. He invited her to have a seat in the living room and offered her a drink.

"Oh I forgot, I need to get something out of my car." She said standing to her feet.

"You want a beer or something?" Alonzo asked as she headed for the front door.

"Yeah that'll be fine." She said not breaking her stride.

By this time Marcus was finishing up his shower and getting dressed. He didn't know Lasaia had made it to the house and was only a few feet away. Nonetheless, he hurried and got dressed to greet his company. At that moment, Lasaia was reaching in her car to grab a surprise that she had brought for her host. She retrieved her gift and made her way back to the house. She got back to the living room and had a seat on the couch just as Alonzo arrived with her beer. He took a seat on the couch next to her and the two of them talked for a minute about his club and her modeling business. About how it had been so long since they had seen each other. Alonzo even told her how Marcus was running around cleaning up before she came.

She got a kick out of that.

She was flattered that he had gone through so much to impress her.

Outside another car pulled into the driveway. It was Lisa. She was back to go with Alonzo to the club. She had already changed and everything. Her skirt clung to her thighs like plastic wrap over leftovers. Her slim curvy frame was only surmounted by her sexy saunter. Lisa had a walk that could give sight to the blind. She didn't know it, but that walk had gotten many men in trouble after she passed by. She walked up to the front door and used her key to get in. She noticed the very expensive automobile sitting in Alonzo's yard and didn't realize it was the same automobile that Marcus had described the night before. She figured it must have been one of Alonzo's business partners or something and paid it no mind. She closed the front door behind her and headed for Alonzo's room to wake him up. As she was walking, she faintly heard a woman's voice coming from the living room. Her nosiness got the best of her and she shifted directions. She came around the corner of the living room to see her man sitting next to a beautiful woman on the couch. In her eyes, he was sitting much too close to her. She couldn't believe her eyes. She just stood and looked at the two of them laughing and talking on the couch for a few seconds until Lasaia saw her standing there.

"Oh, hi." She said to Lisa who didn't have the most pleasant look on her face.

Her hands were crossed and her blood pressure was slowly rising.

Alonzo turned to see who his guest was talking to.

"Oh, hey baby." He said looking back at his woman.

Lisa didn't know what to think. She just turned and walked off, headed down the hall. Alonzo looked back at Lasaia and she just shrugged her shoulders. Neither of them put the scene together but Alonzo knew he had to find out what he had done, or not done, this time to upset her. He excused himself and strolled down the hall behind his woman.

Lisa had just made it into the room as he headed down the hallway. She slammed the door and he marched down the hall and flung it open.

"What is wrong with you?" He said confused.

"Oh, so now you got a lil' girlfriend? Was what went on earlier today really all that bad?" She said in a low but irate tone.

Alonzo just laughed, plopped down on the bed and looked at her. Lisa didn't find the situation the least bit amusing.

"And what's so damn funny?" She asked putting her hands on her hips.

Alonzo stopped laughing but he could barely get his words out without starting back up.

"I'm laughing at you. You just talked shit earlier about me jumping to conclusions, now you doing the same thing. You mad because I was in there with that woman?"

"And I'm not supposed to be mad if I see you alone in your house with another woman?" She said answering his question with a question.

"You don't even know who that is," He said trying not to laugh in her face again, "that's Lasaia, the girl my brother ran into last night, the one that lived next door to us as kids. She stopped by to see him."

Lisa felt about as big as ant notebook paper. She was in shock.

"That's her?" She whispered like Lasaia was at their door listening.

She couldn't believe that she had just done the same thing she got upset with him for doing.

And, on the same day no less.

"Wow, she is really pretty," She said putting her hands on her hips, "I should have known she wasn't here for you. Ain't no way you could pull a girl that good lookin'."

Alonzo stopped laughing and gave her a strange look, not really sure he heard her comment right. She tried, but couldn't hold in her laugh.

"What? Anyway, I got you didn't I?" He said standing up and wrapping his arms around her waist.

"And what exactly makes you think you *got* me?" Lisa said trying to resist his charm.

"Because if I didn't have you, you wouldn't have been mad when you saw me in there with her." Alonzo said pulling her body closer to his.

Lisa loved when she held her tight. His strong body pressed against hers felt like acing a test, everything was right.

"Oh really?" She said unable to think of anything else to say.

"Yes, really." Alonzo said as he moved in and gave his woman a slow sexy kiss on the lips.

Their quick little make out session began to heat up and Lisa began to moan as Alonzo pulled her closer. Alonzo's thought of getting to work had gone out the window and was only focused on one goal now.

After a few more seconds of slow kisses Lisa pushed him back, "Easy, easy cowboy. We have to get ready to get outta here. You know you need to get to work on time."

Alonzo looked a little disappointed and gave her his patented puppy dog face. After she didn't push him away he went back at her neck and began kissing her again.

"Alonzo…mmm…Alonzo, come on baby, we need to get going." Lisa said trying to get him to stop but really not wanting him to.

Alonzo let out a disappointed groan, which was muffled by her neck.

"Come on, you have to get ready to go. You can play with *Lady K* later on tonight." Lisa said finding the strength to push him away.

Alonzo gave up his attempts and started to get ready for another night at work. He gave her another hug and kiss and Lisa jumped on the bed and turned on the television.

By now Marcus was just leaving his room and heading for the kitchen. He heard Lisa and Alonzo in their room talking as he entered the hallway but had no idea that Lasaia was in the living room waiting on him. As he passed, Lasaia saw him but Marcus was so busy rushing that he didn't even glance at the beautiful creature sitting on the couch in his brother's living room. She jumped up and followed him trying to walk as lightly as possible. She caught up to him just as he turned the corner to the kitchen. Marcus still hadn't seen that his company was already there and less than 5 feet behind him. He grabbed a cup from the cabinet and turned on the cold-water faucet to get drink. He didn't hear her heals on the tile floor with the water running and she was able to sneak up right behind him. She reached up and put her hands over his eyes and said, "Guess who?"

Marcus just smiled and turned around.

There she was.

Smile brighter than any of the actors in the Crest commercials.

She opened her arms and they laughed as they shared a hug.

"How long have you been here?" He asked as they separated.

"Not long, me and Alonzo were sitting her on the couch until like five minutes ago. Then this girl came in and just stood there watching us and ran off and he went after her. I guess she thought I was trying to get with him or something. Anyway, I've just been sitting here waiting on you."

"I was wondering why they were in the room talking. I figured he was just getting ready for work or something."

"Oh, before I forget again, I have a surprise for you." Lasaia said while grabbing him by the hand.

She pulled him back to the living room and over to the couch where her present awaited them. She passed him the brown paper bag that she had gotten out of her car. He put down his water, unrolled the bag and looked inside. He couldn't do anything but smile and laugh at what he saw. Lasaia smiled and laughed along with him. She was grateful that he liked his gift.

Five

Marcus reached into the brown paper bag and pulled out a pint sized bottle of *MD 20/20*...Mad Dawg. When he first started drinking at about 16 years old, that was his drink of choice, even though it made him sick every time. He would try and impress Lasaia with his ability to "hold his liquor," as he would always say he could do, but it always backfired. She thought he would get a kick out of seeing that familiar bottle. After all the years, it still looked the same.

"You still remember huh?" He said laughing.

"You never forget what your friends like." She said giggling with him.

The two of them had a seat on the couch.

Alonzo finally finished getting ready and he and Lisa walked into the living room just as the two of them had sat down.

"Lasaia this is my girlfriend Lisa...Lisa this is Lasaia." Alonzo said introducing the two women.

They shook hands.

Lisa gave Lasaia a remorseful smile as she spoke to try and make up for her behavior earlier, and Lasaia mirrored her salutation.

The four of them had a seat.

Marcus and Lasaia sat on the couch and Lisa sat in Alonzo's lap on the recliner.

"So how you been doing?" Alonzo asked, starting over their conversation earlier. More for Lisa than to get the information.

"I'm good, it's been a long week but everything is going pretty good." Lasaia responded.

The small group engaged in a little light small talk for a few minutes, then Alonzo started to joke about how Marcus was frantically cleaning up before Lasaia came over again.

They all had a laugh at that.

The conversation quickly shifted to their childhood. Alonzo brought up Marcus's dream and Lasaia brought up her dream as well. They laughed and talked about the different things they had done as kids and tried to get caught up to the present as best they could.

Alonzo brought up a memory that they both had long forgotten about.

"Hey, you remember that time you almost killed yourself trying to get to that play?" He asked his brother.

"Oooh, man!" Marcus said laughing and thinking about that night's events.

"Killed yourself? You told me your car broke down." Lasaia said surprised at this newfound information.

"It did, but he almost got killed right after that." Alonzo said still laughing at brother. Marcus started the story with him getting home from a short basketball practice after school on a Friday afternoon.

Marcus walked through the front door and the house was buzzing with a vacuum and teeming with the scent of Pine Sol and bleach. Marcus had forgotten that his mother was having a neighborhood dinner party that evening. She did that every so often just to be nice to the neighbors and so they all could have a pleasant evening together. Obviously, this time she had gotten off work late and was hustling to get the house clean and decorated. Alonzo was in charge of cleaning the bathrooms and the living room, and was scrubbing out the tub as Marcus walked by. Why he had to scrub the tub was a mystery to the both of them. Nobody ever asked to take a bath when they came over but their mother demanded it so it had to be done. She couldn't stand the thought of someone coming over, going into her bathroom and seeing a ring around the bathtub. Mrs. Downing prided herself at keeping a nice, clean house for her family and didn't want others to think otherwise.

Marcus walked to his room and put his things on the bed and walked back into the hall. He headed to the living room to hang out until Alonzo finished with the bathroom so he could get showered for the night. He told his mother two weeks prior that he had to go to the play that night but the present situation had changed. Marcus didn't know it but so had his afternoon.

His mother caught him as soon as he passed the kitchen.

"Marcus! I need you to run to the store and get this stuff." She said handing him a list and some money.

"Ma, I told you I got this thing at the school in a little bit and I still need to get ready."

"Marcus I know, but I can't leave and I need that stuff to finish the dinner. Gon' now. It'll only take a few minutes." She said as she turned and walked over to the bubbling pots on the stove. The steam took to the air in three large pillars and the smell of fried chicken, greens and several other soul food aromas filled the kitchen.

Marcus was in a tight spot.

He knew he had to do what his mother wanted because his father wasn't home yet and Alonzo wasn't old enough to drive. And, if he would have let her go she would have been at the store forever looking at everything and talking to everybody. He also knew that he had to be there for Lasaia before the curtain went up because he promised he would. Marcus figured he would just rush to the store as fast as he could and rush back to get ready.

Marcus sped to his room, grabbed his keys and wallet off the bed and ran out the front door. He ran to his car and jumped into the driver's seat. He turned the key of his 1975 Chevrolet Caprice that his parents bought him for his 16th birthday. They said they bought it for him because they trusted him and wanted to give him a little more independence and a way to school. Marcus knew they bought it because they didn't want him banging up their cars.

He pulled out of the driveway and headed to the store. It was already 5:45 and the curtain was scheduled to go up at 7:00 and he still had to get to the store, get the groceries, get home, take a shower, and get to the auditorium. Marcus didn't take very good care of his car and it picked today to act funny. His temperature gauge slowly began creeping its way into the red zone.

"Come on baby, not now, not now, not now." Marcus said trying to encourage his car to just make it to the store. The car decided to let Marcus make it to his destination and he pulled into a space in front of the store. There was a small amount of smoke coming from under his hood, but that happened often and Marcus paid it no mind and darted into the store. He quickly grabbed a buggy and flew up and down the aisles, grabbing things off the shelves that were on the list. He caught a break when he went up to the front to check out. He ran into a classmate who opened her register and let him be the first person to checkout. Marcus dashed out of the store and rushed over to his car. He put his mother's bags in the back seat and jumped into the front. The car started followed by a loud backfire that sounded like a gun shot but Marcus didn't pay it any mind and threw it in gear and sped home. He slowed his driving down when he reached his street so his neighbors wouldn't see him speeding and tell his parents. He pulled into the driveway and rocketed from the car. He grabbed the bags off the back seat and scampered into the house like he was on fire. He dropped the groceries down on the kitchen table and her change on the countertop.

He looked at the clock over the stove. It was 6:25. He had 35 minutes to get out of his uniform, get a shower, and get back to the school. It would be close but he could do it. The school was only about a six or seven minute drive up the street anyway.

Then it happened.

Marcus's mother seemed to appear out of thin air like a magician.

"Marcus, go help your brother finish cleaning up the living room." She said passing by him in the hall.

"Ma, it's almost 6:30, the play starts at 7:00, and I ain't even had a shower yet." Marcus said trying to get her to understand

"Marcus I know, but your brother is taking forever and people are gonna start showing up pretty soon and I need to change. Please, this is the last thing. It'll only take a minute." She said before quickly shuffling off to her room to get ready. Her minutes were starting to eat up a lot of Marcus's time but he did as she asked and rushed back to the living room. Alonzo was in the room watching more television than cleaning and he looked up as his brother approached him.

"Come on man, get up. I need to get outta here and momma said I gotta help you before I can go." Marcus said turning off the TV before grabbing some of the things off the floor. The room wasn't that bad, but this detour shaved valuable minutes off his prep time.

They finished cleaning the room and Marcus left Alonzo to vacuum the floor. He rushed to his room and tried to find an outfit to put on. He was digging through his drawers when he glanced at the time on his alarm clock. It was 6:40. Marcus knew Lasaia was probably getting nervous by now since he wasn't there with her. He just replayed the conversation that they had before he talked her into agreeing to try out for the part of Juliet in their high school's rendition of the Shakespearean classic.

The two of them were sitting, discussing different things in her drama class. The theater always captivated Lasaia but she never did much more than watch as her classmates acted out scenes. The idea of being someone other than herself, if only for an hour, was what really drew her to it. She loved it when they did scenes from *Romeo & Juliet* the most. She told Marcus how she loved the story and how her teacher, Mrs. Andrews, was going to put on a production of it using people from all of her classes. Marcus told her she should go out for Juliet but she wasn't sure she could do it.

"Come on, nobody else has the passion for the character that you do, and I've seen some of her other classes. You the best looking girl in all of em'." Marcus told her.

She just gave him her usual flattered smile that she would get on her face whenever he would say something sweet like that.

"You really think I should?" She asked not sounding too confident.

"I know you should, and I know you can do it too." He said trying to boost her up.

"Ok," She said after several seconds of thought, "BUT…you gotta promise to come see me if I get it."

"Oh, you know I'll be front row center." He said.

"No, I'm serious. Promise me you will come see me before I have to go on if I get the part." She said.

"Ok, I promise." Marcus told her.

The thought of his words echoed through his ears as he burrowed through his drawers looking for something to wear. Marcus knew there was only one way he could make it there on time. He gave up his search and ran out of his room, out the front door, and to his car. He figured he would just take a shower after they got back to the house. He turned the key in the ignition and the engine turned over but won't start. He tried to start the car three more times and still nothing. He banged his palm against the steering wheel and said, "No, no, no, not now, come on!"

He turned the key one more time not giving up.

"Come on, come on, come on baby." Marcus said as the engine continued to try to start.

The car must have felt charitable and finally started. He pulled out of the drive way and flew down his street.

❧ ❧ ❧

By this time Lasaia was a nervous wreck. She paced back and forth back-stage wringing her hands in her Juliet costume. Her teacher saw the look on her face and walked over to her.

"You ok?" Mrs. Andrews asked.

Lasaia had never done anything even closely related to performing in a play in front of a room full of people. Even though the place was full of actors, stage-hands, and a wall-to-wall audience, without Marcus there she felt completely alone. Lasaia looked at her with tears forming in her eyes and said, "I don't know if I can do this," in a quivering voice.

"You'll be fine. If you do half as well as you did at the tryouts and in rehearsal, the show will be amazing." Mrs. Andrews said.

Lasaia played the part so well in tryouts; she almost made Mrs. Andrews cry.

"This is your role Lasaia. You can do this. Ok?" She said finishing her abridged pep talk.

Lasaia felt a little better but she was still too nervous to go on.

"Ok." Lasaia said reluctantly nodding her head.

Her real feelings were to just flee through the back stage door and disappear.

Mrs. Andrews reached in her jacket pocket and handed her some tissue and Lasaia wiped her eyes.

"Ok people it's almost time!" Mrs. Andrews yelled backstage to the other actors as she walked away from Lasaia.

The second Mrs. Andrews walked away the little bit of confidence she had given Lasaia jumped out of her body and ran away. Lasaia was feeling unsure of herself again and the one person that could calm her down and get her to focus was nowhere to be found. She just kept pacing and looking at the big clock on the wall backstage.

Marcus was about a mile from the school when his engine started puffing out thick white smoke. He slowly started losing power and soon after that his car completely died. He swerved to avoid hitting a car that was in front of him that was stopped at a red light and found himself coasting through a busy intersection with no power at all. Cars coming through the intersection swerved to avoid hitting his slow moving Caprice and he was able to make it through the intersection, but his car was still dead. He drifted into a closed gas station parking lot at the other end of the intersection and into a parking space. He put his car in park and tried to start it again. The engine just knocked and kicked out more and more white smoke. The smoke was so thick that Marcus could barely see out the front windshield. He popped the hood, jumped out of the car and lifted the heavy metal covering. Smoke soared from under the hood like Marcus was sending smoke signals.

Marcus looked at his watch.

6:45.

He knew that there was nothing he could do to fix the car in time so he decided to leave it in the space and find another way to the school. Marcus figured he could hitch hike to the school but there was no one pulling into the gas station. And, why would they?

It was abandoned.

The immediate chance of him getting a ride that way was slim to none. He only had 15 minutes to get to the school auditorium before the curtain went up and he didn't have much time to think. He figured it was just a mile and he had run plenty of those in practice easily, so this couldn't be a huge task.

Marcus was running with all he had and he didn't have much left after going to school all day, basketball practice after school, running through a grocery store, hurrying around helping his brother clean, and now running full speed back to school. He got tired quickly but he refused to give up. He had made a promise to his friend that he would do something and he was going to do it or die trying. The night quickly came overhead and the streetlights began to buzz. Marcus had slowed down a little, but was still running his heart out. Ahead of him he saw an intersection that he thought he could make it through with no problem, but he wasn't paying attention to one car that was trying to make it through the light before it turned red. He was in the middle of the crosswalk when the driver slammed on the brakes. The tires yelled at him to get out of the way but Marcus hadn't seen the car before that moment. It was headed directly at him and he had nowhere to go. He somehow found a small burst of speed and ran fast enough to dive out of the way of the car as it skimmed through the crosswalk, missing him by only about a foot. Marcus looked back at the car as it screeched to a halt, then sped off into the dark. They didn't even know if Marcus was ok or not but they didn't care, at that point neither did her. Marcus jumped to his feet and took off running down the street again. He was only about 200 yards from campus and he could see the school sign in the glow of the streetlights.

He made it to the campus about five minutes to seven. He ran to the side of the auditorium and saw a friend of his that was a stagehand on the play.

"What's up Marcus?" He said as the tired Marcus ran up.

"What's up man...hey...where's Lasaia..." Marcus asked between deep breaths.

"She's back here, come on."

Marcus followed the boy into the backstage area of the auditorium. After passing a few props they turned a corner and there she was. They heard another student on stage giving the monologue of the play so Marcus knew that things were already underway. She was just standing with her back to them.

She wasn't moving.

She looked like a statue.

Marcus jogged up behind her.

She jumped when she heard the footsteps and turned to see him standing there with his hands on his knees breathing heavily. Marcus was tired and smelled terrible, but he had made it. Her eyes were full of tears, but to Marcus she was still beautiful. He never knew she could look as beautiful as she was in her costume. He was used to seeing her in blue jeans or shorts and a T-shirt but never anything like this. Her shoulders were exposed and her hair and makeup were flawless. Marcus couldn't believe his eyes. She reached down and wrapped her arms around him and began rambling like she always did when she was nervous.

"I didn't think you were coming, I thought…I was getting scared and…"

Marcus finally caught his breath and stopped her.

"Ok, ok, I'm here. You ready?" He asked.

"I don't know Marcus, I don't think I can go out there." She said looking in the direction of the big curtain separating her from the audience.

"You can do this. Don't worry. We have been over this a million times."

The two of them had practiced almost every evening since she had won the part. Marcus knew the lines almost as well as she did.

"Don't worry, I'm gonna be right here and you can just look at me if you get lost. Ok?"

Lasaia started to calm down and she could actually breathe normally now.

"Ok…now, what's your first line?" Marcus asked and they quickly went through her first scene.

Lasaia took her position on the side of the stage ready to make her entrance and Marcus was right behind her. As *Juliet's* mother frantically rushed around the stage with the nurse looking for her daughter, Lasaia looked back at him and then walked out onto the stage. Marcus could almost hear the students in the crowd go silent as they realized who the beautiful young woman playing *Juliet* was. When it was time for Lasaia to say her first line she froze. There was a short pause and she looked over at Marcus. She knew it was time for her to say something but she went blank. Marcus immediately started mouthing her line to her. She picked it up immediately and she was on her own from there.

Lasaia knocked the audience dead. They had no idea that she was that talented. She had half of the audience in tears by the end of her final line and got a standing ovation for her performance. Mrs. Andrews even brought her back on stage after everyone else had walked off and the crowd went wild again. Lasaia couldn't do anything but cry with joy at all of her classmates standing there cheering and screaming for her. She had never felt anything like that before...a room full of people, clapping only for her. She wished it could have lasted forever.

❧ ❧ ❧

Marcus was waiting on the side of the stage behind the curtain when she came to the side and she dove into his arms.

"You did it! You did it! You were amazing!" He said holding her and spinning in circles. He put her down and she hugged him again. She wanted to thank her friend so much for everything he did for her, but she didn't know how. She was never good with words. She didn't have to thank him though. The smile on her face was all the thanks he needed. She looked at him and saw that he still had on his jersey and realized she hadn't noticed it until then. He told her the long version of his afternoon as they made their way to her dressing room. How his mom gave him everything to do as soon as he got home, then how his car gave out on him, then how he had to run to the school. She just smiled and laughed; flattered that he did all of that trying to make it there for her.

And it had all been for her.

If it hadn't been for him making it there, she probably would have left the play and made a laughing stock of herself and all the other actors. What was *Romeo & Juliet* without *Juliet.* After she finished changing, she met back up with Marcus outside her dressing room and the two of them walked toward the front doors of the auditorium. Marcus's princess was gone, but he still had his friend.

As the night air greeted them so did another round of applause. This time given by Mrs. Andrews and all of the other actors from the play. They all told Lasaia how well she had done and congratulated her on her success. Everyone said goodbye and Marcus and Lasaia started on their walk home. With Marcus's car injured at the gas station up the street, it would be a long walk home. They didn't mind.

As long as they had each other the walk wouldn't be long enough.

As they made it to the big sign at the entrance to their high school, Mrs. Andrews pulled up beside.

"You guys need a ride?" She asked through the car window.

They accepted the ride and got in. Lasaia showed her teacher where they lived and she took them to Marcus's house. She let them out in front and they thanked her for the ride. Mrs. Andrews congratulated Lasaia again, told the two of them goodnight and pulled off down the street.

They could hear the party inside the house from the driveway. A lot of laughing and music broke through the night air. Al Green was serenading the neighborhood, telling people he was *Tired of being Alone.*

"You headed home?" Marcus asked.

"I guess." She said not really wanting to walk through her door after such a great night.

She didn't want anything to ruin its perfection.

"Why don't you come in for a minute?" Marcus asked her.

Lasaia couldn't turn down a chance to go into Marcus's house. His parents treated her like she was the sweetest little girl in the world and she felt more at home over his house than at her own. They walked through the front door and there were people from all over the neighborhood hanging out in the living room and kitchen. Marcus's mom saw the two of them and rushed over to meet them.

"Heeeey yall." She said rushing over and giving Lasaia a big hug.

Lasaia loved Mrs. Downing so much.

"So…how was it?" She asked still holding on to Lasaia's hands.

Before Lasaia could get a word out Marcus cut in.

"Ma' you shoulda' seen her, she hit every line perfect. She had half the audience cryin' by the end of the show. And then they gave her her own standing ovation and everything. She did great!"

Mrs. Downing just looked at Marcus in a way that he knew it was time to shut up. Then she looked back at Lasaia and asked, "Did you have fun?"

Lasaia just looked at her and gave her a humble nod and smiled. Marcus's mom gave her another hug and kissed her on the cheek and walked off to find her husband. Then out of nowhere Lasaia's mom walked up.

"Heeey baby." She said giving her daughter a hug.

Lasaia had no idea that her mom was over there that night. She figured she would be home getting drunk or high with her abuser.

"How was the play baby?" She asked.

"It was fine, why didn't you come?" Lasaia asked, with almost no feeling in her voice.

"Well I was…I mean I wanted to…but I…" Her mothers words were cut short by the entrance of the one person Lasaia hated in the whole world. Lasaia knew if her mother was there that he was lurking somewhere in the shadows and it was only a matter of time before he appeared. He stepped between the two of them and looked down on Lasaia like he always did.

"So…we got a lil' actress here?" He said, in a not so laudatory way.

He was the reason that her mother didn't get to go see her perform. He made her stay home with him knowing that Lasaia was performing tonight. It was the first time her daughter had ever had the nerve to do anything like that and she had to miss it. Lasaia knew why her mom didn't come. Marcus could almost see the hatred percolating through Lasaia's body as she kept her eyes on his. The play must have given her some newfound confidence because she would have usually backed down by now.

This time she just stared at him.

He stood there and laughed at her as if he knew he could crush her with one swing.

"My daughter! The lil' Angela Bassett!" He yelled, followed by drunken chuckle.

The focus of the party seemed to shift from having fun to the battle of wills between the two of them.

"You been stupid for this long. 'Bout time you do something right." He said followed by another hacking laugh as he put his hand on her shoulder and squeezed.

The look on Lasaia's face told Marcus that his grip hurt but she straightened up and tried to show no fear. She looked over at her mother, wondering how long she was going to let him talk about her like she was nothing. Marcus took as much of it as he could and that last statement took him over the edge.

"At least she doin' something. Not just a drunk like you."

The man that was twice Marcus's size turned toward him. Marcus felt no fear in his heart for this bully. Most likely, Marcus would have been no match for him but he knew he had to be weak. He only beat on women.

Out of nowhere Marcus's father stepped into the picture.

"What's the problem here?" Daniel Downing said in his deep, commanding voice. He was about twice the size of Lasaia's stepfather and wasn't about to let anyone disrespect him or his home.

"Nah, Danny, no problems brotha…we just talkin'." Lasaia's step dad said knowing that was a fight he definitely couldn't win.

"Go outside and get some air Willy." Daniel told his drunken neighbor.

Lasaia's mother grabbed her man by the arm and pulled him outside. She looked back at her daughter who was almost in tears as they crossed the threshold with an apologetic look on her face. She didn't want her daughter to have to go through this, but she didn't do anything to stop it. They got outside and Marcus's dad turned back to the two teenagers. He put his big strong hand on Lasaia's shoulder where Willy had grabbed her and rubbed softly. Lasaia just dropped her head.

"You ok sweetie?" He asked.

Lasaia just nodded her head and tried to keep from crying. Marcus put his arm around her and took her to his room. After he had a chance to finally take a shower the two of them went outside and sat on the porch for the rest of the evening. Marcus was able to get her back in good spirits and made her remember what a great job that she had done that night and to forget what her step dad said.

Six

The three of them sat and listened to Marcus finish his story. Lasaia remembered how her stepfather had ruined one of her most triumphant nights but she had gotten over it now and was able to laugh about it.

"I can't believe you almost got hit by a car." She said laughing.

Alonzo looked down at his watch and said, "It's 9:45. I guess we better get rollin'."

Lisa climbed off of her man's lap and the two of them stood up.

"It was a pleasure meeting you." Lisa said shaking Lasaia's hand again.

"Yeah, don't be a stranger." Alonzo said giving her a hug.

"Oh, I won't." Lasaia said as they turned to leave.

Marcus got up and walked them to the door like they were visitors in his house.

"Hey, remember your vows man." Alonzo said in a low tone as he tapped his brother on the chest. Lisa giggled and opened the front door. She looked at Marcus and said, "Yeah, control the testosterone."

Marcus chuckled at her comment and said, "Anyway, yall get out."

"You kickin' me out of my own house?" Alonzo said joking as Marcus shoved him over the threshold and quickly shut the door behind them. Alonzo lightly tapped on the door and said, "Marcus…Marcus…I know you got another woman in there," in a very bad impression of Sherise. Alonzo starts to act like he's crying and kept knocking.

"I dun birthed you two babies and you gon' treat me like this? Why Marcus…Whhhyyyyy?"

Marcus heard his foolish brother as he leaned his back against the door and smiled. Lisa pulled her silly man away from the door and they got into the truck and left.

Marcus walked back to his company in the living room and had a seat on the couch. As hard as he tried, Marcus couldn't get over the fact that Lasaia had grown into this attractive woman sitting next to him. She finished her drink and Marcus offered her another. She accepted and he got up and headed for the kitchen. He brought back another beer for her and one for himself. They sat and talked about old times. How they really started hanging out and had such great times together. Then Lasaia said, "You know what I wanna know?"

"What's that?"

"When you went off to college, why did you stop calling and emailing me?"

Marcus hadn't thought about that in years. He never did know why they lost contact the way they did.

"I didn't. You stopped contacting me. I mean I slowed down a little when I started getting in different organizations and stuff but I emailed you at least once a week"

Lasaia thought back and had a revelation.

"You know what? I don't remember getting any emails from you after I changed my email address."

Marcus remembered that he too had changed his email address on his birthday during his sophomore year. His parents had gotten him a new computer and he had problems logging on to his old account. He gave his explanation and she revealed that she too had changed her email that same day. Since neither of them could access their old accounts, their "My New Address" emails never actually made it to the recipients. Further analysis into the situation showed that with Marcus switching dorms rooms because of a fight with his roommate caused him to miss her calls. After a few months of no contact they both gave up and decided to try and catch each other during the summer or something. The problem with that was that Lasaia never came home for the summer. She spent 18 years of her life trying to get out and when she did she swore she would never go back. Lasaia's mother and step father moved to the other side of town and no one in the neighborhood knew where they were so Marcus had no way of contacting them to get to her. A series of unfortunate events had separated the two of them for almost a decade but they were together again now and that was all that mattered.

Marcus asked Lasaia what she had been doing over the past 10 years. She told him after they lost contact she decided that she wanted to do something in fashion. She wanted to model, but agencies always told her too short, so she figured if she couldn't work for the agency, she would own the agency. She told Marcus how she graduated at the top of her business class and immediately went home to tell her mother. Of course her mother wasn't allowed to go to her graduation. Another mission completed on Willy's agenda to completely separate the two of them. When she got home she got into a huge fight with him and he kicked her out and told her never to come back. She was grown now and his threats of violence didn't faze her any longer. She told Marcus about one situation where he tried to push her and she hit him across the face with a broom handle. They both just laughed as she told the story. She had finally stood up for herself and he got what he deserved. Her stepfather knew the only way to get rid of her now was to erase her from his sight. Lasaia tried to convince her mother to leave too but that was a losing battle. For some reason her mother took those punches to the face as a form of love and he had convinced her that no other man could or would have anything to do with her. To save herself, Lasaia had to leave one of the only two people that she loved behind. It hurt her to her heart to do it, Marcus could tell by the way she told the story, but she knew it was the only way she could really live. She actually hadn't heard from her mother in three years and the last time she went home for a visit her mom had quit her job and they had moved out of Albany. None of her old friends or co-workers had heard from her and she had basically dropped off the planet.

At first, Lasaia tried to track her down and didn't get anywhere. Then she figured there was no point in looking for someone who obviously didn't want to be found. She missed her mom a lot though. Even through the drug abuse, her mom really did love her. The two of them would have great times together when her step-devil wasn't around. It seemed like the whole atmosphere of the house would change the minute he stepped through the front door. But, that was in the past and Lasaia wanted to know about Marcus.

"So, what's been up with you? I see you have a wedding band on so my dreams of sweeping you off your feet have been crushed."

Marcus looked down at his hand and laughs. He had forgotten that he even had it on. They both had a laugh as Marcus told his story.

After they lost contact Marcus became a collegiate machine. He too graduated at the top of his business class. He didn't take on the ownership route Lasaia had but he was a major name in a very reputable company. Lasaia didn't know much about advertising but even she had heard of 'Streamline' advertising. Marcus told her about his wife and how they met his sophomore year in college. They met shortly after the two of them lost contact. She reminded him so much of Lasaia that he couldn't let this one get away. Lasaia was flattered that he held her in that high of a regard that when he found someone else like her, he refused to let her go. Then Marcus told her that he also named his first-born little girl after her and that almost brought her to tears. She couldn't even talk and just wrapped her arms around his neck. She had no idea that Marcus would do something so sweet to keep the thought of her around. He obviously had no intention of ever forgetting her. After their embrace, Marcus took his wallet from his pocket and showed her pictures of his family.

"Oooo Marcus, they are so beautiful!" she said in a whispering, thrilled voice.

Marcus smiled and thanked her. Lasaia just looked at Marcus with that same affectionate look she had that night he showed up at her window to help her study.

"I'm so proud of you." She said.

She gave him another adoring gaze and there was a moment of silence. The only noise for a few seconds was from the television as the sports legends discussed the upcoming pre-season game in Atlanta.

Marcus looked down at their drinks and they were both empty. "You want another one?" He asked pointing at the empty bottle. She snapped back into reality and said, "Um, yeah sure."

Marcus grabbed the empty bottles and started his expedition to the kitchen.

"You got anything stronger?" She asked before he got more then a few steps.

Marcus stopped and looked back at her.

"Yeah, I got some Mad Dawg." He said with a laugh.

"Yeah right, I don't think so."

Marcus made his way to the kitchen, "What you want?" he yelled as he opened the cabinet to check out Alonzo's arsenal.

"What cha' got?" She yelled back, from the living room.

Marcus looked through the bottles.

"Um…I see Gin, Cognac, Rum, Brandy, Vodka, and Scotch." He said reading the bottles like a liquor menu.

"Um…A Gin and juice will be fine." She shouted back.

Marcus grabbed the bottle of *Seagrams* from the shelf and mixed her drink. He made one for himself and headed back to the living room.

"So, tell me." He started as he sat down.

Lasaia gave him her full attention just like she always did.

"Who is the lucky man?" He asked.

"What lucky man?"

“The man that has swept you off your feet. The one that makes your heart skip a beat. I know you got somebody out there wondering where you are tonight.”

“Well, I have only had one of those in my life and I just recently found out that he’s married so…” She said throwing a flattering hint.

Marcus smiled and said, “Come on now. I know you have had a fiancé, boyfriend, male equivalent of a mistress, stalker…something since college.”

“Well, I mean I have had guys that I talked to, date or whatever but none of them ever seemed to fit. You know? It’s like with you, when you found your wife. She fit into your life. I still haven’t found that perfect Lego piece yet.”

“Well, what about boyfriends? I know you have had some kind of long term relationship.”

Lasaia thought for a few seconds.

“I have dated guys but they never could be honest with me long enough to make it to boyfriend status. One guy had a girlfriend and tried to be with me too. Another guy would always lie to me for no reason. He would say he was going home to go to bed because he had to work in the morning, and then come to find out he is out at the strip club with his boys. I didn’t care about him going to a strip club but it’s the fact that he felt he had to lie to me about it.”

Marcus listened to her list a few other guys that did her wrong and sat there wondering how any man could treat a woman this gorgeous the way she described. Then she thought of one guy in particular.

“Oh, there was this one guy though. His name was Greg. I really like him.”

She stopped the story at that and Marcus sat there waiting for her to continue.

“And?” He said, expecting more.

“And, he was cool. What?”

“That’s it? He was cool. You really liked him because he was cool?”

“No. I mean…he was a younger guy, about Alonzo’s age. He was so sweet. He managed a hall here in Atlanta where we held a fashion show once. He asked me out and I was working so much he seemed like the perfect outlet so I was like, “Why not?” He treated me so nice though. He gave me flowers and made me laugh.” Lasaia said gazing into mid air like she slipped into a brief flashback.

After then she went silent.

“So? What happened to him?” Marcus asked thinking he might have found her dream guy.

“He stood me up for a date and I never talked to him again.” She said like that explanation was worthy of praise.

Marcus's head tilted to the side like the RCA dog and his mouth dropped open. Marcus couldn't understand what could have been so bad about this guy that she seemed to be in love with a few seconds earlier.

So he missed one date.

"You broke up with him because he stood you up?" He asked.

"Mmh hmm." She nonchalantly said as she sipped her drink.

Marcus was speechless at the fact that she would let a guy she talked so highly about go that easy.

"So, was it a real important date? Did he at least give you a reason why he couldn't make it?"

"No, it was just an ordinary date. Nothing special. I think we were going out to BED restaurant downtown or something like that. He said he had a flat tire or something and didn't show up because he didn't have a spare."

"So why didn't you believe him?"

"I didn't say I didn't believe him but you don't do that to me. You don't tell someone something then don't follow through on it."

Marcus thought she was joking and let out a slight chuckle.

"So you're telling me, if I were to offer to take you out, and we set a date, you would stop talking to me if I didn't show up?" He asked hypothetically.

"No," She said finishing off her drink, "I wouldn't have to worry about that with you. You didn't let me down like that."

She slowly moved over closer to Marcus and looked deep into his eyes. Marcus didn't know what her intentions were and he wasn't sure he would be able to fight the temptation if she were to try something with him. She leaned over and put her head on his shoulder. Marcus breathed a silent sigh of relief.

"You used to be my security blanket. You were the only person in my life that was stable. From the first time I met you in your parent's shed, I always saw you as this honest, trustworthy, reliable guy. I always fantasized about just…riding off with you into the sunset."

Marcus figured that the alcohol was doing the talking for Lasaia now. He had never known her to be this out spoken, even with him. *A drunk tongue speaks sober words*, Marcus's grandfather always said. She was feeling the effects of the alcohol but all of the words were her true feelings. Marcus was at a loss for words. They did have a little romantic episode in their senior year in high school, but he didn't know it went all the way back to their first encounter. All kinds of emotions ran through his head as they sat there in silence.

Lasaia lifted her head from his shoulder and looked into his eyes again. Without saying a word she slowly leaned forward and kissed Marcus on his lips. Her mouth was just as soft and inviting as it looked. Her lips were full and voluptuous and felt amazing pressed against his. Marcus was lost in the moment and couldn't stop himself from kissing her back. Lasaia felt his acceptance of her action and took this opportunity to get back a small piece of what was once hers. Their slow passionate kiss continued for a few seconds and Lasaia began to tease him with her tongue. He didn't stop her. Ancient emotions surfaced. Body temperatures rose. Lasaia decided to pull out all the stops and separated her lips from his. They gazed into each others eyes. Silent fires burned inside each of them.

She rose from under him and threw her sexy brown leg around to the other side of Marcus, straddling him. The heat from their passion began to warm up the room and their juices began to flow. Marcus had his hands on Lasaia's wide hips and slid them up her back. Her skin was so soft. The fabric of her dress was so thin he could feel every curve of her body. He reached up, grabbed her hair, pulled her head back and attacked her neck with his mouth. Erotic vampires. Lasaia showed her aggressive side and grabbed him by the side of his head and pushed it back. She pressed her lips against his again and plunged her tongue into his mouth. Marcus was turned on even more by her forceful performance. He grabbed a handful of her soft bottom with one hand while pulling down the top of her dress with the other, exposing her perfect D-cup breasts. Marcus took her erect nipple into his mouth and ran his tongue over her areolas.

Lasaia began to moan with pleasure.

Their make-out session lasted for only about thirty seconds before Marcus realized what he was doing. Pictures of his wife and kids quickly flashed through his mind.

"Wait, wait, wait…" He said pushing Lasaia back.

"What?" She whispered, before she pursued another kiss.

Marcus stopped her again.

"I can't do this." He said realizing he was about to make the worst mistake of his life.

He used his strong arms to lift her off of him and placed her back in her spot next to him on the couch. She pulled her dress back up around her breasts and grabbed her purse. She reached inside and pulled out a comb and a miniature makeup kit. She immediately started combing her hair and got it back to its original look. The incident didn't seem to faze her at all. Marcus couldn't believe himself. This was the first time in all the years of being married that he had actually touched another woman in that way. He stood up and straightened his clothes.

"Still a good boy I see." She said putting up her comb away and opening her makeup. She fixed her face and looked just as flawless as when she entered the door.

Before Marcus could form a sentence the front door open. Marcus looked at the clock on the wall. It was 3:45 in the morning. They had been talking for almost 6 hours straight. If they had continued with their escapade, Alonzo and Lisa would have surely walked right in on them. Lasaia quickly stuffed her makeup into her purse just as Alonzo and Lisa walked into the room. If they had been ten minutes earlier they would have seen everything but now the scene was back to normal. Marcus just stood there trying to look natural with Lasaia on the couch, legs crossed.

"Yall still up?" Alonzo asked as he walked in.

"Yeah um…" Marcus said just trying to stop Lasaia from getting a word in, "We were just looking at the clock talking about how fast it got late."

Neither Alonzo nor Lisa noticed Marcus's scramble for words. It must have been the alcohol or they were just tired. Lasaia tried to stop Marcus from giving himself away and said, "I think I better get going. It was really nice meeting you again Lisa. Bye Alonzo."

They both told said their goodbyes and Marcus walked her to the front door. He was happy to get away from them. He felt like their eyes were watching his every move. They got to the front door and Marcus opened it.

"Can I at least have a hug?" She asked quietly.

Marcus reluctantly gave her a hug but she didn't try anything funny. She was going to let him of the hook…for now. She turned to walk out the front door but stopped and turned back.

"Look Marcus, I'm sorry. I didn't mean to…I mean I wasn't trying to…I mean I didn't want…I'm sorry, I just…"

Marcus stopped her words. She reminded him of her younger self at that moment. The Lasaia that could never express herself well with words. She really did look apologetic and Marcus gave her another, more genuine hug. He couldn't blame her. It wasn't like she was on the couch making out with herself. He played a part in the whole thing.

"It's ok, really." He said with his arms around her slim waist.

"You sure?" She asked looking up at him with what looked like tears forming in her eyes. She reminded him so much of how she was with him back when they were kids that for a split second he wished they were back to being 16 year olds in Albany. Marcus instinctively shifted into his protective role of her. He gave her one last squeeze and she laid her head on his shoulder one more time. "I better get going." She said as Marcus released his grip.

She walked out the door, to her car and got in. She gave him a quick wave through the windshield as the Jaguar engine came to life. He watched as she pulled out of the driveway and onto the street. He didn't move until her tail-lights disappeared from sight.

He walked back through the house, headed for the living room and ran into Lisa. It was obvious that she had been drinking as she held onto the walls as she moved.

As she passed she asked, "Were you able to control the testosterone?"

Marcus gave her a nervous laugh but didn't respond.

She wouldn't have heard him if he had. She kept her broken stride, using the wall for support and disappeared into Alonzo's room.

Marcus walked back into the living room where his brother was standing, watching highlights on ESPN. He heard Marcus come in and looked at him briefly then turned back to the television.

"Man, it's looking like this game tomorrow is gonna be more exciting than a regular season game." Alonzo said.

Marcus just sat on the couch and tilted his head back. He couldn't believe what he had just let happened. He just put his life and family at risk. But, to him that wasn't the worst thing. The worst thing about it was that he actually liked the way she felt in his arms. He liked the way her lips felt against his, the way her skin felt, the way her body felt pressed against his, the way she kissed him, the way her strong legs wrapped around him, the way her butt felt in his hands, the way her nipple felt in his mouth…hell, he even liked the way her saliva tasted. That hurt him most of all.

A sin is easy to forgive with repentance, but he couldn't even repent. He did feel ashamed, but he wasn't sorry and he couldn't even say that if he had it to do over he wouldn't do it again. He hated himself for thinking that way. He actually wanted to feel bad, but didn't. Alonzo continued his conversation with his brother but Marcus didn't hear a word he said. After a few seconds Alonzo looked back at his brother and saw him sitting on the couch with his head back staring off into space.

"Marcus!" He said trying to get his brother's attention.

"Huh?" Marcus snapped back into reality.

"Man, you alright?"

"Huh? Yeah, I'm cool."

Alonzo looked at his brother, tilted his head in thought, then slowly walked over and sat next to him. Out of nowhere Alonzo leaned over and started sniffing Marcus's shirt. Marcus pushed him away but not before he had collected his evidence.

"Ooooo!" Alonzo said as Marcus pushed him. "Yall did it didn't you?" He said in an excited whisper.

"No! We didn't do anything." Marcus said in a low tone as if the house was full of people and he didn't want anyone to hear them.

Lisa was the only person in the house that could possibly hear them, but she was most likely passed out by now.

Alonzo looked around the room and began sniffing the air.

"Nah, yall ain't do nothing. At least it doesn't smell like it. I know you did something though." Alonzo said pointing at his big brother.

"I was just a kiss. That's it." Marcus said quietly after a few seconds of Alonzo's stare.

"Uh huh, then why your shirt smell like her perfume? Must have been a pretty long kiss," Alonzo said, "And you need to wipe that lipstick off your lips."

Marcus rubbed his lips and looked at his finger and saw the same shade of lipstick that Lasaia had on. He quickly grabbed one of the napkins from around the cups they had been drinking from and wiped his mouth.

"See, I thought you were smoother than this. Your playa card got dust on it bruh. Now your girl had it together. Hair was fixed, clothes on straight, makeup done…flawless. Looking at her, I wouldn't even be able to tell. You the dead giveaway." Alonzo said joking with his brother.

Marcus only had to try and cover up something like this one time before and that was in college. And since Sherise found out about that time he obviously wasn't good at it then either.

"I'll see you in the morning bruh." Alonzo said getting up from the couch and tossing the remote in Marcus's lap.

"Ole elementary school playa ass," Alonzo said with a laugh as he rounded the corner leaving the living room.

Marcus just sat on the couch staring at the spot where it all took place. He replayed the scene over and over again in his head. He still couldn't believe that he didn't feel the guilt he figured he would in a situation like this. Of course, he was disappointed in himself for letting it go as far as it did, but he still liked it. He turned off the television and lights and headed for his room. He fell back on the bed and closed his eyes but she was there too. He couldn't get Lasaia off of his mind. It was like their short interaction opened a Pandora's Box of emotions for him and he couldn't get it to close again. He wondered if she was going through the same thing. He could still smell her scent in his nostrils. After a few minutes he couldn't take it any longer and jumped up to take a shower. He decided a cold shower would probably help get his mind off of her. Marcus got into the shower and had to stop himself from yelling. The water was colder then he expected, but it did the trick. All of his thoughts of Lasaia seemed to rinse off of his body and go down the drain. He felt a lot better after getting out of the shower. The way he figured it was, yes, he made a mistake but at least he stopped it before it went too far. That was his reasoning. He jumped out of the shower, dried off and got dressed for bed.

As Marcus sat down on his bed, he grabbed his wallet off the night stand. He opened it to the pictures of his family that he had shown Lasaia a few hours earlier and began to smile. He pulled his daughter's drawing out from in between two twenty-dollar bills and unfolded it. It still had that same green fox, red ducks, and blue grass. He stretched out on the bed and looked up at the picture in his hands. He hadn't noticed before, but there was a little message written in the sky. He must have been in such a hurry that he didn't notice it before. Sometimes we go through life so fast that we miss out on the little things that make us smile. Marcus could barely read the scribbled message between the crayon marks but he was soon able to make it out. "I love you daddy" was written in the sky. Marcus just smiled and thought about his little girl. He folded up the drawing and put it back in his wallet. He actually went to bed with a clear mind. Thinking about his family always made everything else seem secondary. He closed his eyes and put an end to his second day in Atlanta.

Seven

Marcus woke up around 10:30 on Sunday morning and got out of bed. Alonzo and Lisa were still asleep and the entire house was silent. He walked to the kitchen and poured himself a glass of orange juice. After fiddling around the house for about 10 minutes, he decided to make breakfast for the sleepy heads. Marcus put together a nice breakfast for the three of them. It was nothing as extravagant as Lisa's breakfast but he was proud of it. Just as he was pulling the last pancake out of the pan, Lisa strolled into the kitchen in a long nightshirt and her Tweety Bird house shoes.

"Wow, you cooked breakfast for us?" She asked looking at the food on the stove. Marcus just smiled and nodded his head.

"Your little date last night must have been better then I thought." She said joking with him.

He wasn't sure if Alonzo told her what happened or not, but he didn't want to give himself away in case she didn't know. He just laughed it off.

"Well I was coming to cook for you guys, but I guess I don't have to."

Alonzo slowly struggled into the kitchen dragging his feet and yawning.

"You ready to eat man?" Marcus asked his half-awake little brother.

Alonzo rubbed his eyes and said, "You cooked," with surprise in his voice.

Lisa didn't wait for an invitation and immediately grabbed a plate. She left the two of them in the kitchen and turned on the television in the living room. Marcus grabbed Alonzo by the arm and pulled him to the side.

"Did you tell her about what happened last night?" He asked, whispering.

"What? Nah. Why? She say something to you about it?" Alonzo said pulling his arm from Marcus's grip.

"Nah, she just came in here and said my little date must have been good because I was up cooking."

"Aw, nigga. She just joking wit you. I could see if she came in here asking if you liked the kiss or something. You soundin' real paranoid right now."

Marcus thought about how he was acting and realized he may have been overacting. On any other day that little comment wouldn't have ruffled his feathers but today he was jumpy.

"You right, you right…ok." Marcus said.

"What yall doin'?" Lisa yelled from the living room wondering where her company was.

"We comin'," Alonzo yelled back to Lisa, "Both yall 'bout to get on my nerves. It's too early for this shit."

Alonzo wasn't a morning person. If they hadn't been going to the game that day he would have probably still been asleep. The two brothers grabbed their plates and went into living room and had a seat.

After their meal Lisa collected their plates and took them to the kitchen. She ran some water and started to wash the breakfast dishes.

"So what time the game start?" Marcus asked.

"Um, like 2:00 I think." Alonzo said. It was almost 11:45 now and Marcus knew that they probably had a small journey ahead of them.

"Shouldn't we get ready to go then?" Marcus asked.

"We got time. I got a hook up."

The two of them sat there for a few minutes watching ESPN when the phone rang.

"I got it!" Lisa yelled from the kitchen.

A few seconds later Lisa appeared and handed Marcus the phone.

"Hello?" Marcus said into the phone. He wondered who could be calling him.

"So you can't call nobody now?" Said a voice with an attitude through the line. Marcus immediately recognized his wife's voice.

"Hey baby."

"What happened to you yesterday?"

"I'm sorry, I forgot."

"Uh huh, so what did you do yesterday that was so important that you just forgot about your poor, lonely old wife?"

"Me, Alonzo, and his girlfriend went to a car show somewhere downtown."

Marcus chose not to tell her about the small scuffle they had gotten into and just told her that they went out there for a little while to hang out with some of Alonzo's friends. He knew if she knew about the altercation that she would not be happy about him fighting.

"So what did you do after that?" Sherise asked as if she already knew about Marcus's little escapade with Lasaia and was just giving him the chance to tell on himself.

"Well, we came home and Lisa went to her mom's house, Alonzo went to sleep because he had to go to work last night and I sat on the couch and watched TV." He said hoping to avoid having to bring up his evening with Lasaia.

"So you didn't go to the club with him?" She asked.

"Nah, he club too hard for me." Marcus said joking.

Marcus dodged the opportunity to tell her about Lasaia's visit a second time. He figured that since he was away from home, alone with a very attractive woman, and at Alonzo's, who she didn't trust anyway, it would be best to just let that piece of information slip through the cracks.

Marcus stood up and walked to his room to get a little more privacy.

"So you didn't call your friend?" She asked.

"What friend?" Marcus asked trying to get a few seconds to think of a good answer to that question.

He knew exactly who she was talking about but he wasn't sure how to answer.

"Your friend that you ran into, Lasaia" She said.

"Oh Lasaia. Yeah I called her yesterday and we got a chance to talk."

Third strike.

He still didn't tell her

"That's good." She said.

"What you and the girls been up to?" Marcus asked trying to change the subject.

"Well, let me tell you about *your* children…" Sherise started off.

Marcus knew he was in for a long descriptive story about everything that had gone wrong since the last time they talked. Sherise told him about how *his* daughters were getting on her nerves again and how it would be a long time before he left her alone with those two mischievous little girls again. Marcus just sat there on the bed and threw in a, "Yeah", "Uh huh", "Ok", "Mmm hmm" every now and then.

Marcus lost track of time sitting there, listening to the story, and out of nowhere Alonzo walked into the room already in his Falcon's jersey. He waved his hand and got Marcus's attention. He pointed at his watch and snapped his fingers signaling Marcus that it was time to get moving. Sherise was still on the phone venting and Marcus broke in.

"Baby, baby, baby…I'm sorry but I need to get going. It's time for us to get on the road to the game."

She stopped her rant and said, "Oh, ok well just call me later."
"Ok"
They exchanged their "I love you's" and he hung up the phone. Marcus took a deep breath, shook his head and stood up.
"Come on man, get dressed, its time to ride." Alonzo said laughing.
He left the room and Marcus got dressed for the game. When he finished he walked back into the living room and found Alonzo on the couch.
"You ready?" Alonzo asked when he realized his brother was in the room.
"Yeah, let's ride."
Alonzo got up and they headed for the front door.
"We gon' baby!" Alonzo yelled as they headed for the front door.
A muffled, "Alright, yall have fun," was heard coming from down the hall behind Alonzo's door.
The brothers walked outside and jumped into Alonzo's truck and drove off.

It took them about 45 minutes to get to the stadium and through the traffic. Alonzo showed Marcus what he meant when he said he had the hook up. He pulled from behind the caravan of cars, trucks and SUVs packed with fans willing to pay insane prices just for a spot in the parking lot and pulled around the side of the huge stadium to the delivery entrance. After three quick honks of the horn the huge chain link fence sprung to life, opening. Alonzo drove through the back receiving area and parked next to a short row of cars.
"Man, what is this?" Marcus asked.
"This, my brother, is the hook up." Alonzo said with a grin.
They jumped out of the truck and were greeted by a familiar face.
"What's up boss?" Ricky said walking over to shake Alonzo's hand.
That was how Alonzo got his hookup.
Ricky was the mini-mountain sized bouncer at *Cloud 9* that handled the front door but this was other job, working in the shipping area at the dome. On game day there were no deliveries allowed so he pretty much did nothing but sit in his office, watch the game and secure the receiving area. He also had the inside track on seat hookups. Alonzo loved having Ricky working for him.
"It's all good man." Alonzo said shaking his friend's hand.
"How's the game going?" Alonzo asked.
"Just started…and I got a surprise for you." Ricky said walking them through a door leading to a hallway.
"What?"
Ricky dug into the shirt pocket of his uniform and pulled out a key.

"We had a business cancel like an hour ago to use one of the skyboxes, they already paid for it so, you can use it if you want." Ricky said handing a small golden key to Alonzo.

Alonzo's mouth dropped open and he stopped dead in his tracks. Marcus and Ricky looked back to see the stunned Alonzo just standing there looking at the key like it was the "Holy Grail". Alonzo just extended his fist, with his head lowered like he was paying homage to his savior.

"You gotta gimmie one folk." He said in a humble tone.

Ricky smiled and gave Alonzo a pound.

"'Preciate this big dawg." Alonzo said as they continue their trip through the back hallways of the Dome.

They could hear people cheering and screaming through the concrete walls as they made it to the elevator. Ricky gave the two of them directions on how to get to their skybox and turned back down the hallway to head back to work.

"Thanks again man." Alonzo said as the elevator bell rang.

"No problem," Ricky yelled out, "Yall have fun."

The two of them looked at each other and ran into the elevator. They were as giddy as two kids waiting on Santa Claus in that elevator. They had never been in a skybox before and they couldn't wait to get upstairs. The bell rang and the elevator doors opened. The two of them raced out the elevator and down the hall like the last one to the room wouldn't be allowed inside. They found the room and the two of them just stood there looking at the door. They weren't sure if they were even worthy of putting the key in the lock.

"Wait, I think we need to have a moment of prayer for the homies who ain't here…" Alonzo couldn't finish his sentence before Marcus shoved him and said, "Open the damn door." Alonzo laughed while he put the key in the lock and tried to turn it. He jiggled the key back and forth like the door wouldn't open.

"I know this the right door." Alonzo said looking at the golden number on the door that separated them from a sports fan's heaven.

Marcus's hopes of getting in the skybox started to sink, thinking that the door must have been double locked or something. Alonzo looked at Marcus with a heartbroken expression on his face.

"Sike!" He said as he threw the door open. Marcus pushed his brother into the room and walked in behind him.

They both stood a few steps inside the door and were amazed at the layout of the skybox. There was a huge glass window that looked down at the field below, 2 televisions on either side of the window where people that wanted to watch the field could see the replays. There was another big screen television behind the window seats where people could watch the game as it was being taped. There was a big sofa and a few chairs for people to sit and watch the game. Alonzo found a stocked bar and a huge buffet set up with every sports fan's favorite foods. Everything from nachos and hot wings to hamburgers and sausages was on that buffet. Heat lamps over everything, keeping it warm. Alonzo grabbed a small card off one of the covered dishes.

"Thank you Jamison, Lincoln, and Mays Law Firm. We appreciate your business." Alonzo said reading the card. "I wanna thank Jamison, Lincoln, and Mays too." He added as he tossed the card to the side.

There were sodas and bottled water in the refrigerator, and beer in a cooler. This room was equipped with everything that you would need to have a good time at the football game. The best thing about it was it was all free. Since Jamison, Lincoln, and Mays had canceled at the last minute they had to pay for the room anyway. The two of them ran over every inch of that skybox looking for anything and everything that it was equipped with. After they got over their initial hysteria, they calmed down, fixed some food, grabbed some beer and had a seat.

The game was very exciting. Atlanta was down for the first half, and then exploded in the third quarter to come within one touchdown. By the forth quarter, the Falcons were still down by six with seven seconds left on the clock. Marcus and Alonzo stopped everything they were doing and focused all attention on the game. The ball was snapped and the last play of the game began. Michael Vick dropped back and started looking for anyone to pass to. It seemed like an eternity but it couldn't have been more then two seconds before one of the defenders broke free and started charging at Vick. He finally saw a man breaking free down field and wound back to throw the ball. Alonzo and Marcus saw the huge man barreling down on Vick and started yelling for him to throw the ball. Vick got the ball in the air only a second before being blindsided by the large opponent. The ball floated through the air in a perfect spiral. That was a moment when every Falcon's fan took a deep breath. The ball slowly dropped from the sky and right into the hands of the receiver. He took a few victory steps and dove into the end zone. He had long left his defender in the dust. The entire stadium went crazy. Players were jumping up and down on the side lines, the Falcon's coaches threw their hands up in victory, the fans couldn't sit down in the stands, and Marcus and Alonzo were jumping all around the skybox. You would have thought this was a Super Bowl game the way people were acting. But, the game wasn't over, that touchdown only tied the score. They set up for the extra point and the kick was off.

"It's Good!" could be heard on the speakers and flashed on all the giant screens throughout the dome. This was arguably the best game the two brothers had ever seen. They finally calmed down and started straightening up the skybox. Even though the janitors would probably have done it, they knew they were blessed to have the place all to themselves and wanted to help someone else have a better day.

They finished their task and walked out of the room. They talked about the game all the way down the hall and in the elevator. When they got downstairs they walked through the back hallways of the dome and made their way back to Ricky's station. They walked into the office and Ricky looked up from a pile of papers.

"Yall have a good time?" He said.

"Man that was the shit!" Alonzo said handing him the key. They talked for a few minutes about the highlights of the game and then the two brothers exited the office.

"Alright man, we gonna get outta here. I'll see you on Thursday." Alonzo said walking through the doorway. "'Preciate that again man." He added before they walked off.

"No problem." Ricky said, not looking up from his papers. The two of them walked back to Alonzo's truck and jumped in. They pulled back up to the delivery gate, honked the horn and the large chain link Frankenstein sprung to life again. They left the dome and avoided the parking lot traffic by leaving through the back exit. Since no one was allowed to park back there during a game, there was no one to fight for position with. They quickly got back to the highway and head for home.

They talk about the game and the skybox and the whole experience all the way and before they knew it they were pulling into Alonzo's driveway. The smell of delicious food smacked them as soon as they got a few feet inside the house. R & B music was blaring from the living room and it was so loud that it sounded like Lisa was giving a concert.

"We home!" Alonzo said walking through the house. They made their way to the living room and found the whole area spotless. Lisa had gotten in one of her cleaning fits. She was in the middle of the room wrapping the cord around the prongs on the back of the vacuum cleaner when she looked up and saw them.

"Oh hey yall, I didn't hear you come in." She said with a smile.

Alonzo walked over to the radio and turned it down to a whisper.
"How could you?" He said.
She gave him a quick attitude filled look and jumped back to her happy self.
"So how was the game?" She said taking the vacuum to the closet.
"Aw baby, it was tight. Let me tell you..."
Alonzo was still amped up about the game and he had to explain every detail. He told her how they had gotten to the dome and Ricky hooked them up with the skybox. Then he had to describe the whole layout of the skybox and all the food and drinks that were there. Then he told her about the game and the last second victory.

Lisa just listened attentively even though she didn't really care all that much. She just wanted to know that he had a good time but it was something that he was excited about so she didn't want to bring him down. Now, if he would have told her about a 80% off Gucci sale they saw on the way home, she would have been just as excited as he was.

Alonzo finished his story and asked her what she had been doing while they were gone. Marcus had a seat on the sofa and started flipping channels. She told Alonzo that she had just got the urge to clean and then decided that she would get dinner started. The house looked and smelled great. Alonzo needed to marry this girl. It wasn't often that a man came across a woman that would do all of these kinds of things for him and expect nothing but love in return...and maybe the occasional shopping spree.
"The food's almost ready if yall wanna eat." She said heading to the kitchen to check on her meal. The brothers had stuffed themselves at the dome but the smell of Lisa's food cleared their stomachs quickly.
"Oh Marcus, before I forget!" Lisa yelled from the kitchen.
"Yeah" Marcus called back to her.
"Your friend called. The one from last night. She said something about being sorry for what happened and she hoped you call her again or something. I wasn't really listening."
Marcus and Alonzo just looked at each other and Alonzo cracked a smile and shook his head.
"I couldn't find the phone in time to answer it, but the message is on the machine." Lisa finished. Marcus was almost scared to listen to the message, but he got up and pressed the playback button. The brothers heard Lasaia's sexy voice emerge from the answering machine speaker, this time sounding like her 16 year old self.

"Hey Marcus, um I just wanted to call and apologize for what happened last night and say that it shouldn't have happened. I hope that you can forgive me and call me again. It's just that it has been so long since I've seen you and I guess I let my emotions take over. Anyway, I hope to here from you. Bye."

Alonzo looked at Marcus in astonishment.

"Man you sure all yall did was kiss?" He asked, a laugh building inside him.

Just then Lisa walked into the room and saw the two of them standing there over the machine.

"What's wrong? Did you get the message?" She asked.

"Yeah, I just heard it." Marcus said reaching down and deleting the message, destroying the chances of it ever being played again.

"She sounded sad or something didn't she? Talkin' bout she sorry about last night. What yall do? You didn't control the testosterone did you?" Lisa said joking with Marcus.

She really found his "hormonal" explanation the other night at the club amusing. Marcus just stood there with a fake smile on his face. He didn't know what to expect if he decided to call her. Alonzo broke the brief silence and asked, "What's up wit' the food?"

"It's ready." Lisa said and the two of them headed to the kitchen. Marcus just stood there looking at the phone. He decided that he wasn't up for calling her and followed them, shaking the thought out of his head.

The three of them had a wonderful meal, and the food was delicious. After they were finished and the dishes were done, the three of them planted themselves in the living room, just hanging out.

"So Marcus…" Lisa began. "Did you enjoy your trip to Atlanta?"

"Oh yeah, I had a great time. I needed this. All I do is work. I needed some time to myself."

"That's good."

"What time you pullin' out tomorrow man?" Alonzo asked.

"I don't know, I guess whenever I wake up."

"Well I'm goin' to bed early tonight. I'm tired as hell." Alonzo said with a yawn.

It was only 8:30 but Alonzo looked like he had spent the night at the club. They had a 30 minute conversation about Marcus's visit before Alonzo said, "Aight man, I'll holla at you before you leave." He stood up and gave his brother a pound before walking out of the living room yawning.

"You comin' to bed baby?" Alonzo said from the hall.

"Yeah, in a minute." Lisa said.

Alonzo walked down the hall to his room and closed the door.

"Sooo…what *really* happened last night?" Lisa asked Marcus after she was sure they were alone. Marcus looked at her with a confused look on his face. He knew what she was talking about but he tried to play it off.

"What do you mean?" He said.

Lisa was being nosey and she knew something had happened between Marcus and his friend. She didn't mean any harm, she just wanted to know.

"You know what I'm talking about. I know something happened. I can feel it. Yall looked like two kids who just got caught making out when we walked in."

Marcus just smiled and chuckled a little.

"And you had lipstick on your lips too. So, either yall kissed or you're into some real freaky shit." She said giggling.

Marcus stopped his smile and looked at her amazed. He couldn't figure out how she knew that. She must not have been as drunk as he thought.

"I won't tell nobody, promise." She said trying to convince Marcus to trust her.

After a few more pleads from Lisa, Marcus said, "Ok, yea we kissed but that's all." in a whispered voice.

"I knew it!" she said in an excited whisper. "Did you like it?"

Marcus gave her another stunned gaze. He couldn't believe this woman he just met two days ago was asking him if he liked kissing a woman besides his wife. But, he was still intrigued that she was so excited about it, instead of putting him down for his actions.

"It was aight. I mean…" Marcus cut his sentence short and just shrugged his shoulders.

"You liked it, yeah you did," She said with confidence, "I knew something looked suspicious when we came in here. So the two of you used to date or something?"

Marcus told her that in their senior year of high school the two of them were hanging out at his house talking about relationships. Lasaia was feeling down, calling herself ugly, because she was seventeen years old and had never even had a boyfriend. Marcus had recently broken up with his last girlfriend because she would always get mad when he would make time for Lasaia and it seemed like she had to wait in line. Lasaia was supposed to be there comforting him through his break up but when she realized she had no idea what he was going. That flipped the focus of the conversation to her love life. Marcus saw Lasaia as one of the most attractive girls in school, not just physically but she had a beautiful personality as well. Before that moment he never had the courage to tell her. He couldn't get the words formed in his mind and didn't know how to tell her now. He just sat and listened to her talk. The emotion ran so deep in Marcus that he had to do something. Then, in the middle of her sentence, he just leaned over and kissed her. It was the first kiss that the two of them shared, Lasaia's first *real* kiss with any boy. The last time she could remember kissing a boy on the lips was in third grade. She kissed him on a dare and he pushed her to the ground for it. This was something completely new to her. She had never experienced anything like this but she liked it. She was a little lost at first but it didn't take her long to get the hang of it and the two of them kissed for about three minutes straight. After their lips separated she looked into Marcus's eyes and he just smiled. They never really verbally agreed on being in a relationship, but after that moment it was understood. They went from introducing each other as "This is my friend…" to saying "This is my girlfriend/boyfriend…" The two of them grew closer and closer everyday it seemed and they were even more inseparable than ever. Lasaia always talked about getting married and having kids, which scared Marcus a little, but he didn't mind. They were just a young couple in love.

Eight

Marcus finished his story and Lisa sat there with an aww-that's-so-sweet look on her face. "So what happened to you guys?" She asked.

She was really interested in getting to know Marcus. After all, she did plan to be his sister-in-law some day. Marcus told her about their discovery of how they lost contact.

"Wow, that's crazy. It's like yall weren't meant to be together, but yall were meant to be friends. I mean, you were in her life long enough for both of you to learn something from the other. She learned that not all men are like her stepfather and you learned that even though some people might not look like 'part of the crowd', they could still be nice. Like, don't judge a book by its cover."

Marcus had never thought about it that way, but it must have been true because he was already teaching his daughters not to judge people without knowing them.

"It's like when I met your brother. I could have stopped at any gas station on that street, but for some reason I wanted this lil' slushy thing and I could only get it from one place. So I went there and got some gas even though I didn't need it and started walking inside. Then I see this cute guy coming out of the store as I'm going in, right? So I look back to see if he is checking me out and your brother is just standing there like a deer about to get hit by a truck. So, I give him a lil' flirty smile and walk in the store and get in line. Your brother comes back in and says the stupidest lil' line I have ever heard. He said something like, 'Can I get your address because I need to know where I'm gonna send my next dozen roses.'" Lisa giggled through her story. Marcus couldn't help but chuckle at how lame of a line his brother used. But, it must have been good enough because she was sitting right there.

"I couldn't help but laugh. He pulled me to the side and asked if he could take me out. I just thought he couldn't be any worse then my last boyfriend so I gave him my number and we have been together pretty much ever since. It's kinda like that with yall two, just in reverse. Everything happens for a reason. So that's why the two of your were separated like that. I think yall weren't meant to be together, just be friends." Lisa said.

Marcus actually liked their little talk. She wasn't trying to belittle him at all, she just wanted to talk to someone and Alonzo would have definitely backed out of the conversation by now.

"Well I'm gonna go to bed, I'll see you in the morning." Lisa said as she got up from the couch.

"Good night."

She patted Marcus on his shoulder as she passed him and disappeared.

"Nite." Marcus said as she left.

She walked down the hall and into Alonzo's room and closed the door. It was almost eleven o'clock by now, and Marcus's eyes were starting to get heavy as well. He turned off the television and the lights and headed to his room. He picked out some things to wear to bed and walked to the bathroom to take a shower. After he had gone through his nightly ritual, he left the bathroom and was halted by the sounds he heard coming from Alonzo's room.

Muffled R&B music squeezed through the cracks around the wooden door. *Must not be as tired as you thought,* Marcus thought to himself as he walked to his room.

He walked back into his room started getting his things together for an early escape back home. *One less thing to do in the morning,* he thought as he packed his bag, only leaving out the clothes he planned to wear home the next day. After he finished he climbed into the bed and stretched out. As he lay there he realized he hadn't called Lasaia back. It was 11:15 now and he figured he would give her a call the next day before he left.

Around 10:45 the next morning, Marcus woke up. He looked at his watch and jumped out of the bed. He had planned to be halfway home by this time so he could get home in the early afternoon. Marcus rushed to put on his clothes and grabbed his bag. He gathered all his items from the room and walked down the hall into the dining area where he met up with Alonzo.

"Hey bruh, I was just coming to ask if you wanted some breakfast."

"Nah, I'm supposed to be almost half way home by now."

"I thought you said you were leaving whenever you woke up." Alonzo said. "Man, have a seat and at least eat something before you go."

Alonzo took Marcus's bags and put them under the table. Marcus figured he was going to get home late now anyway so he decided to get some food in his stomach for the ride. Lisa's cooking was better than any stop he would have made down the road anyway. The two of them had a seat in the living room and about a minute later Lisa walked in with a plate in each hand. She handed each of them a plate and Alonzo said, "Oh, we gettin' the presidential treatment today?"

"Yeah it's only because Marcus is leaving, don't get used to it. I want him to see how good I take care of you, sometimes." She said with a giggle.

The two of them started eating and were shortly joined by Lisa. The all enjoy the breakfast and talked about how Marcus had to bring a Sherise and the kids up to Atlanta next time. Marcus joked about how Alonzo would have probably moved a few times by then so they would have to send him the new address. Alonzo fired back and said that it wouldn't matter if he had the address anyway, he would probably leave the directions at home again. They laughed and Marcus finally said, "Alright, let me get on this road." He stood to his feet and walked over to grab his bag. Alonzo and Lisa got up from the couch to see him off.

"You know how to get to 75 from here?" Alonzo asked.

Marcus realized he had no idea how to get to the highway and Alonzo gave him some directions as he opened the front door. Marcus gave both of them a hug and walked out to his truck.

"Call us when you get home man." Alonzo said as Marcus opened the door to his truck.

"Alright." Marcus said and threw his bag in the passenger seat. He jumped in and started his truck. Alonzo and Lisa were on the front porch and he honked the horn two times as he drove off down the road. They waved until he got out of sight and then headed back into the house.

Marcus had very little trouble navigating his way to the interstate and headed for home. He made it to Jacksonville's city limits around 6 p.m. and his phone started beeping. "Oh, now you wanna work." He said talking to his phone. He reached into his bag, pulled out his phone and looked at the display. *Nine messages?*, Marcus thought, confused. He wondered who could have called him that much over the weekend. He had told everyone he was going out of town for a few days.

He dialed his voicemail started listening to the messages. The first one was from the night before, when Lasaia was over. It was received at 4:30 in the morning so she must have sent it as soon as she got home. It was basically the same message on Alonzo's answering machine. She was saying that she was sorry about what happened and she hoped he wasn't mad at her. The next two were from her again and they were only ten minutes apart. They came in around the time Marcus was at the game with Alonzo. She just kept saying how sorry she was and wasn't sure what he was thinking and hoped he would forgive her. Marcus thought it was a little strange that she would call back to back like that. The next message was from his wife. She had her regular upset tone that he had heard all during his trip. All he heard was his two daughters screaming in the background and what sounded like pots and pans banging around. Then Sherise came on the line and said, "See what you left me with, I hope you are having a *real* good time." Then she hung up the phone. Marcus couldn't help but laugh. His wife was so overly dramatic.

The next message was from one of Marcus's friends and co-worker. He said, "Yooooo, dawg this Mike. I know you just saw that last play. Anyway I was just tryin' to holla at you bout this game. I know you outta town hangin' at the dome. Where you sittin'? We was looking for you. Anyway, hit me up when you get back. Peace." The last four messages were from Lasaia again. This time there was only about three minutes between each one. She was basically saying the same thing but she seemed to get more upset with every call. She kept asking why he wasn't calling her back. They all were received shortly after he left Atlanta.

"Oookaaay." Marcus said to himself after listening to and deleting all his messages.

He was a little unnerved at the fact that she called that many times. He didn't know what to think. First, he ran into her and she was this confident, high-powered, sexy business owner. Then, she came to visit him and turned into this sex crazed aggressive beast. Now, she called and turned into a 16-year-old little girl who sounded like she has just been dumped by her first boyfriend. She had worn three different masks in the span of a weekend. He wasn't just going to give up on his friend like that though. He figured that maybe the reunion made her freak out a little bit, it certainly had his insides doing flips. *Just give her a chance to chill out. Just play it cool and she'll even out. Everything will be fine.* All these thoughts rushed through Marcus's head as he made his way down the city streets, headed home.

Around 6:35 Marcus pulled into his driveway and turned off his engine. He was tired but happy to finally be home. He just looked at his big beautiful house and couldn't wait to get inside. He grabbed his cell phone and bag and jumped out of the truck. While walking to the front door he flipped open his phone to call his brother and let them know he had made it. After a few rings, Alonzo's answering machine started up and Marcus left him a message. He walked into his house and the first person to see him was his oldest daughter, Lasaia. She looked over at him from the family room couch and her eyes instantly grew as big as her face. She jumped to the floor and screamed, "Daaaadddiiiiieee!" Marcus dropped his bag and knelt down to give his daughter a hug. She jumped and threw her arms around his neck and he stood up holding her in his arms.

"Hey sweetness, where's your mom?" He asked.

"In there giving Angela a bath." She said pointing to one of the downstairs guest rooms. He carried his daughter to the room and opened the slightly cracked door. He could hear his wife in the bathroom talking to Angela while she was giving her a bath. Angela's nightclothes were arranged on the bed ready to be put on. Marcus put his finger over his mouth signaling his daughter to be quiet, he put her down. The two of them tiptoed, hand in hand, over to the bathroom door and stood in the doorway. Sherise was on her knees in some sweat pants and a t-shirt rinsing Angela off. Angela looked up and saw her daddy standing in the entryway. She started to point and smile at her daddy and Sherise didn't know what she was so excited about.

"What? What are you looking…" Sherise said looking over her shoulder. "Heeey baby!" She said grabbing a towel and pulling Angela out of the tub. She turned around and walked over to Marcus and gave him a kiss.

"Here, I got her." He said taking the little girl out of Sherise's arms. Sherise had a look of relief now that he was home. She always said she would have never made it as a single parent and this weekend had only confirmed her right.

Sherise and Lasaia walked out of the room and headed upstairs to get her ready for a bath. Marcus put Angela down on the bed and started drying her off. "You been good for mommy?" Marcus asked his daughter while he started getting her dressed. "Yeah." The little girl said nodding her head up and down. He knew she was probably the ringleader of the trouble that Sherise had been complaining about all weekend but she was daddy's little girl, she could do no wrong in his eyes. The two of them laughed and played for a little while as he got her dressed. When they were finished, Marcus carried his baby girl upstairs and he could hear Lasaia splashing around in the tub singing as he passed. He took Angela into her room and put her down on her Barbie Corvette bed. She was almost asleep and Marcus asked, "You wanna read a story?" Her eyes were barely open but she mustered the strength to nod. Marcus grabbed one of her many books and kneeled down next to her bed. Before he could get halfway through the second page, Angela was sound asleep. Marcus saw his little sleeping princess and kissed her on her forehead and whispers, "Goodnight baby," in her ear. He turned off the light and left the room.

At the other end of the walkway Lasaia was just getting out of the tub and giving her mother a hard time about putting on her clothes. Sherise tried to put her clothes on for her, but Lasaia wanted to do it herself. Marcus slipped over to the top of the stairs and scurried down before they saw him. He rushed to the back door and opened it. He walked onto the back deck and grabbed a pair of pruning shears that were sitting on the rail. He rushed over to one of the four rose bushes that cornered their backyard and clipped about four roses before rushing back into the house. He darted up the stairs and quietly passed Lasaia's room again without being seen. Sherise and Lasaia had switched their argument from putting on clothes to why she had to go to bed if she wasn't sleepy. Sherise couldn't wait until the school year rolled around again. That would give her the arsenal she needed to get her in the bed without a fight.

Marcus ran into their bathroom and started running some bath water in their big Jacuzzi tub. He poured in some bath crystals, a little bubble bath and filled the tub with a nice hot bath. He pulled the pedals off two of the roses and sprinkled them on top of the bubbles. Then he lit some incense and candles and dimmed the lights. Marcus made it to the bed and turned on the television right before Sherise walked into the room.

"That little girl know she can work a nerve." She said as she closed the bedroom door and walked over in front of her husband. Marcus stood up and put his arms around his wife, giving her a hug. After a few seconds all of her frustrations and aggravations went away and she saw a flickering light shining from the bathroom. She let go of her husband and started walking slowly toward the bathroom. Marcus followed behind her waiting to see the expression on her face when she saw what he had done.

Sherise walked to the door and saw the scene her husband has put out for her. She turned and looked at him stunned and giggled.

"You know I was about to ask you why you ain't come help me with that little crazy girl." She said. "Come here."

Sherise motioned for him to come to her with her finger. Marcus walked over and wrapped his arms around her again and they shared another, more passionate kiss. That kiss reminded Marcus how much he missed his wife and also why he loved her. Her fingers slowly moved down to the small of his back and began lifting his shirt. Her warm hands squeezed his love handles, letting him know she was *ready*. Marcus slowly moved his kisses from her lips to her neck, being sure not to let a single inch of skin pass without tasting it. Marcus knew exactly where her spot was and wasted no time getting to it. The corner of her neck directly below her earlobe where her neck met her shoulders...that was Marcus's target. As soon as he hit that spot Marcus could feel her getting weaker and weaker with every smack of his lips. She lets out a low moan.

"Mmmmmh, you know you wrong for that." She said as he laughed, his mouth never separating from her skin.

After a few kisses he decided to show mercy on her and let up. As soon as he stopped she grabbed him by the front of his pants and unbuttoned them. She slowly unzipped them and slid her hands between him and his boxers. She tilted her head back and looked him in the eyes and slowly started caressing his penis from base to tip. Marcus closed his eyes and began to enjoy the pleasure. With her free hand, Sherise started lifting her husband's shirt. Marcus was turned on. He didn't wait for her to fight to get his shirt off. He reached down and in less than a second was throwing his shirt to the floor. She continued to stroke his manhood while kissing him on his chest. She slowly started to work her way down. First his chest, then his nipples, then his stomach, then that area directly below his belly button. His happy trail. Marcus's sexual arousal was hard to contain. He was at the point where he just wanted to pick her up, throw her on the bed and slide inside her. But, he was patient and she rewarded him for it.

She slowly stroked his now erect large penis while kissing and licking the shaft. After her little tease session she finally grabbed it by the base and wrapped her warm mouth around it. She worked her way down as far as she could go and slowly came back. After only a few seconds of this Marcus got weak in the knees and was barely able to stand. Sherise slowly worked her mouth and hand back and forth, getting faster and faster with each stroke. Marcus started to groan and sway back and forth. He even had to brace himself on the doorway at one point to keep from falling over. After about five minutes, she stopped. She didn't want him to climax just yet. She stood up and started kissing him on his neck. Marcus couldn't wait any longer and grabbed her by the waist and pulled her body next to his. He pulled down her sweat pants and panties and squeezed her nice soft bottom with both hands. He removed one of his hands and slipped it under her shirt. Ah, no bra...easy access! Marcus started to squeeze her breasts and kissed her on the neck. Sherise took off her shirt and now it was her turn to be pleased. Marcus spun her around, brought her back against him, his rock hard penis pressed against her soft backside. He kissed her neck while squeezing her breasts. Sherise just closed her eyes and leaned her head back against his chest, moaning. He took one hand from her chest and slowly ran it down her stomach between her legs. Marcus knew every spot on his woman's body that turned her on and tonight he was trying to hit every one of them. He gave her clitoris a few quick flips with his middle finger before thrusting a few digits inside of her. Sherise squealed with delight as he slowly worked them in and out of her. After a few strokes Marcus removed his fingers and turned her back around and started sucking on her breasts. He ran his tongue back and forth over her nipples causing her arousal switched to flip to the on position.

Marcus figured it was time to take this affair to a more relaxed setting. He grabbed her by her waist and took her in his arms. "Whoa." Sherise said with a giggle, not expecting him to pick her up. She wrapped her legs around his midsection and he walked with her in his arms through the doorway and over to the waiting bath. The water was still steaming hot and the incense and candles set the scene for their romantic encounter. Marcus placed her on the side of the tub where there was just enough room for her to sit and he got down on his knees. He gave her another kiss and slowly worked his way to her breasts again. After a few quick kisses on both nipples he started working his way down. He kissed her stomach and worked his tongue around her belly button before heading even farther south. He slowly kissed and licked both sides of her vagina teasing her. The feeling tickled Sherise and she let out a low, erotic giggle. Marcus decided it was time to give his wife what he knew she wanted. He spread her vagina lips exposing her clitoris and gave it a few quick flicks with his tongue. This made a sound come out of his wife that he loved to hear. That turned him on even more and he pressed his face into her pelvis jamming his tongue deep inside her opening. Sherise quickly flung her body forward and let out a scream of passion. Her voice echoed off the walls of the bathroom. Marcus knew he had her right where he wanted her and continued with his oral assault. He let her moans guide his tongue.

After a few minutes Sherise started feeling an orgasm coming. "No baby wait…I…I don't wanna come yet…wait, wait…" she said between deep breaths. She tried to push Marcus's head away but her small arms were no match for his upper body strength. Marcus could feel her thighs tightening around his head as her moans started to get louder and louder. She pleaded with him to stop but he didn't. Then in an instant, Marcus felt her entire body tense up and begin to shake. Marcus didn't show any mercy and proceeded to attack her clitoris.

"Baby please, please…I want you to fuck me. I wanna feel you inside of me." She said as she recovered from her orgasm. Marcus slowed his slurps down and slowly worked his way back up her body to her mouth. Sherise kissed her juices from his lips. After her body-quakes stopped her turned away from him and climbed into the tub. She sat down and the warm soapy bubbles rose just above her nipples. She cupped her hands and poured three handfuls of water over her face and it ran down her neck and over her breasts. Marcus just stayed there on his knees admiring his wife in the glow of the candlelight. Sherise motioned for him to come to her with her usual finger motion and stood to her feet. Marcus watched as the bubbles slowly made their way down her body leaving a trail of glistening skin that shined in flicker of the candlelight. He knelt there, looking up at her for a second, admiring this beautiful goddess in front of him. He stood to his feet, removed his socks and stepped into the tub. He sat down and looked up at her, towering above him. She slowly climbed into his lap. They kissed. Sherise rose up a little, grabbed him and slowly lowered herself onto her husband, pleasure making its way to her face.

As she began to move in his lap, Marcus reached around and started squeezing Sherise's bottom. Her moans graduated into screams as Marcus started moving his hips, in rhythm with her, intensifying the power of each stroke. He moved his hands up to her shoulders and pulled her down as he lunged his pelvis up, pushing his hard penis deep inside her.

"Oh shit!" she screamed in pleasure as Marcus did it over and over again. He felt her vaginal walls begin to contract and he knew she was about to orgasm again. Marcus sped up his rhythm and a few seconds later Sherise was screaming and shaking in his lap. She had to brace herself on the side of the tub. Marcus loved to see her orgasm. He pulled one of his hands from her shoulder and brought around to her front and started squeezing and sucking her erect nipples. This turned Sherise on even more. Her screams were only contained by the bedroom door. She started riding Marcus harder and harder trying to make him orgasm too. He was already up by two orgasms in their ongoing sexual challenge, and now he had two more to add to the list. She grinded on him so hard that the water in the tub started to splash over the sides. This didn't distract Sherise at all and she continued to ride Marcus harder and harder. Marcus removed his face from her chest and leaned his head back and let his wife handle her business. Sherise was more turned on then she knew and she started bouncing even harder. Her uncontrollable screams flowed from her throat like a poetic song of seduction. The two of them were so far into the throws of passion that the house could have been on fire and they wouldn't have stopped. Marcus started feeling the sensation of an oncoming orgasm and could feel his muscles tensing. He ran his hands up her thighs and around to her ass and started to squeeze. Sherise could tell by the way he grabbed her that she had him now.

"You wanna come?" She leaned forward and whispered in his ear as she kept hammering his penis.

"Yes...hell yes." Marcus stuttered, barely able to form words at this point. Sherise didn't miss a beat as she kept her sexual rhythm going in his lap. About a minute later Marcus felt the sensation coming even stronger and put his hands on her breasts and squeezed again. He couldn't deny the feeling any longer and felt his little soldiers escape from his loins. Their simultaneous orgasm shot through their flesh.

Everything around them disappeared.

It was just the two of them, connected as one.

Alone.

A sexual being too powerful for this earth.

Surpassing the laws of physics in this dimension.

After a few minutes of long breaths and short kisses, they returned to their home planet, drained. They had just visited the universe but now it was time to go home. Sherise put her mouth close to Marcus's ear and whispered, "I win," before laying her head on his shoulder. He was still inside of her. He could feel her insides quivering, lightly squeezing his penis every couple seconds. She was still coming. He envied her at times like that. Even though his orgasms were amazing, hers lasted. He threw his arms around her and could feel her trembling. That was the best sexual encounter either of them had ever had. They both just sat there breathing hard, barely able to move. Even after a few minutes of motionless panting, they were still high from the act. Sherise lifted her head from his shoulder, looked Marcus in the eyes and gave him a slow sexy kiss.

"Sooo, you wanna go out of town next weekend too?" She said joking with him.

They both laugh and shared another kiss as Sherise slowly lifted herself off of him. She climbed out of the tub, walked over to the closet and grabbed two towels. She noticed it was a little harder to walk now. She could feel every step she took in her pelvis. She awkwardly walked back over to the tub and handed a towel to her husband who was standing there. He stepped out and saw the mess they had made all over the floor. They decided that would be a job for in the morning and they dried each other off. Marcus noticed, as they were leaving the bathroom, that Sherise's steps were slow and very light, indicating that their little episode had caused a little sensitivity in her lower region. Without warning, he picked her up and walked her into the bedroom, placing her on the bed. She removed her towel as he walked around to his side of the bed. The simple vision of her naked body on the sheets got his juices flowing again. He wants to attack her but he knew she was in pain so he decided to wait until she could handle another round. He took off his towel and climbed into the bed next to her. She scooted over to him and they shared a kiss as they lay there next to each other. Marcus slowly ran his hand up her thigh and rested it on her hip. Sherise pushed him on his back and climbed on top of her husband.

"You ready for round two?" She asked.

Marcus took that as a challenge and rolled her onto her back and started kissing her neck. They made love for the next hour and slowly drifted off to sleep. Even though it was slightly painful for Sherise, she never had pain that felt so good.

Nine

Marcus woke up to an empty spot in the bed next to him. He jumped out of the bed and put on a pair of comfortable shorts and a t-shirt. He left the bedroom and walked downstairs, following the sound of his family's voices to the kitchen. Sherise was fixing breakfast plates for the girls as they sat breakfast table, reciting a verse of *Twinkle Twinkle Little Star*. As soon as he walked through the doorway he heard, "Daaaddiiieee". Sherise just smiled at how excited they always were to see him, like every time was their first time.

"Morning ladies." He said to his little ones, headed for his wife.

"You feeling alright this morning?" He whispered with a cocky overtone.

"Oh, you trying to be funny," She said, laughing, "I ain't the one who was sleeping so hard I didn't feel my wife trying to wake me up this morning."

She was implying that she had tried to get a little early morning action before the girls woke up. Marcus kissed her on the cheek and laughed. He picked up the plates from in front of her and took them to his little girls. He said a quick prayer with them, trying to teach them that they should always bless their food before they ate. The two little ones dug in and Marcus walked back over to his wife. Sherise was finishing up some plates for the two of them and they joined their daughters at the table.

Over breakfast, Marcus told his wife about his trip. He told her the story of how they got the hookup at the game and he told her about Alonzo's club.

"Oh so you went out huh," she said, playing with him, "You see any cute girls?"

"Oh yeah, everywhere…none I would want to spend 10 years and have two kids with though." he said.

She giggled.

They talked a little bit more about his trip and everything that went on at the house while he was gone. Turns out things were not as bad as she had made them seem. They finished their meal and the girls left the table and ran to the family room to play. Marcus and Sherise gathered all the dishes and started washing them.

"What you got planned for today?" He asked from his position in the dish washing assembly line.

"Not much. I know I need to go by the salon today and make sure Lele put in my inventory order like I asked. Probably do a little paperwork but I really want to go shopping. I need a new dress and we need to find a gift for a certain someone's birthday." She said handing him a dish to rinse. They finish with the dishes and headed out of the kitchen.

"So why don't you go find a dress, go by the salon and get the gift and I'll stay here with the girls and try to get some work done." Marcus suggested.

"You think you are actually gonna get some work done with those two awake?"

"We'll be fine." Marcus said trying to give her a chance for some time to herself. Sherise decided that she did need a break from the girls and headed upstairs to get ready. Marcus walked into the living room and had a seat next to Lasaia. The three of them sat there watching cartoons until Sherise reappeared in the doorway.

"Ok, I'm gone." She said.

Marcus got up to walk her out.

"Bye Mommy." Lasaia said from her position on the couch. They walked to the front door and Marcus gave her a kiss and she left. He tried to sneak to his office to work on his project that he blew off for his weekend vacation. He didn't get to sit down for more then two minutes before he heard the doorbell. Marcus looked at the clock on his desk.

It was 11:30. He wasn't expecting company. Who could this be? Marcus opened the front door only to find a pint-sized person struggling to reach for the doorbell to ring it again.

"Hi Melissa." Marcus said in a sassy little voice as he leaned against the doorway, his arms crossed over his chest.

"Hi, Mr. Downing, is Lasaia home?" Melissa said in her cute little five-year-old voice. Melissa was the daughter of Marcus's next-door neighbor. Tiny little white girl with big blue eyes and long blond hair. The spitting image of her mother.

"Yeah, she's in there." Marcus said pointing to the family room. Melissa bolted by him and into the house. Marcus barely had time to move out of the way. He closed the door and heard their usual greeting as he made his way back to his office.

"Missiieee.", "Laacciiieee"
Marcus wasn't seated for more then five minutes before he heard Lasaia and her little sister arguing. Lasaia wanted to play with Melissa, but Angela kept following them.
"Hey, hey, hey, what's the problem?" Marcus said emerging from his office and finding them at the bottom of the stairs. Lasaia told her daddy what was going on and he picked up the little one and let the two friends go upstairs to play. Angela had a pouting look on her face as Marcus took her to his office and sat her down. Her facial expression hadn't changed and wasn't happy about not being able to follow the *big* girls.
"You wanna draw daddy a picture?" Marcus said grabbing a pen and some paper. Angela just crossed her arms refusing to take her father's compromise.
"What do you wanna do baby?" Marcus asked getting a little frustrated. Angela poked out her lip again and pointed out the door to the steps telling him she wanted to go play with her sister.
"Baby, you can't go up there. They wanna play big girl games." He said trying to comfort her. Angela's eyes started to water and she began to whine.
"Ok, ok, ok. How about you and I go play in your room, ok?" Marcus said trying to avoid the tears that were about to fall from her eyes. She kept the same look on her face and started to nod her head signaling him that he had come up with an acceptable solution.

He took her in his arms and gave up trying to do his work for the moment and headed upstairs. He stepped into Angela's room and put her down on the floor. She ran over to her tea set and sat down. Marcus took a deep cleansing breath and walked over to play with his daughter. After a tea party with her teddy bear, a horsy ride on his back, some coloring, a couple rides around the room in Barbie's corvette, and half of the Lion King movie, Angela was sound asleep. Marcus picked her up and placed her in her bed. She was breathing lightly as he turned out the light and walked out of the room. Marcus had gotten only a few steps out of her door when he heard, "Daadddieee!" as Lasaia and Melissa ran up.
"Shhh," Marcus said, "Your sister is sleeping."
"Daddy, can I go over Melissa's house?" She asked in a whisper.
Marcus saw his chance to get some peace and quiet and granted her request. The two little girls slowly walked to the top of the staircase and ran down giggling. They went out the front door and the house was silent. Marcus went downstairs and watched as the girls made it safely across the grass and into

Melissa's house. He gave a quick thanks to the Lord and rushed over to his office.

Twenty minutes later Marcus heard his cell phone ring. It was coming from his bag in the corner of his office. Sherise must have put it there when she saw it lying in the middle of the family room doorway where he had dropped it the day before. Marcus just dropped his head and took a deep breath. He just wasn't going to get anything done with all these interruptions. He got up from his chair and walked over to his bag and pulled out his phone. He looked at the display and it was a 404 number.

"Atlanta?" Marcus said to himself. He figured it was Alonzo calling from the club or something.

"Hello?"

"Hello?" said the voice on the other end.

"This is Marcus."

"Hey, Marcus. This is Lasaia."

"Oh, what's going on girl?"

"Nothin, look...I am really, really sorry about what happened...I mean I..."

"Wait, wait, wait. You don't have to apologize for anything. I was part of it too, and..."

"I know, I know but it's just that I hadn't seen you in so long and a lot of old emotions I thought were gone just came rushing back. Believe me, I didn't come over there with that in mind. I mean you have a family now. I wouldn't think of doing anything to mess that up for you. And I..."

She was speaking so fast that her words began to run together, like they did when she was a kid.

"Me too, me too. Trust me, I understand. I don't know what I was thinking. But forget all that. Let's just start over. It was great seeing you again."

"I'd like that. It was great seeing you too. I really hope that we can keep in touch."

"Oh most definitely, I got you back now, you ain't running away again."

Lasaia giggled at his comment.

"Ok well good, cause I don't plan on leaving."

Marcus laughed and said, "You had me scared, calling all those times though. Had me scared to call you back."

Lasaia laughed and said, "Thought you had you a fatal attraction, huh?"

"I wasn't sure if I was dialing the right number, so I kept calling. I figured I would either get you or somebody that would tell me to stop calling their house," She said laughing,

"Anyway, I wanted to call and let you know that we are actually doing a casting call in Jacksonville this weekend and usually I don't go on them, but if you don't mind, I would like to come visit you and your family."

"Definitely," Marcus said enthused, "That's cool, I want yall to get a chance to meet."

"Ok, I can't wait to see my little girl."

"Your little girl?"

"My little girl. She got my name all over her. She's mine." Lasaia said followed by a laugh.

Marcus chuckled and said, "Oh yeah, if you want her you can have her. I guarantee you'll want a refund in a couple days."

They both laughed and talked for a little while longer and Lasaia says, "Ok, well I'm not gonna take up your time. If you are still the Marcus I remember, I'm sure you're busy."

"Yeah, just trying to get a little work done." He says.

"I knew it. You're always into something. Well I'll call you on Friday when I get in town."

"Ok."

"Alright, talk to you then."

"Ok."

"Bye, bye."

"Bye."

Marcus hung up the phone and set it on his desk. He was happy to speak with his friend again. He missed the inconsistency in what she just told him and goes back to his work.

At that moment Sherise was pulling up to her shop to check things out. She walked through the front door and was greeted by her receptionist.

"Hey Miss Sherise." the young girl said hanging up her phone.

"Hey Peaches, how you doin' girl?" Sherise said as she walked around the waist high counter. Sherise heard her best friend before she even made it around the wall behind the receptionist. Alicia Carmichael, but to her, Lele. Her and Sherise had been friends since her freshman year in college. They were roommates and became inseparable. Alicia was the one that warned Sherise about Marcus. She also told Sherise about the little "tramp" that he cheated on her with. She always had her girl's back, and always would. Alicia was what you might call a full-figured woman, and loved it. She didn't let anything take away from the fact that she knew she was sexy. Her most famous quote was, "Thin bitches ain't cute. They ass always look hungry." She was the most honest, reliable, straightforward, funny person that Sherise knew and she wouldn't trade her for the world.

A real friend.

She would be on Sherise's side when she was right, and tell her about herself when she knew Sherise was wrong. She didn't candy coat anything and Sherise loved her like a sister.

Alicia was having a conversation about why men cheat with some of the patrons and stylists, and she was being loud, as usual.

"See that's why yo' crazy ass can't keep a man. You don't cook, you don't clean, you don't fuck...what he need you for?" Alicia yelled to a woman getting her hair braided. She loved to be the center of attention and everyone was laughing and having a good time, even her victim.

"All you do is get your hair done. You here more than me, and I'm the manager. Usin' up the baby's lunch money on perms. Bitch, you need to be shamed."

She had the whole room dying, and even some of the stylists have to stop doing hair to keep from burning their client's head.

"Yo' child can't eat no updo. Put that shit in a pony tail and buy that baby some cereal." Sherise just stood behind her and watched, laughing. Alicia turned around and left the group in stitches. Business went back to being as close to normal as it got in *Sherise's*. Visiting this salon was always an adventure. There was always some good conversation. It looked pretty much like most salons, but it was the atmosphere that brought people in. Sherise knew that a woman could get her hair done pretty much anywhere, but if you give them somewhere that's comfortable and affordable and people feel at home then they will come back.

"Heeey sista." Alicia said, seeing her best friend standing there.

They shared a hug and walked through the shop to the office.

"Girl you a trip. Why are you in here messing with these women?" Sherise asked, closing the door as she laughed.

"Girl, somebody gotta teach these hoes that looks and actions ain't gonna keep no man. He gotta wanna be with you to stay with you. The goal ain't to hold on to him, but to make him not wanna leave."

"You right, you right. Ain't no way to keep a man that ain't trying to be kept." Sherise said looking through her file cabinet.

She grabbed a file and walked over to her desk.

"So did you put in the order for next week?" Sherise asked.

"Order? What order?" Alicia asked.

Sherise looked up from her pile of papers with a shocked look on her face. Alicia baited her along for a few seconds then smiled and laughed.

"Girl, you know I sent out the order. How long have we been doing this now?"

Sherise's expression went from surprise to attitude.

"Don't play like that." She said, cracking a smile.

Alicia sat in the chair in front of Sherise's desk across from her.

"So how are my little girls doing?"

"They're fine, got on my nerves all weekend."

"What happened?"

"Nothing out of the ordinary. It's just that Marcus was in Atlanta visiting his brother and those two lose their minds when he's not around."

"Girl you let your man go to Atlanta without you? Atlanta is like…hoe-central. Hoes at the clubs, hoes at the grocery store, hoes swingin' from poles…shit, you can room service order a hoe in 'Hoe'-lanta."

Sherise laughed at her friend.

"Girl you are gonna be alright. My man knows where he lives."

"Alright, come nine months and he pop up with some lil' hoelettes runnin' around."

"Whatever. He didn't do nothin' but go to a football game. I'm gonna need you to calm down."

"A game huh? Mmmh hmmm. That's how it starts. Next thing you know he'll be running into some old girlfriend from college or some shit." Alicia said, digging through the candy dish on Sherise's desk.

Sherise paused from her work and looked up at her friend.

"What?" Alicia said, catching the expression on her face.

"Marcus met his old girlfriend from high school when he was up there."

"Uh huh. See. I told you." Alicia said, unwrapping a piece of candy.

"Anyway, I ain't listening to you anymore. You trying to have me following that man around the whole city." Sherise said, returning to her work.

"That's alright, don't listen, but you better keep that bitch away from your man. I ain't going to jail because the bitch jumped on you and I had to stab her. I don't dig the prison issue shit."

Sherise laughed at her and started going over some more of the paperwork.

After about an hour, they finish their work and got everything filed away. "Alright girl, I'm gonna head to the house." Sherise looked at her watch. "It's 4:30 and I know that man ain't fed my babies yet. Call me if you need me. I'll be home for the rest of the night."

"Ok girl, you gonna be here tomorrow?"

"Yeah, I'll be here all day tomorrow. Gonna try to get here early."

"Ok, sista."

Sherise opened the door and it was like she opened a Ziploc bag full of laughter. The two of them walked out and heard the same conversation still going on and even more women had come into the shop and joined in. Alicia's previous victim was still in the stylist's chair and Alicia couldn't resist the opportunity.

"Bitch you still here? Your ass here so much we about to start gettin' your mail...I know what I'mma do, I'm gonna start chargin' yo' ass rent."

Alicia regained her spot as the center of attention, where she loved to be. Sherise walked by her laughing and headed for the front door.

"Bye girl!" Alicia screamed as Sherise made it around the front counter. Sherise threw her hand up to say goodbye and walked out the front door. She walked to her car and started her journey home.

Ten

Angela woke up from her nap and got out of bed. She walked to the hallway and slowly wandered down the steps. She heard her daddy typing away on his computer and started for his office. She walked through the doorway rubbing her eyes and he looked up from his papers.

"Hey baby girl, you up from your nap?" He asked while saving his work and getting up from his desk. She let out a low groggy, "Yeah," as he walked toward her.

"You want a snack?" he asked, kneeling down.

The little one just nodded her head and they made their way to the kitchen. He sat her at the table and gave her some cut up pieces of banana while he started the dinner. He didn't realize how long he had been in his office working.

A few minutes later, Marcus heard the front door open and shut. Then he heard little person footsteps headed his way and knew Lasaia was home.

"Hi daddy." She said with a short wave, not breaking her stride. She shuffled over to her sister and snatched a piece of her banana out of her bowl and heaved it into her mouth. Angela let out a quick but loud whine and Marcus turned around and said, "What you doin' to her?" With a mouth full, Lasaia said, "Numphin."

"Uh huh, go in the living room and watch TV. You ready to eat?"

"Yeeeesss." She said leaving the kitchen.

Marcus was almost done with preparing the meal when his wife stepped through the front door. Marcus heard the door close and Lasaia greet her mother. She walked into the kitchen and smelled the aroma from the stove.

"Baby, that smells good."

"Well thank you, thank you. How things at the shop?"

"Fine. Lele acting up as usual." She said taking Angela out of her seat and putting her down. The little one ran off to join her big sister in the family room.
"Figured that. Did you get her gift?"
"Yeah, it's in the car. I'm gonna wait until she goes to sleep to bring it in."
Sherise got some water from the refrigerator as Marcus put the finishing touches on his meal.
"Oh, guess who called today." He said.
"Who?"
"Lasaia. She said she has a modeling thing going on here this weekend and wanted to know if it would be alright if she stopped by and met you and the kids."
Sherise stopped in her spot and thought back to the conversation she had with Alicia in the salon. Marcus turned around after a few seconds of silence and no response. He saw his wife standing there staring at him with a strange look on her face.
"What's wrong?" He says confused by her silence.
"What? Nothing. Sure ok. When she comin?"
"Friday I guess, she said she was gonna call."

Sherise set her glass down and left the kitchen without saying another word, joining her daughters in the family room. Marcus figured it's a woman thing and let her go. He finished the meal and turned off the stove.
"Food's ready!" He shouted to the three women in the living room. A few seconds later they all filed into the kitchen and Sherise fixed the little ones their plates. They all sat down at the table and had a nice dinner. Lasaia told her parents about everything that she did at Melissa's house and how much fun she had there. She loved playing with her friend. They finished their meal and Marcus started gathering their dishes to wash them.
"No siiiirr." Sherise said bumping him away from the sink with her hip.
"I had them all weekend, it's your turn." Marcus laughed at her catching his obvious attempt to avoid fighting with the girls about going to bed.
"Come on ladies." He said grabbing Angela from her chair and sitting her on the floor.

The small party marched out of the kitchen and up the stairs. Marcus told Lasaia to go clean up her room so she could get ready to take a bath after he was done with Angela. After a small protest, Lasaia eventually submitted and went to start on her room. Marcus took Angela into her room and picked some nightclothes for her to wear. He placed them on the bed and picked her up. They headed for the bathroom and Marcus started to run her water.

"You have to use the bathroom?" He asked while the bath tub is filling up.

"Nope." She said shaking her little head. Marcus took off her clothes and placed her in the water. After a little splashing around and a lot of soap, he was finally able to get her completely bathed and rinsed off. He took her out of the tub and wrapped her in a towel. Marcus carried her into her room and dried her off. He got her lotion, put it on and got her dressed for the night. Marcus didn't mind putting Angela to bed. She was the easy one, it was the other one that he had to brace himself for. Angela climbed into her bed and got under the covers.

"You wanna read a story?" Marcus asked.

She nodded her little head and Marcus grabbed her favorite book, *Cinderella*. He got all the way to the night Cinderella was going to the ball and looked over at his daughter. She was sound asleep. Marcus closed the book and kissed her on the forehead. He turned off the light and walked out of the room.

As he stepped closer and closer to Lasaia's bedroom he prepared himself for the battle ahead. Marcus stepped through her doorway and saw Lasaia in the middle of the floor playing with her dolls.

"Little girl what are you doin'?" Marcus said scaring her to her feet. She started picking up toys and throwing them in her toy box.

"Girl, come on here." He said in a commanding voice.

Lasaia dropped the toys in her hands and quickly walked out of the room. She rushed over to the bathroom, sat on the toilet lid and started taking off her socks.

"Daaadddiieee" she shouted from the bathroom. Marcus walked into the bathroom and saw her standing there over the tub.

"Daddy that's used water." She said pointing at the tub before putting her hands on her hips. The tub was half full of water, but what she was talking about was the soap bubbles floating around in it.

"Girl, that water is fine." He said.

"I don't wanna use used water." She said, in protest. Marcus started to regret the fact that he used to call her his "Little Princess".

"Look its germs floatin' in it." She said putting her hands on the edge of the tub and looking over into the water. Marcus didn't have the strength to fight this battle, he gave in.

"Ok, ok. Fine." He let out the water and ran her a new "fresh" tub of water.

"Now get in the tub." He said turning off the water.

"Can I pleeeaaase have some privacy…Gosh." She said pushing him by the legs to get him out of the bathroom. Marcus backed out of the bathroom and she closed the door. *You did it to yourself,* Marcus repeated to himself in his head as he stepped into her room. He decided to pick up her room and put her things away so she wouldn't have one more thing to delay her getting to bed. As he was throwing the last of the toys into her overflowing toy box he heard, "Daaaddiiieee."

What now, he thought as he headed for her. He walked into the hall and saw a little head peeking out from the cracked bathroom door.

"Yes, sweetie?" he said.

"I don't have any nightclothes."

"Hold on." Marcus said taking a deep breath.

He walked back into her room and picked out some clothes for her to wear. He brought his selection back into the hall and as soon as she saw him she said, "Daddy no, I can't wear that to bed. Get me the long purple shirt with the bear on it."

Lasaia was starting to work her dad's nerves but he decided to avoid another battle and went to get the shirt she wanted. A few seconds later he emerged from her room and she saw he had what she wanted and said, "Daddy stop!"

Marcus stopped and looked around thinking she saw something he didn't.

"What?"

She wrapped her arm around the door and held her palm out.

"Throw it here." She requested.

"What?" Marcus said, confused.

"Throw it to me. I'm naked in here." She said with the door closed so tight that she could barely squeeze little her arm through the crack.

Sherise had finished her dishes and was making her way toward them. She saw Marcus standing there with a purple shirt in his hand and her daughter's arm stretched out the bathroom door. She made it to the top of the stairs, patted him on the shoulder, wished him luck, and walked into their room, giggling. Marcus turned back to his current battle and Lasaia still had her arm stretched out the bathroom door.

"Throw the shirt daddy." She said getting tired of holding out her hand. Marcus thought for a minute.

"Girl I used to change your diapers, I already seen every inch of you and…"

He started toward the door.

Lasaia let out a quick loud scream, pulled her arm back through the crack, and closed and locked the door. Marcus got to the door and saw that she had locked it and knocked on the door.

"Little girl open this door and put on this shirt."

"Daaddiieee, I'm naked. Leave it by the door and close your eyes."

He heard her muffled request come through the door. Marcus figured he couldn't get her out without breaking the lock so the best solution was to give her what she wanted to get her to open the door. He dropped the shirt on the floor in front of the door and took three steps back.

"Ok, the shirt is by the door." He heard the lock click and her eyes appeared through crack again.

"Close your eyes." She said from her mini-fortress.

Marcus took a deep breath again and closed his eyes.

"Now cover 'em."

Marcus continued to follow the directions and put his hands over his eyes.

"Ok, turn around."

Marcus had enough and dropped his hands, opened his eyes and said, "Girl if you don't…"

"Daaaddiiiee"

Marcus gave in, turned around and placed his hands over his closed eyes. He heard the door slowly open, the slight rustle of her snatching the shirt from the floor and the bathroom door quickly closing.

"Daddiiieee?"

Marcus dropped his hands, opened his eyes and turned around.

"Yes baby?"

"I need underwear."

That was it.

He wasn't going through this all over again. He rushed over to the door and opened it. The surprised Lasaia jumped back. She had forgotten to lock the door to keep him from getting in a second time

"Little girl, get in that room and get in the bed." He said trying his hardest to keep his cool. Lasaia quickly left the bathroom and went into her room with her father on her heels.

She figured she still had one last line of defense. Her dad wasn't going to let her go to bed with her room in a mess. She figured she could squeeze at least twenty more minutes out on that alone. She stepped through the doorway to her room and stopped a few steps inside. Marcus stood behind her leaning against the doorframe waiting to catch her reaction. Lasaia just looked around her room in amazement. Her spirit to fight had been broken. She walked over to her dresser, grabbed some underwear from a drawer and slipped them on under her long nightshirt.

"Night daddy." She said giving him a hug before climbing into her bed. Marcus almost felt sorry for her. He walked over and gave her a kiss on the cheek.
"Night baby." He said before turning off her light and walking out.

Marcus walked into his bedroom with his hands up in victory and found Sherise on the bed watching television. "No problems?" She asked looking over at him.
"I think I hurt her feelings." He said sitting down next to her in the bed.
"What you do?
Marcus explained how he cleaned up her room while she was in the tub and the look on her face when she saw her plan had been foiled.
"That little girl is a trip." Sherise said giggling.
Marcus got up from his spot and went into the bathroom to take a shower. When he finished and was brushing his teeth, Sherise asked, "What time are you going in tomorrow?"
"I have a meeting at 10, so I need to get ready for that…Umm probably try to get there around 8:30 or 9"
"Ok well I need you to drop the girls off at the daycare before you go. I told Lele I would be at the salon early."
"Ok."
Marcus finished his nightly bed-prep routine and walked back into the bedroom. He got into the bed and watched a little bit of the show his wife was watching. Sherise had something on her mind and was trying to find the words to say it.
"Marcus?" She said, reluctantly.
"Hmm." He said, still watching television.
"Why…why did you tell her she could come before you asked me?"
Marcus slowly turned his head from the television.
"Huh?" It took a few seconds for what she said to register.
"What do you mean?" He asked.
"I mean you didn't ask me before you told her it was ok for her to come here."
"I didn't think it was a big deal. She just wants to meet you and the kids. It ain't like she movin' in."
"I know but…I don't know." Sherise said.
She was confused as to why it bothered her as well.
Marcus started to smile.
"What did Lele say?"
Marcus knew this had to be the handy work of Miss Carmichael.
"She didn't say nothin'. She just said…"

"I knew it." He said with a smile.

"She just said something that got me thinking."

"What did she say?"

They were talking about men who cheat when I came in and…"

"Oh lawd." Marcus said joking.

"Shut up. Let me finish." She said pushing him and laughing.

They were talking and me and Lele went into the office to do the payroll and orders and stuff. So, we were talking and it came up that you had run into your old friend."

"Here it comes."

"Stop now, listen. She was like 'What he doin' in Atlanta? That's hoe central.' and blah blah blah. So she says 'Next thing you know he gonna be talkin' about he ran into an old friend.' And I was like, he already did. Then she said 'See, watch yo' man girl. That's how it starts.'"

Marcus was laughing by now and Sherise was starting to hear how ridiculous she sounded. In her head it was serious, but after she said it out loud she couldn't hold back the laugh. "Ok, ok, ok…so let me make sure I got this. Alicia told *you* to watch Lasaia so she doesn't *take* me."

"Basically."

"Baby, she's just a friend from back in the day. You know everything about her. We talked about her all the time when we first started dating. You must have thought she was nice, you let me name our daughter after her."

"Well, she sounded nice, but I didn't think that I would ever have to meet her. It just seems, I don't know, uncomfortable"

"Well, just do it for me. Please?"

"Ok, ok."

"Why are you so worked up about meeting her anyway?"

"I don't know. I just…"

"Ok, let me ask this. If I had ran into Calvin or any of the other guys from my high school, would you be this reluctant about meeting them?"

Sherise thought for a second and said, "No."

"So, it's the fact that it's a woman?"

"No, it's the fact that she is your old girlfriend."

"Yeah, from like 11 years ago, and we only dated for a few months before we went off to college. So, is it that you're jealous?"

"No, I'm not jealous. I'm just…"

"Jealous?"

"Anyway."

They laughed at the strangeness of the conversation.

"Well baby. Don't worry about it. You know I love you, and I'm not going anywhere. Plus it's cheaper to keep you."

She was almost feeling bad about bringing it up until that statement.

"Oh, anyway" She said.

The two of them laughed and watched a little more television before Sherise asked, "How does she look?"

"Who?"

"Your friend."

"Lasaia?"

"Yes"

"She looks *good*." Marcus said before remembering who he was talking to. Sherise's face changed and Marcus tried to back pedal.

"I mean she looks like she owns a modeling agency."

"Mmh hmm"

"Oh lawd, here you go."

"What? I'm just sayin'. You talkin' bout she all fine and stuff."

"I just said she looks good."

"No you said she looks *good*. Like men say when they're talking to your friends."

"Ok, well she is an attractive woman. How about that? Why don't you ask the question you really want to know?"

"What?"

"Does she look better then me?" Marcus said impersonating Sherise.

"Anyway. I know she don't look better then me."

"Nah she is in no way as beautiful as Sherise Downing."

"Anyway." She said trying not to smile.

"Baby I just want you to meet my best friend from the time I was like 14 years old. If you don't want to meet her, that's fine. But, I do want her to at least meet the kids."

Sherise thought for a second.

"But then I look like the "bad guy". How is that gonna look? She would be meeting everyone but me."

"Well it's not like I'm asking you to take her out with you. I just want yall to meet. Hang out. Maybe some dinner. You might actually like her."

She paused again.

"Ok, I'll meet her. But, I don't have to like it."

"Don't get sent to your room for being rude." He said laughing.

"Imma be good."
They talked for a little while longer about what they needed to get done in the next couple of days and then turned out the light and fell asleep in each other's arms.

Early the next morning Marcus woke up to the sound of the alarm clock. He hit the off button and got out of bed. He walked to the bathroom and washed his face, then stepped back into the bedroom and saw Sherise sitting on the side of the bed.
"Morning." He said walking over to her and giving her a kiss on the cheek.
"Morning baby." She said followed by a grunt. Marcus went over to his closet to pick out a suit for work. He selected his attire and walked back over and placed it on the bed. Sherise was still sitting in the same spot, head down, arms bracing herself, eyes closed.
"You alright baby?" Marcus said feeling concerned.
She usually beat him out of bed in the morning but every now and then she would lose her steam.
"I'm fine. My stomach just hurts a little bit. Think I must have slept wrong or something." She said standing up and stretching. "What you want for breakfast?"
"Anything is fine with me." Marcus told her.
She left the room and walked down the walkway to both of the girl's rooms to wake them. Marcus saw a slow moving Lasaia follow her mother out of her room.
"Get your sister and take her downstairs." Sherise said before descending the staircase. Lasaia walked her sleepy little sister downstairs to the family room and flipped on the television.

Marcus finished getting dressed and went downstairs to get his work in order and ready to go. He passed the family room and forgot to greet his little girls, but Lasaia didn't let it slide.
"Morning daddy" she shouted as he walked toward his office. Marcus put on his brakes, made a U-turn and headed back the way he came to the family room.
"Morning ladies." He said with a kiss on each of their foreheads before he turned and continued his journey to his office. He walked through the door and started gathering his papers and notes and put them in his briefcase. He started looking for one particular CD containing a presentation that he had been working on for months and had to present today. He couldn't find it any-

where and even the backup copy he made was nowhere to be found. Marcus started to panic.

"Girls, the food is ready!" Sherise shouted from the kitchen.

Marcus heard their little feet on the floor headed for the kitchen. He looked all over his office for the CD but couldn't find it anywhere. He walked to the kitchen and found the girls at the table eating and his wife making their plates.

"I was wondering what you were doing." She said.

"Baby, have you seen a CD with 'Coke presentation' written on it?"

"It's in your office isn't it?"

"I can't find it anywhere."

"Did you check your laptop?"

Without saying a word Marcus turned around and hurried out of the kitchen. He took his laptop out of its case and placed it on his desk. He turned it on and prayed that his CD was in the drive. Before the computer could load completely Marcus pushed the eject button and the tray opened. Marcus let out a sigh of relief as he carefully took the CD out and put it in a case. He shut down his laptop, placed it back into his bag and put the CD in the side pocket.

Marcus walked back into the kitchen and sat down to join his family. "You find it?" Sherise asked.

"Yeah."

She laughed.

As the little ones finished, Sherise got up from her seat and took them upstairs to get them dressed while Marcus ate. He finished his meal and ran into Sherise and the girls coming down the stairs.

"That was fast." He said seeing them already fully dressed. It was about 7:30 by now and Marcus marched his little ones out to his truck with Sherise right behind them. The girls climbed into their seats while Marcus grabbed Angela's car seat out of Sherise's car. He brought it back and got her buckled in and Lasaia put on her seatbelt. Marcus kissed his wife and leaned over and whispered, "Don't forget to hide that present in your back seat." Sherise had forgotten all about Lasaia's birthday gift in her car. It was a good thing they didn't get in her car; the surprise would have been ruined. Marcus climbed into the truck and pulled out the driveway. He honked the horn as the kids waved goodbye to their mother. After they were out of sight Sherise walked to her car and removed her daughter's gift. She headed back into the house so she could get ready for her day.

Marcus dropped the girls off and headed to work to get ready for his meeting. Sherise got dressed and headed for her salon. They both had a great day at work. Marcus knocked his online presentation with Coke out of the water, which could mean millions of dollars for his company and a huge bonus for him. Sherise's had lots of new clients make appointments with her due to a new marketing strategy that Marcus told her and she didn't have nearly as much paper work as she thought she did. She even had time to take a lunch with Lele which hadn't happened in months. Marcus picked up the girls and they all met back home that evening. That day, and the two following, were pretty average days in that household. The only difference was on Wednesday and Thursday Marcus received emails from his friend Lasaia counting down the days until she would be there. She seemed to be more excited about visiting them then he was. Marcus paid it little attention to it and went on with his family life.

On Friday afternoon, Marcus rushed home to get things set up for his out of town visitor. After getting out of his suit he went to work. He cleaned the bathrooms, kitchen, family room and even did a little dusting. Sherise and the girls made it home to a fresh smelling house and ran into Marcus coming out of the kitchen. He had started cooking and was speeding around the house checking all the rooms, sometimes two or three times to make sure they were clean. As if the filth elves had come through and messed something up.

"Hey sweetie." He said, giving his wife a kiss on the cheek before shuffling by her to check the family room again.

"Help your sister take her stuff to her room." Sherise said to Lasaia.

The two girls headed up the steps to put their things away. Marcus flew back from the family room and jetted into the kitchen. Sherise gave him a funny look and followed him.

"You alright babe?" She asked, walking around their kitchen island, to the stove where Marcus was mixing his dish.

"Yeah, why?"

"Cause you're running around the house like you're crazy." She said laughing.

"Oh," he chuckled, "I'm fine, just tryin' to make sure everything looks good for our company."

"Mmmh hmmm. Your little girlfriend comes to town and you clean up the whole house. I can't even get you to mop the bathroom floor." She said, joking.

"Whatever." He said, puckering his lips, signaling her.

She gave him a quick peck on the lips and left the kitchen. She made her way upstairs to change into something more comfortable.

Around 7:30 Marcus heard his cell phone ringing in his office and left the kitchen to answer it. He grabbed it off the charger and flipped it open.

“Hello?” He said.
“Hi. Marcus?”
“Yeah.”
“Hey, this is Lasaia.”
“Hey, what’s up?”
“We are in Jacksonville now and I wanted to make sure I’m going the right way.”
Lasaia told Marcus where she was and read off the directions she got off the Internet.
“Yeah, that’s it.” Marcus told her.
“Ok, cool. I guess I’ll see you in about twenty minutes.”
“Ok. I hope you’re hungry, cause I’ve been cooking.”
“Oooo, you cooked for me? How sweet. That’s good because I’m starved. Hey…is it alright if I bring a friend?”
“Oh yeah, definitely. You guys, come on. Who is it?”
“It’s a surprise.”
Marcus laughed.
“Ok, see you in a little bit.”
“Ok.”
They hung up the phone and Marcus started to get a little nervous. He was feeling the butterflies growing in his stomach just like when she came to visit him at Alonzo’s house. Marcus finished his meal and turned off the stove. He rushed out of the kitchen and was headed upstairs when he saw the two little ones in the family room. Lasaia was coloring and she had put in Angela’s Disney video. Angela was in her usual Indian style seated position, staring at the screen.
“Yall be careful in here. Don’t mess up this room, we have company coming.” He said.
They said, “Ok,” and Marcus continued upstairs.

Marcus entered his room and Sherise was sitting on the bed reading a magazine. She looked up and saw him come in and disappear into his closet. She could hear him shuffling around in there for a few minutes and finally asked, “What you looking for?”
“Something to wear. She just called and said they are like twenty minutes away.” He said from inside his walk-in closet.
“So you’re about to put on a suit?”
“No, no. Just change out of the clothes I’ve been cleaning and cooking in.”
“Oh.” Sherise said returning to her spot on the page.

Marcus finally found a decent outfit, brought it into the room and set it on the bed. He put on his clothes and looked over to his wife sitting there in her sweat pants and t-shirt.

“You gonna wear that?” He asked.

Sherise looked up at him and down at her clothes.

“You want me to change?” She said, not believing he just asked that.

“No, I mean…I was just asking.” He says realizing in his haste he might have just crossed the line. Sherise got up and walked into her closet and Marcus didn’t even try to stop her. He knew that would have been the beginning of a fight.

“I’m going downstairs.” Marcus said walking out of the room. He made it downstairs and into the kitchen when he saw lights reflect off of his wall, indicating a car had pulled into the driveway. Marcus’s heart jumped into his throat. He turned around and headed for the front door. He opened the door to a shiny jaguar resting in front of his house. The soft murmur from the engine came to a halt. Marcus saw another figure slowly rise from the passenger side of her car. He took a few steps out from the doorway and Lasaia saw him.

“Heeeey Marcus.” She said waving from beside her car waiting on her companion. The figure walked around the car and into the light next to Lasaia. They started their walk toward the house and Marcus was finally able to make out the figure beside her. It was a man! The woman that would dismiss any man at the drop of a hat had a date. Marcus was confused but he waited to greet them as they walked up. The first question on Marcus’s mind was, *Who is he?*

Eleven

The two of them walked up to the walkway admiring the house and the yard, pointing the whole way. They finally made it to porch and Lasaia gave Marcus a big hug.

"Heeeey buddy." She said, squeezing his neck. Marcus hugged her and acted happy to see them but in the back of his mind he was thinking about who this guy could be. Their meeting brought back more emotions for Marcus then he thought. He had slipped right back into protective mode and didn't even realize it. Lasaia let him go and introduced the two of them.

"Marcus, this is Greg. This is the guy you told me I was crazy for not calling. Greg this is Marcus, my old friend I have been telling you about for like, the last seven hours."

Marcus was somewhat relieved and offered the man his hand. She had talked so highly about him and about how good he treated her, he couldn't help but accept him. Greg shook his hand and said, "Nice to meet you man. Lasaia has told me *everything* about you."

They shared a brief chuckle.

"Good to meet you too. Yall come on in." Marcus said and the three of them walked into the house.

"Marcus your house is beautiful." Lasaia said looking up at the inside of the foyer.

"Yeah, this is real nice." Greg said.

"Thanks, it's a blessing." Marcus said humbly.

They walked into the family room and the girls were still in their spots, Lasaia in her coloring book and Angela watching her tape.

"Come here girls, I want you to meet somebody."

Lasaia got up off the floor and Angela stood to her feet. They walked over and stood next to Marcus and Greg kneeled down to speak to them.

"Hey, how are you guys doing?" He said.

"Fine." Lasaia said.

He extended his hand and said, "I'm Greg. What's your name?"

"My name's Lasaia Downing," the little one said, with pride, shaking his hand like a grown up.

Lasaia reached down and picked up Angela and held her in her arms.

"Aren't you the prettiest thing? Marcus they are gorgeous." She said.

"Thank you."

Lasaia sat Angela back on the floor and the little one just stood there looking up at her.

"Hi, Lasaia." Marcus's old friend said. "My name is Lasaia too."

The little one didn't say a word and just backed up slightly behind her father's leg.

"What's wrong with you? You not shy." Marcus said trying to get her to speak.

Lasaia just stood there looking up at this woman who she was frightened of and didn't know why.

Just then Sherise came down the steps. She had changed into a nice comfortable sundress. "Hello everybody." She said as she reached the bottom of the steps. The three adults turned around to see Sherise walking over to them. She extended her hand to Lasaia who looked down at it and said, "Oh no you didn't." she stepped forward and threw her arms around Sherise's neck.

"I can't just shake your hand," Lasaia told her, "You have to give me a hug."

"Nice to finally meet you." Sherise said hugging her back.

After their embrace, Lasaia introduced her companion.

"And this is my friend Greg."

Sherise shook his hand and they all walked into the family room. The girls returned to what they were doing and the grown folks had a seat.

"So how was your trip?" Sherise asked.

"Lon," Lasaia said with a laugh, "But everybody made it here safe, so it's alright." "Marcus told me you were coming for something to do with your agency?"

"Yeah girl, looking for some new faces, trying to expand, you know? You ever thought about modeling, cause you wearin' that dress." Lasaia said, complimenting Sherise.

Sherise smiled and said, "Thank you, but…."

She paused and a laughed.

"No, no, I'm too short and wide for that." She said blushing.

She was flattered that someone actually thought she looked good enough to model. Sherise wasn't fat, or big boned to be politically correct, but she did have wide hips, thick legs, and a big but nicely shaped backside. She didn't think she had what people were looking for.

"Girl you should, I'm telling you. All these skinny anorexic girls out here struttin'…That's not what a real woman looks like." Lasaia said.

They sat and talked for a little while then Sherise said, "You guys wanna see the rest of the house?"

"Sure." Lasaia said standing to her feet.

The four of them got up and walked out of the family room and Marcus broke from the group in the foyer.

"I'm gonna get the food set, yall go ahead."

Marcus disappeared into the kitchen and they proceeded upstairs. Sherise showed them their bedroom and Angela's bedroom, but before they could walk into Lasaia's room they heard a loud call, "Not my room mommieee!" Sherise looked over the staircase and saw her daughter standing there peaking around the corner. She had been watching them ever since they left the family room and didn't want this strange woman in her room. She didn't know why, but she didn't like her father's friend.

"Girl ain't nobody messin' with your room. Go back and watch TV." Sherise said not knowing why her daughter was acting so strange.

"Mommy noooo." Lasaia said, begging her mom not to take them into her room.

"Ok, well that's Lasaia's room right there." Sherise said pointing to the room with the closed door. She honored her daughter's request and they headed downstairs. Sherise showed them the other two guest bedrooms and Marcus's office and they headed back to the family room. Marcus met them on his way out of the kitchen and asked, "You guys ready to eat?" Sherise got the girls together and they all headed for the dining room. The visitors and little ones had a seat at the dining room table and Marcus and Sherise brought the food. They shared a delicious meal prepared by Marcus and had a little light conversation. Marcus's daughter, Lasaia, seems very unresponsive during the entire meal but he figured she was just sleepy. The girls finished up and Sherise took them upstairs and got them ready for bed.

After about 30 minutes, and a fight with a certain five year old, Sherise finally made it back downstairs. She walked into the dining room and saw Marcus clearing the table while Lasaia and her date collected the dishes.

"Girl, I don't know how you eat like this and stay so slim."

Sherise joined them and tried to hold back the smile creeping onto her face. Sherise was a sucker for compliments. They got the dishes into the kitchen and Marcus ran some dishwater.

"Boy move, what you think you doin'?" Lasaia said grabbing the dish rag.

"I was gonna…"

"You was gonna go sit down. We got this." Lasaia said taking the spot next to Sherise at the sink. Sherise just smiled as Marcus walked over and kissed his wife on the cheek.

"Come on man." Marcus said to Greg as he grabbed a couple of beers out of the refrigerator. Greg started to follow Marcus and Lasaia said, "Hey!"

Greg stopped, but Marcus kept moving toward the family room.

"Where mine at?" Lasaia said.

"Your what?" Greg asked.

"My kiss." She said.

Greg hesitated for a second and said, "Oh," before quickly walking over to Lasaia and giving her an awkward peck on her cheek.

"Thank you baby." Lasaia said as Greg walked out of the kitchen and joined Marcus in the family room.

"How long you two been together?" Sherise asked after she was sure he was gone.

"We talked for a couple of weeks like almost 2 years ago, and I broke up with him over something stupid. But when Marcus was in Atlanta we got a chance to talk and he came up. He made me realize how silly I was being and I called him back like 2 days ago." Lasaia said as they started the dishes.

"Marcus told you to call him?"

"Not directly, but he was talking about how much he loves being with you and having the kids and I felt kinda like I was missing out on something great, ya' know? So, I figured I would stop being so picky and just take a chance."

"So how have things been since you called him?"

"Fine, I think he is still a little scared that I'm setting him up or something."

They laughed.

"But I can't blame him. I was wrong. He's not all that bright but he's just so damn cute." Lasaia said, looking back to make sure he hadn't slipped back in on them.

They shared a girly giggle and kept washing the dishes.

Out in the family room, Marcus and Greg sat and watched some ESPN highlights. Greg took a sip from his beer and said, "This is a really nice house."

"Thanks man."

"How long you and your wife been together?"

"About 10 years now."

"That's beautiful. That's what I'm looking for."

"Well, if you play your cards right I think you might have a chance with this one." Marcus quieted down so the girls couldn't hear him if they were eavesdropping.

"When I was in Atlanta, she told me about you and how good you used to treat her and how much she liked you. You stay on that track, and she's yours."

Greg looked confused then smiled and said, "Yeah, well we'll see."

"She told me about how you two broke up and I told her she was crazy for letting you get away."

Greg just sat and listened to Marcus talk.

"She told me she broke up with you because you had a flat tire and was late for a date."

"Uh, yeah. I didn't understand that one, but I figured she just didn't want to be with me and was looking for a reason so…"

"Yeah, that was crazy, but that's women. They get in their moods and you can't win for losing."

"Yeah"

Back in the kitchen Sherise was really taking a liking to her visitor. "Girl, let me tell you, Marcus used to be like the only guy in my high school that would look out for me. My family was kinda poor. Well not poor, but my step dad would spend all our money on drugs and stuff, so I never had new clothes and stuff and other kids used to pick on me. But not Marcus, he would always get them off of me. He was almost like my big brother."

"Yall were really good friends huh?"

"The best. He was pretty much the only *true* one I had."

They finish up the dishes and Sherise poured them some wine and they had a seat at the breakfast table.

"No disrespect to you sista, but I love your husband, even to this day," Lasaia said with a laugh, "He's a good man girl. Don't let him go. A man like Marcus comes along only once in a lifetime."

Sherise saw the sincerity in Lasaia's eyes and nodded her head. She understood where she was coming from.

"Did Marcus ever tell you about when we went to prom?" Lasaia asked.
"He told me yall went, but never really went into detail."
"Let me tell you how sweet your man is." Lasaia said opening up to her story.

It was lunch time one Monday afternoon at their high school. All Lasaia had seen all day were flyers in the hall, preaching about the prom. She had missed out on prom her junior year and was determined not to miss this one. Her one triumphant moment was her role in *Romeo & Juliet* but she wanted to go out with another precious memory. She and Marcus started talking about it as they ate and she discovered he didn't have plans to go.
"How you not gonna go? It's the SENIOR prom! We're seniors. It's for *us*."
"I went last year and it was busted. I'm just gonna get me something to drink and chill."
"Well I want to go. Not all of us got to go *last* year."
"I'm tellin' you. It's gonna be boring. Don't waste your time."
Lasaia was quiet for a moment.
Sadness began to draw a self portrait across her face.
"It don't matter anyway, ain't nobody gonna ask me anyway."
Marcus looked up from his lunch and saw how serious she was. He fell into the nice guy mode and said, "Do you really want to go to the prom?"
"Yes." She said, tired of repeating herself.
"Well, let's do it."
"Do what?" She lifted her eyes from the flyer.
"Let's do it, let's go to prom. Me and you."
"Don't play with me." She said, knowing how playful he was.
"I'm serious, let's go. Then you can see how bad it is and I can say I told you so."
"You're for real?"
"Yes, man."
"Ok, promise me you will take me to prom and I'll say yes."
"Ok. I promise. You think I'm playin'."
"Ok, well I gotta get a dress."
"Well we can go this afternoon and check some prices."
"You don't have practice?"
"Not anymore." Marcus said, insinuating that he wasn't going to go.

That afternoon Marcus got excused from his practice and they headed to the mall to find her a dress. When they got there, Lasaia had to have tried on twenty different dresses before she found the *one*. It was a tight, soft purple dress that showed off her young but developed figure. It went around her shoulders and had a split that went up one side. That was the one. She wanted the dress so bad but it was $120 and she didn't have that much to spend. She knew asking her mom and step dad for the money would be a waste of time. She might as well have asked the lady that worked in the store to buy it for her. She would have gotten the same response. The lady in the store probably would have been a lot nicer about saying no too. She reluctantly took it off and was ready to leave the mall. That was the dress. If she couldn't have that one she didn't want any of them.

The next day, when Lasaia got home from school, she walked into her room and found a white box with a red ribbon tied around it, sitting on her bed. The note on it only had two words, I PROMISED. Lasaia quickly untied the ribbon and snatched the top off the box. She dropped the box on the bed and let out a quick scream, her hands concealing her excitement from echoing through the house. Tears of joy began to roll down her cheeks. She could barely breathe and her heart was pounding. She could only stand there and look at the contents of the box. There, inside the box, was the dress that she loved in the mall so much. She felt she didn't deserve to have someone, good to her as Marcus was as a friend. Her mom came in the room to check on her after hearing her muffled scream.

"Baby what's wrong?" She said seeing her daughter standing next to her bed crying. Lasaia couldn't even get the words out as her mother stood there looking at her. They sat on the bed and Lasaia showed her mother the box. Lasaia had told her mother about the dress when she had come home from the mall the day before but they weren't able to come up with a plan for her to get it before the prom. Her mother looked into the box and saw the dress and knew why she was crying.

"This is the dress? Marcus brought this box over a little while ago and told me to give it to you, but I had no idea...Oh baby, you are gonna be so beautiful. Here try it on." Her mother said taking the dress out of the box. After Lasaia got the dress on her mother just sat and admired how beautiful she was.

Just as they were starting to have fun and enjoying their mother/daughter time, in walked Lasaia's stepfather. They both went silent as he walked in and a look of fear jumped onto Lasaia's mother's face. It was as if he had warned her that she would be beaten if he saw the two of them happy.

"What the hell is that?" He said in a half drunk voice, taking a sip from the beer in his hand.

"It's her prom dress. Her friend got it for her." Lasaia's mom said in a timid voice standing up from her spot on the bed.

"Hmph," he said, "Somebody actually gon' take *you* to the prom?"

He took another sip from his beer and laughed as he turned and walked out. Lasaia just stood there, her eyes focused in hate at her adversary. She didn't understand how one person could have so much evil in them. His footsteps disappeared into his room and they were alone for another few seconds. Lasaia's mother just turned to her child with a remorseful look on her face. Lasaia stood there with tears forming in her eyes. She knew he wouldn't touch her anymore; he stopped that when people began to notice, but sometimes she wished he would just hit her. The physical pain only lasted until the bruise healed, but the mental pain hurt just as bad every time she thought about it.

"I'm sorry baby," her mother said giving her a hug, "you are gonna be so beautiful," she whispered in her ear.

She kissed her daughter on the forehead, walked out the room and into her own. Lasaia could not understand why she was so drawn to him. He was no good to either of them and she couldn't remember a time that they had actually had fun as a family. She carefully took off her dress and placed it back into the box. She placed the box in the corner and just sat on the bed looking at it for a couple minutes everyday.

The day of the prom came quickly and Lasaia rushed home from school that day. She knew she had to get her nails and hair done, borrow some shoes from someone and be ready by the time Marcus was ready to go. She dropped her things off in her room, held her dress box in her hands for a few seconds, then walked back out the door. She walked three blocks to her friend's house and knocked on the door.

"Hey, what's up?" A girl said unlocking the screen door. Lasaia walked in and had a seat on her couch. Tiffany was a friend of Lasaia's, but they didn't really talk over the past few years like they used to. Tiffany's house used to be sort of a refuge for Lasaia when her stepfather would go on one of his rampages. Anytime things got really out of control, Lasaia's mother would call Tiffany's mother and she would go over there.

"You get the stuff?" Lasaia asked catching a quick rest from her walk.

"Yeah, you ready?" Tiffany asked.

Tiffany spent the next couple of hours perming and styling Lasaia's hair. After that, they worked on her nails and toes. They finished her miniature make over and Lasaia asked, "You have any shoes I can borrow?" Tiffany took Lasaia to her room and opened her closet. There she saw shoes upon shoes of all different colors and styles piled into the closet.

"If you can find a matching pair you can take 'em." Tiffany said laughing. Lasaia rummaged through the shoes and found a pair that went with her dress perfectly.

"Thank you." Lasaia said giving her old friend a hug.

Neither of them knew why they had stopped talking to each other. It was just one of those situations where two people just grew apart. Lasaia left Tiffany's house and started on her way home, hair done and shoes in her hand.

She got back to her street around 6:30 and went over to see what time Marcus would be ready to go. She knocked on his door and his mother answered.

"Heeey sweetie!" She said in her southern drawl.

"Hey Mrs. Downing, is Marcus home?"

"No darlin', he ain't made it in yet."

"Ok, I was just coming by to see what time he wanted to leave."

"Oh, I don't know baby, I'll send him over when he gets in. Your hair is beautiful though."

"Thank you. Ok, see you later."

"Bye, bye sweetie"

Mrs. Downing closed the door and Lasaia started on her way home. She almost got in her yard when a car pulled into Marcus's driveway. Lasaia turned around and saw Marcus step out the car and lean over and look into the window. He was with Samantha Newberry, head cheerleader at their high school. Lasaia just stood there looking at them, getting more and more jealous with each second that passed. Marcus stood up from the car window and looked over to see Lasaia standing there. He left from beside the car and started walking over to her. Samantha cut her eyes at Lasaia and pulled out of the driveway. She sped off down the street as Marcus got to his friend.

"What's up?" He asked as if he didn't just get out of the car with another woman.

"What was that all about?" Lasaia asked with an attitude.

"What? Samantha? She just gave me a ride home." Marcus said.

Lasaia just stood there in silence.

"What? Did you get your gift?" He asked.

"Yes. Thank you." She said still irritated by what happened. Marcus just smiled and said, "It's not what you think. It was just a ride."

She could never stay mad at him for very long and figured she was just acting silly.

It was just a ride.

It wasn't like he kissed her or anything. Marcus reached forward and threw his arms around her. He gave her a tight squeeze and Lasaia immediately melted in his arms. That hug made everything go away. She wasn't sure, but she thought she may have been falling in love with her best friend.

He released his grip around her and she slipped back into reality. "Did you like your dress?" He asked.

"Yeeeess!" She said excited. "How did you…where did you get the money?"

"My little secret." He said winking at her and smiling.

He was glad she enjoyed it.

"So what time you getting ready?" She asked.

"Bout to go jump in the shower now, where you wanna go eat?"

"I don't care."

"Ok, well I'll get some ideas while I'm getting ready. Give me about an hour and I'll be over."

"Ok."

"Ok. See you in an hour." Marcus said turning and hurrying toward his front door. He got about ten feet away and stopped and turned back to her.

"Oh, your hair looks great." He said.

Lasaia just smiled and looked at him. He smiled back and turned to go into the house.

Lasaia was frozen in her spot until he disappeared through the door. It was like her eyes wouldn't let her miss a single second of him while he was still in sight. Lasaia walked over to her house and through the front door.

She walked through the house and to her room. "Moommiiieee," Lasaia screamed as she looked over to the corner where her dress had been for the last week and a half. The box was gone and she knew she hadn't moved it. She had just held it in her hands before leaving to get her hair done, now, it was gone. It had been there for what seemed like forever and had pretty much become like a piece of furniture in her room. Her mother rushed into the room.

"What baby? What happened?" She said, nervously approaching her daughter. The way she shrieked she thought she had hurt herself.

"My dress is gone, and I know it was there when I left! I picked it up for a few seconds and but it back! Now, it's gone!" Lasaia said, hysterically.

"Well baby, maybe you put it somewhere else and…"

"No, no, no. I put it right there." Lasaia said, pointing to the empty spot on her wall. "I put it there before I left."

The tears started to roll from her eyes. She already knew who had to have taken it. He was the only other person in the house.

"Where did he put it mommy?" Lasaia asked, tears in her eyes.

"I don't know. He came home and was in the bedroom for a few minutes, then he left with one of his friends. Baby, I don't think he would've…"

"He took it. I know he took it. I can feel it. He couldn't stand to see me happy for one day!" Lasaia yelled between sobs while she paced.

"Well baby let's look. He didn't leave with it. It has to be around here somewhere."

Her mother didn't fight the thought that her man had taken the box. She didn't want to believe that he would be that evil. This had nothing to do with him. She hadn't asked him for the money to get it, her friend bought it for her. Sometimes she wondered how she could be with someone so heartless.

The two of them jumped from room to room searching for the white, rectangle-shaped box with the red ribbon. They searched from top to bottom. They looked in closets, bathrooms, the kitchen, under sinks, and even under the couch in the living room. They looked in every conceivable hiding place big enough to conceal the dress, nothing. They were sweating and Lasaia's hair do was ruined in the process. She had spent a few hours getting it done and ruined it in less then half that time. Lasaia just sat on her bed and cried. It hurt her mother to her heart to see her child in so much pain. She decided that there was nothing that was going to stop her from finding that dress if it was in that house. She went back over every area that the two of them searched. After about fifteen minutes she figured all was lost. She hadn't found anything even resembling the box. She sat on the side of her bed, fell back, tilted her head over the edge and closed her eyes.

Please lord, help me find my baby's dress. She deserves this. She deserves better.

Her silent prayer was catapulted into the sky above. She could only hope that it would be heard. She opened her eyes she looked at herself in the standing mirror on the other side of the bed. Just stared at herself in the mirror for a few seconds.

She was about to get up when she caught a glimpse of something under the bed. The light shined through the window and caught the edge of something shiny under the bed. She could barely see it but it was there. She got up from her spot on the bed and walked around to her husband's side. She reached under the bed and the only thing under there was a black duffel bag. He would use this if he had to do a job out of town or something like that. Usually it was empty, but this time it had a weird shape. She looked at the zipper and there was a small piece of red ribbon sticking out from under the closed zipper. She slowly unzipped the bag and looked inside. There was a white box with a red ribbon inside the bag. She pulled it out and opened it to find Lasaia's dress lying in it, just as beautiful as when she had it on. She threw the bag on the ground and rushed to her daughter's room. Lasaia was lying face down on the bed still crying her eyes out when she ran in.

"Baby, baby look! I found it!"

Lasaia raised her face from the bed and looked up at her mother. She could barely see through the tears but she saw her dress box in her mother's hands. She jumped up and sat on the bed and took the box from her mother. She opened it and let out a quick laugh of joy while quickly stomping her feet on the floor with glee. She stood up with tears running down her cheeks and threw her arms around her mother's neck. Moments like this made her wish she could be with her daughter more often.

"Where was it?" Lasaia said, not really caring but curious.

"It was," her mother hesitated, "Don't worry about that now. Come on, you have to get ready. Marcus will be here any minute."

She didn't want to tell her daughter that her husband had really taken it. They already despised each other, this was just fuel for the forest fire. Her mother rushed her to get into the shower. As Lasaia showered and her mother was laying the dress out on the bed with all of her accessories, there was a knock at the door. Lasaia's mom rushed to answer it. She opened the door to find a tuxedo'd down Marcus. He was standing there cleaner than Easter Sunday.

"Hey Marcus." She said smiling as she opened the screen door.

"Hi Mrs. Jones. Is Lasaia ready?" He asked, walking into the house.

"Almost, we had a little problem earlier but she's taking a shower now." She said, not able to stop smiling. She was so proud of the two of them she could hardly contain it.

"Have a seat and I'll check on her." She said, leaving the living room. Marcus sat on the couch with Lasaia's corsage, wrapped in a plastic container, in his hand. As soon as she was out of his view, Lasaia's mother darted to the bathroom door. Lasaia was just getting out of the shower and heard her mother knocking on the door.

"Yes?" She said through the door.

"He's here." Her mother said, trying to whisper through the crack of the door.

"Already?" Lasaia said, quickly drying off.

She put on her under clothes and opened the door. The two of them rushed into her room and quickly threw on her dress. While Lasaia twisted and turned to get the dress in the right position, her mom ran to her room and hurried back with her makeup kit. They quickly threw her face together in about seven minutes. Luckily, her nails weren't messed up while they were looking for her dress. The same thing couldn't be said for her hair. They had forgotten about her hair.

"What am I gonna do. I can't get my hair done over in enough time." Lasaia said, about to revert back to her tears.

"It's ok baby, just comb it out." Her mother said trying to help.

They fix her hair the best they can but can't get it anywhere near the way Tiffany had done it. After a few minutes they gave up, pulled it back into a ponytail and walked out to see her date.

They came around the corner and Marcus stood to his feet. "Wow…you…you look great." He said.

Even his *Juliet* princess hadn't looked this good. The dress looked even better on her now then it did in the store.

"Oh, I got this for you." Marcus said, snapping back into reality and opening the corsage box.

"Wait, wait, let me get my camera." Lasaia's mom said running to her room.

"Momma!" Lasaia said in protest.

She disappeared into her room and they could hear her in there throwing stuff around, looking for the camera.

"What happened to your hair? You didn't like it the other way?" Marcus said.

"No, I did. But…that's a long story. There's nothing I can do now." She said.

"My mom can probably hook it up. I mean if you want her to."

Lasaia's eyes lit up.

"You think she would?"

"Yeah, why not?"

Lasaia's mom came back into the room with her camera in hand and put it up to her eye. "Say cheeeeese."

"No mama wait. Marcus said his mom might do my hair real quick."

"Really?" Her mom said lowering her camera.

"Yeah. I mean she might not be able to get it like it was but she can probably do it another way. Let's go see." Marcus said, opening the front door.

The three of them walked out the front door and across the lawn that separated their properties.

"Maaaa!" Marcus yelled through the house as they walked in.

"In here." She called back to him from the living room. The small group walked into the room as she was standing up.

"Awww, look at yall. Let me get my camera." Mrs. Downing said.

"Ma, we need you to do something with Lasaia's hair. It got messed up and I thought you might be able to fix it." Marcus said.

"Oh, baby what happened? It was beautiful." Mrs. Downing said.

"It's a long story." Lasaia said.

"Ok, well we don't have time right now. Let's go." Mrs. Downing said walking by and grabbing Lasaia's hand. The two of them hurried down the hallway and disappeared into her room. Marcus and Mrs. Jones had a seat and waited.

About thirty minutes later they emerged from the back room and head up to meet the other two. Mrs. Jones was so nervous she had just about gnawed all of her fingernails off. They walked into the living room and Marcus and Mrs. Jones jumped to their feet. Lasaia stood there with Mrs. Downing behind her. Her hair looked even more beautiful than before and now they were ready to go. Lasaia's mother could barely contain herself. Her eyes began to tear at how beautiful her daughter was. Mrs. Downing had even touched up their makeup job and there was no way Lasaia could have been anymore beautiful. Marcus walked over and put her corsage on her waiting wrist.

"Come on, come on, picture time." Mrs. Downing said.

They burn through almost a whole role of film on the two of them. It looked like a photo shoot was going on inside that small three bedroom Albany home.

They finished taking their pictures and the small party headed back out the door. They walked over to Mr. Downing's Cadillac. He had loaned it to Marcus for his big night. It was old but it was one of the cleanest and best running cars in Albany. A lot of the young knuckleheads had offered to pay him three to four times what it was worth to buy it but he shot all of them down. He couldn't stand the thought of his baby becoming some low riding, loud music playing toy for some young kid that would show her the respect she deserved.

They almost made it to the car when Lasaia said, "My purse!" In the rush, she had left her purse with her keys in the house. The three of them walked back over to her house and Marcus had a seat while she got her purse. As he waited a car pulled into the driveway and someone got out. It was Lasaia's step-father. He was back. He walked up to the front door and opened it. Marcus saw him coming and stood to his feet. Willy walked in and saw the young man standing in his living room. They stared at each other eye to eye for a few seconds before he said, "The hell you doin' here?" At that exact moment, Lasaia and her mother were coming down the hall talking about the prom and laughing. They both saw him standing there at the same time and froze in their spot. The rage could be seen mounting in his eyes as he realized what was going on. They had found the dress and his plan had been ruined. He figured all he would have to do is hide the dress and stay gone long enough for them to cancel their date, then she wouldn't be able to go. There was complete silence in the house for a few seconds before Mrs. Jones said, "Yall better get goin'. You don't wanna be late."

She rushed Lasaia over to the door while Marcus followed behind them. The two men never took their eyes off one another as they moved. Marcus refused to be intimidated by this man he had no respect for. Willy turned around and went to grab Lasaia.

"Where you think you goin'?" He said extending his arm. Marcus saw it coming and pushed his arm away.

"Boy, you crazy? I'll..."

"You'll what?" Marcus said standing face to face with the tyrant.

Willy knew if he messed with Marcus he would have to mess with his father, and Daniel Downing was the wrong man to play with about his boys. Willy just stood there staring at this young man in the eyes and laughing until Mrs. Jones came and pulled Marcus back.

"Come on baby, yall gonna be late."

Marcus stared at Mr. Jones as he backed out the door and met his date on the porch.

"Yall be careful." Mrs. Jones said as they walked arm-in-arm down the walkway. The two of them walked out to his father's car, got in, and drove off on their way to the prom.

"Girl, we had the best time. I still have pictures from that night." Lasaia said to Sherise ending her story.

Twelve

Lasaia took a sip of her wine as Sherise digested her words.
"Wow! I'm surprised that the two of you even made it. I can't believe your step father actually hid your prom dress."
"Girl, that man was so evil it was a shame. I never understood why. I never did anything to him."
There was a brief moment of silence.
"Well, at least you got there and had a good time."
"Yeah, too bad my mom had to pay for it."
"What do you mean?"
"When I saw her the next day, she had a black eye. He made up some story about her tripping and hitting her head. Yeah, she tripped and hit her head on your fist."
"That's a shame. I have no respect for men like that."
They each took another sip of wine and Lasaia said, "I can't believe Marcus didn't tell you about that."
"No, he sure didn't."
I'm gonna have to ask him about this."
The two of them got up from the table and marched into the living room to get an explanation.
"I was startin' wonder what yall were doin'." Marcus said as they entered and had a seat.
"Marcus, I can't believe you didn't tell your wife about our night at the prom." Lasaia said.
"What you talkin' about? I did." He said, turning to Sherise.
"No, you told me that you two dated and went to the prom, but you never gave me any details."

"See boy, you're missing out on valuable cool points. You didn't tell her about how you got your mom to do my hair, you didn't tell her about how you stood up to my step dad…you didn't even tell her about how you bought my dress."

"Well, I didn't think…" Marcus was cut off.

"How did you by my dress anyway?" Lasaia asked.

"I never told you? I used the money that I was saving to get my car fixed after the little problem I had getting to your play. Well, the guy who was gonna fix it told me it was gonna be like $2,000. So I started saving. But, when you wanted to go to prom I spent it on the my tux, your dress, dinner, pictures and gas. After that, I had like $12 left and ain't no tellin' what I did with that." Marcus said laughing.

"Aawww, you used your car money on me?" Lasaia said followed by a laugh. Marcus laughed with her and said, "Yeah but if it took me almost a year to save a couple hundred dollars, I would probably still be trying to make it to that 2,000 right now."

"So what was up with you riding with that other girl?" Sherise asked.

"What other girl?" Marcus asked.

"She's talking bout Samantha," Lasaia chirped in, "You were with her the day of the prom."

"Samantha?" Marcus thought for a minute. "Ooooh, you mean the cheerleader? Damn you did go into detail."

"Yeah." Lasaia said.

"What about her?" Marcus asks.

"You were in her car." Lasaia said.

"Oh, yeah she gave me a ride home. She came up to me after practice that day, talking about her date bailed on her and she wanted to know if I would go to prom with her. I told her I had a date but she kept bugging me. So then she asked if she could give me a ride home. I figured it beat the walk home so I got in. The whole way home she was talking bout how I would have a much better time at prom with her, and an even *better* time afterwards if I went with her. I was like 'whoa', but I gave my word to you so I turned her down. I guess she was mad because even the guarantee to get between her legs wasn't even enough to change my mind."

"Is that why she was always cutting her eyes at me all the time after that day?" Lasaia asked.

"Could be."

"But she was like the most popular girl in school."

"Yeah, but now she work at a grocery store and got 3 kids. Popularity doesn't guarantee anything."

"Yeah but, at least you would have got some popular booty." Lasaia said and they all laughed. Marcus chuckled and said, "Yeah, but I think I made the right decision."

Marcus and Lasaia's eyes connected for a few seconds and they saw each other back in that small city in Georgia. A young couple, not exactly sure what love was, but enjoying the discovery.

"See girl, that's what I was telling you about. Please hold on to him." Lasaia said, talking to Sherise.

Lasaia snapped back into reality and looked at her watch. It was 11:15. "Oh man, I didn't realize we had been talking for this long. We need to get going. Got a big day tomorrow, and we haven't even checked into the hotel yet. Do yall know how to get here?" Lasaia said pulling a hotel brochure out of her purse. Before Marcus could get out his first direction, Sherise said, "Why don't you guys stay here for the night. I mean, there's no use in paying full price for a couple hours in a room. You can just check in tomorrow morning. We have plenty of room."

"Oh nooo, we can't impose on you guys like that. We can just…"

Sherise cut her off.

"Impose? Girl, I'm going to bed so it ain't like I'm gonna be sleeping on the couch. You're not putting us out at all. Now look, just go get you something to sleep in and put on tomorrow and you can have your choice of the guest rooms."

"Yes ma'am." Lasaia said, laughing a little.

"I like her Marcus. I know she keeps you in line."

Lasaia stood to her feet with Greg right behind her. The four adults headed for the front door. Lasaia and Greg went out to the car and quickly returned with a few clothes and their toiletries in hand.

"Well, there's a bathroom in both rooms and there should be some towels in the linen closets." Sherise said. "If yall need anything, please help yourself or just come knock on our door."

"Thank you Sherise. Really, thank you." Lasaia said.

"No problem girl."

They exchanged a hug and Marcus said, "Night yall."

He gave Lasaia a hug and shook Greg's hand. Marcus and his wife headed upstairs to get ready for bed as Lasaia and Greg did the same.

Around 4:30 in the morning the telephone rang. Marcus jumped out of his sleep and answered the phone.

"Hello?"

"Hello sir. This is Tim with 'Safe Screen' security calling. I have a report of a silent alarm going off in your home. Do you need emergency assistance?"

Marcus was hardly awake but he figured out what was going on.

"Huh? Oh no, no," He said, clearing his throat, "I have house guests and forgot to tell them about the alarm. I'm sorry about that."

"Oh no problem sir. I just need you to verify the security password in order to disarm."

Marcus gave the man his secret code to not have the police dispatched to his home. It was a pretty good feature. Any criminal could pretend they were sleep and give a reason why the alarm was going off. But they wouldn't have security clearance. After getting the code the operator said, "Ok sir, you have a good night, thanks for using Safe Screen, and sorry for waking you."

"Oh, no problem. It was my fault. I should have warned them."

"You have a good night sir."

"You too."

Marcus hung up the phone and rubbed his eyes.

"Who was that baby?" A voice said from under the covers.

"Security system people. Said the silent alarm was going off. I forgot to tell them about that." He said climbing out of bed.

"Where you goin?" Sherise asked.

"To shut it off, otherwise it will reset itself in a few minutes." He said, opening the door to their bedroom. There was a control panel just outside their room and Marcus made his way toward it.

He flipped open the alarm panel and punched in his code. The system produced a long, soft beep and the word *Ready* popped up on the screen, indicating it had been disarmed. Marcus was about to walk back into the room when he felt thirst enter his throat. He decided he would get a glass of juice before retiring.

He walked down the walkway and went down the steps to the foyer. There were beams of moonlight shining through the kitchen windows as he walked in and opened the refrigerator.

The house was silent.

He poured himself a glass and drank it down. He walked over to the sink and rinsed out his glass and placed it on the counter top. He stood there for a moment still not completely awake and leaned forward with his hands on the corners of the sink and his head down.

He took a deep breath.

All of a sudden he felt two hands wrap around his waist and a pair of large soft breasts press against his back. Marcus jumped and spun around. He knew his wife's touch, and that wasn't it.

"What?" Lasaia whispered, inching toward him.

"Are you crazy?" Marcus whispered, "You gonna try this in my house? With my wife, kids, and your boyfriend less than 100 feet away."

"Try what? I'm not trying anything. I just wanted a goodnight kiss."

"What the hell? We did that already and I thought we agreed that it was a mistake."

"No, it wasn't a mistake. It was destiny. We were meant to find each other, don't you see that?"

"See what?"

"Us running into each other wasn't an accident or a coincidence, it was fate. I could have been anywhere in Atlanta that night and so could you. But, we weren't. We were meant to reunite."

"Yeah, reunite. But, as friends."

"We will always be more then friends. You know that."

"Things are different now. I'm married."

"That can be taken care of though baby."

"Taken care of? What are you saying? You think I'm gonna divorce my wife?"

Lasaia stood there staring at him in silence for a second.

"Whatever it takes." She said.

"Whatever it takes for what?"

"For us to be together again." She said, moving even closer to him.

She pressed her body against his and pinned him against the sink. She gave him a slow sultry kiss on the neck and worked her way up to his lips. The only article of clothing she had on was a silk teddy that barely contained her curves. Marcus could feel her soft skin pressed against his and couldn't help liking the sensation that ran through his nerves. Marcus didn't know what it was about this woman that he couldn't resist. In his head he could hear himself screaming, *no, No, NO!!!* But, his body wouldn't stop. It was like he was standing outside of himself watching everything go wrong but was powerless to stop it. He was a cobra in her snake charmer's trance. But, just like a cobra, after being in a trance for too long, they eventually strike.

That's what Marcus was worried about.

Not being able to hold back.
She reached down and grabbed Marcus's crouch and that broke the trance. He pulled his lips from hers and pushed her back. She just looked into his eyes and smiled.
"See, you still love me." She said as she turned and walked out of the kitchen. Marcus just stood there, leaning back against the counter thinking about what he just let happen. He slammed his hand against the counter top and whispered, "Damnit!"
The episode only lasted about 2 or 3 minutes, but it seemed like forever.

Marcus made his way up the steps to his room and into the bathroom. He pretended to use the bathroom to give himself a chance to give his face the once over for any evidence to show what just happened a few short yards away. He flushed the toilet and washed his hands to complete the illusion. He even swished some mouthwash around in his mouth, just in case. As he climbed into the bed he saw his wife was sound asleep.
She must have had a little too much wine.
She was out cold.
Marcus pulled the sheets up over his body and fell asleep next to her.

The next morning Marcus woke up and headed downstairs. He greeted his oldest daughter in the living room. He could hear his wife and Lasaia in the kitchen talking and laughing as he sat next to his little girl.
"Hey little bit." He said to her.
Lasaia looked up at her daddy with a sad look on her face.
"Hi daddy." She said, then turned back to the television.
"What's wrong baby?" He asked, knowing his daughter was usually the most lively person in the whole house.
Something was up.
Lasaia looked back at her father with sincerity in her eyes.
"I don't like her." She told him.
"Who? Daddy's friend?"
"Yeah."
"Why?"
"I don't know. I just don't like her. Is she going to be here long?"
"No sweetie. She's leaving today."
"Can I go to Melissa's until she's gone?"
"It's too early to go over there now baby."
Lasaia just looked down at the floor as if her father took away her favorite toy.
"Can I go to my room until she leaves then?" She asked.

Marcus knew emotions were real. She had never requested to be alone in her room with guests in the house. She usually wanted to be the center of attention. Now she wanted to just disappear into the shadows.

"Yeah baby, go ahead."

She jumped off the couch and slowly walked out of the family room and up the steps. Marcus just sat there and wished he could disappear into his room until she left too. He was still feeling a little guilty about what happened the night before. He got up from his spot and picked up the cordless phone. He dialed his neighbor's number and waited through a few rings.

"Hello?" Bill said.

Bill was Melissa's father.

"Hey Bill. This is Marcus."

"Hey neighbor, what's going on?"

"Nothing much. Hey, are you guys busy over there?"

"No not at all, what's going on?"

"We have house guests and Lasaia isn't happy at all about it. You know how kids are about things."

"Oh yeah, definitely."

"Would it be alright if she came over there until they leave? It'll only be about an hour or so. I know it's early but..."

"Say no more neighbor. Send 'er on over. Do you know how much I would pay to have another child right now for Melissa to play with. I love it when Lasaia is over here, I can finally get some rest."

They both laughed.

"I really appreciate it man."

"No problem. If you like, you can bring Angela too, you know how my wife loves her. We're all going to the mall in an hour. We could give you guys a break to enjoy your company."

"Man, if you ever move, I'm moving right with you." Marcus said.

They both laughed again.

"Don't mention it partner. It's nothing compared to all the things you have done for us. Watching Melissa when my mom died, helping us out when we were in a bind...the way I look at it, we owe you."

"Nah man, you don't owe me anything. But, I do appreciate it. I'll get them ready and come right over."

"Alright buddy. We'll be waitin'."

Marcus hung up the phone and walked up the steps to Lasaia's room. He opened the door and found her sitting Indian style in the middle of her floor looking through her animal ABC's book.

"Hey," He said whispering from the doorway. Lasaia looked up at him.

"Get dressed, Melissa's dad said you and Angela can go with them to the mall."

Lasaia's eyes lit up as if someone told her Santa Claus was coming twice this year. She ran to her drawers and started looking for something to put on. Marcus smiled at her and started back down the steps to get Angela. He was glad that he could make his little girl happy.

He walked into the kitchen and Sherise, Greg, and Lasaia were sitting at the table with Angela, finishing their breakfast. "I was wondering what you were doing. I saw you go into the family room." Sherise said.

"Oh, I was on the phone with Bill and he wants the kids to go with them to the mall." Marcus said, lifting Angela out of her chair.

"Oh, well here, let me get her and you sit down and eat before it gets any colder." Marcus sat down across from Lasaia and her boyfriend as Sherise rushed Angela up the stairs to get her ready to go.

"Did you sleep well?" Lasaia asked Marcus almost giggling behind sipping her coffee.

"I slept alright, small interruption, but it was good." He said, eating.

Lasaia gave him a flirtatious smile.

Greg and Lasaia began talking about the casting call as Marcus ran through his food.

"Well, we better get going." She said, looking at her watch.

Marcus took the last few bites of his food and got up from the table and followed behind them. They grabbed their bags from beside the front door just as Sherise was walking back down the stairs with the girls.

"Yall leavin'?" Sherise asked, sounding a little disappointed.

"Yeah, we still need to check in at the hotel and get to the conference room to get things set up." Lasaia said.

"Oh, ok. Well, I guess we'll see you guys later. You gotta come see us before you leave." Sherise said.

"Sure," Lasaia said as Marcus opened the door, "Hey, you know what? Why don't you guys come by the call? I'm not going to be all that busy. I'm just here to watch. The scouts are going to be handling most of it."

"Um, ok. Where is it?" Sherise asked.

Lasaia showed her the brochure again and got directions to the hotel as well. Sherise gave Lasaia a hug as Marcus and Greg shook hands.

"Yall be safe." Marcus said walking them outside.

"Bye girls." Lasaia said, waving to the children.

"Bye." Angela yelled, waving and smiling. Her sister unwillingly gave them a swift wave and left it at that. Lasaia and Greg walked to their car and got in. They pulled off down the street and Marcus took his little girls over to the neighbor's house. Sherise was already in the kitchen washing dishes when he got back. He walked in and stepped behind her and grabbed her waist. He leaned forward and kissed her on the cheek and she smiled.

"So, what you wanna do today?" She said putting the last dish in the drain. Marcus turned her around, picked her up, spun around, and placed her on the island. When she asked what he wanted to *do,* she had no idea it would be her.

After there sexual interlude that went from the kitchen, to the foyer, to the staircase…the two of them went upstairs to get ready for the day. Sherise convinced Marcus to go to Lasaia's modeling call and, even though he was reluctant, he agreed. When they pulled into the parking lot of the hotel there were people everywhere. People outside, people in the halls, people in the conference room…everywhere. They worked their way through the crowd and into the room. They were in awe at the amount of people that were in attendance just for the chance to be discovered by this agency. The two of them had heard the radio ads on the way over but didn't expect this type of turnout. *Intrigue* modeling must have been bigger than they thought.

After standing in wonder for a few minutes between points and whispers, Marcus felt a tap on his shoulder. He turned around to see Lasaia standing there smiling. Sherise turned to see what caught her husband's attention and saw her too.

"Heeeey!" Sherise said, giving her a hug.

"Hi, I'm glad you guys came." Lasaia said, hugging her new friend.

"This is amazing." Sherise said, in reference to the scene around them.

"Yeah, we got a pretty good turnout today." Lasaia commented.

There were people of all shapes and sizes out in the crowd. Big, small, short, tall, hand models, body doubles, everything you could need a particular individual to look like was there in that room. Lasaia gave them a quick tour of the set up and they ended up in the makeup area. Lasaia grabbed Sherise by the hand and said, "Come with me."

She took Sherise a few steps away to an open seat and sat her down.

"Rico!" Lasaia said, looking up at a skinny black man in a tight, black silk shirt a few feet away. He turned around and walked over to them with a switch in his step.

"Yeeeesss Ma'am?" He said.

"I need you to hook my girl up. She doesn't need much makeup cause she is already beautiful," Sherise blushed, "but I want you to work your magic. Make her look amazing."

Sherise looked up at her and said, "Girl, what have you gotten me into?"

"Girl I just want you to see what I see. You talking about you ain't got what it takes. I'm gonna show you that you have everything it takes." Lasaia said, and left Sherise in the hands of her.

"Okay honey, you heard the boss. You look good but I'm gonna make you look fabulous." Rico said, grabbing a flat iron from the counter.

Sherise sat back in the stylist's chair and closed her eyes and Rico got right to work.

Lasaia walked back over to Marcus and asked, "You want something to drink?" They grabbed some bottled water out of a nearby cooler and found an empty table to have a seat.

"So, what do you really think?" Lasaia asked.

"This is nice, I'm real proud of you." He said.

Lasaia smiled and said, "Well thank you."

There was a brief moment of silence before Lasaia started back up.

"Look Marcus, I know I said this before but…I'm sorry about last night. I don't know what has gotten into me. It's like, when I'm around you, nothing else matters. I do acknowledge your wife and respect her and I don't want you to think I would do anything to hurt what you guys have. But, it's like, I don't know. But, I am sorry. Still friends?" She said extending her hand.

Marcus shook her hand and they put the situation in the past. They sat there and sipped their water until Sherise walked up to them. She was beaming and had a huge smile on her face. Rico had hooked her up to the fullest. Her makeup and hair were perfect and Marcus barely recognized her. Rico only had her for about twenty minutes, but he worked wonders.

"Whooooa!" Lasaia said standing to her feet. Sherise couldn't stop smiling. She loved her new look.

"You like it?" Lasaia asked.

All Sherise could do was nod her head. She couldn't get the words out between her teeth. Marcus was at a loss for words. He had seen his wife with her hair and makeup done before, but this was something different.

"Ok, time for step two" Lasaia said, grabbing Sherise by the hand again and dragging over to the corner where the photographer was located. Lasaia shut down the whole area and had the photographer take a whole roll of film of Sherise. Marcus's wife felt like a movie star. She never got attention like this and loved every minute of it. He just stood back and watched as his wife had the time of her life posing. Lasaia even got in a few pictures with her. After the roll was finished, Lasaia walked over and got it from the photographer. She took it to another man that was organizing the camera equipment and handed the roll to him. She whispered something in his ear and he immediately dropped what he was doing and disappeared through a door.

Lasaia walked back over to the married couple and Sherise was all giggles, talking about her photo shoo with her husband.

"Yall wanna get something to eat?" Lasaia asked. They agreed and the three of them left the busy conference room and went to the hotel restaurant. They were quickly seated and placed their orders.

"So, what are you guys getting into today?" Lasaia asked.

"Just hanging out really." Marcus said.

"Yeah, oh baby, I need to go by the shop before we go home." Sherise said.

"Ok." He said.

Their food came and they had a nice light lunch.

"That was really good." Sherise said putting down her fork. The waiter brought the check and Marcus reached for his wallet.

"What are you doing?" Lasaia asked, snatching the bill off the table.

"I was just gonna pay for our…"

"Aaaa," Lasaia interrupted, waving her hand in the air, "I got this. You guys already saved me a hundred and twenty dollars just by letting me stay at your house last night. And, you fed me twice. This is the least I can do."

Lasaia placed her credit card in the bill wallet and handed it to the waiter.

"Thank you so much." Sherise said.

"No problem. So, what do you think about modeling?" Lasaia asked Sherise.

"It's interesting, I didn't know there was so much to it." Sherise answered.

"Oh this is just the beginning. This is nothing. It can get pretty hectic at times, but that's the beauty of the business. You can hire people to have a headache for you." Lasaia said, laughing.

The waiter brought back her credit card and she signed the receipt.

"Another good thing about business is that the little conversation we just had allows me to write this meal off as a business expense." Lasaia said, giggling again.

They got up from their seat and headed back to the conference room. The scene hadn't changed. There were still people all over the place and the atmosphere was buzzing with model hopefuls.

Before they were able to make it back into the room, a man walked up to Lasaia with a yellow envelope. "Here you go Miss Lewis." He said, handing her the envelope before disappearing through the crowd.

"Thanks Jerry." Lasaia said, as he walked away. Lasaia opened the envelope and pulled out a stack of photos. Sherise covered her mouth and let out a scream of surprise when she saw what Lasaia had. They were the pictures that she had taken less than an hour earlier, and they were amazing. Sherise had never seen such beautiful pictures of herself. It was almost as if she didn't know how pretty she really was until that moment.

"Here you go." Lasaia said to Sherise, handing her the stack. Sherise held the pictures in her hands like she was holding a newborn child. She was in awe at what an outstanding job they had done. A man strolled up to Lasaia and said, "Excuse me, Miss Lewis. We need your assistance inside. We need to go over some things about the call before we close up shop this afternoon."

"Ok, give me two minutes and I'll be right there." Lasaia said.

She turned back to her friends and said, "Well, duty calls." Sherise was still going through her pictures, but Marcus said, "Alright, well we'll talk to you later."

"Ok, Byeee." Lasaia said waving as she headed into the room. Sherise looked up and waved at her and said, "Bye, thank you!" Sherise couldn't take her eyes off of her pictures and almost bumped into several people on her way out of the building.

They finally made it to the car and got in. Marcus had to drive because Sherise could not stop looking at her pictures. She just kept going through them over and over again, finding something more that she liked about them with every rotation. They made their way to the salon and walked inside. The place wasn't teeming with the spicy type of conversation it had earlier in the week but there were a lot of heads being done at the same time. Alicia came out the back room and saw Sherise. She walked over and said, "Hey girl."

"Hey what's u?" Sherise said.

They exchange a hug and then Alicia looked over at Marcus.

"Hey Marcus, how you doing?" Alicia said, as if she really didn't want to.

"I'm good, how bout yourself?" He answered.

"Mmm hmm, I bet you are," Alicia said looking him up and down, "I heard you got a new girlfriend."

"What? Nah…see you the one that…"

Sherise broke in and said, "Lele! Stop it! Now I told you…"

"Stop what? I'm just trying to stop him from getting his legs broke, that's all."

"Anyway, it ain't even like that." Marcus said.

"It ain't like that huh," Alicia said, "Well tell me Marcus, what is it like?"

"She's just an old friend, that's it." He said.

"Ok," Alicia said sucking her teeth, "You just let her know she messin' with a heavyweight."

"Duly noted." Marcus said, having a seat, indicating he was through defending himself from her accusations.

"Come on girl!" Sherise said with a look of aggravation in her eyes. Sherise and Alicia walked into the back office arguing back and forth in a whisper. Sherise couldn't believe that Alicia just brought that up. The conversation they had in her office was private and should have been kept between them. In her effort to protect her friend, Alicia jumped in before she knew the full situation.

They got into the back office and Sherise placed her pictures on her desk. "Oh giiirl, these are some bad ass pictures. I can barely tell it's you. And I love your hair, you gonna have to show me how you did that one." Alicia said.

"I didn't do it." Sherise said, flipping through the invoices on her desk.

"Who did it?"

"One of Marcus's friend's stylists. And, she had them take those picture too."

"I don't understand. Don't tell me you hangin' out with the bitch. I thought you didn't want to meet her."

"Well, I didn't at first but, she is really nice. And the best part is, she has a boyfriend."

"Girl, a boyfriend don't mean nothin'. Hell I've dated married men before."

"Well I like her. She seems like a very nice person."

"So she took your picture…woop-de-do."

"No, she came to our house last night. Me and her got to talk and she has a great personality."

"Girl you don't let the devil in yo' house?"

"What? You are really trippin'. Look, I met her, I like her, she's nice, she has a man, and I'm not worried about it." Sherise said, starting to get a little irritated.

"Mmm hmm." Alicia said still a little suspicious. "Ok, alright, I'll leave it alone. But you still better watch her."

The two of them went over the orders while Marcus sat out front. About ten minutes later they emerged from the room and Marcus stood to his feet.

"You ready baby?" Sherise said walking up to him.

Alicia led the way to the front door as Sherise and Marcus followed closely behind. She opened the door and let them through. She gave Marcus an intimidating look as he passed and all he could do was smile and laugh. Call it instinct, women's intuition, or just plain experience, but Alicia had a bad feeling about this *old* friend.

Thirteen

Sherise and Marcus pulled into their driveway around 4:30 and saw their neighbors pull in at the same time. Lasaia rocketed from Bill's SUV and across the lawn.

"Mommy, Mommy…look!" Lasaia said running up to her mother's feet. She wanted her mother to see her face painting and poster that she got from the mall.

"Hey Bill." Marcus shouted as he got out of his truck.

"What's going on neighbor?"

Marcus and Bill exchanged a greeting as he headed over to get the sleeping Angela from Janet, Bill's wife.

"She couldn't hang." Janet giggled as she passed Marcus the little one.

"I really appreciate it guys, if you ever need anything…"

"Now look Marcus," Bill cut in, "I told you, we owe you more then you know. We are happy to help. That's what friends are for."

Janet stood next to her husband, nodding her agreement. Marcus gave them a silent nod and let it go. He shook Bill's hand and thanked him again before heading back to his house. Bill and Janet were probably the best neighbors that a person could have.

Sherise and Lasaia had already made it inside by the time Marcus made it through the front door. He laid his little princess on the couch in the family room and headed to the kitchen to help his wife with the family meal. He heard Lasaia in her room playing as he left the family room.

"What do you want to eat?" Sherise asked him as he entered the kitchen. She was standing in front of the refrigerator, holding the door open, looking at shelves full of food, not sure of what to make. Marcus walked over behind her and wrapped his arms around her waist and looked into the refrigerator too.

"Anything is fine with me." He said.

"I don't feel like cooking, you?" Sherise asked.

"Nope."

She turned and looked at him and they simultaneously said, "Hotdogs and chips."

A quick easy meal that the girls always loved. Sherise put some water on the stove to boil as Marcus got everything else together and they quickly made up a meal for their family. They called Lasaia downstairs and woke Angela up so she could eat. They got everything together and had a nice family meal in front of the television. Around 7:30 Marcus looked over to his wife and said, "Kitchen or kids?" That was his way of asking if she wanted to do the dishes or give the girls a bath.

"Come on girls." Sherise said after giving him a kiss on the cheek. She must have had a good day because she actually chose to take the kids. Sherise rounded up the girls and the three of them marched upstairs to get ready for bed, as Marcus headed to the kitchen to clean the few dishes they had used.

About halfway through the dishes Marcus's cell phone began to ring. He quickly dried his hands and took it off of his belt clip.

"Hello?" He said, flipping it open.

"Hi, Marcus?"

"Yeah."

"Hey, this is Lasaia."

"Hey, what's up?"

"Nothing. I just wanted to thank you guys so much for letting us stay at your house and for coming to see me today, for just...everything."

"Well it was our pleasure. We enjoyed having you, and I know Sherise had a great time with you today. She talked about those pictures all the way home."

Lasaia laughed and said, "Well good. I'm glad she had fun. I just wanted to call and thank you guys for everything before I left town."

"Well, what are you doing tonight? Sherise is putting the kids to bed now and I know she would love it if you and Greg came over."

"Awww man, I wish I could but, I'm still in this conference room trying to get this thing wrapped up. Now I see why I don't go to these things. I don't know when I'll be getting out of here and we are leaving early in the morning."

"Oh man, well that's alright. There's always next time."

"Oh yes, definitely."

Marcus heard a voice interrupt them in the background of Lasaia's phone, "Miss Lewis we need you for a second."

"Ok Jerry, give me 5 minutes," Lasaia said to the voice, "Hello Marcus?"
"Yeah."
"I gotta go, but tell Sherise thank you and it was really great to get to meet her. These people are about to run me crazy."
"Hold on, hold on. Let me get her real fast."
Marcus darted out of the kitchen and up the stairs to find Sherise. She was in the bathroom with Angela drying her off from her bath. She decided to fight the hardest battle first and got Lasaia out of the way early.
"Baby here." Marcus said, walking up behind her.
Sherise looked at him with a confused look on her face after hearing him rush up the stairs. Marcus took over with the little girl as Sherise grabbed the phone.
"Hello?" She said, not sure who she was talking to.
"Heeey girl."
Marcus finished with his daughter while listening to the one-sided conversation.
"Oh girl please, that was our pleasure.", "Oh yes, I love them!", "Yeap, I shole did, the whole way home." Sherise said laughing. "Well why don't you guys come over?", "Oh.", "Oh, ok. Make that money girl.", "Well it was great to meet you too.", "Ok.", "Yes definitely. Next time you come to visit, no work.", "Ok.", "Ok, talk to you later. Here's Marcus."

Marcus got the phone back from his smiling wife as she started to put on Angela's clothes. "Ok well you handle your business Miss lady and call me when you get back safely."
"Ok. I'll do that. Bye." Lasaia said.
"Bye."
Marcus closed his phone as he walked back into the kitchen to finish his dishes. He completed his task and made his way to the bedroom. He found his wife lying on top of the sheets, fully clothed, fast asleep. The excitement of the day had really taken a lot out of her. Marcus gently tapped her on the shoulder and woke her up. He asked her if she wanted to take a shower before he did and she got up without saying a word. She walked into the bathroom and took a shower, wrapped her hair in a scarf and quickly fell asleep after climbing back into the bed. Marcus took a quick shower and joined his wife.

Shortly after his head hits the pillow, Marcus was in a deep sleep. He must have been more tired then he thought, too. He slept for several hours and then was brought out of his sleep by something making noise downstairs. Marcus was half asleep but it sounded like someone was in the kitchen opening and closing the refrigerator door. Marcus climbed out of bed and looked back at his wife. She was sound asleep. She was not disturbed by the sound and simply rolled over. Marcus lightly walked out of the room and over to his daughters' rooms. He checked on each of them and they were both sound asleep. Now Marcus's heart rate started to go up. He wasn't scared, but he had just realized that he had disabled his alarm the night they had guests and had forgot to arm it again tonight, now someone or something was invading their home. He quickly stepped back to his bedroom and slipped into his closet. He removed a panel behind a row of his suits and reached into the opening and pulled out a 9mm. Beretta. Marcus kept it hidden there so his wife and kids couldn't find it. If Sherise knew he had it she probably would have made him get rid of it.

Good thing she hadn't.

Tonight it was obvious that he would need it.

He hurried back out the room and tiptoed across the walkway, looking over the rail into the dark foyer for any movement. He didn't see anything, but he could definitely hear some kind of noise coming from the kitchen. It sounded like dishes clanking around. Like someone was stacking dishes on his counter. They didn't own any expensive dishes so these must have been some foolish thieves. He checked on his little ones again to make sure they had not moved. He found both of them in their beds still asleep and he quietly closed their doors. Marcus lightly made his way down the steps and cocked his firearm very slowly so that it didn't alert the intruder. He rounded the corner of the steps and heard the noises one last time.

Then there was nothing but silence.

Marcus could hardly see into the kitchen and the only light was coming from moon beams that penetrated the kitchen windows. Marcus slowly stepped closer and closer to the kitchen. He no longer heard the noise but was sure it was coming from a few feet in front of him. He made it into the doorway to the kitchen and reached for the light switch. Every hair on his arm stood on end as he extended his arm. As his fingers touched the switch he heard, "Don't turn on the light." Marcus looked around the kitchen. The voice came from over by the breakfast table, but the large wooden blinds were closed and all Marcus could see was the silhouette of a very *curvashish* figure standing there with their arms at their sides. Marcus pointed the gun in the direction of the intruder and said, "Don't move, I have a gun and I *will* shoot you." The figure slowly moved toward Marcus with its hands raised as a sign of surrender.

"You gonna shoot me baby?" The voice said.

Marcus recognized it.

"Lasaia?"

Marcus's eyes began to focus in the low lighting and he saw his old friend's face appear. She made her way up in front of the end of Marcus's gun and pressed her soft chest against the barrel. She looked down at the gun then up into Marcus's eyes, seductively. He quickly lowered his firearm to his side. She just looked at him and smiled as if he had just followed her command. There, in front of him was his old friend, half-dressed in a thin, white top that looked like a sports bra and a matching pair of boy shorts. The middle of the shirt had been slit to make her cleavage show. Her body seemed to shine in the moonlight. Marcus was shocked to see her there, but at the same time he couldn't take his eyes off of her.

"How did you get in here?" He asked.

"You should really lock your back door. Anyone could just walk right into your house." She said, stepping closer to him.

She made her way within a few inches of him and said, "I couldn't sleep. I just kept thinking about you, so I came over."

"And you decided to break into my house?" He said, frozen in his spot, staring at her. Marcus wasn't sure what her intentions were at this point, but he was a little surprised at her persistence.

"I wanted to see you."

"What if my wife would have been awake?"

"I knew she wasn't."

"How?"

"I have my ways. Just like I knew you would be the one to come downstairs. And, I bet you didn't even wake her up before you came down here did you?" She said, walking next to him and leaning back against the kitchen island.

She was right.

Marcus was silent, which gave her more confidence in her assumption. He was amazed at her courage to even try something this crazy.

"So you got us all figured out?" Marcus said, placing his gun down on the island. Lasaia grabbed him by the sides of his shirt and said, "Something like that. Just like I know that if I kiss you right now, you won't stop me."

"Oh really? Well I know…"

Lasaia cut his sentence short and pressed her lips against his. Just as she had predicted, Marcus didn't stop her advance. It was almost like he couldn't. Somehow, someway…feeling her body against his felt *right.* Their first kiss turned into a second and third until their lips and tongues intertwined in a passionate series of locked lips and wet mouths. Marcus lost all sense of where he was and picked Lasaia up and set her on the kitchen island. She ripped his shirt off and started sucking on his neck as he slid his hands up her thigh. Her cloth shorts were so thin and tight that she could feel his fingers moving back and forth on her crotch, causing her to moan. Her pleasure didn't halt her attack as she continued to kiss his neck and worked her way back to his lips. Marcus grabbed her tight white top by the sides and lifted it up over her head. He stared at how perfect she was. He couldn't believe she was the same girl that grew up next to him, so many years ago.

Marcus moved back toward her to quench her thirst for his love. He felt a hunger deep inside himself, she was what he craved. He leaned down and began sucking her breasts. She began to let out a slightly louder moan. Marcus was turned on even more by her whimper and began to run his hand back and forth between her legs. This intensified her arousal. Marcus stopped before his family was disturbed by their passionate session. Lasaia saw her opportunity and pushed Marcus back. She jumped to the floor in front of him, topless, and pulled down her shorts. She was standing there completely naked. He looked at her for a few seconds before grabbing her around her slim, soft waist, pressing their bodies together. She pulled down his shorts and exposed his rock hard penis. Lasaia took it in her hand and stroked it up and down. Her soft hand made stiffen even more.

"You don't know how long I have waited for this," She whispered between pants, "I want you to fuck me, right now."

Marcus didn't say a word and bent his knees slightly as she spread her legs in front of him. He carefully lined his penis up with her opening and began to rise slowly while pushing inside of her. He held onto her butt to keep her in place and she was so wet that he slid inside her easily. He lifted her into his arms and drove his penis deep inside her. She had to place her mouth over his shoulder to silence her scream. He began to bounce her up and down onto him, bringing it to the very rim of her vagina then shoving it all the way back in. Lasaia felt like he was going to split her in two but this was the feeling she had craved for over a decade. She leaned her body back and placed her hands on the island and Marcus held her legs around his waist, continuing to stroke. Lasaia's canal squeezed Marcus's penis so tight that every stroke seems to make him want to come. It took everything he had to keep from letting loose inside of her. Lasaia tried to mask her screams with a few kisses but a few of them slipped out. Their sexual grunts were kept as quiet as possible but the pure pleasure of the act caused a few of them to break the silence of the house. Lasaia began biting Marcus's shoulder and letting out deep breaths through her nose. Marcus chewed on his bottom lip, trying not to release any noises that would wake his family. He continued to thrust his waist between her thighs, making her jolt like an electric current was being sent through her nervous system with every stroke.

Up the stairs, Sherise tossed, turned and rolled over to get comfortable in her husband's arms. She opened her eyes and looked at the empty spot in the bed next to her. She sat up in the bed and looked around the room, half asleep. She wondered where her husband could be at this time of night. She wiped her eyes, removed the covers from her legs and climbed out of the bed. She walked into the bathroom, he wasn't there. She walked back through the dark bedroom toward the door leading to the girls' rooms. She figured that one of the girls must have had a bad dream or something and Marcus got up to check on them. After she saw that both the girls were sound asleep and no Marcus was around she heard what sounded like something moving downstairs in the kitchen. She figured Marcus was sneaking a midnight snack and decided to catch him in the act. He always made fun of her for sneaking downstairs and having a midnight snack. Now she was going to get him back. She made her way to the staircase and quietly walked down. She wiped her eyes, still not completely awake, yet. She always had a hard time sleeping without her husband next to her so she *had* to find him.

Marcus and Lasaia were still in the kitchen and didn't miss a beat. He was still pounding away at the now weak Lasaia. Her body was limp and she had to lock her arms around his neck to keep from falling backwards across the kitchen island. Her grunts had turned to low groans as Marcus had gone from short, fast strokes to longer, slower ones. Sherise reached the bottom of the steps and rounded the corner, headed right for the kitchen. She could hear something going on in there, but she was still drowsy and didn't realize what it was. She was only about 20 feet from them now and closing. They would have had to stop now to keep from getting caught in the act, but they didn't even hear her footsteps and with every stroke she got a step closer.
How would they explain a scantily clad Lasaia hanging out in the kitchen in the middle of the night anyway?

"Oh Marcus, oh baby…yes…yes…don't stop…oh Marcus…Marcus." Lasaia whispered into his ear.
"Marcus…Marcus…"

"MARCUS!!!"

Marcus jumped up in the bed, Sherise sitting next to him. He was drenched in sweat. He looked around; he was back in his bed. He didn't know what to believe. He looked over at wife and she looked very concerned.

"You ok baby?" She said, rubbing his shoulder.

"Yeah, yeah, it was a dream." He said, getting up and walking to the bathroom. He wiped the sweat from his face and looked into the mirror over the sink. He hadn't noticed it until then but he looked down and his penis was rock hard. It was faint, and probably in his head, but Marcus swore he smelled the same scent that Lasaia had worn the night they made out on Alonzo's couch. He fanned the smell away from his nostrils.

It was just a dream, He thought to himself, trying to convince himself everything was alright. After his erection had diminished, he returned to the bedroom where Sherise was waiting patiently. A nervous look glazed her face.

"You sure you're alright, baby?" She said, as he climbed back into bed.

"Yeah baby, I'm fine." He told her, kissing her on the cheek.

He tried his best to get comfortable in the bed. Sherise slid over next to him, her head on his chest. She detected his fast paced heart beat but didn't bring it up. She had no idea what his dream was about but she did know that he had never had a dream like it before. They fell asleep and rested soundly through the remainder of the night.

The next morning Marcus woke up to his wife's hair in his face. He nudged her with his hand and she slowly moved off of his chest. He got up and went to the bathroom. When he returned to the bedroom he saw that she had disappeared. He figured she had already made her way downstairs to get her coffee. He left the room and headed down the steps to the kitchen where he found her exactly where he knew he would, in front of the coffee pot. He walked over to her, put his hands on her waist, kissed her cheek. She let out a girlish giggle and said, "Good morning to you too."

"Morning baby." He responded.

Marcus went to the cabinet to get himself a glass to pour his juice into. He fixed a glass and downed it right away. Sherise watched him, she knew something was wrong. His dream had really made her nervous and now her intuition was telling her that there was more.

"Baby...you sure you alright?" She asked, hesitantly.

"What do you mean?" He said, pouring another glass of juice.

"Your dream."

He stopped pouring, set the container down.

"It was nothing. Really."

"Well it's just that…you never had a dream like that before. It scared me."

Marcus walked over and gave her a hug. She was really frightened that something seemed to be bothering him so bad that he had a dream about it.

"It's ok. It was nothing. Just a crazy dream. That's all." He said, releasing his grip around her. She felt a little better, but not much. Marcus went back to his juice and downed another glass full. As he was putting the juice back into the refrigerator Sherise asked, "What did you dream about?"

Marcus figured that question was coming and had already prepared himself for it. He knew he couldn't tell her the real plot of the dream, that would be like asking for a fight with Mike Tyson. But, he knew he had to tell her something.

"It was crazy. We were here and I heard something going on in the kitchen. You were sleep, so I tiptoed down here to check it out. I ended up getting into a fight with this guy and then you walked in and he pulled a gun."

Sherise was completely glued to the story as the words flowed from Marcus's mouth as if they were the truth.

"He pointed the gun at you and I jumped in the way just as he pulled the trigger, that's when I woke up." Marcus said, finishing his lie.

Sherise was in awe for a few seconds then said, "Wow, I wonder what that means. They say dreams usually have a meaning of something that you want to do, or feelings that you feel. Either that or they are trying to tell you something."

"Yeah?"

"Yeah, but I don't think that you want to be shot do you? Maybe it means something else, like, it's trying to tell you something."

Marcus remembered something said in his dream and walked over to the door leading to the back deck. He turned the knob and the door opened. He closed it back and locked it. He turned back to his wife with a grin on his face.

"What?" She asked.

"This was how the guy got in. Maybe my dream was trying to say that we need to keep this door locked."

Sherise giggled and said, "Yeah, maybe," before pouring herself a hot cup of coffee.

Marcus had put her mind at ease, but now he felt a little guilty for lying to his wife. He didn't know how the door got unlocked, not to mention how that fact ended up in his dream. He pushed the thought to the back of his mind and soon forgot all about it. He and his wife talked for a few more minutes, then decide it was time to wake the kids so they could get ready for church.

After a few minutes of shaking, they were able to get the girls up and dressed. Marcus took Angela, the easiest, while Sherise fought with Lasaia, the warrior. After a quick breakfast they left the house and arrived at the church just in time for the morning service. They made their way to some empty seats and witnessed a lovely sermon. The preacher spoke about the importance of family. He talked about how someone can take your money, house, cars, anything you own...but they can not take your family away. You have to freely give up on your family to lose it. Marcus and Sherise really enjoyed the sermon. They picked up the kids from their Sunday school classrooms and headed to the car to go home.

They made it home around 2:30 and they saw their neighbor Bill cutting his grass. They filed out of the car and Lasaia asked her mother if she could go see her friend.

"Go ask her dad if it's ok first. If he says you can come over, change your clothes and you can go." Sherise said.

Lasaia darted over to Bill and he stopped his mower when he saw her headed his way. Bill knelt down and Sherise watched as they exchanged a few words. A few seconds later, she was flying back toward the house and met them at the door.

"What did he say?" Sherise asked, as Marcus opened the door.

"He said I could." Lasaia said bouncing with anticipation as her father pushed the door open. She could barely wait long enough for him to get the door open before rushing through a crack only big enough for her small frame to fit through and bolted up the stairs. Marcus and Sherise looked at each other and laughed at their daughter's excitement. You would think she was late for a bus to Disney World the way she moved. It was funny, but they were glad that she had such a good friend so close to her. Marcus took Angela to her room to get her changed out of her church clothes as Sherise went to their room to change into something more comfortable. Lasaia got dressed and told her dad that she is leaving before hurrying down the steps and out the front door. Marcus finished changing Angela and put on a video so she could have something to watch in her room. He walked to his bedroom to change and ran into Sherise on his way.

"What you want to eat tonight?" She said, not breaking her stride.

"Don't matter. Whatever." He said, walking into the room. He changed his clothes and went downstairs to the family room to try and catch a game. Marcus watched television for a while and Sherise came in periodically to watch with him even though she had no idea what was going on. They had a fairly relaxed Sunday afternoon and Lasaia returned home around six o'clock. They had their dinner and lounged around a little longer before Sherise took the girls upstairs for their bath. She got them in the bed around 8:30 and she and Marcus made their way to their room. This time, Marcus was sure to set the alarm before walking into his bedroom. They each took their showers and climb into bed. There was a long day of work ahead for both of them but that didn't stop them from having a quick make-out session followed by a short love making episode. The two of them fell asleep in each other's arms and have a peaceful night's sleep.

Marcus's alarm clock woke him up at 8:00 and he slowly climbed out of bed. He washed his face in the bathroom and walked back into the bedroom, headed for his closet. He saw his wife slumped over, sitting on the side of the bed, just like she was a few days before.

"Stomach hurt again?" He asked, walking toward his closet.

"Mmm hmm." She grunted.

"Alright now, we don't need no morning sickness." Marcus said, laughing.

"Oh anyway, if I am, you're carrying this one." She said, with an uncomfortable laugh, rubbing her stomach.

"I didn't get sick with the other two. I think this is your fault."

"My fault?"

"Yeah. It only happens on days after we have sex. You might need to stop trying to dig so deep. Ain't no oil down there." She said laughing, uncomfortably.

"You used to like when I dug a little too deep."

Sherise giggled.

He walked over to her and kissed her on the cheek as she sat there rubbing her stomach. Marcus got his clothes together and started to get ready for a day at work. Sherise walked to the bathroom and had a seat on the toilet.

"What you want for breakfast?" She said, through the bathroom door.

"Anything. Whatever you want." He said, putting on his suit. He heard the toilet flush and Sherise walked back into the bedroom. She headed for the door leading out of the room and Marcus grabbed her by the arm as she passed. He pulled her close to him and gave her a kiss. She smiled, that was what he wanted to see. He could always find a way to make her smile even when she didn't want to.

Sherise left the room and Marcus finished getting ready for work. On his way down the steps he checked on his little girls. Sherise had turned on their lights, which was the signal that it was time to get up. Angela was still in her bed fast asleep, the light being on meant nothing to a sleeping two-year-old. Lasaia, on the other hand, knew the drill and was climbing out of bed as he peeked in.

"Morning baby." He said from her doorway.

"Morning daddy." She said, still a little groggy.

"Get your sister up and bring her downstairs with you, ok?" Marcus asked.

Lasaia gave him a quick nod of compliance before making her way to the bathroom.

Marcus made his way downstairs and headed to his office to be sure that he had everything in order.

As he was gathering his things his cell phone beeped telling him he had a message. Marcus grabbed the phone off the charger and flipped it open. He had one new text message. It was from one of his friends that worked at his office. Marcus checked to see what time it was received and it was after they had already made their way up to bed the night before. Marcus opened the message and read it, "Hey bruh, I tried to call you earlier, but I guess you were at church. Anyway, I got a call a little while ago and the boss man wants everyone in for some big announcement tomorrow at 9 am."

Marcus flipped his phone closed and looked at his watch.

It was 8:32.

Marcus quickly gathered his things and put them in his briefcase. He rushed out of his office and headed for the kitchen. He saw Lasaia and Angela sitting at the table drinking some milk, Sherise was standing over the stove, cooking a quick breakfast. He rushed over to his wife and she asked, "How many eggs you want," as she opened the carton.

"None, I gotta go. I just got a message that Mr. Lockson wants everybody in by nine for some big announcement. I can still make it on time if I leave now."

"You think they gonna give you a shot at that account you've been working on?" Sherise asked, a little bit of excitement coated her words.

"Nah, I doubt it. It's too early. I just did that presentation last week. He probably wants tell us about some new yacht he just bought or something ridiculous like that. Anyway, I'm going to get out of here."

Sherise laughed and said, "Ok, well I guess I'll see you tonight. Have a good day." Marcus gave her a kiss and walked over to his little ladies who were sitting so politely at the table.

"Bye girls, see you this afternoon." He said, giving each of them a kiss on their foreheads. He rushed out the kitchen door leading to the garage and jumped into his truck. He pulled out of the driveway and made his way to work to hear this *big* announcement.

He made it to his office building just in time and hurried upstairs. He dropped his things in his office and followed everyone else to the conference room. They all filed in and Mr. Lockson began.

"Morning people, morning." Mr. Lockson, his British accent covered his words.

"Morning sir." Everyone said in unison.

"I called you all here today to inform you that we have been selected as on of three companies that are in the running for a major account. This account could take us from the largest advertising company in the southeast, to the third, second, or even the highest ranking advertising company in the U.S." Mr. Lockson said.

Marcus's heart started beating in his chest. Could it really be his account that Mr. Lockson was talking about?

"That account is…Coca-Cola. And, the sole individual responsible for getting us this far is our very own, Marcus Downing." Mr. Lockson, said pointing at Marcus.

The boss began to clap and everyone joined in. The room roared with applause and screams for Marcus. You would think they were at a pep rally back in high school.

"Alright, alright," Mr. Lockson said, walking over to Marcus, "Let's put this puppy to bed, aye? I need everyone to stay focused on this. If Marcus needs any of your help, please help him."

Mr. Lockson shook Marcus's hand and sent everyone out of the conference room, "Ok, ok, back to work. Let's get ready for the big time."

Everyone, that was close enough, gave Marcus a pat on the shoulder on the way out and the room cleared quickly. Mr. Lockson held Marcus from leaving and waited until everyone left before saying, "Good job Marcus my boy, good job indeed."

"Thank you, sir." Marcus said, humbly shaking his hand again.

"Now comes the hard part." Mr. Lockson said.

"Sir?" Marcus said, a little confused.

Mr. Lockson motioned for Marcus to have a seat. They took a seat in the two closest chairs.

"Out of the three companies that are chasing this thing, we are the smallest. So I expect the others to try and cut us out using their money. We're big here, but these other guys are national and international names with much deeper pockets than ours. I believe we have a shot but I want my best man on the job. You, Marcus."

"Sure sir. What do you want me to do?" Marcus asked, eagerly awaiting the challenge.

He probably would have been offended if Mr. Lockson had asked anyone but him to do it. Especially after all of the time he had spent getting the first presentation out of the way.

"I want you to redo your presentation. Not start over, just make it so bloody amazing that it has those Coca-Cola big wigs creaming in their knickers. I want you to go to Atlanta and knock their bloody socks off and bring that account home. Can you do that for me Marcus?" Mr. Lockson asked, his eyes looking for any shred of confidence in his best worker. Marcus didn't know this would involve him leaving town again and knew Sherise wouldn't be happy, but on the other hand this was a big opportunity and he knew it would mean major things for him in the future. It meant a big reputation for him in the company and not to mention a very nice commission for him and his family. Without hesitation Marcus answered Mr. Lockson's question.

"Yes sir, definitely!"

"Great! I knew I could count on you my boy. You leave Wednesday morning." Mr. Lockson said, slamming his hand on the table in excitement.

"Wednesday?" Marcus said, confused.

"Yes, I need you up there by Wednesday for our presentation time on Friday. I need you to be familiar with your surroundings. I need you comfortable, punctual and sharp. I want you to use every angle of that room, if possible, to articulate your point. I want them to see dollar signs in their eyes when you're finished. Truth be told, you are the only one I can rely on to pull this off," Mr. Lockson paused, a look of concern visited his face, "Are you up for it?"

Marcus didn't want his boss to lose the confidence he had in his work and said, "Yes sir, I know I am!"

"Right then! That's what I'm talking about. Take the next few days off and get ready to blow them away. I'll have Rita get you your plane tickets and hotel reservations made immediately. Do you need a rental car?" He asked.

"Probably," Marcus said, "since I won't have my..."

"Right, I'll have a courier bring it all by tomorrow." Mr. Lockson said leaving the room.

Marcus just sat there thinking about what had just happened. He walked out of the conference room and his friend Mike walked up to him.

"Congratulations man." Mike said as they down the hall to Marcus's office.

"'Preciate it, bruh." Marcus said, giving him a pound.

"So what you gotta do now?" Mike asked as they walked through the doorway to Marcus's corner office.

Marcus stepped behind his desk and started looking through some of his papers.

"Lockson wants me to go to Atlanta and pitch the presentation to some Coca-Cola big wigs. I guess they are the decision makers. He thinks we have a shot at getting it, so…"

"Word? That's straight man. You're gonna do it right?"

Marcus looked at his friend with a confused look and said, "Hell yeah, I'm gonna do it. You know how much money they're talking bout? That's a $150 million deal over the next five years. I'll make more off the commission than I would make with my regular salary in that time. Am I gonna do it? Nigga is you sick?"

Mike laughed at his friend.

"Well I better get outta here before Lockson thinks I'm fucking with your creative aura or some shit. I'll holla."

"Alright man." Marcus said, his friend leaving the office.

Marcus started collecting different programs off of his computer and saving them onto a CD so he could get started on revamping his presentation. Mr. Lockson happened to walk by his office, saw him sitting there, and barged in.

"Marcus my boy, what are you still doing here. I need you focused. Go home, get some rest." Mr. Lockson said.

"I know sir, I know. I'm just getting a few things that I'll need to make it perfect." Marcus told him.

"That's my boy. Go show 'em what we're made of." He said, walking out of the office. Marcus just watched him with a strange look. He really worked for a strange man, he thought. He finished gathering his things and left his office. On his way to the elevator he got dozens of handshakes and pats on the back. Everyone was proud of him and backed him all the way. They knew that his success in this deal meant really big things for all of them. Marcus knew it too; he didn't want to let them down. He made it back to his truck and climbed into the driver's seat. He just sat there for a few minutes thinking about the opportunity that had just presented itself. He could barely grasp the magnitude of what it could mean if he made his Mr. Lockson's dream a reality. This meant

more than the money he would get in commission; it meant a national reputation, which could open doors to bigger and better things.
He got it in his head that he would make this presentation the best thing those executives had ever seen. He pulled out of the parking space and left the lot. He decided to drive to Sherise's salon to tell her the good news.

Fourteen

About fifteen minutes later he pulled into her parking lot and got out of his truck. He walked through the front door and the young receptionist said, "Hi Mr. Downing."

"Hey Peaches, how are you doing?" Marcus said.

"I'm fine. You here to see your wife?"

"No, actually…I figured I would get some finger waves, maybe some braids. What do you think?"

The receptionist giggled and started to pick up the phone to call Sherise to the front.

"No, no, no. Don't call. I want to surprise her." He said, walking around the counter. She put the phone down and giggled at him before returning to the magazine book in front of her. There were several women getting their hair done and a few of them that didn't know who he was began to stare. Marcus made his way through the office and heard their whispers, "Mmm, girl who is that?" He must have been looking good because he could hear them as they did their little feminine cat calls. He kept a straight face, but he knew all eyes in the room were on him. A few of the stylists and patrons, that knew him, greeted Marcus on his way and they exchanged a few words before Marcus continued to his Sherise's office.

As he reached for the doorknob, it opened. Alicia backed through the open doorway and didn't see Marcus standing behind her. She and Sherise exchanged a few words and she turned around and almost bumped into him.

"What's up Lele, is my wife in her office." He asked, trying to be hospitable.

"Mmm hmmm." She said, lips tight and full of attitude.

"Good to see you too." Marcus said, walking through the doorway as she stepped to the side. She just stood there looking into the room as Marcus closed the door on her. She stood there for a few seconds with her arms crossed as if she wanted to kick the door open but she knew she would have to deal with Sherise if she did. Marcus never understood why she always acted the way she did towards him. He did mess up, once, but that was a long time ago. It was like she never really forgave him even though what he did was not to her.

Marcus stood there for a minute and watched his wife try and dig herself out from under a pile of papers on her desk. She was so busy that she hadn't even heard his little exchange with Alicia just outside her door. He took a few steps over to her desk and she looked up.

"Heeeey baby." She said, dropping her pen and standing up from her desk to give him a hug. She was hoping for a reason to stop working and he was just the excuse she needed. He hugged his wife and gave her a kiss.

"What are you doing here? Shouldn't you be at work?" She asked, still in his arms.

"Yeah, I got some good news today. Sit down." He said.

The two of them take the seats right in front of her desk and Marcus began to tell her about the meeting. He told her how his meeting really was about his presentation with Coca-Cola and told her that Mr. Lockson told everyone that they were actually in the running to get the account.

"So, he gave me some time off to get my presentation perfect because I have to present it again to the top dogs at Coke." He finished.

"Oh baby, that's wonderful!" She said, leaning over to give him a hug.

"Yeah, and with the commission I'll make, if we get it, we can probably pay off the house."

"Hey, I ain't mad about that." She said, jokingly.

"There's just one thing." He said, preparing to tell her he would have to do his presentation in Atlanta.

"What?" She said, her smile slowly left her face.

"I have to go to Atlanta to present the information at their headquarters."

He tried to gauge her reaction. She just sat there as if she was waiting for him to keep talking.

"Oh, ok."

He looked at her in amazement.

"That's it? Ok?"

"What?"

"I have to leave Wednesday morning."

"Wednesday?"

Marcus thought to himself, *Ok, here we go.*

She paused for a moment, silent, then said, "Ok."
"This Wednesday."
"Ok."
"Day after tomorrow Wednesday."
"I know when Wednesday is." She said, laughing.
"So you aren't mad? You're not going to tell me that you don't want me to go?" He asked, remembering how she had overacted when he told her he was going to visit Alonzo.
"No, I'm not mad. I'm not happy, but I'm not mad. The way I look at it, if there is a chance that you could get this thing done and we could pay off our house early, you could tell me you had to go to the moon to pitch a Coke ad to some aliens and I'm fine with it."
The two of them laughed and talked for a little longer before Sherise needed to get back to work. She gave her husband a big hug and told him how proud she was of what he was doing for his family. Marcus walked back through the salon and out the front door. He jumped into his truck and pulled out of the parking lot, headed home. He got home and went straight to work on editing his presentation.

For the rest of that afternoon and the following day, Marcus did nothing but eat, sleep, and work on his presentation. At times he would be on both his laptop and desktop at the same time. He wanted to get every piece of information that he could about the company to use in his presentation. Past sales, failed marketing strategies, and low production figures were what he was looking for to make his presentation look that much better. Sherise kept the girls away from him so that he wouldn't be disturbed. He only saw his girls when they came home and when they came to say goodnight before bed. Marcus was pouring his soul into this presentation because he knew what it could mean for just about everyone in his life.

Early Wednesday morning Marcus woke up and gathered his things. His wife and children were still sleep as he got dressed for his trip. After he was ready, he called a cab.
"Baby, baby," Marcus said, tapping his sleeping wife, "I'm about to go, the cab is on the way."
Sherise slowly climbed out of the bed and walked with him down the stairs. It was still dark outside and there were a couple of hours left before the girls had to wake up so they let them sleep and had a seat on the couch in the family room. Sherise laid her head on his shoulder and they talked about what he was going to do on his trip. A few minutes later there was a honk from outside and

they saw the taxi's headlights shining through the windows. They both stood to their feet and walked to the front door. Marcus opened it and they stepped out onto the porch. Marcus turned to her and set his bag down to give his wife a hug. He threw his arms around her and they shared a short but sensual kiss. Marcus turned to head up the walkway toward the cab. As he was placing his bag in the trunk Sherise said, "Call me when you get there."

"Ok, baby." He said, closing the trunk.

"I love you." She said, as he opened the door.

"Love you too." He said.

She had the same look on her face that she had almost two weeks prior when he was leaving to visit Alonzo. The cab pulled out of the driveway and she waved to him until he was out of sight. Sherise went back inside the house and up to her room to get a little more rest before she had to wake the girls up.

Marcus got to the airport and made his flight. About 45 minutes after they took off, the pilot's voice came through the speaker letting them know they were about to land at Hartsfield-Jackson International Airport. Marcus got off the plane, claimed his luggage and headed for the car rental counter. He got his keys and directions to his hotel from the clerk and headed for his automobile. About 30 minutes later Marcus pulled into the parking lot of his hotel and grabbed all of his things from the back seat. He walked through the front doors and up to the service counter.

"How can I help you sir?" The attendant said as Marcus walked up.

"Yes, reservation for Downing, first name Marcus. It may be under *Streamline* advertising."

The attendant typed his information into her system and said, "Oookay, we have you in the executive suite, correct?"

"Oh, ummm, I don't know. The reservations were made by someone else." Marcus said.

"Oh ok. No problem. I just need to see your I.D. and I can get your key for you."

Marcus showed the attendant his identification and she said, "Ok. Give me one moment."

"No problem."

Marcus took a moment to take in the scene around him. He had rushed in so fast that he didn't realize how nice the hotel was that his boss put him in.

"So what kind of work do you do?" She asked, programming his key card.

"Advertising, I'm here to bid on a contract with Coca-Cola in a few days."

"Really! Wow, that's great!" She said, with an impressed look on her face.

"Well, here you go."

"Thank you." Marcus said, taking the card.

"Good luck on your presentation." She said as Marcus made his way around the counter. Marcus thanked her again and made his way to the elevator and up to his room. After finding his room he slid the card and pushed the door open.

The room was huge. It came complete with a kitchen, a king-sized bed, a Jacuzzi tub, and a nice sized desk for him to use. Marcus had never been sent out of town on business but if this was what it was like, he could get used to it. He put his bags on the floor in the closet, hung up the bag with his suits in it, and put his laptop bag and briefcase on the desk. He didn't mind staying there for the next 4 days. He took off his suit jacket and threw it over the back of a chair and stretched out on the bed. He took his cell phone from his belt clip and looked at it. He didn't expect it to work after his last fiasco concerning his phone but this time he got a signal. He flipped it open and called home. The phone rang a few times before the answering machine picked up. He closed his phone and looked at his watch. It was almost 12:30. He should have known that Sherise would have been at the salon by now. He flipped his phone open again and dialed the salon number.

"Hello, *Sherise's* hair salon, how can I help you," said the energetic voice over the phone. "Hey Peaches, this is Marcus Downing. Is my wife in?"

"Um, I believe so. She's in her office, I think. You want me to transfer you back to her?"

"Yes please."

"Ok hold on."

Marcus listened to a few brief words from Jill Scott as he sat on hold.

"This is Sherise."

"Hey baby."

"Heeeeeey baby! So you made it in ok?"

"Yeah, just got in and put my stuff down actually."

"See, I knew I would get you trained if I stuck with it."

They both laughed.

"Anyway, so what are you up to?" Marcus asked.

"Nothing, just getting some work done. I'm actually almost finished. What do you have to do today?"

"Nothing really. My presentation is on Friday at noon. So, I'm going to finish fixing my presentation today and go check out the conference room tomorrow."

"Oh ok. Well, I know you're going to do great. I'm so proud of you baby."

Marcus smiled.

"Thank you. Well I don't want to hold you up. I know you have plenty to do. I just wanted to call and let you know I made it."

"You have no idea. Sometimes I think somebody is dropping off papers from some other *Sherise's* in town."

Marcus chuckled.

"Ok, well I love you." He said.

"I love you too. Oh, before you go. Are you gonna go see your brother or Lasaia while you're up there?"

"I'll probably drop by Alonzo's on Saturday, but I doubt I will get to see Lasaia. She most likely has a lot of work to do, since she just had that call and everything. I'll probably just call her and see how she is doing."

"Oh, well tell her I said hello and your brother too."

Marcus chuckled and said, "Umm, ok."

"What?"

"Nothing, you really liked her huh?"

"Well, she just seems really nice."

"See, and you didn't even want to meet her."

"I know. But, I'm glad I did. Now, I can get some juicy details on some of the things you did as a kid. I know, if she wasn't there, you told her."

He laughed and said, "Anyway, let me give you her number."

He pulled her card from his wallet and gave her the number.

"Ok baby, I think I'm gonna take a quick nap before I start working on this presentation."

"Ok, call me later."

"Ok."

"Miss you."

"Miss you more."

Sherise laughed and said, "Ok, bye."

Marcus closed his phone and decided to change before his nap. He unpacked his suits, hung them up so they wouldn't wrinkle. He unzipped his suitcase and picked out some comfortable clothes to lounge around in. He turned on the television and flipped through the channels for a few minutes then slowly drifted off to sleep.

His eyes opened around 3:30. He sat up in the bed and rubbed his eyes. The television was the only noise in the room and Marcus decided to get back to working on his presentation. He booted up his laptop and dove in. Marcus streamlined his presentation to contain every piece of pertinent information needed to show that there was no question his offer was the best for the job. He dotted every *i* and crossed every *t*. Then checked, double-checked, triple-checked, and then just to be sure he checked again, just to be sure everything was perfect. He didn't want a single word misspelled or a single animation to come in a second late. He didn't want to show a single sign of weakness in presenting his information. If they couldn't sell themselves to these executives, there was no way they were going to walk away with the contract. Marcus put the finishing touches on his visual presentation and made three back up copies. He put one in his briefcase, one in his laptop case, and one in his suitcase for safe keeping in case something somehow happened to the other two.

Marcus needed to find a conference room or somewhere that he could practice his presentation before having to do it for real. He figured the hotel probably had one that he could slip into for a few minutes. Marcus changed into some more suitable attire to go out in and threw his lounging clothes on the bed. As he was walking out the door his cell phone began to ring. He flipped it open and put it to his ear.

"Marcus Downing." He said into the phone.

"So you're just gonna come to town and not tell nobody huh?" A voice said. Marcus recognized it immediately.

"What's up girl? I see my wife is working fast as usual." He said, laughing, walking toward the elevator.

"Uh huh, she sure did. It's a shame she had to tell me that you were here, and I didn't even grow up with her. You know you're wrong, right?"

"I was going to call you. I've just been working on my presentation for the last couple hours. I was just headed downstairs now to and see if they have somewhere I can practice."

"Uh huh. So, when am I going to get to see you?"

"Oh um, I figured you would be busy after your modeling call, so I wasn't going to bother you on this trip."

"Bother me? Boy, you wouldn't be bothering me. I will *always* make time for you. When is your presentation?"

"Friday at noon."

"And when will you know if they picked you?"

"Probably that afternoon. My boss told me they are ready to get the ball rolling on this thing and won't be wasting any time picking somebody."

"Ok well after they tell you that you have the account, we can go out to celebrate."

Marcus smiled at the confidence that she had in him. Everyone seemed to be so sure that he could pull this off. Mr. Lockson, Mike, Sherise, everyone at work, and now Lasaia. Marcus knew he had to win this contract now.

"So you think I got it like that huh?"

"I know you do. And, after you get it, we're going out."

"Well it doesn't seem like I have much to say in the matter so, I guess I'll just be ready."

"Great! It's a date," She said, excited, "Well I'll let you get back to work and I'll call you on Friday to let you know where we're going."

"Ok, sounds like a plan."

"Ok, bye."

Marcus hung up his phone as he rounded the corner of the front desk in the lobby. He saw the same girl he saw earlier still at her post.

"Hello again. What can I do for you?" She asked.

"Hey, I was wondering if it was possible for me to use one of your conference rooms to practice my presentation that I have in a few days. It'll only take a little while." Marcus asked.

"Oh, um, we're not really allowed to let people in there unless they rent them." She said.

"Really?" Marcus said, disappointed.

He didn't put up a fight and understood her position. He didn't want to get her in any trouble and thanked her anyway. He figured his hotel room would have to be good enough. He began to leave the counter and the girl watched him for a few seconds. Just as he was about to get out of sight she said, "Hey, sir...wait." Marcus stopped and turned back to her.

"You know what?" She said digging through some things behind the desk. "My supervisor isn't here today and no one is back there anyway so," She pulled a key from behind the counter and walked around to where Marcus was standing, "I'll let you in and you can practice. But, if anyone asks, I didn't do it."

"Scouts honor." Marcus said, holding up his three finger salute. She took Marcus to the conference room and let him in.

"Just let me know when you're done so I can lock up." She said, pushing the door open.

"Definitely. Thanks again." He said, walking into the room. She closed the door and returned to her post. Marcus got into the room and set his things up just like he planned to do for the presentation. He found spots that he could improve and made some changes. He practiced over the next hour and a half and left the room when he felt a little more comfortable with his work. He caught the desk clerk just as she was about to end her shift. He told her he was done, thanked her again, and went back up to his room. He sat on the bed and turned on the television. After flipping through a few channels he looks at his watch. It was 7:45. He figured his wife was most likely fighting with Lasaia over bath time right about now and decided to call his brother. He grabbed his phone and dialed Alonzo's number.

"Hello?" A female voice said, answering the phone.

"Hey, what's up?" Marcus said.

"Who is this?" The voice said with an attitude.

"Marcus."

"Oh, hey Marcus, what's up?"

"Damn girl, I thought you were about to jump through the phone at me."

"Sorry," She said laughing, "Things have been a little crazy around here since you left."

"Why, what happened?"

"You remember that guy y'all got into it with at the car show?"

"Yeah, Richard right?"

"Yeah, well he's been asking around about me and he's trying to find out where we are. I can't even go to my mama's house 'cause I don't want him to see me and follow me back."

"Really, like that?"

"Like that."

"That's crazy. You doing alright though, besides that?"

"Yeah, I'm fine. Just sick of being in this house all the time. I feel like I'm under the witness protection program or some shit."

"Did you call the police about him?"

"Yeah but they said they can't do anything because I don't have any proof that he is trying to hurt us. All I have is what other people tell me. I can't even get a restraining order because they say he hasn't done anything to me. All they say is, 'There isn't a crime in asking about someone'. I guess I have to wait until he tries to kill me before they lift a finger."

"Does he know about Alonzo's club?"

"Not yet, I don't think. But it's only a matter of time before he goes and finds Alonzo there. It's not like *Cloud 9* is a secret. Everyone goes there. And, you know your brother, he can't just stay in the back. He has to walk through the club and let everybody see him."

"So he still goes in to work?"

"Yeah! He won't listen to me. I keep telling him to chill out, but he always say, 'I ain't lettin' no Rasta nigga run me out my own shit.' I think he wants to run into him again."

"That sounds like Zo. Is he there?"

"Yeah, let me get him."

Lisa walked to Alonzo's room and handed him the phone.

"Whassup?" Alonzo said, into the phone.

"What's going on bruh?" Marcus answered.

"Oh, what's up man. I didn't know this was you. Not shit, about to get ready to head to the club in a few."

"I heard you got a little stalker up there lookin' for you." Marcus said, laughing.

"Yeah, he can look, but he ain't gonna like what he finds, ya' know?"

"Yeah, yeah…you be careful though bruh. Don't start nothing."

"Nah man, you know me. I'm just gonna finish it. So what's up with you? How's Duval treatin' y'all?"

"Good, can't complain. I'm actually in Atlanta right now though."

"Oh, for real? What you doing up this way?"

"Business. I have a presentation on Friday with Coca-Cola."

"Oh ok, that's good man. Good luck with that."

"Thanks. I just wanted to holla at you man. I know you're resting up for the night ahead, but I wanna come through and see you guys on Saturday, before I leave."

"Oh yeah, you know you gotta do that."

"Alright brotha, I'll holla at you later."

"Alright man, take it easy."

"Later."

"Peace."

Marcus hung up the phone and laughed at his brother. Even when Alonzo was trying to be good, he always managed to get wrapped up in something. Marcus figured he should get some rest for the day ahead and took a shower to prepare for bed. He completed his nightly ritual and jumped on the bed to call his wife. The two of them discussed their day and everything they did and Marcus even told her about Lasaia's offer to take him out after his presentation. Sherise didn't think twice about it and told him he should go. They talked for a few more minutes before Sherise told him she needed to get ready for bed. They said their good-byes and hung up. Marcus watched television until his eyes pretty much closed on their own and he drifted off to sleep.

Fifteen

Marcus woke up the next morning with the television still playing in the background. He climbed out of bed and started getting ready for his day. After putting on one of his suits and gathering his things, he made his way to the Coca-Cola headquarters to preview the room where he would be doing his presentation. After a brief conversation with the front desk, Marcus was led up to the conference room and left in peace. He surveyed the room to be sure that he would be able to reach anyone that was in front of him, noted a few adjustments he could make, and gathered his things. He returned his visitors pass to the front desk after he was finished and headed back to his hotel. He got to his room around noon and spent the next five hours going over his short 20 minute presentation. He knew it inside and out. He knew what kind of people he would be dealing with (the kind that saw your mistakes far more clearly than your successes) and left nothing to chance. He had his PowerPoint slides perfectly choreographed with his words and had the whole thing memorized. After getting everything exactly how he wanted it, he decided it was time for a break. He pulled up directions to Alonzo's house from the hotel on his laptop and jotted them down. He grabbed his keys and wallet and headed out the door.

About 20 minutes later he pulled into Alonzo's driveway. He got out and knocked on the door. Alonzo opened it, saw his big brother and smiled.

"What's up nigga," Alonzo yelled, excitedly, "I thought you said you weren't coming through until tomorrow."

They gave each other a hug and walked inside.

"Yeah I know. I just had to get out of that hotel room." Marcus said, following Alonzo through the house. Lisa was lying on the couch watching television as they walked in. She looked up and said, "Heeey Marcus." She got up from her spot and gave him a big hug. They all had a seat and talked for a while about Marcus's trip and how his family had been doing over the last few weeks. Marcus told them about Lasaia coming to Jacksonville and meeting Sherise and the kids. Alonzo teased Marcus about letting his wife meet his mistress and they all had a laugh. Around 8:30 Marcus thought to call his wife to see how things were going at home. He took his cell phone from his belt clip and flipped it open.

"No signal? This phone is trippin'. It was working fine at the hotel, but I come over here and now I can't get a signal. It must be something about Decatur." Marcus said.

He closed his phone and put it back in his clip.

"Here, you can use mine." Alonzo said, standing to his feet.

"Nah, that's alright. I need to get out of here anyway," Marcus said, getting up, "I need to get back to the hotel and get some rest for my presentation tomorrow."

"True, how much is that thing worth anyway?" Alonzo asked.

"About $150 million." Marcus said.

"Daaaa-yuuum-maaa," Alonzo said shocked at the amount, "And how much of that you get?"

He didn't realize that for a big company that was nothing to spend on advertising. Hell, those 30 second ads during the Superbowl were easily thirty million, plus.

"Um, I get ½ % of the total amount in commission, and then if I work on the account I get whatever salary is budgeted. But, my commission alone would be like almost eight hundred thousand dollars." Marcus said.

Alonzo whistled at the amount as they walked out.

"Bye Marcus." Lisa yelled to him as the brothers headed for the front door.

"Later." He called back to her.

Alonzo opened the door and said, "Good luck on that thing tomorrow man. I already know you gonna get it though."

"Thanks man. I'm going to do my best." Marcus said.

He walked out the door and over to his truck and got in. Marcus left his brother's house and headed back to the hotel.

He pulled into the hotel parking lot and got out. He got up to his room and began preparing for bed. He called his wife to wish her a goodnight and went over his presentation one more time before deciding it was as good as it was going to get and got in the bed. He drifted off to sleep around 10:00 after lying in the bed trying to stop himself from getting up to work on his presentation. He needed his rest for his big day coming up.

Marcus woke up the next day around 9:45 and got out of bed. He got dressed for his day and checked to make sure he had everything he needed for the presentation. He gathered his things, said a prayer, and started on his way to the biggest event of his career. He made it to the Coca-Cola headquarters around 11:15 and made his way through security to the conference room. Marcus signed in with the receptionist and had a seat to wait until he was called to present. It seemed like a new butterfly jumped into his stomach with every minute that passed. He felt like he was back at high school basketball try-outs, while the coach read off the names of who made the team. All Marcus could think about was everyone that was counting on him. His wife, his kids, Mr. Lockson, all his co-workers...he even thought about Alonzo, Lisa and Lasaia. They wouldn't be affected by it directly, but they had confidence that he could do it and he didn't want to let any of them down. The silence was broken by a beep on the receptionist's phone and she picked it up.

"Yes sir...yes...he's right here...ok...right away sir." She said to whoever was on the other end of the phone.

She looked over to Marcus and said, "They're ready for you now."

"Thank you." Marcus said as he quickly gathered his things and headed for the huge double doors. As he passed her desk she looked over to him smiling and said, "Good luck."

Marcus smiled back and thanked her again before taking a deep breath and grabbing the handle. When he got into the room Marcus came face to face with three of the most stone-faced individuals that he had ever seen. They just watched, in silence, as Marcus walked over and introduced himself and his company. They shook his hand, introduced themselves, and then went silent. It was clear that this presentation would be strictly business. No fun and games. Marcus felt a little intimidated, but he wasn't going to show it. He quickly set up his laptop on the television at the front of the long conference table and began his presentation. He was flawless. He didn't forget a single word. Every slide seemed to hit the screen just as Marcus was getting to that point. This is what he had practiced for. Even his little joke that he threw in got a short, distinguished chuckle out of the straight faces. He finished his presentation and the three executives shook his hand and thanked him for coming. Their poker faces gave no indication that he was even in the running. That was probably how they wanted it. All he could do now was wait.

Marcus walked out the double doors and closed them behind him. He closed his eyes and took a deep breath with his back against the door. The receptionist let out a tiny giggle and asked, "How'd it go?"

Marcus looked over at her and smiled. There was another gentleman sitting in the chair where he was before, looking just as nervous as he did an hour ago.

"Tough crowd. I think I handled it well though." He said smiling.

Her phone beeped again and Marcus waved goodbye. She waved back and told the next candidate it was his turn. Marcus left the Coca-Cola headquarters and headed back to the hotel.

He got back to his room and flopped down onto the bed looking up at the ceiling. He smiled at the great job he knew he had just done and couldn't wait to hear the decision. It hadn't been more then 45 minutes since he shook the hands of those men but he was already sitting by the phone, waiting for it to ring. He paced around his room in his suit and even lifted the receiver a few times to make sure there was a dial tone. Marcus hadn't eaten all morning but he didn't dare leave the room or even pick up the phone to order room service. He didn't want to take the chance that his boss would call while he was ordering a sandwich or something. He could have probably called room service from his cell phone but his mind was so focused on getting the call that the thought didn't even cross his mind. He was too anxious to eat now anyway. He worried himself crazy for another 45 minutes before the phone rang. Marcus jumped to his feet and picked up the receiver.

"Hello…hello? This is Marcus." He said into the phone as soon as he struggled to get it to his ear.

"Marcus." Said the voice on the other end.

"Yes sir, Mr. Lockson." Marcus said, giving his boss his full attention.

Marcus's heart began to pound harder and harder in his chest. He knew this was the call he had been waiting for.

"We just received word from Coca-Cola." Mr. Lockson said, his words not coated with the excitement Marcus had hoped for.

Marcus sat down on the bed and barely took a breath while he listened.

"They say that they have decided to go with *Perimeter* instead." Mr. Lockson said.

Marcus dropped his head and his heart fell to his feet. What could he have done wrong? What did he forget? Question upon question ran through his mind. He couldn't believe what was happening.

"Those bloody bastards had so much money that they offered to do the deal for half as much as everyone else just so they can have Coca-Cola's name on their books. 75 million bloody dollars...that's what those wankers gave up. They offered us a chance to match it because they really liked your presentation, but there is no way we could take that big of a loss." Mr. Lockson continued.

Marcus just sat on the bed with his head down scarcely listening.

"Good news is, we will have another bid in 5 years. We'll show those blokes who we are and steal that bloody contract back."

There was silence on the line for a few seconds before Mr. Lockson said, "Marcus? You there?"

"Yes sir...yes I'm here." Marcus said, a disheartened tone in his voice.

"Look, Marcus don't beat yourself up about this ole' boy. They loved your work. I know you. You've probably been working on this thing nonstop since I last saw you. I know you were great. But, we can only do what we can do. Those bastards just pulled a dirty trick. Threw everything into a shambles, they did. I told you about those sneaky bastards. But, that's the business we're in. Cut throat, you know." He said, trying to lift his spirits.

Marcus tried not to get dejected about the whole situation but he got lower and lower with every second. He masked his true feelings and told his boss that he wouldn't worry about it just to get off the phone.

"Ok then, that's the spirit. I'll see you on Monday alright then?" Mr. Lockson said.

"Yes sir. Bright and early." Marcus said before hanging up the phone.

Marcus stretched out on the bed and closed his eyes. The reality of the situation had set in and Marcus couldn't imagine having to look his wife and kids in the eyes knowing he couldn't make their dreams come true. Then he thought about his co-workers and how their faces lit up at the thought of getting the contract. Marcus felt even worse after thinking about them. He lay there in the bed with his eyes closed, feeling bad. He felt as if he had let everyone down and there was no way to fix it.

Marcus didn't move from his spot on the bed until about 5 o'clock when his cell phone rang. He slowly reached over and answered it. He put the phone to his ear and said, "Hello?"

"Hey buddy, have you heard from the top dogs yet? Lasaia's voice came through the phone.

"Yeah." Marcus said, the same dejected tone ran in his tone.

"What's wrong? What happened?" She asked, concerned.

"Another company under bid us and we lost the contract."

"Aaaawww. Oh, I am so sorry to hear that. You doing ok?"

"Yeah, I'm cool. A little disappointed about it, but I'll be fine."
"Aaaww, poor baby. I'm really sorry to hear that. Can I still take you out tonight? I know you didn't get it but I want to be there for you."
"I…I don't know. I think I just want to be alone tonight."
"Aw, come on. You need to be with a friend right now. I know this was important to you. Please let me be there for you like you were always there for me."
Marcus thought about his friend's plea, and then thought about spending the rest of the night in the room by himself, thinking about the presentation. He figured he might as well have some fun before he had to leave the city. If he was to sit in that room all night he would definitely drive himself crazy. He really needed a drink right about now.
"Come on, pleeeaaase." She said after a few seconds of silence.
Marcus finally gave in and said, "Ok, where are we going?"
"Yeaaaaa, ok, ok. I want to go to this new jazz bar thing they just opened in Buckhead like a week ago. I heard it's really nice."
"Ok, well what time do you want to leave?"
"How about I pick you up around 9? Is that cool?"
"Yeah that's fine."
"Ok. Well I better get back to this paperwork so I'll be able to go out," Lasaia said with a giggle, "I'll see you later?"
"Ok."
"Great, bye."
Marcus hung up the phone and he actually felt a little bit better than he did before she called. He knew it wasn't his fault that they didn't get the contract, but after being boosted by everyone else's praise, he felt bad for not getting it.

After sulking around for about 30 more minutes, Marcus decided he should call his wife and tell her what happened. He flipped open his phone and dialed home. After a few rings he heard his wife's voice come through the receiver, "Hello?"
Marcus went silent and was tempted to hang up. He had the courage to dial the number but it all went down the drain when he heard her voice.
"Hello?" She said again. Marcus still couldn't speak. He didn't want to tell her that he had failed.
"Marcus, hello?" She said after another few seconds of silence. She knew it was him, she saw his phone number on the Caller ID, but he was frozen. Marcus finally broke out of his petrified state and took a deep breath.

"Hey baby." He says trying not to let the depression swathe his words. Sherise knew her husband though; she could tell when he was mad or upset, just by the pitch in his voice.

"Hey, what's wrong?" She asked.

"Nothing. I'm cool."

"Yeah right. Marcus you know I know you better then that. What happened?"

Marcus was silent for another few seconds, then took another deep breath and said, "I didn't get it."

"It what? What it? Ooooh, you didn't get the contract? Oh baby, I'm sorry," She said feeling bad for her husband, "What happened?"

"Another company took a huge loss just to get the Coca-Cola name on their books and we couldn't match it." Marcus told her.

"Aw baby, I'm sorry. Well, it's alright. You'll get it next time."

"Yeah. Mr. Lockson says we can bid again in 5 years."

"See, and I bet you will get an even bigger and better contract then."

Marcus smiled at his wife's support. That's one thing he loved about her, she would always have his back. Marcus could have been selling toothpicks on an interstate off ramp somewhere and she would say something like, *Baby you got the best toothpicks on this side of town.* They talked for a little longer about the kids and everything that had been going on since he left and then he got off the phone. Marcus felt even better now that he got the chance to speak to his wife. She could always make things right.

Around 8:30 Marcus heard his cell phone ring. He flipped it open and said, "Hello?"

"Hey, you ready?"

Marcus had completely forgotten about promising Lasaia that she could take him out.

"Hey, oh man. Nah I'm not ready yet, but…give me a few minutes."

"Ok, well you want me to call you back, or you can call me?"

"Nah, nah, I can be ready by the time you get here."

"Ok, well where are you?"

Marcus told her the name of the hotel he was in and she said, "Oh ok. I know exactly where that is. I can be there in like 20 minutes."

"Ok, I can be ready by then."

"Ok, cool. See you in a few."

"Ok."

Marcus hung up the phone and sped over to the shower. After he got out he brushed his teeth and started putting on his clothes. He got on his slacks and undershirt and then heard a knock on the door. Marcus looked over at the clock on the nightstand. It was 8:48. *She couldn't be here already could she?*, Marcus thought. "Yeah, who is it!?" He yelled from beside the bed.

"Room service!" A muffled voice said from the other side of the door.

Room Service, Marcus thought to himself as he walked to the door. He hadn't ordered anything, they must have had the wrong room. He opened the door and his eyes got wide as he saw Lasaia standing there smiling.

She looked amazing. She had on a tight blue and white long-sleeved shirt, which was only kept together by a small knot tied in the ends that connected between her breasts, exposing her nicely toned stomach. She had on a matching skirt that went just below her knees with two slits on the sides that wasted no time exposing her thick, sexy thighs as she walked into the room. Marcus wondered if she owned anything that didn't cling to her skin like plastic wrap.

"How'd you get here so fast?" Marcus said as she walked pass him.

He just stood there with his t-shirt on and his belt unbuckled and hanging from the loops. His muscular arms were still a little wet from his shower. Marcus wasn't paying attention, but Lasaia was scanning every inch of him as he closed the door and headed back to his clothes. He threw on his shirt, tie and jacket to complete his look.

"I'm ready." He said and they grabbed their belongings and left the room. They made it to *Passion* a little after nine o'clock and parked. They walked through the front door and the scene was pleasant.

Passion was a dimly lit jazz bar that was a new edition to the Atlanta nightlife. It was a small bar that had plush seating and decent drink prices. The two of them walked in and were greeted by a woman that asked them if they wanted a table or a seat at the bar.

"Hungry?" Lasaia asked her date.

"I could eat." Marcus said.

Passion had a short gourmet selection, but Lasaia had heard good things and wanted to try it out. The waitress seated the two of them and gave Marcus a quick flirtatious smile as she said, "How is this," referring to the seats she selected for them.

"This is fine. Thanks." He said.

The stranger touched Marcus on the shoulder and said, "You two get comfortable and I'll be right back."

The woman walked off and Lasaia gave her a dirty look. Marcus paid her actions no attention, but Lasaia saw it all.

"Oh, no she didn't!"

"What?" Marcus asked.

"You didn't see how she was looking at you? Then gonna walk off throwing her hips all in your face."

"Huh," Marcus laughed. It felt good to laugh, "You're paranoid. What are you talking about?"

"That waitress"

Marcus was joking but Lasaia was very serious.

"What about her?"

"Eyeing you like a piece of meat. Like you don't have a woman with you."

Marcus laughed and said, "You jealous?"

"No, I'm just saying, she doesn't know we're just friends. I could be your girlfriend or wife or something and she's just gonna flirt with you like that, right in front of me."

"She probably just friendly like that. Or wants a big tip." Marcus said laughing again.

"Oh, I'll give her a tip alright." Lasaia said, a smile creeping back onto her face. They took in the scene around them for a few minutes before the waitress came back.

"You ready to order?" The waitress said, her eyes never leaving Marcus.

She paid no attention to Lasaia and Lasaia cut her eyes at the woman again. The woman slid down every word that came out of Marcus's mouth and never took her eyes off of him, except to look down at her ticket. Marcus finished his order and the woman turned to Lasaia and said, "And for you?"

The waitress rushed through Lasaia's order, never looking up at her and walked off when she was done. She disappeared and Lasaia sat in shock at how this woman was practically throwing herself at Marcus. He just sat across the table and laughed after seeing the expression on Lasaia's face. The waitress brought their drink order and they talked for a short period about Marcus's presentation. Marcus felt himself getting upset again and changed the subject.

"So, how are you and Greg doing?" He asked.

Lasaia laughed briefly and said, "Yeah, um. I need to tell you about that..."

Just as she said that and took a sip from her drink, the waitress came back with their food. She placed their orders on the table and said, "Enjoy!" before walking off. Both the entrees look delectable. Lasaia had lobster and crab legs and they were as delicious as they looked. Marcus's T-bone was very tender and flavorful. They enjoyed their meal as they listened to the jazz band on the stage at the other end of the club. *Passion* was really a nice place for people to hang out who were not looking for a fast paced atmosphere. As they were finishing up their meal, Lasaia felt a tap on her shoulder. She looked up and saw an attractive caramel skinned man standing there looking down at her. Marcus watched as she realized who he was. It was the man Lasaia brought to Marcus's house when she was in town.

"Heeeey Tony." She said, jumping to her feet.

Tony?, Marcus thought to himself, *I thought his name was Greg.* She gave him a hug and kissed his cheek.

"What are you doing here?" She said surprised.

Marcus looked at the two of them oddly. They didn't seem like a couple, more like friends. The guy looked over to Marcus and extended his hand.

"Hey man, how you doing?" He said.

Marcus stood up and shook his hand.

"Confused?" Marcus said, keeping his smile.

Marcus *was* confused. First, the two of them showed up at his house talking about they're together, now they see each other out and seem to be more friends then anything else.

"I thought the two of you were…" Marcus's words were interrupted when another man walked up and pinched Lasaia on the butt. Marcus recognized him too. It was Rico, the man that had done his wife's hair at the casting call. Lasaia screamed with delight again and gave Rico a hug. Marcus sat down trying to figure out what was going on. First her boyfriend walked up, doesn't get mad about her being with another man in a very revealing dress, they talk, then Rico comes in and him and this guy act like they have known each other for years, now all of them were standing there laughing and talking. Marcus downed his third rum and coke and went back over it all again.

"Well you guys have a good night." Tony said waving to Marcus and giving Lasaia another hug. The smile on his face didn't seem authentic. It was a concealing smile. Like he knew something that Marcus didn't. Marcus waved back with a fake smile on his face as they left. The two men walked off, together. As they got a few feet away Rico wrapped his arms around Greg's waist like a woman would do in a crowd to tell all the other women that this one was taken. Marcus's face changed and he raised his eyebrow. He was completely out of the loop now. Lasaia looked at him and laughed.

"You ok?" She asked.

"I thought that was, I mean isn't that the same…" Marcus cut his sentence short.

Lasaia jumped in to clear the air.

"Yeah, that's Tony. He's Rico's boyfriend. I've known those two since I graduated from college." She said.
"Well why did you bring him to my house and tell me he was a guy you dated?" Marcus asked.
"I only did that because I didn't want your wife to not like me before she even knew me. Not many women would welcome their husband's ex-single-girlfriend into her house. I figured if she thought I already had a man, she could get to know me instead of looking at me as somebody who wants her man. I just wanted her to be at ease, so, Tony was traveling with Rico and I asked if I could borrow him for a few hours. He did get in trouble for spending the night though." Lasaia said, followed by another laugh.
"So you *borrowed* his boyfriend?" Marcus asked.
"Yeah."
If Marcus wasn't already pretty much drunk that might have sounded strange to him. But, the two of them had a quick laugh about it and continued to talk about the music and scene around them.

An hour and several drinks later the two of them were laughing and talking about old times. Marcus had completely forgotten about not getting the contract and was just enjoying a night of fun and drinking with his old friend.
They were both beginning to feel a little tipsy. Lasaia stopped laughing and just sat across from Marcus, staring at him, adoringly. She really loved this man, always had, but now it was too late for them. Marcus's vision became a little impaired, but he could see her looking at him.
"What?" He said, with a chuckle.
Lasaia snapped back into reality from his question and said, "Huh, oh nothing. I just can't believe that we ran into each other again. I have really missed you," She paused, "I mean it's been so long, and I...I'm just so happy for you, but...at the same time, I feel like, with you being married...I feel like I missed out on something."
Marcus didn't know if this is the alcohol talking or if this was just something that she had wanted to say for a long time. He moved his chair around the table beside hers and put his arm around her shoulder. She was almost in tears as she rested her head on his shoulder. Everything in the club was still going on but to them no one else was around. Everything seemed to disappear. The music, the people, the club...gone. All that mattered was that she was in the arms of the man she loved.

Lasaia composed herself and lifted her head from his shoulder. "I'm sorry," She said, wiping her eyes, "I really shouldn't drink. I always get so emotional."

"It's alright." Marcus said.

"It's just that you have always been there for me when I needed you, and I always saw the two of us together one day." Lasaia grabbed a napkin and wiped her face. She saw her makeup smeared on the napkin and cleaned the rest of it off. She figured it was time for a quick touch up job and excused herself from the table, headed for the restroom. Marcus sat there still wondering what just happened.

Not more then 2 minutes after she was gone, the waitress popped up at the table. They hadn't seen her for at least 45 minutes; she seemed to appear out of nowhere. Marcus looked up at her through his hazy eyes.

"What happened to your date?" She asked, not sounding all that concerned.

"Oh, she's not my date," Marcus said, with a chuckle, "Just old friends. We grew up together."

Marcus was still a little shaken by the fact that she had appeared like that. It was like she was standing by, waiting for the opportunity to catch him alone.

"Oh Really?" The waitress said, a smile rested on her lips, "Well, my name is Camille."

She extended her hand.

"Marcus." He said, shaking her hand.

At that moment Lasaia could be seen headed back from the bathroom. She had fixed her makeup and looked just as good as she did when Marcus opened his hotel room door. She saw the waitress, who at this point was wearing razor blade shoes as she ran across her last nerve, standing there hovering over her date and walked back to the table and stood on the opposite side of Marcus looking at her.

"Would you like anything else?" The waitress asked, quickly thinking of reason to be there.

"Yes, please. Two more drinks." Lasaia said.

The woman walked off and Lasaia cut her eyes at her again.

"What was she doing over here?" Lasaia asked.

"She was asking what happened to you." Marcus told her.

"Uh huh. I think she likes you."

Marcus laughed.

"But she's out of luck, cause you're mine tonight." Lasaia said, taking her seat.

Marcus had moved his chair back to his side of the table just as the waitress brought out their drinks. A new jazz band had taken the stage and they were playing some nice slow melodies. A few couples had already found their way to the dance floor and Lasaia looked over to Marcus and said, "Would you like to dance with me?"

Marcus, not in full use of his mind, looked at her and accepted. Lasaia grabbed him by the hand and led him to the dance floor. She took him into the middle of the crowd and turned around. She threw her arms around his neck and he placed his hands on her hips. They slowly rocked side to side to the soft music. Lasaia rested her head on Marcus's strong chest as they listened to the jazz band release a lovely ballad from their instruments. She disappeared into her own little world in his arms where he was her man and she was happy. Marcus, still tipsy from his drinks, seemed to forget who he was with, because he started to squeeze her tighter and tighter against his body. The end of the song brought them back into reality and they joined the other dancers in applauding for the band. The group took a break and Lasaia and Marcus returned to their table.

"You know what that reminded me of?" Lasaia asked as they had a seat.

"What's that?" Marcus said, finishing his drink.

"Prom," She said, "I had so much fun with you that night. Do you know I still have our pictures?"

"Really," Marcus said, surprised, "I do too. At least I'm sure my mom still does. That woman every picture ever taken of me and Alonzo since birth."

"I still can't believe that you turned Samantha down to go with me." She said.

"Well, I promised you I would take you and I had always kept my word to you."

"Yeah I know. Even when I thought you would never make it. You came through. You remember that time we were studying for the S.A.T.'s and you promised you would go with me?"

"Yeah I remember that. I still owe Alonzo a kick in the head for unplugging my alarm clock. That's why I woke up late."

They talked about a story that took place before they had gone to prom.

It was the week before S.A.T.'s and Lasaia was nervous. She knew that test would determine whether she could escape her hell of a home or whether she would have to stay in Albany and make do with whatever happened. She knew as soon as he could, her step dad would kick her out, so scoring low on this test was not an option. She struggled through study sessions and preparatory books, but nothing was sticking. At least, not until Marcus stepped in. He offered to help and she jumped at the chance. For six days straight the two of them spent hours going back and forth over the study guides and she finally began to retain the information. The night before they had a quick refresher session and at the end as Marcus was leaving Lasaia stopped him.

"Marcus." She said.

Marcus turned around and returned to her porch.

"Yeah?"

"What time are you going tomorrow?"

"I don't know. The test is at 10, so I guess about 9 so I can study some more."

"Ok, can I study with you then?"

"Sure, if you want to."

"Ok, well meet me in front of the lunchroom at 9:00. Ok?"

"Ok."

"Promise?"

"Promise."

Marcus had gotten used to her asking him to promise to do everything she wanted him to do. It actually motivated him to get the job done. He didn't know how important he was to her. He walked home and got ready for bed so he could be refreshed for the test.

The next day Marcus was nowhere in sight. The test was scheduled to start at 10:00 a.m. that Saturday morning. It was 9:20 and Marcus was A.W.O.L. At the Downing household, Marcus was sound asleep in his bed. Alonzo had tripped on the cord to his alarm clock when he snuck into Marcus's room to get some cologne and didn't plug it back in. Lasaia was in a panic at the school and Marcus was sound asleep at home. She became more and more nervous as the time passed. Marcus woke up a few minutes later and looked at the arms on his clock. 8:47. Marcus slowly got out of his bed and went into the bathroom. On his way out he ran into his mother.

"I thought you had S.A.T.'s to take this morning?"

"I do, at 10:00"

"Boy do you know it's almost 9:30"

Marcus gave her a confused look and walked into his room and looked at his clock again. Still 8:47. He followed the clock cord to the wall with his eyes and saw that it was unplugged.

"Aaaw man!" Marcus yelled, throwing his clock on the bed. He rushed over to his dresser to try and find something to wear.

"What happened?" His mother asked from his doorway.

"My clock is unplugged."

"You think you can still make it?"

"Yeah if I hurry. If I don't, I have to wait until this summer to take it again. Can you drop me off?" Marcus said, snatching a quick outfit out of his dresser.

"Ok, hurry up I'll be outside." She said leaving his doorway to get her keys.

Marcus put on his clothes and grabbed his registration form off the dresser. He rushed to the living room and ran into his brother.

"Were you in my room this morning?" Marcus asked.

"Huh, nah. What do you mean? Nah." Alonzo said, sounding guilty.

Marcus leaned over and smelled Alonzo's neck.

"You been in my cologne again? If I wasn't in a hurry…" Marcus's sentence was interrupted by a honk from his mother's horn. She was already in the car and had it running. "I'll deal with you later." Marcus said, sprinting out the front door and over to his mother's car. It was 9:47 when they pulled out of the driveway and Mrs. Downing hurried off down the street. The school wasn't far, but it seemed like they caught every light on the way. Marcus didn't want to have to wait until after he graduated to take the test and risk not getting accepted to college right away. Like wise, Mrs. Downing didn't want him to miss his chance to start college. She had something to lose as well if Marcus didn't make it to this test. She wanted him to go off and have the college experience and everything like she never had the chance to, but she also wanted him out of the house so she only had one knucklehead to deal with. He was looking at education and life, but she was also looking at freedom.

They made it to the high school parking lot at 9:57 and Marcus bolted from the car before it even stopped moving.

"How you gettin' home!" His mother yelled from the open car door.

"I'll walk!" He yelled back, not even turning around or slowing his stride.

He ran to the first set of doors he saw and tried to open them, but they are locked. He ran to the next set and they were locked as well. Marcus started to panic but luckily he saw a janitor open a service door a few feet away. He yelled for the man to hold the door and rushed over to him. He explained that he was late for his test and the janitor let him in. Marcus ran down the hall toward the cafeteria but there was only one person in the foyer leading into the lunchroom. It was Lasaia. She couldn't even bring herself to walk through the doors without him. She was just in the hall, pacing back and forth, wringing her hands. She was so nervous she couldn't think straight and was on the verge of breaking into tears. She saw Marcus running up to her and her eyes lit up. He ran up to her and she threw her arms around his neck. He didn't realize how happy she was to see him. Marcus could feel her heart beating rapidly as her chest pressed against his. One of her teachers and a few other students had tried to talk her into going into the room but she couldn't walk through the doors, not without Marcus…her other half. She knew that she was facing getting kicked out of her house after she graduated. And, the test was the only way to guarantee a way for her to go *somewhere*. And, she knew that if she didn't take it that she was pretty much signing up for the newly homeless list, but she still couldn't walk into that room without him.

"What you still doing out here?" Marcus asked, as she released his neck.

"I couldn't go…I mean, I…"

Lasaia's words were cut short as her teacher stuck her head out of the door to try and coax her into the room one more time. She saw Marcus there and knew that he could probably talk some sense into her.

"Y'all come on in," Mrs. Banks whispered from the cracked door, "They are about to start."

The two of them walked through the door and Mrs. Banks led them to their seats. They sat down, listened to the instructions and started the test. After a few grueling hours of math, science and just plan analytical thought, the test was over and they had a nice walk home together.

Sixteen

The old friends laughed over the story and Lasaia said, "See you almost always came through every time I needed you. That's why I wanted to do this for you." The drunken Marcus finished off another drink they had ordered during the story and thought about what she just said.

"Almost? I always came through with what I said I would do." He said.

His speech was beginning to slur. He had clearly consumed his limit. Lasaia was feeling the effects of the liquor as well and had no problem saying what was on her mind.

"You did make things happen 99.99% of the time but I can't give you a perfect score because there was one *very* important promise that you didn't fulfill."

Marcus tried to think but his brain was not running at full capacity at this point.

"And what was that?" He asked.

Lasaia leaned forward to told him. She layered her hands on top of one another on the table in front of her and leaned forward not realizing that she was pressing her breasts against them making her cleavage even more noticeable. Marcus tried to look her in the eyes but his eyes started on her chest and slowly worked their way up. When Marcus finally made it to her face she was sitting there looking at him smiling and she started laughing. She knew what he was looking at and it was amusing that she caught him.

"What?" Marcus said, trying to play off the fact that he had just been caught looking down her shirt. He tried to change the subject by saying, "You gonna tell me what I didn't do or what?"

Lasaia just looked at him and said, "Not now, not here."

Marcus smiled and said, "Ok, well I'm gonna go to the bathroom. I'll be right back."

As he stood up from the table Lasaia said, "Hey, can I see your little girls again?"

"Of course, just call whenever you get to town and…"

Lasaia cut him off.

"No, no no," She said, laughing, "I mean your pictures."

"Oh." He said, laughing while he reached into his pocket.

He handed her his wallet and headed for the bathroom. On his way out Marcus looked at his watch. It was 11:50. They had been there for almost three hours and Marcus didn't even realize it. He walked back to the table after leaving the restroom and saw Lasaia sitting there watching the band. She looked over as he reached for his wallet that was sitting on the table.

"I had to stop looking at them. I started to get jealous," She said, giggling, "But for real, they are very beautiful girls."

"Thank you." Marcus said, taking his seat.

"I asked for the check. I'm getting a little tired. I hope you don't mind. Did you know it's almost midnight?" She said.

Yeah, I just saw that. Time just flew by. I didn't even realize it either. I was about to ask you if you were ready." He said, with a chuckle.

"I have never spent this much time in a club before."

"Well you know what they say, time flies when you're having fun."

"So you are having a good time with me?"

"Oh yeah, being a family man…I don't get to go out and just relax all that often. This was a much needed break."

"Well good."

The waitress that had been flirting with Marcus all night walked up, handed him the bill and walked off without saying a word.

"Now how does she know who's paying?" Lasaia said, offended.

That woman had been giving her the cold shoulder all night and she was being pushed to the limit. Marcus opened the bill wallet and a small piece of paper fell to the table. Marcus picked it up and unfolded it. The waitress had written him a note. Marcus's eyes slowly scanned the paper.

~

I know you don't know me and I don't know you, but when you walked in I felt that there was something between us. Maybe I'm crazy but since you said that the woman with you is just your friend I figured, What the hell? Anyway, if you are interested, you can come see me anytime. I'm usually here from 6–2 every

weekend or you can call me at 404-555-1134. I hope to hear from you soon.

After reading the letter Marcus let out a flattered smile.

"What is that?" Lasaia asked.

"Nothing." Marcus said, handing her the envelope.

The bill was $99.30 and Lasaia placed a $100 bill in the wallet and placed it on the table. She usually tipped big but the woman's attitude didn't make her feel very generous. They gathered their things and walked out of the club, headed for her car.

"What did that paper say that had you smiling all big?" Lasaia asked again, being nosey. Marcus figured it was safe to show her now that they had left the club. He took the note from his jacket pocket and handed it to her. The two of them stumbled back and forth in an intoxicated gait as Lasaia tried to open and read the note. She read the contents of the quarter page letter and said, "Oh, no she didn't. I told you she liked you."

Marcus just smiled and tried to stay vertical as they headed for her automobile. They had only been walking for about 30 seconds but it seemed like forever before they made it to the car. Lasaia made fun of the waitress as they made it around the bumper of her Jaguar. She reached in her purse to get her keys and slipped on a shallow puddle of water. She fell back into Marcus and he instinctively tried to catch her but he was off balance too and both of them toppled backwards to the ground. Lasaia landed on top of him and both of them laid there on their back looking up at the sky. There was a few seconds of silence before they couldn't help but to burst out laughing. There they were, two grown folks, laying down in a parking lot. Both of them face up, one on top of the other.

After a few seconds of all out laughter, Lasaia slowly climbed off of him and made it to her feet. Marcus climbed using the car bumper for support. They were both still laughing at what happened when Marcus asked, "You sure you can drive?"

"I don't know, I don't think I should." She said, between laughs.

They decided it would probably be better if they caught cabs home tonight and just worried about the car in the morning. They headed back out to the main street that ran in front of the club and were lucky enough to hail a cab immediately. He opened the door for his friend and she slowly made her way over.

Before she entered the cab she wrapped her arms around his neck and they shared a hug.

"It was great seeing you again." She said, kissing him on the cheek.

She climbed into the cab and closed the door.

Before the cab drove off, Lasaia rolled down the window and said, "You have enough money to get back to the hotel?"

"Yeah, I believe...um..." Marcus reached in his pocket and pulled out his wallet to check his funds. He opened it, looked in, then started patting his pockets and digging in all of them.

"What is it?" Lasaia said.

"My credit card is gone." He said, looking around, confused.

"What," she said, opening the door, "Are you sure you brought it?"

Marcus's mind wouldn't allow him to think past the last few hours and he just stood there going through his pockets again. Lasaia opened the door and told him to get in. Marcus knew there was no way he could find his card in his present state of mind and didn't want to be left somewhere, in a city where he had no idea where he was, without any money. He climbed into the cab and they drove off down the road.

Lasaia gave Marcus her cell phone. "What's this for?" He asked.

"So you can call and have your card deactivate. Just in case someone finds it, they can't use it."

Marcus hadn't even thought about that. He dialed the number from his palm pilot and was able to cancel the card and have a new one sent out. Luckily, there were no new transactions showing so if it was found it would just be a useless piece of plastic. After he handled his situation, Marcus looked out the front window of the cab and saw that they were in a nice neighborhood with large houses on both sides. Marcus wondered what they were doing in this ritzy downtown neighborhood at this time of night. The cab driver followed Lasaia's commands of left's and right's until she directed him to pull into the driveway of a beautiful home.

"Thank you so much," Lasaia said, handing the driver some money, "Keep the change."

She opened the door and stepped out of the car. Marcus was stuck in his seat, staring out of the front window at the huge house in front of him. *This couldn't possibly be where she lived*, he thought.

"You coming?" Lasaia asked, looking through the cab window.

"If he don't, I will." The old cab driver said, joking.

Lasaia giggled at the man's comment and Marcus finally opened the door and left the cab. The car backed out of the driveway and pulled off down the road as the two of them headed for the front door.

"This is your house?" Marcus asked, shocked.

"No, I just figured we could knock and ask if we can stay here for the night. Of course I live here. Just paid it off last year...finally." She said.

Marcus was astonished as she turned the key to the lock and they walked into the house.

The alarm system yelped out a long beep letting her know that she had a few seconds to put in the security code before the authorities would be on the way. Lasaia punched her code into a panel just inside the door and the system disarmed. "Welcome home Miss Lewis." A computerized voice spoke from the speaker.

"Damn." Marcus said, shocked at the new age technology. The inside was even more amazing than the outside. A beautiful marble foyer led to a pair of staircases that wrapped up the walls and met in the middle, leading to the upstairs area. On the upper level there was a U-shaped walkway that led to three different doors. One on either side, and two huge double doors in the middle. The rooms must have been huge, Marcus thought. Judging by the size of the house, if there were only three of them up there, they had to be gigantic. To his left was a large open den. There was a very large flat screen television mounted on the wall and furniture so beautiful he could tell it was expense from where he was standing. Beside the staircase on the right was a hallway, which Marcus could see led to the dining room and kitchen, and to his immediate right was another hallway, which looked like it led to more rooms. Marcus was amazed at how beautiful Lasaia's house was.

"You want another drink or a beer or something?" Lasaia asked as she walked into the house.

"Um, yeah sure. A beer would be fine." Marcus said, still shocked by his surrounding.

"Ok well have a seat in the den and I'll be right back."

Marcus walked to his left to the large den and was about to sit down when he remembered that they had fallen on the ground and didn't want to dirty up her furniture. He took off his jacket and laid it on the floor and had a seat on it with his back against the couch. A few seconds later Lasaia walked in with his beer and a glass of wine for herself.

"Boy, what are you doing on the floor?" She asked, looking down at him.

"I didn't want to get your furniture dirty from my clothes. My jacket's still dirty from the fall and…"

Lasaia cut him off and demanded that he sit with her on the couch. She turned on the television and they sat and watch for a few more minutes before Marcus remembered something.

"Oh ok, now you can tell me what I didn't do that I said I would." He said.

Lasaia laughed and took a sip from her drink. She was hoping that he would have asked her that.

"Ok, ok. You remember when I got accepted to Howard and you got accepted to Florida A & M?"

"Yeah."

"Do you remember the party we went to that your friend threw a few weeks before we left?"

"Yeah, the party Rick had. I remember."

Lasaia started the story about how the two of them had become more then just *friends* after prom. That was pretty much the beginning of their relationship. After prom the two of them moved from friends to girlfriend and boyfriend. There was a night that a friend of Marcus's had thrown a graduation party and invited the new couple. Rick's parents had gone out of town for the weekend and left their only son at home. Rick couldn't pass up the opportunity to have a little parental-less fun. Marcus and Lasaia arrived at the party and the yard was full of graduates blowing off steam. There was drinking and dancing and everything through the front door of the house. After a few drinks, and a couple dances, Marcus and Lasaia ended up in the kitchen.

"You having a good time?" The semi-drunk Marcus asked his girlfriend.

"Yeah." Lasaia said, smiling at her sweetheart.

She was actually having a good time in a place where, a few years earlier, she would have been too nervous to even move. Marcus had brought her out of the terrible world she knew as a young girl, and into a new and exciting world that she loved having him in.

A few minutes later a group of Marcus's teammates rushed into the kitchen. After a few yells and chants, Calvin, Marcus's old friend said, "Bruh, it's been a pleasure having you on the team, and since you the only senior, we gotta send you out with a bang. We know you gonna be down in Tallahassee knockin' down all types of scattered ass, but we gonna get you right tonight." His words were followed by a group yell from the other guys behind him. Marcus looked back at Lasaia and before he could say anything the boys grabbed him and pulled him out of the kitchen, causing him to drop the plastic cup he was holding. Lasaia was shocked at what Calvin was implying. She knew Calvin never really liked her, but she didn't know he would go to this extreme to get under her skin. They dragged Marcus through the house to the back, to the door leading to Rick's parents' room. They push him into the room and closed the door behind him. A few seconds later Samantha appeared out of nowhere and worked her way through the crowd of boys. Samantha was barely clothed with her mini skirt and half-shirt on. Her clothes were tight and showed no shame in displaying young but well developed figure. Samantha got to the door, opened it, and disappeared into the room. It was almost as if she had set the whole thing up, and she had. Lasaia had a look of shock on her face as the events unfolded in front of her eyes. As the boys heard the lock click they let out a final round of, "Oooooo", before going back to the party as if nothing happened.

The party pretty much went back to normal and everyone returned to having their fun, everyone except Lasaia. She just stood there petrified, peaking around the corner of the kitchen doorway. Her stronger half had been taken away from her and she didn't know what to do. She could only stand there staring at the door hoping that Marcus would emerge from the door any second. All she knew was her boyfriend was locked in a bedroom with another woman doing God only knew what. *Go open that door right now!,* Lasaia's voice told her in her head. But, she couldn't move. She just stood there too scared to go to the door and knock but too scared to leave her spot.

Inside the room, Marcus was standing there in front of the bed looking at Samantha. She walked over to him and didn't say a word. She put her hands on his cheeks, looked into his eyes and pressed her lips against his. Marcus pushed her back and said, "What are you doing?"

Samantha refused to give up and grabbed Marcus around his waist.

"Giving you your going away present." She said, trying to kiss him on the neck.

Marcus broke free again and pushed her back.

"You set this up?" He asked, anger in his voice.

"Yeah, I've been trying to get with you for the longest, but you're always with *that girl*."

"That girl is my girlfriend. Who else am I suppose to be with?"

"Me. You can't tell me you actually like that punching bag."

Samantha knew about Lasaia's abusive stepfather, everyone who had a pulse did. Marcus just looked at her with an appalled look on his face, not believing the fact that she just said that about his girlfriend. He tried to walk away from her and leave, but she grabbed him by the sleeve.

"No, Marcus wait." She said, pulling him back.

Marcus tried to snatch his arm free and his sleeve ripped. He looked back at her with anger on his face and she let go. She looked scared.

"I'm sorry…I…Marcus." She said as Marcus unlocked the door and opened it. He walked out of the room and slammed the door behind him. A few of the guys spot him come out and started chanting, "Marcus, Marcus, Marcus!"

They rushed over and slapped him five and gave him pounds like he had just made the winning shot in a championship game. Marcus instinctively accepted the praise and held out his hands, a smile on his face. Big mistake. Samantha walked out of the room and saw the group standing there. She looked over at Lasaia who was watching their every move and gave her a devilish smile. She walked over to Marcus, kissed him on the cheek and walked out the front door. It all happened so fast that Marcus didn't have time to react. The boys went wild again, chanting and cheering for him. Marcus looked over to the kitchen doorway and saw Lasaia standing there watching everything. She couldn't believe that he was in there with that girl and claimed to love her and be her boyfriend. Her feelings finally overwhelmed her. She ran from the kitchen, out the front door, into the night air. She didn't want anyone to see the tears as they fell. Marcus saw her retreat and made his way through the crowd to go after her.

He made it to the porch and looked around the yard, trying to see where she could have gone. A few seconds later he saw a lone figure walking up the street in the dark. He darted from the porch and through the front fence yelling, "Lasaia!"

He called out to her as he ran but she didn't stop. After a few calls, she turned around and saw him running to her. She turned back to the road in front of her and started to run away from him. She could barely see through her tears but she ran with everything she had left. Marcus poured on more speed and she was unable to out run him. He got in front of her and stopped. He put his hands on her shoulders and made her look at him.

"Where are you going?" He asked.

Lasaia pushed his hands off of her and said, "I figured you wanted to be alone with your new girlfriend."

She could barely control her sobbing but was able to get the words out.

"What are you talking about," He said, "Nothing happened."

Lasaia started to go from upset to angry. She thought he was trying to insult her intelligence.

"Then why is your shirt ripped, why do you have lipstick on your lip, and why do you smell like her then, if nothing happened, huh," She asked, rage built in her voice, "Obviously you weren't in there playing Twister. Or, maybe you were."

"Nothing happened. I swear. She tried to kiss me, I pushed her away. I tried to leave and she grabbed my shirt and ripped it. That's it. We were only in there for like 2 minutes." Marcus said giving her a brief synopsis.

Lasaia wanted to believe him. He was the only person that knew her the way he did and she didn't want to lose him.

"You swear to me that you didn't do anything?" She asked.

"Yes, nothing. I never want to hurt you."

"Promise me that you didn't do anything." She said.

"I just said I didn't..."

Marcus was cut off.

"Just...promise me." She said, closing her eyes.

"Ok, I promise. I promise on my granddaddy grave I didn't touch her." He said, seeing that she was willing to hear his side.

Lasaia took a deep breath and opened her eyes. It wasn't until he said he promised that she could believe him.

He had never let her down when he graced his sentences with those words.

"Ok, but I don't want to go back." She said.

"Me neither. It was lame anyway." Marcus said.

"What do you want to do?" Lasaia asked.

"I know where we can go." He said leading Lasaia through the dimly lit back streets.

She had no idea where they were going but she felt safe as long as he was there.

After about an hour of walking they ended up on the street next to the school. Marcus led her to the softball field and they had a seat in the dugout. They talked about how weird it was going to feel not to be in Albany the next year. Neither of them really liked high school while they were going but now that they were leaving, a piece of each of them wished they could stay. They talked about all their different experiences and what they would miss. Then Marcus said, "You know what I'm gonna miss most?"

"What?" She said, moving the dirt on the ground around with her foot.

"You."

She looked at her boyfriend and was astounded. He had never really switched into the *boyfriend* mode. Of course, he would hold her hand and they would kiss, but he was never big on conversations dealing with his feelings. To her he was just the same old sweet, caring Marcus. Lasaia was at a loss for words. Someone was actually going to miss her. She didn't even think that her mother was going to miss her when she was gone.

"I'm gonna miss you too." She said, smiling.

Marcus just looked deep into her eyes without saying a word. He slowly leaned forward and kissed her on the lips. That first kiss turned into a second and a third, until the two of them had worked themselves into a frenzy that ended with Lasaia on Marcus's lap and his hand up her shirt.

"No, no, no…stop." She said, reluctantly.

Marcus looked up at her, disappointment on his face.

"What's wrong?" He asked.

She climbed off of his lap and sat down beside him.

"I don't know. This just doesn't feel right." She said.

"What doesn't?"

"This. This whole situation. I mean…I…I have never done this before and…"

Marcus figured she was a virgin. He had never seen her around many guys, but he didn't know for sure until she spoke the words.

"I mean I want to, but not like this. Out here in the open." She finished.

Marcus understood that she wanted her first time to be special and even he wanted their first time to mean something.

"I want you to promise me something though." She said.

"What?"

"I love you a lot. I have always loved you. And, since we are going off to different places in a few weeks I want you to promise me that you will be my first."

"First what? Oh, oooohh." Marcus said figuring out what she was talking about.

Lasaia giggled at him.

"Yeah, I promise. Definitely." He said, fumbling over his words, trying to hurry them out before she changed her mind.

Lasaia's smile widened as she wrapped her arms around his neck and kissed him on the cheek.

"Come on, let's get outta here." He said.

They stood to their feet, exited the dugout and left the field. They took the back roads and were home in about fifteen minutes. Marcus, being a gentleman, walked his lady to her porch. They gave each other a goodnight kiss and

Lasaia went inside. It was around midnight when Marcus walked into his house. His parents had long gone to bed since they had to work in the morning and Alonzo was asleep on the couch. Marcus walked to his room and flopped down on his bed and slowly drifted off to sleep.

Lasaia ended her story with a sip of her wine. Marcus sat there on the couch beside her stunned. He had forgotten about the last part of that evening, including his promise. Lasaia just looked at him and said, "Mmh Hmm, see…99.99%"

She stood to her feet while Marcus continued trying to register what she just reminded him of.

"You want another one?" She asked, referring to his empty beer.

"Huh, oh yeah, sure" He said, snapping back into reality.

Lasaia grabbed his empty bottle and walked toward the foyer.

"It's gonna be a minute, I'm gonna go change outta this outfit." She said, leaving the den.

Marcus was so far in thought that he didn't even hear her. Until that moment he had always seen their entire friendship/relationship as perfect. He remembered himself as always doing what he said he would. It wasn't that big of a deal, but it did bother him that he really wasn't how he thought he was.

Marcus waited for a while for Lasaia who seemed to have disappeared. He pulled his wallet from his pocket and removed his daughter's artwork. He still had it from his first visit to Atlanta. He saw that same strange wilderness scene. Red ducks, a green fox, and blue grass. Marcus smiled as he read her message in the sky again.

I love you daddy

Marcus sat there staring at the picture for 5 more minutes before Lasaia finally walked back into the room.

As she walked in Marcus looked up at her and his eyes grew large in their sockets. She had changed clothes but what she had on wasn't modest by any means. She had on the exact outfit that he dreamed her in that night they had sex in his kitchen. She stepped over to him and handed him a glass and said, "That was the last beer so I made you a drink instead. You want it?"

"Yeah." Marcus said, trying to play off the fact that he was just ogling her.

She reached out to hand him the drink and saw the picture in his lap.

"What's that?" she asked, sitting close to him, her breast pressed against his shoulder.

"Oh, this is a picture my little girl colored for me before I came to Atlanta the last time."

"Let me see." She said, looking over his shoulder.

She laughed at the scene and said, "Awwww, see that's what I want. Someone little that loves me like that."

Marcus really was lucky to have his family. Not everyone was fortunate to have the things he had.

Seventeen

Marcus and Lasaia sat on the couch sipping their drinks when Lasaia said, "Hey, you know what I remember?" She started laughing before she could get the whole question out.

"What?" Marcus said, chuckling with her, not even knowing what he was laughing at.

He was just laughing because she was laughing, and probably even more so because he was drunk. Lasaia took his daughter's artwork from his hand and placed it on the end table.

"I left out the best part of the story. You remember what happened later that night, after you left my house?"

He thought for a minute.

"Ooooh," He said, knowing exactly what she was laughing at now.

Marcus reminisced about that night.

He had fallen asleep quickly after getting in the bed that night. He was brought out of his slumber by a light tapping sound. He slowly rose and propped himself up on his elbows. He looked around the dark room wondering where the noise was coming from.

"Marcus!"

He heard an exclaimed whisper from over by his window. He rubbed his eyes and tried to focus on who was calling to him. He saw Lasaia's head and shoulders at the bottom of his window looking into his room. He jumped out of the bed, rushed over to the window and opened it.

"What's wrong?" He asked, thinking there must have been a problem.

She had never shown up at his window like that.

"Nothing. My mom and her husband are gone. You wanna come over?" She asked.
Her words were laced with a nervous overtone.
Marcus smiled and said, "Sure, I'll be out in a minute".

He closed the window and walked back through his silent house. He had just left her house a little over an hour earlier. Alonzo was still knocked out in front of the television as Marcus walked through the kitchen and out the back door. He greeted his girlfriend with a kiss and they crossed into her backyard, hand in hand. They got to the back door and entered the house. The two of them walked over the old hardwood floor in silence, into the only bedroom with a light on, her room.
They had a seat on the bed.
Lasaia looked sad and Marcus didn't understand why.
"What's wrong?" He asked.
"Nothing. I was just here by myself. I was lonely." She told him.
She lay her head on his shoulder and they sat in silence for a few seconds. Marcus figured there was more to this than what she was giving up but he didn't know what to say to get her to open up.
Lasaia finally said, "Marcus, do you love me?"
"Of course." He said, without hesitation.
Lasaia raised her head from his shoulder and looked into his eyes.

She had a look of fear on her face and Marcus asked her again, "What's going on?" She just sat there in silence for a few seconds with her head down then looked back at him with a little more courage on her face.
"Ok…well, I want you to have something. It's something that I have been saving for, like forever, and I said I would only give it to someone I love and who loves me." She said, her eyes glued to his.
She stood up before Marcus could ask what she was talking about and walked over to her dresser. He had no idea what she had to give him but he just waited patiently to find out. She reached on top of her dresser and turned on a small boom box radio. She flipped through a few channels and stopped on a station that played all R & B classics.

As Teddy P. crooned his melody through the small speakers, she followed his instructions. She immediately walked over and turned off the light. And, if she had one, she would have lit a candle. The room went completely dark. The only light was from the moon coming through her window. Marcus started to realize that what she wanted to give him was not a watch or a new shirt or anything like that…it was much more, something special. Tonight, she wanted him to follow through on his promise. She started to walk over toward him. In the darkness, she tripped over her book bag and stumbled forward, into his lap. Marcus caught her in his arms and the two of them fell back onto the bed. They laughed at that for a few seconds before silence surrounded them again. This wasn't the uncomfortable silence you felt when you were in an elevator with a group of strangers or sitting in a small doctor's office.

Words weren't needed.

Their hearts had been carrying on this conversation for years.

Lasaia lay there on top of him, looking down, trying to focus her eyes in the darkness. As soon as she was able to make him out, she lowered her head, kissing his lips. They shared several romantic smooches before she decided it was time to take the session to the next level. Even though he was more experienced in this realm, Marcus didn't try to take charge, he just followed her lead. He knew she was already scared out of her mind for even going this far, even though she was playing it cool. She slowly raised her body off him and he followed her. She sat in his lap and pulled his shirt over his head. She began kissing his neck and chest, softly, teasing him with her tongue.

A few minutes and many kisses later, the two of them were completely naked and under her covers. They hadn't done anything yet, Lasaia was just lying there on top of him as they made out. She removed her lips from his and sat on top of him, looking down.

"You sure you're ready for this?" He asked.

His body wanted her, badly, but he would have waited, if she changed her mind.

She nodded her head and returned to kissing him. Marcus was just about to enter her when they heard the front door open and shut. Both of them jumped up and looked at her closed bedroom door. Her mother would surely hear the music and come in. They heard one set of footsteps get closer then turn into her mother's room. The two of them sat there quietly as they heard the muffled conversation of her mother and stepfather. They had returned from wherever they had gone and were less then 20 feet away from the two naked teenagers.

"Oh shit, get up." Marcus whispered, trying to nudge Lasaia off his lap.

She climbed off him and he tiptoed around the room, trying to find all of his clothes. He gathered all of his things under his arm and rushed to the window, struggling to open it. It wouldn't move at first, but then, all of a sudden, it flew open and made a loud screeching noise before banging into the top of the window frame. At that exact moment, Lasaia's mother was about to walk into her room with her husband.

She hadn't heard the music.

If the two of them had waited another 20 minutes, Marcus would have been able to walk right out the front door and neither of the drunken pair would have been conscious to see him.

But, she heard the sound of the window come from her daughter's room and wondered what was going on. Marcus made it outside, a naked Lasaia wrapped in her comforter, standing by the open window.

"I'll see you tomorrow, ok?" He said, giving her a quick peck on the cheek.

As their lips separated, they heard Lasaia's inebriated mother fumbling with the knob. Marcus ran from the window as Lasaia rushed over and jumped into her bed. Mrs. Jones got into the room only a second after the sheets had settled from her daughter's dive into the bed. She walked into the dark room and looked around to find out what the noise was. She looked over and saw the open window and figured the noise must have came from outside. She walked over and reached up to close the window. As she was looking through the glass, she caught a glimpse of what looked like a naked man run around the corner of her neighbor's house. She figured it was just the alcohol distorting her reality and closed the window. She looked over at her sleeping daughter and smiled.

"Woman, what the hell you doin'?" A deep commanding voice came from down the hall. Mrs. Jones just rolled her eyes, sighed a tired sigh and walked out of the room, closing the door on her way out. Lasaia had to cover her face with a pillow to keep her mother from hearing her laugh.

The two of them sat in the beautiful den of Lasaia's home and laughed about that night.

"I wish I could have seen you running naked through the yard." Lasaia said, laughing.

"You should have seen my Alonzo's face when I walked in the backdoor with my clothes in my hands." Marcus said, joining in on the laughter.

"And I think my mom saw you, but she was too drunk to know what you were." Lasaia said.

They laughed together for a few more seconds, then, silence. Lasaia took another sip from her drink and looked at Marcus.

"See, told you…99.99%."

She giggled.

Marcus chuckled with her.

She took the final sip of her drink and asked, "You wanna see the house?"

"Sure".

The two of them stood and headed out of the den. They walked back into the foyer and Lasaia showed him her two downstairs guest rooms, her office, the dining room, and the kitchen. Lasaia placed the glass in the sink and asked, "You want another one?"

Marcus had already had way too much, but against his better judgment he said, "Yeah, why not."

Lasaia quickly mixed him another drink and they headed out of the kitchen and over to the stairs. They walked upstairs and Lasaia showed him her other two guest bedrooms. These rooms were located on both sides of the walkway at the top of the steps. They were huge. They looked like a suite at a 5-star hotel. Plush furniture and bedding, each had their own bathroom and huge window that looked over the neighboring houses. Even though they were immaculately kept, they, like the downstairs guest rooms, didn't look like they had been touched in quiet some time. It was clear that Lasaia didn't have many visitors. After leaving the second room, the two of them made their way to the middle doors.

"And now, ta-daaaa…" She said, throwing open the doors.

It was Lasaia's bedroom, and it was exquisite. There was another 50" flat screen television mounted on the wall, across from her huge king-sized canopy bed, which looked like it came straight out of medieval times. The ceilings were at least 15 feet high and vaulted. There was a beautiful couch that sat by a gigantic picture window with a view of a lake behind her house. She had a full professional makeup area and Marcus couldn't see much of the bathroom but it looked like it was about half the size of the bedroom. The whole room looked like a picture out of *Good Housekeeping* magazine. It was so big it actually looked like another den, except there was a bed in it. The drunken Marcus walked around the room admiring the layout and stopped at the foot of the bed. He looked back at Lasaia and said, "This is beautiful."

As he continued to look around, she walked over in front of him, took his drink out of his hand and said, "You wanna make it 100?"

The intoxicated Marcus was confused, but before he could say anything she placed her hands on his cheeks and kissed him. He didn't resist her and they stood there kissing for a few seconds. She removed her lips from his, downed the rest of his drink and threw the glass to the floor. She pushed Marcus back onto the bed and climbed into his lap. On any other day, her small frame could never have toppled Marcus's physique; but with the amount of alcohol he running through his blood, it was amazing that he was still able to hold himself up. She leaned down and began to kiss him on his neck. The feeling of her soft lips against his skin began to turn Marcus on but before he got too deep into the act he pushed her up by her shoulders and asked, "What are you doing?"

"Just helping you keep your promise.", She said, going in for another kiss. Marcus held her back.

"But my promise was to be your first. You're not still a virgin, are you?"

Lasaia sat there on his lap with her hands on his chest looking down at him for a few seconds, and then said, "Yes, I am."

A puzzled look formed on Marcus's face. "Wait, wait, wait." He said as he sat up and pushed her off his lap. Lasaia stretched out on her luxurious bed, her knees in the air, slowly rubbing her thighs."

"So you have never had sex before…ever?" He asked.

"Nope."

"No oral no nothing?"

"Nope."

"Not even a little…"

Marcus made a motion with his finger and she knew exactly what he meant.

"I could do that myself." She laughed.

"Why?"

Lasaia got up off the bed and stood in front of him, her belly button lined up perfectly with his eyes.

"Because *you* promised to be my first and I wasn't gonna let anything ruin that. I knew, that if I waited, one day you would come back and keep that promise…like you always did. And, here you are," She said, followed by a moment of silence, "You promised me hundreds of things before, and you always came through, every time. I knew all I had to do was wait and you would come back to me. And here you are. That's how I know it was destiny that we ran into each other."

She placed her hands on his shoulders. Lowered her self a little, and began kissing his lips again. Marcus knew that what was going on was wrong but he couldn't resist her. He found the strength to finally push her back.

"But, I'm married now." He said.

"She doesn't have to know. I'm over 400 miles away. This can be our little secret," Lasaia continued to kiss him as she whispered in his ear, "Please, I need this…I need you. If I can't have you, at least give me this."

Marcus knew he needed to stop this, right now, but he couldn't. It was like she had cast some kind of spell over him. This time was much worse than the times before. There was no threat of any interruption. At Alonzo's, they had to be careful. At his house, they had to be careful. But, now they were all alone. Marcus couldn't restrain that side of him that was crying out for the love of this woman. His lust, coupled with the alcohol, caused Marcus's thought process to void out any logical thoughts and all he could think about was how good it felt to have her in his arms again.

Lasaia climbed into his lap, again. This time his strong arms squeezed her closer instead of pushing her away.

She had him.

He stopped resisting and gave into her temptation. She ripped his shirt open, sending his buttons flying to the floor. Their unrestrained passion seemed to seep from their pores and fill the room with the scent of desire. They had hungered for each other, and the encounter brought out feelings that they had never felt for anyone else. Lasaia could feel him begin to grow between her legs as she started to gyrate in his lap. Her shorts were so thin that she could feel the rubbing of his penis against her clitoris. It was a feeling that she was unfamiliar with but it felt amazing. Marcus reached around and placed both of his hands on her butt and squeezed. He moved his hand in rhythm with her motions and his added pressure caused deeper sensations to shoot through her. She felt a tingling sensation begin to build up in her pelvis. She didn't know what it was, but it started to get stronger and stronger. Lasaia's moans got louder and that turned Marcus on even more. She didn't have to suppress herself now, she didn't have to hold back. He started to move her body harder and faster against him. The tingle became more and more intense until she felt an electric vibe shoot through her entire body and she began to shake, uncontrollably. Her screams could be heard echoing through the house. It was her first orgasm. She knew exactly what happened but didn't know it felt that good. She just laid her head on his chest, breathing heavily.

After she had a few seconds to recoup, her breathing slowed. She lifted her head off his chest and looked at him. For a brief moment, they were back in her room at her mother's house, late at night, before her parents got home. Marcus began to run his hands up and down her back, lightly tickling her skin with his fingertips. Lasaia closed her eyes and smiled, enjoying his tease. Really, she just enjoyed feeling his touch. After a few seconds, Lasaia started back after him. He had given her an orgasm, but she still had her virginity. That was what she wanted him to have. She began kissing him on his chest and reached between her legs, stroking his penis. Marcus could tell that she didn't know exactly what to do. He took over and pulled her hand from between his legs and sat up. He grabbed the small shirt that she had on and pulled it up over her head. Her beautiful hair fell onto her bare back and reached just above her breasts in the front. Her body was as perfect as a woman's body could be. Marcus began to suck on her large breasts, which turned Lasaia on even more. Her unrestricted moans ricocheted off the walls around them, filling the room with the sounds of pleasure. Lasaia flinched every time Marcus would nibble on her nipple. The feeling was new and strange to her. Marcus grabbed her by her wrists and wrapped her arms behind her back, causing her to push her chest forward. She had nowhere to run now. Marcus bombarded her chest with a barrage of kisses, licks, and sucks. She loved it.

"Wait…wait…," she whispered, causing him to stop.

He released her from her capture and she stood up in front of him. She began to take off her shorts when Marcus stopped her. He pulled her closer to him as he moved to the edge of the bed. Marcus removed her hands from her shorts and began to slowly remove them, kissing her waist as he pulled them down. The middle of her shorts were soaked with her juices. The feeling of his lips in that area tickled and she let out a short erotic giggle. Marcus worked her shorts down her legs to her ankles. She lifted one leg out of the shorts and kicked them to the side with the other. Marcus rubbed and squeezed her backside as he kissed her around her belly button. Lasaia stopped giggling and started to moan again.

It was time to stop playing games.

He was ready.

He pulled down his pants, guided her into his lap again. After the exchange of several kisses, Marcus slowly moved backward until they were completely on the bed. Then, he flipped her over and started kissing her on her neck. He slowly worked his way down to her chest and after a few quick kisses on her breasts, he moved down to her stomach. Lasaia's nipples were erect and every kiss made a new sound escape from her mouth. Marcus gave her a few quick licks and kisses on her stomach before he packed up and headed even further south. He slowly flicked his tongue back and forth several times across her clitoris. This quickly worked Lasaia into a frenzy. She grabbed the back of his head and started to scream. It wasn't long before Lasaia felt the tingling begin to build again. This time she knew what it was and thought she was ready for it. But this time the feeling was more intense, no clothes blocked her sensation. Marcus felt her begin to tense up and start to shake in his arms.

She had come again.

That one felt even better then the first.

Marcus wanted to feel her. He slowly worked his way back on top. He reached between his legs and grabbed his penis. He probed it around her opening, slowly pushing in. It took a few several attempts before he was able to enter her. Her tightness was a combination of virginity and anxiety. She had never had one in there before, and his size didn't help matters much. She was only able to get halfway in at first but his long, slow strokes ignited another tingle in her pelvis. As another orgasm visited her loins, she finally moistened up enough for him to slide all the way in. It was pleasure and pain at the same time

She loved it.

Marcus began to stroke her slowly at first, then sped up after he figured she was ready. Her screams of passion flew from her mouth as Marcus moved in and out of her. This was what she had longed for all these years.

After he made her come again, he rolled over and let her take over. Lasaia didn't know what to do, but she began to move her waist in his lap. With every move she made she could feel Marcus's rock hard penis shift inside her. She felt what seemed like an electric surge shoot through her body with the slightest motion. Marcus let her wiggle in his lap for a few minutes while he rested, then he started to move the two of them to the edge of the bed. He put his feet to the floor and sat up, Lasaia still doing her thing. He grabbed her by her bottom and stood up. Lasaia felt like he was pushing into her chest as he held her in his arms and began to stroke in and out. Marcus made his way over to her couch by her window and lay her down on her back while he got on his knees. He began to pound his penis inside of her. It was almost like he was trying to hurt her. Marcus was so overcome with his passion for her that he forgot that she was just a virgin only minutes ago. Lasaia didn't care, his aggressiveness turned her on even more and she had forgotten all about the pain. Marcus turned her around and entered her from behind. Lasaia threw her face into a pillow as Marcus moved in and out of her. She felt another one coming, and so did he. They both came, the final time, together. Neither of them had felt a level of ecstasy this great. Even crack heads were envious of this level of high. He kissed her back.

Like he had done with his wife so many times before.

The two of them just lay there, resting, unable to move.

Their deep breathing was the only sound.

After a few seconds, Marcus pulled out of her and she turned to him. No words were exchanged, just deep, sensual kissing. After they finished their game of tongue hockey, Lasaia fell back against the couch. She looked as if she had passed out. Her breasts rose and fell as she took in deep breaths of air. Marcus leaned down and began sucking her nipple. She flinched. He knew she was done for the night. He picked her up, walked her over to her bed, and set her down. Lasaia instinctively climbed under the covers and was asleep before Marcus could say a word. He stood there, looking at her. The woman he had loved so many years ago. The woman he thought had been his perfect match. The woman he had just probably ruined his current life for.

Against his better judgment, Marcus climbed into the bed next to her.

Eighteen

Forty-five minutes later, Marcus's eyes opened. Lasaia was lying on his chest with her arm and leg draped across him. The effects of the alcohol had finally worn off. He lay there with tears falling from his eyes. He was beginning to realize the true horror about what he had just done. He had put his life, as he knew it, in jeopardy. That short episode could cost him everything in the world that he knew, and loved. He could lose his wife and kids, who were everything to him. Marcus began to panic and tried to finagle his way out of the bed. At first, he tried to slowly slide his body from under her, but when he moved, she moved right along with him. She was still asleep and he didn't want to wake her, so he gave up on that. He tried lightly tickling her but that only made her giggle in her sleep. He gave up on that idea and decided he was just going to wake her up. He tapped her on the shoulder until she woke up.

"Hey, I need to use the bathroom." He said, thinking quickly.

She rolled over and was asleep again before he got out of the bed. Marcus scurried around the room, picking up his clothes, then disappeared into the bathroom. He hurried to put on his clothes and opened the bathroom door. He slowly and softly walked back into the room. Lasaia was still unconscious in the bed. Marcus checked to make sure he had all his things before tiptoeing across the huge room and over to the door leading to the foyer. He lightly turned the knob, keeping his eye on the bed. He opened it enough to slip through the crack and peeked inside the room one last time before closing it. He made his way down the stairs and into the den. He could barely see in the dark house and stumbled a few times before finding the phone. Luckily, there was a phone book under the phone and he was able to call a cab to come get him. He gave them her address off a magazine on the coffee table and hung up the phone.

As he paced back and forth, waiting on the cab, Marcus realized he didn't have any money to pay the driver. Marcus spotted Lasaia's purse on the floor by the couch and rushed over to get it. He reached into the purse and fumbled around looking for some money. He found her wallet and took it out. As he snatched it out a bunch of her things fell to the floor. Some makeup, a couple dollars, her cell phone and one of her credit cards. He swore under his breath and quickly began gathering her things. As he got everything back into her purse he looked at the credit card. It wasn't one of her cards, it was his! The one he *thought* he had lost at the club. But how did it get there? Why didn't she tell him she found it? And why didn't she…

Marcus's thought process stopped and everything began to come together. Every event since the time the two of them saw each other had been aimed at the act that he just committed. The episode at Alonzo's house, having that gay man pose as her boyfriend to get on Sherise's good side, spending all that time with Sherise at the model call, taking him out for a so called *friendly* evening, stealing his credit card so he couldn't get back to the hotel, then getting him drunk enough to submit to her will.

It was all a plan.

But when could she have gotten it, it was in his wallet. He had his wallet all night, except when…

The Bathroom.

Marcus remembered that the only time his wallet was not in his pocket was when he gave it to her before he went to the bathroom. She didn't want to see his daughters; she wanted to complete her plan.

And, why would she tell him to get into her cab instead of just giving him a couple dollars to get to his hotel. Why would she bring him to her house instead of telling the cab driver to drop him off first? Marcus felt betrayed at the fact that she would stoop to such a level of deceit, but he couldn't blame her. He was as much a part of the whole act as she was. He was just as responsible as she was, but he had much more to lose then she did. What would Sherise do if she found out? What would happen to his little girls? To his entire family? Questions began to flood Marcus's head.

As he stood there in a daze thinking about all of the horrible effects his act could have on his life, he saw two headlights pull into the driveway. He jumped to his feet, shoved the card in his pocket and rushed to the door before the driver honked. He didn't want Lasaia to wake up. He opened the front door and rushed out to the car.

"You call a cab, buddy?" The driver asked.

"Yeah, um, do you take credit cards?" Marcus asked.

"Yeah sure, I just gotta run it first." The driver said.

Marcus gave the driver his card and the driver called it in. Marcus nervously looked back at the house every few seconds hoping the activity in the driveway wasn't enough to wake the sleeping Lasaia. The driver got a response and told Marcus that his card had been declined. Marcus had completely forgotten that he had called and had the card terminated after he thought it was lost.

"Ok, hold on. I'll be right back," Marcus said, turning and jogging back to the house.

He slowly opened the front door and quickly stepped back over to Lasaia's purse. He grabbed her wallet and all she had was three crisp $100 bills. Marcus took one of the bills and rushed back to the door. He locked and closed the door behind him before jumping into the backseat of the cab.

Marcus sat in the back of the cab with his head back against the seat, eyes closed. He looked like an expensive hobo. His suit was wrinkled, his shirt was open from all the buttons being ripped off, and his clothes were still a little dirty from the fall earlier. All kinds of questions flooded his mind as he rode back to his hotel.

What should he do?

Should he tell his wife?

Should he try to forget it all happened?

What would he do without his family?

Marcus was extremely disappointed in himself. He mulled over the whole situation all the way to the hotel. He gave the cab driver the whole $100 bill and jumped out. His ride only cost $12.89 but at that point he didn't care about the money. He walked through the front sliding door of the hotel. The front desk girl, who checked him in was at work and she looked at Marcus with a raised eyebrow. He walked through the lobby, eyes focused in front of him, over to the elevator. He made it to his room and pulled his card out of his pocket. He couldn't stop thinking about how stupid he was for falling for her trick. Of course, she was beautiful, an old friend, and he did fantasize about her, and he did promise her but all of that meant nothing. He made an even bigger promise to his wife in front of a church full of people and God, that she would be the only one for the rest of his life. Now, that promise was broken and there was nothing that he could do to change that.

It was almost five in the morning when Marcus turned the shower knob in the bathroom. Marcus was able to wash away the dirt from his body but he couldn't wash away his thoughts. He wished he could let that warm water flow through his ear and take away that pain he felt inside. He got out of the shower and walked over by the bed. He lay on his back, towel around his waist, staring at the ceiling. He couldn't get the images of Lasaia out of his mind. Different scenes flashed in front of him over and over again. He could still see the look of ecstasy that she had on her face as clearly as when it happened. He was upset that he actually wanted to have sex with her. Marcus lay there for a few hours, thinking about the situation he had put himself in. His whole life was different now. He had been up for nearly 20 hours, but the thoughts streamed through his mind every time he closed his eyes. Sleep wasn't happening, not tonight.

Around 8:00 a.m., Marcus couldn't take it any longer and got up. He packed up all of his things and rushed downstairs. He walked around to the front counter and checked out, then went outside and jumped into his rental car. He drove to the airport, turned in his vehicle and headed for the check-in counter. Marcus needed to get out of Atlanta. As long as he was there he wouldn't be able to think. Even though he wasn't supposed to leave until Sunday, he couldn't stay in that room for one more minute. He felt as if he had failed in his job, then in his marriage. Marcus wished he had a remote control like Adam Sandler in that movie, Click. He would rewind everything, all the way up to that night at the Waffle House. If he had it to do over, with the knowledge he had now, he wouldn't even stop at that diner. He would have rather stayed lost that night and drove all the way back to Jacksonville. At least that way he would have never run into her. He wouldn't have had the chance to make the worst mistake of his life.

He didn't want to think about it anymore but nothing else came to mind.

It was all he thought about.

And, every time he thought about it, a new knot was tied it self in his stomach.

After a brief incident at the counter, Marcus was able to get a boarding pass and headed for his gate. Since his ticket was for the following day, the clerk didn't want to honor it until then. Marcus demanded to speak with the manager and was able to get his flight switched. He made it to his gate and had a seat to wait for his flight to be called. They called his flight number and he boarded the plane. After a short flight, Marcus landed in Jacksonville. He claimed his bags and jumped into a cab in front of the airport. The cab pulled into his driveway around 11:45. After getting some cash from inside and going back out to pay the driver, Marcus was *finally* home. Being home almost made him feel better, but not much.

The house was silent.

Sherise had taken the kids out for the day. Marcus took his things up to his room and put them away. He was so exhausted that he could barely stand. He had gotten less then an hour of sleep in the last 25 hours and his body couldn't take much more. He changed into something more comfortable and jumped onto his bed. His bed was the best feeling he had felt in the last few days. Marcus was able to finally get some rest, but it wasn't peaceful. The only thing that he could think about was his act of infidelity. He woke up several times, but the final time was around 4:30. He couldn't take the dreams anymore and climbed out of the bed. He walked down to the kitchen and poured himself a drink. He heard the garage door open as he was putting away his juice. A few minutes after, he heard the most beautiful sounds in the world, the voices of his wife and children. The door to the garage opened.

"Daaaadddiieee." Lasaia said running over to him when she saw him standing in the kitchen. Marcus knelt down and scooped her up into his arms.

"Hey, baby girl."

Sherise walked in with a pizza box and some rental movies in her hands followed by another little person.

"Heeeey, baby!" She said, walking over and putting the pizza and movies down on the kitchen island.

She wrapped her arms around his neck and gave him a kiss.

Marcus could barely look her in the eyes. He felt like he didn't deserve to be with her after what he had done. Marcus put his little girl down and she looked back up at him, oddly. She has a perplexed look on her face, as if she wanted to say something but didn't know what words to use.

Something just wasn't right to her.

"Baby, take your sister in the living room for me, please." Sherise said, to Lasaia.

The two little girls walked out of the kitchen and disappeared around a corner. Sherise waited for them to leave then turned to her husband and threw her hands around his neck, again. After a few kisses she said, "Couldn't stay away, huh?"

Marcus laughed.

She released him and walked over to one of the kitchen cabinets. She took out some plates and got some pizza for the girls. Marcus just stared at his beautiful wife unable to understand how he could risk doing anything that could possibly jeopardize their relationship.

Marcus knew he needed to tell her.

He wanted to tell her.

He wanted to just get it out, let her yell, and get through it.

But, he knew that it wouldn't be that easy. He wished he could just forget it ever happened.

They took some of the pizza to the girls and they all had a family dinner watching the movies Sherise had rented. About half way through the second movie Lasaia stood up from her spot on the floor. She walked over to the couch where her parents were sitting, stood in front of them. She looked at Marcus with the same strange look she gave him in the kitchen, then climbed into Sherise's lap, resting her head on her shoulder.

"What did you do to her?" Sherise whispered, giggling.

Lasaia would usually sit with her father during the movies, but today she chose Sherise instead. Marcus just shrugged his shoulders and reached over grabbed his wife's hand.

After the movie was over, Marcus said, "Come on girls", signaled them to get up for bath time. Angela jumped up and ran to her daddy's arms, mouth wide with a smile.

Lasaia didn't move.

She stayed in Sherise's lap.

Marcus stood up with Angela in his arms and started walking out of the family room. Lasaia still hadn't moved.

"Come on, Lasaia". Marcus said.

Lasaia looked at her mother and said, "I want you to give me a bath, mommy."

"Baby, your daddy can give you a bath. He…"

Sherise was cut short.

"Nooooo. I want you to do it." Lasaia said almost whispering.

Sherise saw the sincerity in her daughter's eyes and looked over to Marcus.

"I'll get her, you two go ahead." Marcus turned and left the family room and started up the steps to get his little one ready for bed. Sherise and Lasaia sat on the couch for about another minute before Sherise said, "You wanna help mommy with the dishes?"

Lasaia seemed like a whole new person and jumped out of her mother's lap and picked up her plate. They gathered the dishes and headed to the kitchen. Sherise ran some dishwater, then filled the other sink with some cool water. Lasaia was in charge of rinsing. Sherise pulled a chair from the breakfast table and put it against the sink. Lasaia climbed into the chair and the two of them had a good time washing dishes together.

When they finished with the dishes, they headed upstairs to get Lasaia in the tub and ready for bed. Marcus finished with Angela and turned off her light.

He walked out of her room and heard his wife and daughter talking. He heard one question in particular that caused him to sneak over to the door and eavesdrop on their conversation.

"Why didn't you want your daddy to give you a bath?" Sherise asked.

She had seen the way Lasaia looked at her father in the kitchen and how she didn't want to sit with him during the movie, and now she didn't want him to give her a bath. She knew something was up. Lasaia was daddy's little girl. The two of them had been inseparable since the day she was born.

Lasaia was quiet for a few seconds. Marcus stood with his back to the wall outside the bathroom waiting to hear her reply. Lasaia chose her words the best she could.

"Daddy's dirty."

"Dirty?" Sherise said, giggling.

"Yeah."

"What do you mean?"

"I don't know. He's just dirty."

Marcus stood outside the door with a confused look on his face. Dirty? What could she mean? Marcus thought about it for a second and realized that there was only one thing that had happened that she could possibly be talking about. But, there was no way she could have known what he did. Marcus snuck away from the door and into his room. He couldn't believe that his daughter felt that way about him. Marcus jumped into the shower and took a quick bath. As he was walking back into the bedroom, Sherise was walking into the room.

"So, what *really* made you come back so early?" She asked.

This was his chance. He could say it now and get it all out. The kids were in bed and they were all alone. All he had to do was say it.

"I got tired of being in Atlanta." He said.

He couldn't bring himself to tell her. He didn't want to break her heart and that is all telling her would do. She walked over and kissed him before heading to the bathroom to take her shower.

"So, I'm dirty, huh?" Marcus asked.

Sherise stopped in the bathroom doorway and turned around.

"Huh?" She asked.

"I'm dirty. That's why she didn't want me to give her a bath?"

"You heard that?"

"Yeah."

"I don't know what she's talking about. You know how she gets sometimes."

Sherise turned and walked into the bathroom without giving it another thought. She had chalked it up to her daughter being the silly little girl that she always was. Very picky, very opinionated, very Lasaia. But, Lasaia did know something was wrong, she just didn't know what. Her "dirty" comment really bothered Marcus, though. He heard the shower start up and Sherise climb in. He flipped on the television and watched it until she returned to the room. She walked in with her hair wet and curly and a towel wrapped under her arms. She was still a little wet and had beads of water on her shoulders and chest. Marcus looked over at the beautiful creature he married and wanted nothing more than to throw her on the bed and make love to her. But, now he didn't think he was worthy of even touching her. He just sat there and watched as she looked through her drawers for something to put on. She felt his eyes on her and looked up at him.

"What you lookin' at?" She said, jokingly.

"Huh? Nothing." Marcus said, turning back to the television.

"Uh huh. Ok." Sherise said, undoing her towel and throwing it to the floor. "Now, what are you looking at?"

Marcus looked over at his wife standing there naked. She was truly the most beautiful thing in the world to him. All thoughts of his actions the night before went away. She crawled on her hands and knees across the bed to him and pressed her lips against his. At that moment Marcus thought about nothing else but her. He pulled her on top of him and she began to take off his clothes.

After a few minutes of lovemaking, Sherise began to scream out his name. Marcus flashed back to the night before when Lasaia was on top of him. Sherise was on top of him enjoying herself but he couldn't get the image of the other woman out of his head. He closed his eyes and tried to think about his wife, and it worked for a minute…until he opened them again. He looked up at his wife and instead of seeing the gorgeous woman he married, he saw Lasaia, plain as day. Marcus freaked out and pushed Sherise off him, jumping out of the bed. Sherise was surprised by his outburst and just looked at him standing there. He looked at the woman in the bed again and it was his wife.

"Baby, what's wrong?" Sherise asked, confusion in her eyes.

He had never done anything like that before. Marcus just stood there wiping his eyes, not sure about what just happened. Sherise sat there for a second on the bed looking at him. He was starting to scare her. He walked back to the bed and sat down with his back to her. She slid over behind him and wrapped her arms around his waist, her head on his shoulder.

"You ok?" She asked, giving him a kiss on his shoulder.

"Yeah. Yeah, I'm fine. I just...I don't know. I was...I'm fine."

They sat there in silence for a few seconds before Marcus broke her grasp and got up.

He grabbed his clothes from the floor and put them on.

"Where are you going?" She asked.

"To get something to drink. I'm sorry, I'll be right back."

Marcus walked out of the room and Sherise watched him leave as she climbed under the covers. Marcus made his way downstairs and went into the kitchen. He poured himself a drink and downed it, greedily. Marcus just stood there in the kitchen, leaning against the island, wondering what could have happened to him in his room. This situation was really taking its toll on his mind. He was in the kitchen for a few minutes before he heard his cell phone ringing in his office. He left the kitchen, headed to his office. Before he got there, the phone stopped its whine. He picked it up off the charger and looked at the screen.

1 missed call

Marcus flipped the phone open and looked at the number.

It was Lasaia.

What could she want?

Before he had time to think about it, the phone rang again. Marcus looked at the display. She was calling back. Marcus didn't know whether to answer it or not. He didn't know what to expect from her at this point.

Nineteen

Marcus flipped open the phone and pressed the answer key.

"Hello?"

"Heeey, sweetie. What's up?" Lasaia said on the other end.

"Sweetie? Nah, this ain't your sweetie. What do you want?"

"Baby, what's wrong? I was just calling to see what you were doing tonight."

"I'm not your baby. Do you realize what we did last night?"

"Yeah. You kept your promise to me, just like I *knew* you would."

"No. I cheated on my wife. Don't you realize that?"

"Yes. But she won't know unless you tell her."

"It's not that simple. I can't get it out of my mind."

"Baby look, don't worry about it. We had sex, that's it. You don't have to worry about anything. I'm not going to tell her. You have her in Jacksonville and whenever you are here you can have me."

"You just don't get it do you? That can never happen again. I regret doing it the first time."

"Men do it all the time. My step dad used to cheat on my mom all the time and..."

"I'm not your step dad and this is not gonna work. I love my wife."

"But you love me too."

Marcus went silent for a second.

"See, every time I bring us up, I can tell that you still have feelings for me." She said, breaking the silence.

"I do but, it's not something that I want. I mean, yeah 10 years ago, maybe...but I'm different now. Things are different now. I love my wife and don't want to do anything to hurt her."

"Then why did you sleep with me?"

"I don't know. It was a mistake. It shouldn't have happened."

Lasaia was quiet for a few seconds.

"Look, why don't you come over here so we can talk?"

"I'm not in Atlanta anymore and even if I was, I don't think that would be a good idea."

"You're not here? I thought you weren't leaving until tomorrow morning?"

"I wasn't, but I left today. I had to get out of there."

"But I…I don't understand. You're not supposed to be gone yet."

Marcus could hear the frustration building in her voice. It was as if he had squashed her Plan B.

To get him to her house again for a second helping.

"When…when are you coming back?"

"I'm not. Not any time soon, that's for sure. I need to handle this. I have to find a way to tell Sherise the truth."

"But…but what," Lasaia reverted back to fifteen years old, struggling to get her words out, "but I wanna see you. You can't just come back into my life, fuck me, and leave."

"I told you, that was a mistake. A mistake that you caused. I was fine with the two of us being just friends, but you didn't want it that way." Marcus said, starting to get angry. He didn't like the way she expected him to just forget about his life and become a part of hers.

Lasaia jumped on the defensive. "I didn't what? Hold on, how is this my fault? Nobody pushed your dick inside of me. As I recall, you were the one that did most of the fucking. Then you left me in the middle of the night, like I was some kinda hoe or something. How am I supposed to feel about that? You didn't do anything that you didn't want to do. Don't even try and make it seem like everything was on me."

"Ok, so who was it that jumped in my lap at Alonzo's house, who set off my alarm and tried to fuck me in my kitchen with my wife and kids right upstairs, who brought a gay man to my house to posing as her boyfriend, and who stole my credit card so I wouldn't be able to go home? Huh? Who was it that did all that?"

Lasaia was silent.

She didn't know he had found out about the card.

If it hadn't been for that, Marcus probably wouldn't have even linked the events.

"Ok, ok, ok. Yes I did take your card, but that was only because I didn't want you to go back to your hotel so early. I wanted to spend more time with you.

But I didn't *jump* into your lap, you were as much a part of that as I was. And, I didn't try to fuck you in your kitchen, I did try to kiss you and you let that happen too, didn't you? And, I brought Tony to your house, yes, but that was because I didn't want Sherise watching me every minute around you. All I wanted was to see *you* and spend time with *you*."

"Well the time we spent together has cost me more than you know. I don't think it would be good for us to see each other again, ever."

"So, what are you saying? You're just gonna disappear from my life again?"

"Yeah, that's pretty much exactly what I'm saying. After Sherise finds out what happened, I will have a lot of making up to do, if she doesn't leave me all together."

"But Marcus, I can't…I *won't* let you leave me again."

"Well, I'm sorry but that's how it's gonna have to be."

"But Marcus…"

"Bye Lasaia."

"Baby, wait. Just…"

Marcus closed his phone as she tried to speak. He placed it back on the charger and walked out of the office. He couldn't believe how indifferent she was about the whole situation. He made his way back up to his room. Sherise had gotten tired of waiting for him and was under the covers, asleep. Marcus climbed into the bed and fell asleep next to his wife.

The next morning Marcus woke up and walked down the stairs to the kitchen where he found his family. Sherise was finishing up breakfast and the kids were sitting at the table coloring. Sherise grabbed some plates from the cabinet as he walked in. He walked over to his little jewels, said good morning, and gave each of them a kiss on the forehead, like he always did. Angela laughed as he kissed her but Lasaia wasn't as enthused as she usually was to see him. All she gave him was a, "Hey daddy," out of courtesy, and returned to coloring in her book. Marcus didn't think too much about her attitude and walked over to his wife. He kissed her on the cheek as she picked up the girls' food and took it to the table. After breakfast, the family got up from the table and started getting ready for church.

The service was just as good as the one they had heard a week earlier. The preacher spoke about trust. Trusting in God as well and trusting in others. Marcus couldn't help relating the sermon to himself. He knew his bond of trust with his wife had been broken and if she needed to lean against it now, it would surely topple. They left the church and headed home. They had a fairly normal Sunday afternoon, except for the fact that Lasaia didn't want too much to do with her father. He was still *dirty* to her. As Sherise was putting the kids to bed, Marcus rushed over to his office to try and get a little work done on a few of his projects. He decided to check his email, after searching around on the Internet. He logged onto his account and pulled up his new mail. There, on the screen, were four new messages from Lasaia. All of them were pretty much the same. Between the apologies, requests for him to call, and pleas for him to come to Atlanta; they were asking why he wasn't calling her and why he was treating her like this. Marcus finally came to the realization that she might not be wrapped too tightly. He deleted the messages just as Sherise walked into his office.

"Are you coming to bed?" She asked from the doorway.

"Yeah, just getting some things together for tomorrow."

Sherise walked over and gave him a kiss on the cheek and left the office, headed for bed. Marcus finished opening his emails and turned off his computer. He made his way upstairs, took a shower and climbed into bed. He fell asleep cuddled up next to his wife.

Marcus woke up the following morning and after the family went through their usual morning ritual, he was off to work. He walked out of the elevator door and was immediately greeted by all of his co-workers standing in the entryway. They gave him a round of applause as soon as they saw him. They cheered and clapped their hands and smiled and rooted for him. He didn't understand what was going on until his friend, Mike, quieted everyone down and said, "Brotha' we know that you didn't get the contract, but we wanted you to see how much we appreciate you going up there fighting for us."

Mike's words were trailed by reverberating screams of, "That's right," and nodding heads.

"And to show our appreciation...we got you this."

Mike turned and grabbed a fruit basket from one of the women behind him, handing it to Marcus. The audience gave Marcus another round of applause and cheers. Mr. Lockson worked his way through the crowd and shook Marcus's hand, followed by a hug. The congregation slowly broke up and Marcus headed for his office, Mike right along side him. They walked into his office and Mike had a seat in the chair in front of Marcus's desk.

"So, besides the presentation, how was the weekend? You get to holla at your brother?" Mike asked.

"Yeah, yeah. It was cool." Marcus said, starting up his computer.

Mike looked at his friend with a suspecting glance.

"Man, what did you do?" He said out of nowhere.

Marcus looked over at him from his chair with a baffled look.

"What?"

"Man, I have known you for over eight years, worked with you for five. I can tell when you're hiding something, and right now, you're hiding something."

Marcus looked at him in amazement, but didn't let the expression stay on his face for very long. Was it that obvious that something was up?

"Whateva' man. Don't you have some work to do?" Marcus said, laughing it off.

"Come on man, I know you up to something. What you do? Go out to the strip club and lie to Sherise about it?"

"What? No."

"I know what happened. You went to your brother's club and got a lil' too freaky on the dance floor huh?"

"Nah."

"You kissed her didn't you?"

"Kissed who? What are you talking bout?"

"Brotha, I am a no good man and I can spot an amateur no good man from a mile away. Y'all get all quiet and nervous and shit. I know you're up to something. What's her name?"

Marcus couldn't believe it. How could he have possibly known he had done something with another woman? Marcus got up, walked to his office door and closed it.

"Alright, you gotta keep this on the down low, 'cause I have really messed up."

Mike listened attentively to his friend.

"I cheated on Sherise." Marcus said, whispering.

"What?" Mike yelled, jumping out of his chair.

"Shhhh…" Marcus said, grabbing him by the shoulder, pushing him back down into the chair. He didn't want to draw attention to the two of them.

Mike calmed down.

"Man, I was just joking wit'chu. I ain't know you did something for real." Mike said, whispering, looking around like someone was eavesdropping on their conversation.

Mike could see that the situation had Marcus on edge.

"Ok, ok, ok…so what are you gonna do?" Mike asked.

"I don't know. I need to tell her."

"No, no, no, no, no, no…Hell No! You can't tell her that. Sherise ain't ghetto enough to stay with you after finding out you slept wit another woman."

Marcus was silent for a few seconds.

"So, what am I supposed to do?"

"Ok, ok...Who is this other woman?"

"My old girlfriend from high school."

"Aw, hell nah. Ok, first off, you gotta make sure the two of them never meet."

"They already met."

Mike looked at Marcus with a strange look on his face and said, "Are you trying to break some kind of divorce record?"

"Nah, nah. When they met I didn't think it was gonna go down like this. I just wanted the two of them to get to know each other."

"Well, it looks like you did more *getting to know* than Sherise did. Ok, well first thing is to cut the ties with this old girlfriend."

"Yeah, I did that. She called me last night and I told her we can't see each other any more."

"Be careful how you do it though brother. You don't want to piss her off and then have her make a little courtesy call to Sherise. She could go nuts. I usually recommend that you keep seeing her and just be an ass until she gets tired of you. That usually works."

"I don't have time for that. She's not gonna get tired."

Marcus remembered that he had turned his phone off and pulled it out of his jacket pocket.

"Man she's already sending me emails and..."

After his phone powered up, he saw that he had 14 new voicemails.

"See, this is what I'm talking about."

Marcus turned his phone toward Mike.

"Aw, hell nah. You need to talk to her. That bitch crazy." Mike said, flipping through the voicemails and seeing that they were all from Lasaia.

"Talk to her and say what," Marcus asked, "what else can I say besides leave me the hell lone?"

"See if y'all can come to an agreement or something 'cause she's obviously not gonna just let it go. I can tell you that now. If all of those messages are from her, she's obsessed. Those types are the hardest to get rid of."

Mike got out of Marcus's chair and headed for the door.

"And what if she doesn't want to compromise?" Marcus said as his friend reached for the doorknob.

"Say a prayer and hold on tight bruh, 'cause you're gonna be in for a long, bumpy ride." Mike said, walking out of the office.

Marcus just stared at the door, thinking about the words that had just come out of his friend's mouth.

He wished more than ever that he had never run into Lasaia that night at the diner.

Twenty

Marcus finished out his day at work and headed home. The rest of the week was routine. Marcus went to work, Sherise dropped Lasaia off at school and Angela at daycare before heading to the salon, and they all met back home in the evening. Lasaia still didn't pay too much attention to her father and still wouldn't let him give her a bath. Even though her birthday was on Saturday, she acted as if it didn't really matter anymore. Marcus checked his e-mails everyday and everyday he had a minimum of four e-mails from Lasaia, begging him to call her. Marcus wrote her a few e-mails back trying to get her to let it all go, but she wouldn't take no for an answer. He didn't want to upset her and cause her to call his wife, so he made dates with her to call and never did. Then he came up with an excuse why he didn't call. One e-mail that Marcus received on Friday worried him a little more than all the others he had received throughout the week. It was an e-mail with the words, *I love you*, repeated 3,652 times. At the end she wrote, *One for everyday of the last 10 years.* Marcus sat and actually calculated the total. He thought that she had over counted until he realized that she had actually added in two extra days for the leap years. That e-mail made Marcus really begin to question her mental stability.

The following day was Lasaia's birthday and Sherise had a hard time getting the excited little girl to calm down and go to bed. Every time she walked by her room, Sherise would hear her in the bed in the dark singing Happy Birthday to herself. Sherise would tell her to go to sleep and she would quiet down for a few minutes, then start right back up again. After a while, she was no longer able to fight the Sand Man and dropped off to sleep. Marcus and Sherise rushed by her room and down the stairs to get things set up for her party. They worked for a few hours, running streamers and putting up decorations all over the bottom level of the house. After they finished, they snuck back upstairs and into their room where they fell asleep.

The next day, Sherise and Marcus woke up and went downstairs to start cooking food for the party. Marcus went into the backyard and got his grill ready, while Sherise started making her dishes. They worked for about an hour before Lasaia walked into the kitchen in her pajamas, rubbing her eyes. She was up so late the night before that she slept longer then usual and was still a little drowsy. Marcus walked in through the back door and had a seat at the breakfast table. Lasaia walked over to him, still rubbing her eyes, and climbed into her daddy's lap. It was the first time in a week that she actually allowed him to touch her. She didn't say a word, just sat there and laid her head on his shoulder. Sherise looked over at the two of them and smiled. She had no idea why her little girl didn't want anything to do with her daddy and, for that matter, Lasaia didn't know herself. Sherise was just glad to see her daughter's phase was over.

"How much meat you gotta cook?" Sherise asked.

"I don't even know. I'm just gonna cook until kids start passin' out. Then I'll cut it off." He said.

Sherise laughed at her silly husband and they all sat there for a few minutes talking about what the birthday girl wanted to do on her big day. After Sherise finished preparing two large pans of lasagna, she placed them in the oven and turned around to start on her potato salad, macaroni and cheese, finger sandwiches and Garden salad. Marcus was handling all of the meat, so she was in charge of sides.

Around eleven they all took a break and Sherise went upstairs to wake Angela before serving breakfast. They had a quick meal before Sherise sent Lasaia upstairs to get dressed for the day. The doorbell rang on Lasaia's way back downstairs and she rushed over to answer it. She struggled with the big door a little, but managed to get it open. On the other side of the threshold was her best friend and next-door neighbor, Melissa, along with her parents. The two girls screamed, threw their arms around each other and started jumping up and down in the doorway.

Bill and Janet looked at the girls and smiled. Sherise looked around the corner of the kitchen to see what all the yelling was about and saw her neighbors standing there.

"Heeey guys. Y'all come on in." Sherise said, waving from the kitchen.

The girls let each other go and took off into the house. Bill and his wife made their way to the kitchen where Sherise greeted them with a hug. Janet immediately picked up Angela from her seat at the table and held her in her arms. She loved that little girl.

"Thank you guys so much for coming. Nobody's here yet but we're getting started around 2:00." Sherise said going back to preparing her dishes.

"Oh, we're here to help." Bill said, in his usual chipper voice.

"Ooooh, gon' head now. Well if y'all here to get dirty, then we can definitely get you dirty." Sherise said.

They all had a laugh as Marcus walked in. "Y'all laughin' at me?" He asked, joking. Marcus walked over, shook Bill's hand, and gave Janet a peck on the cheek and a hug. Bill gave Marcus the gift he had in his hands and Marcus took it to the gift table in the family room. As Marcus walked back into the kitchen Sherise said, "Baby, they said they're here to help."

Marcus looked at the two of them and said, "Oh, we can definitely get you dirty."

Sherise, Bill and Janet laughed at him for saying the same thing his wife already said.

The men headed into the back yard by the pool to decorate the deck and set up the games while Sherise and Janet rolled up their sleeves and finished the sides. The four of them got everything set up and the food ready before the guests arrived. Sherise disappeared upstairs for a quick change into what she planned to wear for the party. She threw on her favorite shirt and Capri jeans and put on her shoes but saw one shoe was shinier then the other. She rushed over to Marcus's closet and looked around for his shoe polish. After she found the polish she headed out of the closet and saw one of Marcus's sleeves sticking out of his suitcase. She was always getting on Marcus about not putting his clothes in the dirty clothes hamper. She let out a grunt and opened the suitcase. She pulled the shirt out and saw that five of the buttons down the front were missing. Sherise got aggravated by Marcus always messing up his clothes and was in so much of a hurry that she didn't even put much thought into how the shirt got like that. She shoved it back in the suitcase and decided to let Marcus handle his own dirty laundry. She headed back downstairs to finish all the little things to get ready for the party.

By 3:30 that afternoon there were about 30 kids running around the Downing family backyard. Almost every child from Lasaia's class, a few from Angela's daycare, some kids from church and a few children of friends of Marcus and Sherise were there. Sherise's best friend, Alicia, came and Marcus's co-worker and friend, Mike, brought his son. They all had a good time talking and laughing as the children ran around the huge backyard.

Sherise got a call on her cell phone around 4:30 and Marcus saw her disappear into the house. She reemerged about five minutes later, with a companion. Marcus looked at the person with her and his heart almost jumped out of his chest.

It was Lasaia.

What was she doing here?

Who told her about the party?

"Look who I found," Sherise said, smiling, as she walked up with Lasaia.

Marcus reluctantly gave her a hug.

"What are you doing here?" Marcus asked, trying to sound excited in front of his wife.

"I invited her. When I called to tell her you were in Atlanta I told her about us getting ready for the party…"

Lasaia cut in and said, "And I told Sherise I wouldn't miss it for the world. Now, where is the birthday girl?"

Sherise called her daughter over from her group of friends and she came running. Lasaia kneeled down as she reached their feet and said, "I heard it's your birthday."

"Yeah." The little girl said, shyly.

Lasaia stood up and reached into her purse. She fumbled around for a few seconds and pulled out a small wrapped box and gave it to the little girl standing in front of her.

"What do you say?" Sherise said, reminding her of her manners.

"Thank you." Lasaia said, looking up at her father's friend.

"Take it inside with your other gifts, baby, and we'll open it later." Marcus said.

Lasaia took off toward the house and went through the back door.

"Come on girl, I have some people I want you to meet." Sherise said, grabbing Lasaia's arm. Lasaia winked at Marcus and gave him a conniving smile as Sherise pulled her off. It was like she was bragging on how brave she was to come into his house after what they had done. The two of them walked over to a crowd of Sherise's friends and she began to introduce Lasaia. Mike walked up to Marcus and said, "Ooooo wee, who is *that*? That girl finer then fly antennas."

Marcus looked at his friend and said, "That's *her*."

"Her who?" Mike asked.

"Her, her."

Mike had a moment of enlightenment and his eyes grew big in their sockets.

"That's her? That's the one you…" Mike said in an exclaimed whisper before Marcus cut him off.

"Shhhh…" Marcus said, quieting him down.

"Man you ain't tell me she was that fine…Damn!"

"Yeah whatever, that *fineness* could cost me my marriage."

"Yeah, but what a way to go."

Mike fantasized for a few more seconds before looking at the serious look on Marcus's face.

"Sorry man, what she doin' here anyway?"

"Sherise invited her."

"Aw, hell nah. Well, did y'all at least come to some kind of agreement?"

"Nah, I wrote her back like you said, asking her what she wants. She said she doesn't want anything but me."

"Damn, you in some hot water brotha."

"You think she'll say something?"

"Nah, if she wanted to tell her she could have been did that. And she knows if she does that, there is no way you would get with her. She's just testing the waters, waiting for a time to strike. Don't show fear man…they can smell it."

"They who?" Marcus said with a chuckle.

"Women fool. They know when you're scared of them."

Marcus looked at his friend with a strange look.

"What are you talking about?" Marcus said, laughing this time.

"Think about it. She has your cell number, your house number, your e-mail address, hell…even your house address right?"

"Yeah."

"And if Sherise invited her she probably has her cell phone number too. If her goal was to tell her, she could have done that by now. That ain't what she want. See, the way she sees it is if she was able to wear you down before she can do it again. All she has to do is just keep showing up and she got you. And as fine as she is…I probably would have jumped on her in front of my ex-wife. You got the upper hand bruh. *She* wants *you.* Not the other way around. You just gotta play it cool. She's not gonna try anything."

Marcus just looked across the yard at his wife as she and Lasaia talked and laughed with a group of the other parents.

As Sherise was talking with the parents and Lasaia, Alicia appeared out of the back door. "Excuse us everybody." Sherise said grabbing and dragging Lasaia by the wrist. They walked over to Alicia, who was fixing herself a small plate and Sherise said, "Lele, I want you to meet somebody." Alicia looked up from the table and saw her best friend standing there smiling with a stranger standing next to her. She sat down her plate and extended her hand to the woman.

They shook hands as Sherise said, “Lele, this is Marcus’s old friend Lasaia from high school…Lasaia this is my best friend and business partner Alicia, but I call her Lele.”

Alicia’s facial expression changed for a quick second as she realized whose hand was in hers.

“Hey, how are you doing?” Alicia said, jumping back into her manners mode, but barely acknowledging Lasaia. This is the woman that she already didn’t like, but she knew Sherise did and didn’t want to upset her by snatching her hand back before the evil crept over from this woman onto her skin. After they shook hands Alicia said, “Sherise can I talk to you for a second?”

“Yeah um…”

“Oh, don’t let me interrupt…” Lasaia said breaking in.

“Sherise can I use your bathroom?”

“Sure girl, you know where it is.” Sherise said.

Lasaia walked to the back door and disappeared in the house.

“Girl, what is she doing here?” Alicia asked.

“I invited her.”

“Why?”

“Because she’s my friend and she wanted to come.”

“Girl, do you see the body on that bitch. You can’t have her over here flauntin’ that shit in front of your husband.”

“So what are you trying to say…I can’t flaunt?”

“No, that’s not what I’m saying. We are talking about men, and men are visually stimulated animals and they can only see something for so long before they start to want it.”

“Girl, anyway. She’s not even thinking about my husband. She has a new boyfriend, a good career, and lives in a different state. She can’t help that she’s an attractive woman.”

“Ok. Well explain to me how this bitch is supposed to ‘know’ where your bathroom is?”

“Because she spent the night here when she was in town last time.”

“You let that woman stay in your house?”

“Yes. I told you she came here.”

“You said she came by, you ain’t say the bitch spent the night.”

“It wasn’t that serious.”

"Ok. I'm gonna let it go. But, I don't like the bitch."
Sherise started laughing at her crazy friend as her oldest daughter ran up with Melissa and a few other girls from her class.
"Mommy, Mommy...can we cut the cake." She asked with a bunch of little eyes wide behind her.
"Ok, sweetie." Sherise said and the small crowd started to cheer.
Sherise called Marcus in from the yard. He and Mike had rounded up six of the boys and were playing a three-on-three game of football, the adults playing the quarterbacks. They all rushed over and gathered around the big buffet table. Sherise put Lasaia in a chair in the middle of the table as Marcus headed inside to get the cake. They had bought a huge sheet cake with a picture of Lasaia's class scanned on top. As Marcus picked up the cake, Lasaia appeared around the corner of the kitchen.
"A fine man and a lot of sugar. This is my type of party."
Marcus looked back to see her standing there with a grin on her face.
"Why did you come here? I told you it's not a good idea for us to see each other." Marcus said, turning toward the door.
Lasaia walked over and opened the door for him while smiling and said, "I told you I wasn't going to let you leave me again."

As Marcus walked through the door she walked behind him, grabbed a hand full of his butt, and said, "You're going to be mine again. Just watch and see." Marcus didn't flinch from her action even though his insides were jumping all over the place. Everyone was looking at him with that huge cake in his hands. He walked over to the table and placed the cake in front of his daughter. The kids' eyes lit up as some of them realized that they were on the cake. They all sang Happy Birthday to the birthday girl and she blew out all her candles. Everyone clapped and cheered and Lasaia smiled at all the attention she was getting. Sherise cut the cake while Marcus scooped ice cream from a gigantic tub. After everyone had gotten a treat, they all made their way inside to watch Lasaia open her gifts. The kids gathered around as Sherise and Lasaia sat in the middle of the family room while Marcus piled the gifts around them. Sherise read off the names of the people who gave the gifts as Lasaia ripped the paper from the presents. Lasaia had stacks of dolls and books and other toys piled around her by the time she got to the last box. It was the small wrapped box that her father's friend had given to her. Lasaia carefully opened the small box and looked inside.

Inside the tiny box was a pair of 3-stone dangling earrings. Sherise's eyes lit up as she looked inside the box.

"Whoa! Girl you're gonna be stylin'." Sherise said.
Sherise showed the earrings to the crowd and there was a series of "Oooo's" and gasps. Jokingly, Bill yelled out, "How many carats is it?"
"Just one." Lasaia said, from her spot in the crowd.
"Those are real?" Sherise asked, snatching the box back from her daughter.
"Yeah." Lasaia said.
"Oh no, girl we can't take these. It's too much. We…"
Lasaia cut her off.
"Uh uh, when I was a little girl I wished I had some earrings like in Cinderella. I bought those for her and I'm not taking them back."
"Please mommy?" Lasaia said, begging her mother.
She hadn't taken her eyes off of them since she opened the box. Sherise looked back at Marcus who had a shocked look on his face. He just shrugged his shoulders not knowing what to say. Sherise looked back at her daughter's big pretty eyes and said, "Ok, but you have to take real good care of them, alright?"
"I will. I promise." Lasaia said, smiling, as her mother gave the small black box back to her.
"Shoot, mama might have to put those on." Sherise said, as everyone laughed.
"Well, that's all of them. Thank you guys so much."
The crowd clapped and they started to head back into the backyard for a little more fun before it was time to go.

People started to leave about an hour later as their children began to get sleepy and it started to get dark. The party had been exceptional and the kids had a great time playing together. By 6:30 everyone was gone except for Alicia, Mike and his son, Bill, Janet and Lasaia. They were all sitting in the family room as Lasaia and Melissa played with Lasaia's birthday loot.
"Well, I guess it's clean up time." Sherise said, standing up.
"Here, let me help you." Lasaia said, getting up behind her.
"No girl, you're a guest. You just relax."
Sherise looked over at Alicia sitting on the couch next to Mike and his son. Mike seemed to have taken a liking to this full figured female and the two of them were having a quiet conversation while his son slept with his head on the arm of the couch.
"But you, you come with me." Sherise said to Alicia.
"What? I'm a guest too." Alicia said.
"Nah, you be here too much to be a guest. And, you said you were coming to help me get ready and didn't so you owe me."

Alicia let out a long sigh, told Mike she would talk to him in a minute, and followed Sherise into the kitchen. Lasaia went with them and the three of them disappeared around the corner.

"You need some help, good buddy?" Bill asked from his seat in the recliner.

"Nah, I'm just going be the trash man tonight. Gotta get all the stuff they throw out so I have to wait until everything is done anyway. You guys can head on out if you want. I can handle it." Marcus said.

"Alrighty, well it was a pleasure." Bill said as Janet climbed out of his lap and he stood to his feet. They shook hands and Marcus gave his wife a hug and Bill said, "Come on Melissa, time to go." Melissa jumped to her knees, gave her friend a hug, and rushed to her parents' side. Bill yelled a farewell to Sherise and she appeared around the corner and waved. She thanked them again for coming and Bill took his family home.

Mike and Marcus started taking down all of the decorations and piling them in the family room. They gathered all the wrapping paper and miscellaneous paper plates from around the room and got it all together. Marcus sent Mike to the kitchen to get a big trash bag to put it all in. He entered the kitchen and saw Alicia washing the last few dishes while Sherise wiped down the countertops. Lasaia was seated in a chair at the breakfast table sipping on some wine because Sherise wouldn't let her do anything.

"Um, Sherise, Marcus says we need a big trash bag." Mike said.

"Ok, there are some big black ones under the sink."

Mike walked over to where Alicia was standing. She looked at him out the corner of her eye and tried to hold back her grin. The two of them looked like teenagers who liked each other and didn't know how to say it.

"Excuse me." Mike said, leaning down as Alicia moved out of his way.

He didn't take his eyes off of her as he knelt down and grabbed the bags. Sherise and Lasaia looked at each other and giggled.

"Thanks." He said, closing the cabinet.

Mike left and they waited for him to get down the hall and into the family room before Sherise and Lasaia burst out laughing.

"What y'all heffas laughin' at?" Alicia said putting her dish down and turning around with her hand on her hip.

"Nothin', nothin'. Y'all just look so cute." Sherise said.

"Yeah, it was like seeing a little boy bring a little girl a flower." Lasaia said.

"Both you bitches trippin'." Alicia said, laughing right along with them.

She knew she was caught. She was just as smitten as he was.

In the family room, Mike and Marcus were throwing trash into the large bag.

"Baby, start taking your gifts to your room for me." Marcus said to Lasaia who was still in the middle of her Pile O' Presents. She got up from her spot, grabbed an arm full of stuff and headed upstairs without saying a word.

"And check on your sister too." Marcus yelled to her as she made her way up the stairs. Angela had fallen asleep much earlier from all the running and playing with the bigger kids. The two men finished picking up the trash and tied the bag. Lasaia made it downstairs for another load and Marcus asked, "She still sleep?"

Lasaia nodded her head and grabbed some more things to take to her room. Marcus spotted the box that her earrings came in and grabbed it. He didn't get to get a good look at them before, but as soon as he opened the box he saw how beautiful they were. Mike walked over and stared into the box with him.

"Maaaan, she's good." He said.

"What are you talking about?"

"First, she got your wife, now she tryin' to get your daughter."

"Man, you crazy. Lasaia doesn't even like her. Last time she was here Lasaia didn't even want to be in the same room with her."

"Call me crazy if you want, but even I can't tell you how far this broad would go. She could be dangerous. You need to watch yourself."

"Yeah, I'll do that." Marcus said sarcastically as Lasaia walked into the room to make her final trip. Marcus gave her the earrings and told her to put them on her dresser so she could wear them to church in the morning.

"You ready to take your bath?" Marcus asked.

"Daddy…since I'm six now, can I take a bath by myself?" She asked.

"Well…ok but be careful with the water, don't make it too hot."

She smiled and rushed over and hugged his leg with her free hand, then took off up the stairs before he changed his mind.

Marcus grabbed the bag of trash and headed for the backyard. The two men entered the kitchen and found the group of women talking and laughing as they finished up their cleaning. Marcus headed to the back door, trying to ignore Lasaia's staring, and opened it.

"Wait, Marcus, take this trash too." Sherise said, walking over to the full kitchen trashcan.

"I got it." Mike said as he picked it up out of the can.

Alicia and Mike exchange another quick admiring glance before he headed outside behind his friend. The two men finished taking down all the outside decorations and got all the trash up. They took the bags to the side of the house and put them in the large trash containers. As they walked back into the house they heard the women talking in the foyer. They walked toward their voices and found Sherise trying to convince Lasaia to stay for a while.

"Do you really have to go back now?" Sherise asked.

"Yeah, I have to finish up some work before Monday so I need to go ahead and get back home."

"Awww, I was hoping you would be able to stay longer."

"Yeah, I wish I could too," she said looking pass Sherise, at Marcus, "but you know, duty calls."

"Well ok, I guess we'll see you next time."

Sherise and Lasaia shared a hug and even Alicia gave her one. Lasaia shook Mike's hand and told him it was a pleasure to meet him. As Marcus extended his hand, hoping she would accept that as a farewell, Lasaia said, "I know you didn't just…Boy, give me a hug."

Marcus reluctantly gave her an awkward hug and Lasaia said, "Well, thank you guys so much for having me. I'll see you later."

She walked out the front door and headed for her car.

"I better get going too." Alicia said.

"Hold on, I'll walk you out." Mike said rushing to the family room to get his son who was still fast asleep on the couch.

They each said goodbyes to Marcus and Sherise and Mike walked Alicia out. Marcus and Sherise congratulated each other on a wonderful day. It had been a total success. All the kids seemed to have fun, all the parents got a semi-break from the usual Saturday of aggravation and their daughter had a great birthday. The two of them headed upstairs and found Lasaia already in her bed asleep. She had taken her bath and climbed into bed all by herself. No arguing, no slow moving, no series of questions…she had just climbed into her bed and was out like a light. Angela still hadn't woken up and it didn't appear as if she would. Both of them were knocked out and Marcus said, "Maybe we need to do this every Saturday."

They laughed as they headed into their bedroom.

The next day they all got up and went to church. The preacher spoke on friendship and how everyone who says they are your friend really isn't.

Another great sermon.

The family left the church and headed home. The following week was routine, except for the change in the attitude of the e-mails Lasaia was still sending to Marcus. Before, they were pleading with him to call her and begging for him to visit. Now, they were filled with phrases like, "Who do you think I am?", "You need to stop ignoring me." and "You better stop treating me like this…or else." Marcus paid little attention to her e-mails and went on with his days as usual.

One Friday he finally decided he would write her back because he was growing increasingly tired of her threats. He figured that Mike was right. If what she really wanted was him, there was no way that she would tell Sherise. He would resent her and not be with her for that reason alone. Marcus sat at work and wrote Lasaia an e-mail.

Look, I told you. You and me CANNOT happen. Years ago, maybe, but just because we ran into each other again doesn't mean anything. I LOVE my wife, and there is nothing you can do or say to change that. We fucked…so what? That doesn't make me yours. And if I had been sober, it would have never happened. Who are you to think you can just come in and change my life? If you think I'm going to leave Sherise for you, you must be a fool. I'm sick and tired of your threats and if you think by trying to intimidate me you will make me come to you, then you really must be crazy too. Stop e-mailing me, stop calling me and stop calling my wife. Disappear and forget you ever saw me again. It will be a cold day in HELL before me and you get back together.

Marcus put all of his anger and feelings into that e-mail and sent it. After the mail was sent, he felt a little more confidence than ever about the whole situation. He finished out his day and went home. Later that night, after the kids were in bed, Marcus ended up in his office doing some research on a company whose contract his company would be bidding on in a few months. While he was sitting there, he received a new e-mail. He clicked on his new mail icon and the only new e-mail was from Lasaia. There was only one word in the subject line.

Ok.

Marcus figured that she must have finally got the point.

He opened it.

There were only six words.

Today's Forecast: Cold Day In Hell!!!

Marcus sat and stared at the words.

Slowly, the confidence he had began to feel drained out of his body.

He just sat there staring at the screen until Sherise came to his door and knocked on the frame. He quickly snapped back into reality.

"I'm gonna get some ice cream, you want some?" She asked.

Before he could answer the phone rang.

"I'll get it." Sherise said, darting to the kitchen.

Most times he had at least one of the house phones in his office. But today, fate had dealt him an ugly hand. He heard her pick up the phone and say, "Hello?" She was a good distance from him but he could hear her say, "Oh, hey Lasaia."

Marcus flew from around his desk. His heart started to beat in his chest. What could she be calling about? He stood in his doorway where Sherise couldn't see him and tried to hear what was going on.

"Girl, what's wrong. Why you crying?" Sherise asked.

Marcus's eyes got big.

This was it.

He had pushed her over the limit. She was calling to tell her everything and was probably blaming everything on him. Telling his wife how he *made* her do it and she *tried* to stop him but he seduced her. Marcus couldn't hear the words, but she could hear Sherise begin to cry. Marcus figured he could probably go upstairs and start packing now, but he was too scared to leave his office. He looked like George W. Bush in Fahrenheit 911 when the secret service guy came into the classroom and told him the planes had hit the Twin Towers.

Worried.

Scared.

Knowing that if he walked out that door, he would have a lot of shit to deal with.

Wishing he could stay in there for the rest of his life.

He paced back and forth in the office until he heard the beep from his wife hanging up the cordless phone. His heart pounded even harder as he heard her footsteps, headed his way.

Marcus walked around the corner of his office and stopped a few feet in front of his wife. Tears were running from her eyes like villagers trying to escape the big volcano.

Marcus started to panic.

He tried to beat her to the punch.

"Baby, look I…"

Twenty-one

Sherise cut in and said, "Lasaia's boyfriend broke up with her."

She walked over to him and threw her arms around his waist. She pressed her head against his chest as he hugged her.

Lasaia hadn't told her.

She had lied to her and told her that Greg broke up with her.

But why?

Marcus figured it had to be part of some greater plan.

But, what did she have up her sleeve?

Sherise didn't like for anything bad to happen to her friends and she felt really bad for her.

"It's ok. She'll be alright." Marcus said, trying to comfort his wife.

They went upstairs and got ready for bed. Sherise fell asleep in her husband's arms, still sniffling. The way she acted, you would think she had just lost him or something. Marcus was awake for a while after she fell asleep, lying there, thinking about what would have happened if she had told Sherise the truth. He wasn't prepared. It hurt him to see her cry for a friend. If she were to find out about his actions, there would be no level of comfort that he could give her.

The following day Sherise felt a little better and they decided to have a family day out. They took the girls to Chuck E Cheese, caught a movie, and had dinner at Sherise's favorite Chinese restaurant. They got back to the house around 8:30 and Sherise sent Lasaia upstairs to start her bath. She had really enjoyed being able to take a bath by herself. She even cleaned up the bathroom after she was done so her parents wouldn't take away her new privilege. Sherise gave Angela a bath in their bathroom and let her play in the bubbles of the Jacuzzi tub. She took her out of the tub and got the girls off to bed. Marcus and

Sherise got their showers in and the two of them watched television before deciding to turn out the lights. Marcus slid over to his wife in the dark and started running his hands up and down her back. She knew what he wanted because he would always do that when he wanted sex. She just laid there and let him beg for a minute before she turned over. They made love and fell asleep peacefully.

Around 4:30 in the morning the phone broke into their bedroom silence. Marcus jumped out of his sleep and fumbled around in the dark for the receiver. He finally found it and brought it to his ear.

"Hello?" He said, groggy, still half asleep.

"Oh my God! Marcus…Hello?" A hysterical voice screamed through the phone.

Marcus had to take it away from his ear. He heard sirens and a lot of activity in the background.

"Who is this?" Marcus said, rubbing his eyes.

"Marcus, this is Lisa…Alonzo just got shot."

Marcus jumped out of the bed.

"What? When? What happened?" He said, standing next to the bed.

His outburst woke Sherise. Lisa's distressed voice filled his ear. She was crying, trying to talk to the police and trying to talk to Marcus all at the same time.

"At the club. We went out. I thought it would be alright because he's been going all this time and nothing happened. But, tonight…tonight Richard was there and…it's all my fault."

Lisa's tears consumed her.

"No, it's not your fault. Calm down. Is he ok?"

"Yeah…No, I don't know. He was talking to me when they were putting him in the ambulance. But, the police wouldn't let me leave with him because they wanted a statement from me."

"Ok, ok…where did they take him?"

Marcus got the name of the hospital and directions to get there and told Lisa he was on his way. He hung up the phone and threw it on the bed. Sherise had been watching him pace around the room since he woke her up and said, "Baby what happened?"

"Alonzo got shot." Marcus said, putting on some pants.

Sherise gasped deeply and said, "What? Oh my God, is he ok?"

"I don't know, she said he was talking to her when they put him in the ambulance. I gotta get up there and find out."

Sherise jumped out of the bed and started to throw on her clothes. After she got dressed she grabbed some extra clothes to change into and threw them on the bed.

"I'll get the girls, you get some clothes to put in a bag." Sherise said walking out the room.

The two of them work together like a well-oiled machine. Marcus packed up all of their things, grabbing toothbrushes, deodorant, and all the toiletries. As he made it out of the room and to the top of the stairs, he saw that Sherise had already packed the girls a bag, complete with some activity books for them to play with.

Damn she's good, He thought to himself as he grabbed the bags and headed to the garage. He threw the bags in the back of his truck and got Angela's car seat out of Sherise's car. Then he hurried back inside to help Sherise with the girls. Lasaia was just putting on her shoes as he made it to the top of the steps. He saw Sherise walk out of Angela's room with a sleeping girl in her arms. Marcus went into Lasaia's room and said, "Come on baby girl, time to go".

The half-asleep Lasaia finished tying her shoe and said, "Daddy can I take my earrings?"

"Baby we're going to Atlanta. I don't want you to lose them."

"I'll be careful, I promise. You said I could wear them today."

"Ok, ok. Get them and let's go." Marcus agreed to her request just to get her to come without an argument.

Lasaia dashed to her dresser, snatched her box, and rushed back to her father. They all filed down the steps and into the truck. They had to have set a new world record for preparation. Two adults, two children, fully dressed, three bags packed and out the door in thirty minutes. Even the Guinness people would be impressed.

After 6 ½ hours, 3 bathroom stops and 1 food stop, they made it to the Atlanta city limits. Marcus followed the directions Lisa gave him and they pulled into the parking lot of Grady Hospital. They walked to the front counter and the receptionist said, "Hi, what can I do for you?"

"Yeah um, which room is Alonzo Downing in?" Marcus asked.

The receptionist typed the name into the computer and said, "He was in Urgent Care until about 10 minutes ago. Um, he's probably not in his room yet but you can go up and wait if you like. He'll be in room 316."

Marcus got directions from the receptionist and they hurried to the elevator. They reached the hallway where Alonzo's room was and Lisa saw Marcus coming down the hall. She got up from her seat and rushed over to him. As she got closer, Marcus could see the tears and make up smeared all over her face. It was clear that she had been there all night. She still had on the same outfit she had worn to the club. She walked up to Marcus, still sniffling, and gave him a hug.

"Heeey, are you alright?" Marcus said.

She just nodded her head and said, "I'm better, but they won't tell me anything. We were in the Emergency Room and they wouldn't let me in the back to see him. And then they told us that they were moving him up here and…"

Lisa started to get hysterical again and Marcus stopped her sentence. "Whoa, whoa, whoa…ok, it's ok. Calm down. If they are putting him in a room, chances are he is alright. You said he was talking to you before right?"

"Yeah."

"Ok, he'll be fine. Come on, let's have a seat."

They walked toward the chairs in front of Alonzo's room that Lisa was in before. There was an older woman sitting there already, working on a cross-stitch pattern. She was Lisa's mother. As soon as Lisa called and told her about what happened, she rushed right to the hospital. She had been there with Lisa since she was in the Emergency Room. She loved Alonzo too. She was happy that her daughter found someone who treated her with respect, and someone who got Lisa out of her house, but mainly it was because he treated her right.

"Everyone, this is my mom Pearl Ann Moore. Ma', this is Alonzo's brother Marcus and…"

"Oh, this is my wife Sherise and my daughters Lasaia and Angela." Marcus said realizing he hadn't introduced his family to Lisa.

Usually Sherise would have made a slick comment about that but her mind wasn't in its usually playful mood. They all exchanged hugs and had a seat. Ms. Moore went back to her stitching. Lasaia watched her for a second and couldn't hold back her curiosity any longer.

"What's that?" Lasaia said, walking over to her.

Ms. Moore smiled and showed her the quilt and even showed her how to do it, while the adults talked.

"So, what happened?" Marcus asked.

Lisa started the story and told him every detail of the night.

Alonzo started getting ready at 9:30. Lisa was still lounging around the house preparing for another night alone while Alonzo went to work. She got up from the couch and walked back into the room where he was.

"Baby, why don't you stay here with me tonight?" She asked.

"Girl you know I got a club to run. I got too much to do to stay home."

"But what are you going to do if Richard comes in there. I don't want you to get hurt."

"Baby, I can't close down my club because some fool doesn't like me. What do you want me to do? Close up shop and get a job at Pizza Hut or something? I have the tightest security in Atlanta, plus it's been over a month. If he was going to come in there he would have been there by now."

"I just don't want anything to happen to you."

"Nothing is going to happen. Why don't you come out tonight and you'll see. You been in the house for all this time, I know your juke bone is itching."

Lisa laughed.

"Come on out and have some fun." Alonzo said.

Lisa thought about what he said and decided that he was probably right. Maybe she was being too cautious. She hadn't seen or heard from Richard since that day at the car show and even the people that used to tell her that he was looking for her hadn't told her anything new. And, she was tired of being in that house all the time. Lisa got ready and the two of them hit the street, headed for *Cloud 9*.

The night was going great. Lisa got to see a lot of her club friends that she hadn't seen since she stopped going out and even got Alonzo on the dance floor a few times. She was having a great time. She had really missed going out all the weeks she was on her hiatus. Around 2:30, one of the bouncers tapped Alonzo on the shoulder and whispered something in his ear. Alonzo told Lisa he would be right back and left her at the bar. He left with the bouncer and disappeared through the door leading into the back office area. Lisa was having a good time hanging out at the bar alone. A couple guys tried to talk to her and she shot them all down. Even though she didn't really like being bothered, she loved the attention. Alonzo had been gone for almost an hour and Lisa was getting tired of waiting.

Just before she was about to go to the back room, she heard a voice in her ear.

"Wha' gwan likkle one?" The voice said.

Lisa's whole body tensed up. It was the voice of the one person she wished she would never see again. Lisa spun around and looked at Richard, standing right there in front of her. Her heartbeat quickly sped up and she could barely breathe. She couldn't speak, all she could do was look at him. He moved closer to her and she jumped off the stool, backing up against the bar rail. Just as he was about to take another step toward her, Alonzo appeared out of nowhere with Ricky by his side

"Still don't know your place, huh bruh?" Alonzo said.

Richard didn't recognize Alonzo at first, then he said, "Oooh, de' tiny boyfrien' again. You ready to sign 'er ova to me bredren?"

Alonzo didn't like his woman being talked about like she was a car title. And, by saying it he felt that Richard was disrespecting him as well. Alonzo didn't waste any time and lunged forward punching Richard in the face. Richard was caught off guard and fell back into some people standing by the bar. Ricky rushed over to the two of them to try and break up the fight, while Lisa screamed for them to stop. While they were struggling, 3 shots rang out in the confusion. This sent the club into a panic. People started screaming and running for the exit doors. In the confusion, Richard broke free from Ricky's grasp and disappeared into the crowd. As the area began to clear, Lisa saw Alonzo lying on the floor by the bar struggling to get up. Ricky got back on his feet after being knocked down by the terror-stricken crowd. Even his size was no match for the mob of people pushing and running to get out of the club. He made it to Alonzo and dragged him into the middle bar area to avoid the crowd rushing by. He flipped Alonzo over on his back and saw two large bloodstains on his shirt and his arm was bleeding too. Lisa saw the blood and lost it. She started screaming uncontrollably flailing her hands frantically. Ricky grabbed some clean towels from under the bar and handed one to Lisa. He was able to calm her down enough to get her to take the towel and said, "Wrap this around his arm and put pressure on it!" Ricky unfolded the other two towels and pressed them on Alonzo's wounds as he yelled down the bar to two women bartenders who were hiding below the counter.

"Call an ambulance!" He yelled to them and one of the women pulled out a cell phone and called 911.

Lisa finished her story saying, "I called you as soon as they drove off with him".

Twenty-two

Sherise's cell phone rang as soon as Lisa got her last word out. She stood up from her seat and walked down the hall a little as Marcus and Lisa tried to figure out what was happening. Lasaia and Angela were still watching attentively as Lisa's mother worked on her project.

"Hello?" Sherise said, into her phone.

"Hey Sherise girl. This Lasaia."

"Hey girl."

"I'm sorry about last night. I had just got off the phone with him and needed someone to talk to and..."

"Oh, girl that's alright. I'm here anytime you need me."

"Thank you. What are you guys up to?"

"Girl, we're in Atlanta."

"What are y'all doing up here?"

"Girl, Alonzo got shot last night in his club."

"What? Oh my God! Is he ok?"

"We don't know yet. We just got here. They were supposed to be moving him to a room, but we haven't seen him yet."

"What hospital are you guys at?"

Sherise read her the name of the hospital off an information board in the hallway.

"Um, Grady."

"I'll be right there!" Lasaia said.

Sherise hung up the phone and walked back to where Marcus and Lisa where, had a seat.

About 10 minutes later the elevator door opened at the end of the hall and a nurse pushed a wheelchair into the hallway, followed by a doctor. Alonzo was in the chair talking with the doctor about his club. Only Alonzo would think about club promotion being wheeled through a hospital. Lisa jumped up and ran over to him. The rest of the family stood up and watched as they rolled him into his room. They all walked in behind the doctor and waited while they got Alonzo situated. After Alonzo climbed out of the chair and into the bed, the nurse left. Lisa was stuck on her man. After she made sure he was resting comfortably, she practically climbed into the bed with him. She just kept rubbing his head and kissing him on the cheek. She was just happy to see him alive.

"How are you feeling, bruh?" Marcus said, walking over and giving his brother a pound.

"I'm cool. Aches and pains, but I'm living." Alonzo said.

"Mr. Downing, I'm gonna head down to get your test results and I'll be right back." The doctor said, walking out the door.

"Thanks doc." Alonzo said.

Lisa still had not left her man's side as he looked around the room.

"Heeeeey Mama Pearly." Alonzo said, realizing Lisa's mother was in the room. The elderly woman walked over and gave him a soft hug and a kiss on the cheek.

"How you doin' baby?" She asked.

"I'm alright. Just happy to be alive." Alonzo said.

Ms. Moore told him she was happy to see he was all right and told him that she would be praying for him. Ms. Moore gave Alonzo another kiss on the forehead and left the room. She just wanted to make sure that he was alright, and now that she knew he was and her daughter's mind was at ease, she could leave. Alonzo looked around at his family standing in the room and saw Lasaia standing next to her father. He acted like he didn't see her and said, "Wait a minute, where is the birthday girl?"

"Right here, right here!" Lasaia said, waving her hand, jumping up and down.

"Come here baby girl." Alonzo said.

Lasaia rushed over to his bedside and couldn't stop moving. She loved her uncle a whole lot.

"Did you have a good birthday?" Alonzo asked.

"Yeeeesss."

"Did you get a lotta presents?"

"Yeaaaah."

"Are you gonna share them with your sister?"

"Oh no Uncle Zo, she breaks stuff."

Everyone laughed at her statement and Alonzo said, "What did you get?"

Lasaia started naming off different gifts she received from her friends. She told Alonzo about her earrings and pulled the box out of her pocket.

"Look what I got." She said, showing him her beautiful gift.

Alonzo and Lisa looked into the box and both of them were impressed.

"Wow, who gave you get those?" Alonzo asked.

"Daddy's friend."

Alonzo looked over at Marcus trying to find out whom she was talking about.

"Lasaia." Marcus said.

"Those are really pretty, baby girl." Alonzo said, complimenting her gift.

Lasaia turned to her mother and said, "Can I put them on?"

Sherise nodded her head from her seat and Alonzo helped her put on her gift.

"Wow, those look really pretty on you." Lisa said from her spot next to Alonzo.

A grin that would rival the Cheshire cat jumped onto her face.

"Yeah those are really nice," Alonzo said, "but I still have a gift for you too, ok?"

"Ok." Lasaia said.

Alonzo looked over at Sherise who was sitting in a chair behind Marcus, just watching the whole scene. She wasn't saying anything and didn't look comfortable at all. Her expression wasn't one of anger, but she didn't look happy either.

"You alright sis?" Alonzo asked.

"Yeah I'm fine. I just…I just don't like hospitals that much." She said.

When Sherise was a little girl she wanted to be a doctor, but her mother died in a hospital and ever since then just being inside of a hospital would creep her out. They all sat and talked about Lasaia's birthday party for a few minutes until two men in suits came through the open door. They looked around the room and walked over to Alonzo's bed. One the men looked down at a clipboard in his hand and said, "Excuse me Mr. Downing, I'm Detective Meeks, this is Detective Jennings, we need to ask you a few questions".

"Ok." Alonzo said.

One of the detectives pulled out a small notebook, while the other talked.

"Our reports show that witnesses stated that you got into an altercation with another gentleman right before the shooting. It that correct?"

"Yeah."

"Did you know this man?"

"Yeah, he's her ex-boyfriend," Alonzo said, pointing at Lisa, "We got into a little fight about a month ago at a car show downtown, but that was nothing."

"Did he pull out or show you a weapon that day?"

"Nah. I got into it with him and his homeboys, then my brother and a couple of my homeboys got into it with them. Wasn't nothing though." Alonzo said, pointing at Marcus.

The detective turned to Marcus and said, "And your name sir?"

"Marcus Downing, his brother." Marcus said, as the man wrote in his notepad.

"And did you see any weapons the day you guys got into the fight?" The detective asked.

"Nah, it was just like he said. Nothing really."

Marcus could feel Sherise's eyes piercing the skin on his back. He had told her about going to the car show, but he didn't tell her about getting into a fight.

The detectives turned back to Alonzo and one of them said, "Ok, and do you know this person's full name?"

"Richard Winston Marcell." Lisa quickly spoke up.

"And an address where we can find him?" The detective asked.

"Um, I don't know. He used to hang out in the West End in some projects over there. But, that was before he went to jail. There's no telling where he lives now."

Just as she finished her sentences, the doctor walked in and said, "Ok Mr. Downing, we have your results and…"

The doctor looked up from his papers and saw the two men standing there.

"I'm sorry, I didn't mean to…"

The detective cut in, "That's fine, we were just finishing up. We just needed to get his statement."

"Mr. Downing, we're gonna try and find this Richard person and bring him in for questioning. We'll be in touch."

The two detectives turned and were about to walk out of the room when the doctor said, "Hold on a minute, officers, you might want to hear this."

He flipped through Alonzo's report on his clipboard and turned back to Alonzo, as the detectives stopped in the door.

"You said that you were wrestling with the man like this right?" The doctor said, reenacting the struggle.

"Yeah." Alonzo said.

"Well according to our tests, you were hit three times. Twice in the abdominal area and once in the arm. Now, luckily the ones that hit your body didn't hit anything like your kidneys or liver or anything like that. You'll be fine, probably feel some strong pains for a few weeks and you'll probably feel them months down the road when you turn a certain way, but I'll give you some mild painkillers to help with that. The strange thing is that we can see where the bullets entered and exited, but the way they came in and the angle they traveled would make it impossible for the man you were fighting with to have shot you. There were no powder burns on your skin, which tells us the attacker was at least a few feet away. If he was close enough to wrestle with you then that meant he was close enough to leave some type of evidence."

The detectives walked over to the doctor and requested to see the reports. After a quick review one of them asked, "Did either of you see someone else with this Richard Marcell?"

Both Lisa and Alonzo shook their heads no.

"Ok, thanks doctor." The detective said before they turned to leave.

"I'm gonna head back down and check on your X-rays and other tests Mr. Downing. I just wanna make sure no bones are fractured and there is no major tissue damage. You should be ok, if you need anything just call the nurse." The doctor said.

"Ok doc. I appreciate everything." Alonzo said.

"Not a problem, you just feel better…and get outta my hospital." The doctor said joking, with Alonzo as he left the room.

They all had a quick laugh as Marcus took the seat next to his wife.

"So," Sherise said, slowly turning to him, "You got into a fight, huh?"

Marcus knew this was coming after the detective asked him questions about it.

"Yeah but, I was just trying to help my brother."

"And you felt you couldn't tell me about this?"

"I didn't want you to be all worried and look at me the way you are now."

"Yeah but baby, come on now, you know you can tell me about stuff like that. I get more upset then I would have when I have to find out things like this."

"I know. Ok, when we get home I'll tell you all about it. Can we just talk about it then?"

"Ok."

Sherise and Marcus sat and watched the girls interact with their uncle for a minute. Even though he had three bullet wounds he still had the energy to play with his nieces. He picked Angela up and sat her on his lap and Lasaia climbed into Lisa's lap. The four of them sat there laughing and playing. Alonzo didn't get to see the girls that often and wanted to enjoy every moment.

A few minutes later, a woman rushed into the room. Sherise looked up and saw her new friend standing there. Lasaia looked over at her and Marcus and waved quickly before turning to Alonzo and walking to his bed.

"Are you alright?" Lasaia asked, in a concerned voice.

"Yeah, I'm cool. Hurts a little bit but I'm living."

"When Sherise told me you got shot I almost dropped the phone."

Marcus's oldest daughter slowly climbed out of Lisa's lap and slipped over to her mother's arms.

"So, how are you feeling? Do you need anything?" Lasaia asked.

"Nah, I'm cool. Just glad to be alive. Thanks for coming by."

Lasaia stood there talking to Alonzo for a minute, while the little girl in Sherise's lap turned to her mother and said, "Mommy, I'm hungry."

"Ok sweetie, I'm a little hungry too." Sherise said, as the two of them got up.

"I'm gonna go get the girls something from the cafeteria or something. You want anything?" Sherise told her husband.

"No, I'm fine. I'm just gonna chill right here." Marcus said.

Sherise called Angela from her uncle's lap and asked if anyone else wanted something from the cafeteria while she was going.

"I'll go with you. I haven't eaten since yesterday." Lisa said, separating herself from her man for the first time since he got in the bed.

"You want something baby?" She asked Alonzo.

"Yeah, just get me whatever you get."

She leaned over and kissed Alonzo on the lips and he slapped her on the bottom as she turned and walked off. Lisa stopped, turned back and gave him a look as if she couldn't believe he had just done that in front of everyone.

"Sorry, muscle spasm, uncontrollable." Alonzo said, joking with her and pointing at his arm.

"Mmh Hmm." She said, smiling as she walked out into the hall.

"I'll go with y'all." Lasaia said as Sherise grabbed the girls and walked out the door.

The women disappeared out the room and Marcus got up from his seat and took the one next to his brother's bed.

"Damn she fine as hell." Alonzo said.

"Who?" Marcus asked.

"Your girl Lasaia. Make me wish I would've tried to holla at that when she didn't have any self-esteem." Alonzo said, laughing.

"Yeah well, just because she's fine doesn't mean she's stable." Marcus said, thinking about what he had on the line because of what they did.

"Yeah, true, but...DAMN she fine. I'm sitting in his bed hoping that Lisa don't see the sheets start to move downtown, you know what I'm sayin'," Alonzo laughed, "And if you think she's fine now, you should've seen her last night."

"Last night?"

"Yeah, she came through the club in this little low cut dress with the splits up the sides. Titties was like BAM! Ass shaking like a Jell-O shot with every step."

"She was at your club last night?"

"Yeah, I saw her twice. Once before I realized who she was. She was up front and all I saw was her walking through the club and I was like *Damnit man*. Then, I saw her again right before I ran into that Richard muthafucka. I was coming out the back room and she was just standing there like she was waiting on something. That's when she said my name and I realized who she was."

"Did she say anything to you?"

"She just told me how you and her went out that Friday after your presentation, how did that go by the way?"

"I didn't get it, but we get another chance in a few years." Marcus said, quickly trying to get back to the story.

He wanted to know exactly how much information Lasaia was volunteering to people.

"Oh that's too bad, um anyway…she told me you guys went out to some jazz bar and about how some dame was trying to holla at you and she was getting mad. Ummm, oh, she did tell me that you went to her house afterwards. You better hope she don't tell Sherise about that."

Marcus was silent for a few seconds then said, "I need to tell you something, but you can't tell anybody, not even Lisa."

"What's up man?"

Marcus moved closer to the bed and lowered his voice.

"I cheated on Sherise."

"What," Alonzo said sitting up, "Nigga, is you crazy? With who?"

"Lasaia."

"Awww nigga. What the hell are you thinking?"

"I know, I know…"

Marcus told Alonzo the whole story about that night. He even told him about all the crazy things Lasaia did to make it happen. When he was finished, Alonzo just shook his head and said, "Man, she might be crazy. But, that don't change what you did. You need to tell Sherise. Out of respect, if for nothing else."

"But Lasaia isn't gonna say anything." Marcus said

"That doesn't matter. Some how, she gonna find out and it's gonna be a lot worse if she hears about it from someone else."

"You right, you right. But, I just don't want to lose my family."

"I hate to be the bearer of bad news but it's too late to worry about that now. That's for Sherise to decide. You gotta tell her, and let her make her decision of whether she is gonna stay with you or if she is gonna leave. You already made your decision, now it's her turn." Alonzo said.

To be as young as he was, Alonzo was a little bit of wisdom under his belt. It was probably more experience talking than anything but he was right and Marcus knew it. Just then Sherise, Lasaia, Lisa and the girls came back into the room, and Marcus and Alonzo shut down their conversation.

"Here you go baby." Lisa said, handing Alonzo a bag of food.

She took her spot next to him in the bed and Sherise walked over to Marcus and said, "Can I talk to you for a minute?"

Marcus looked at Alonzo strangely, as he stood up from his chair. They walked outside into the hallway and Sherise said, "Would it be alright if me and the girls get out of here for a little while?"

Marcus's heart slowed down and he said, "Um, yeah. Is the hospital getting to you?"

"Yeah, a little." She said, nodding her head and looking a little nervous.

"Where are you going to?" Marcus asked.

"I was telling Lasaia about how hospitals really freak me out and she said we could go over her house for a little while."

Marcus didn't want her to be anywhere near Lasaia or her house, but he didn't have a legitimate reason for her not to go. Lisa wasn't going to leave her man and he didn't want to go back there with them. He truly believed that Lasaia wouldn't tell her so he gave in.

"Ok sure. When are y'all leaving?"

"Now, I guess."

They walked back into the room and Sherise said, "Come on girls, we're going for a ride."

The girls got up and went to Sherise's side.

"Go give Uncle Alonzo a hug before we go."

The little ones rushed over to their uncle and he reached over the bed to give each one of them a hug. The bending hurt a little but even if it had been 10 times worse, he would have still done it to hug his nieces. The girls returned to their mother and she kissed her husband before they walked into the hall. Lasaia walked toward the door, following Sherise, and got in front of Marcus.

"Where's mine?" She said, just loud enough for him to hear, before she smiled and walked out the door.

Marcus watched as they got into the elevator and kept his eye on them until the doors closed. He didn't know whether Lasaia had something up her sleeve or not, but he did know that he didn't trust her.

Twenty-three

Lasaia pulled into her driveway and Sherise pulled in behind her. Her eyes exploded at the sight of her house.

"Girl, this is beautiful." Sherise said, getting the girls out of the truck.

Sherise was in awe at how exquisite the foyer was. They walked into the den and Lasaia turned on the television. She flipped right to Cartoon Network and the girls wasted no time jumping to the floor in front of the large screen.

"You want some coffee?" Lasaia asked.

Sherise accepted her offer and the two of them made their way to the kitchen. Sherise didn't get a chance to get her morning fix since they left so early, so she was really craving her Columbian delight. After her first few sips, she started to perk up. The two of them laughed and talked about the birthday party and various other womanly things.

About thirty minutes into the conversation Sherise asked, "When can I see the house?"

"Oh girl, you ain't said nothin' but a word. Let's go." Lasaia said. They refreshed their coffee supply and headed out of the kitchen. Lasaia showed her the entire bottom floor of her home. She showed her the dining room, guest rooms, and her office. Sherise loved every room she went into. They passed by the girls who had not moved from their spot in front of the television and headed toward the back of the house. Lasaia showed Sherise her backyard, which was bordered at the back by a beautiful lake. They headed back inside and up the stairs. Lasaia showed her both of her huge upstairs guest rooms and they ended up at the middle door, Lasaia's room. Lasaia pushed the handle and threw the huge door open. Sherise peeked around the corner of the door and looked in. Her eyes got big as she saw how beautiful Lasaia's bedroom was. She walked into the same scene that Marcus saw a few weeks earlier. The room was spotless. Sherise walked around the bedroom looking up and turning around like someone walking through the Vatican for the first time. She walked around touching all of the furniture. She loved it all so much she just wants to know how it felt. She loved her huge bedroom windows and couldn't take her eyes off the view of the lake through it. Of all the things in the room, she loved the bed the most. It looked like something a princess would have. The same canopy bed that her husband broke their wedding vows in was the same bed she was now sitting on. She ran her hands back and forth over the comforter and admired how soft and comfortable it felt. She complimented Lasaia on having a lot of beautiful things. She had no idea that Lasaia had slept with her husband and the life she thought she had was totally different now because of this woman standing in front of her.

Lasaia's phone rang and she rushed over to answer it. "Hello?"

Sherise just sat on the bed envying Lasaia's room.

"Oh hey Tony. What's going on?" Lasaia said.

It was Tony, or "Greg" as Sherise knew him. Sherise really had no idea about all the deception that had been going on behind her back. All she knew was she had a new friend. She had no idea that same "friend" was really not a friend at all.

"No, no…Tell Rico we can't change that. The client has it set the way they want it." Lasaia said as Sherise got up and looked around the room some more. Lasaia was busy with her business call and didn't see Sherise looking at a beautiful vase that had caught her eye. It was a beautiful handmade vase that Sherise could tell had to be from another country. As she was admiring the vase her eyes dropped a few inches to the base. There, on the nightstand, were 5 little buttons. Sherise didn't pay them much attention at first until she remembered seeing the same design on the buttons that were on the shirt hidden in Marcus's closet. Sherise picked up one of the buttons and had a closer look. It was the same design. Sherise couldn't believe it. She dropped the button back on the nightstand and sat on the edge of the bed. Her heart rate started to rise as all kinds of thoughts came flooding into her head.

Those couldn't be Marcus's buttons. No, no…it can't be, Sherise thought to herself.

She refused to accept the thought that those buttons could have come from her husband's shirt.

They probably make thousands of those shirts everyday. It's just a coincidence, that's all…a coincidence.

Sherise got weak sitting on the side of the bed, thinking about the possibility that something may have happened between Marcus and Lasaia. She looked over at Lasaia standing across the room on the phone and saw how beautiful she was.

No, no...my husband loves me. He wouldn't do that.

Sherise started to try and come up with different scenarios as to how Marcus's buttons got on her nightstand, but none of them made much sense. She started to get short of breath and stood up. Lasaia had her back turned and Sherise walked out of the room without saying a word. She tried to block out the thought of her husband doing anything sexual with Lasaia. She made her way back to her little girls and had a seat on the couch.

Lasaia looked up as her mother sat down and rushed over. "Mommy Mommy...Look...my picture!" She said handing her mother a folded piece of paper. Sherise tried not to let her daughter see the distress in her face while she started unfolding the sheet.

"You drew mommy a picture?" She said, opening it up.

"No, it's daddy's picture." Lasaia said, bouncing up and down, excited to show her mother the picture. Sherise's eyes opened wide as she looked at the picture and realized it really was her husband's picture. Tears began to form in her eyes as she looked at the crazy discolored scene. Those same red ducks, green fox, and blue grass. *I love you Daddy* etched into the sky.

"Where did you get this baby?" Sherise asked.

"From right here." Lasaia said tapping her finger on the end table next to the couch.

This woman, who had been smiling in her face, was secretly sleeping with her husband and she had just gotten all the proof she needed. Sherise's emotions went from denial to sadness. She couldn't believe that she had given this man the last 10 years of her life, 7 of them in marriage, and he threw it all away on this tramp. Then, didn't have the decency to tell her the truth. Sherise wanted to cry. She wanted to run to her room, jump under her covers and let it all out. But she couldn't, she was in a different town, hundreds of miles away from home, sitting in the house of the woman who was fucking her husband. Sherise kept her composure and was able to calm herself down over the next few minutes. She couldn't take being in that house any longer and said, "Come on girls, we have to go."

The girls reluctantly got up from their television show and walked over to their mother.

"You ok Mommy?" Lasaia asked, looking up at her.

She could tell that something wasn't right with her.
"Yeah baby, everything's fine, it's just time for us to go." Sherise said.

As they turned to leave the den, Lasaia came around the corner. "Girl, I was wondering where you disappeared to…" She said, smiling.

There was a few seconds of silence while Sherise just stood there staring at her. She had all the words lined up in her head to throw at this woman but…in her heart she knew it wasn't worth it. If she could be this friendly person in the light and this man stealing whore in the dark, her words would mean nothing to her and she would just be wasting her breath.

Lasaia looked down and saw the two little ones holding their mother's hands.

"What's going on?" Lasaia said, confused.

"We really need to go." Sherise said.

She wanted to drop her daughters' hands and punch the woman standing there in front of her. She felt betrayed, confused and angry, all at the same time. All kinds of emotions overflowed Sherise's body but she stayed calm.

"Well let me get my purse and I'll…"

"No, you stay here. We're just going to leave."

Sherise and the girls walked out of the house and made it up the driveway before Lasaia said, "Sherise wait, what's going on?" Sherise didn't say a word and got Angela strapped into her car seat. Lasaia climbed into the seat next to her as her mother's former friend walked toward the truck. Sherise finished with Angela and closed her door. Lasaia made it to Sherise's door just as she was reaching for the handle.

"Sherise, what's wrong? What happened?"

"What happened? What happened," Sherise gave her a nervous sounding laugh, "You have the nerve to ask me what happened? You must really think I'm stupid don't you?"

"I don't know what you're talking about. What did I do wrong?" Lasaia said, sounding confused.

She had no idea about the items Sherise had found in her house. She thought she had just gotten upset because she was on the phone for so long.

"What did you do wrong? Hmm, let's see. Well, how about lie to me, make me believe you were my friend, or how about fuck my husband? Yeah, I think that's it. You fucked my husband!" Sherise said, slamming the truck door.

Lasaia just stood there in shock. She didn't understand how she could have found that out.

"Lele was right. She told me I couldn't trust you. But, I thought you were so nice. I thought you were my friend. But, obviously you're not."

Sherise opened the driver's side door to the truck and climbed in. She backed out of the driveway and sped off down the street.
Lasaia's face slowly formed into a grin.

❧ ❧ ❧

Sherise drove through the streets of Atlanta, tears escaping her eyes. She couldn't believe that her husband had been unfaithful to her. She couldn't believe that for the last three weeks he had been hiding what he did. She couldn't believe how she could not have realized that something was going on. She was so happy to meet an old friend of his that meant so much to him that she never expected things to end up this way. She thought she could trust her husband to keep his vows sacred. She thought back and realized how many signs she should have seen to tell her that something was going on. Her energetic, friendly, usually loud little girl wanted nothing to do with this woman. She noticed how Marcus's attitude toward her quickly changed after he came back from his business trip. Then there was the way Lasaia turned on her father and didn't even want him to touch her for a week after he got back. Her little girl's words, that night in the bathroom, kept ringing in Sherise's ears.
Daddy's dirty.
Then there was the dinner she encouraged him to go to, that she never heard anything about. Now she found the buttons to a shirt he tried to hide in his closet and their daughter's picture inside this woman's house. That was enough proof for her to think that something was going on. Lasaia hadn't even denied it when she brought it up. A real friend, one that isn't sleeping with you man, would have told her that she was being foolish and she would never touch her man like that.

She tried to control her tears but didn't do a very good job. The pain was too heavy. She could feel the pain shoot through her heart like a lighting bolt every time she thought about it. Lasaia could see the side of her mother's face from her seat and could see that she was crying. She didn't understand why, but she didn't want her mom to feel sad.
"It's ok mommy, I don't like her either." The little voice said from the back seat.
"Thank you baby." Sherise said, trying to calm down and not cry in front of her daughters. She grabbed a few napkins from the reservoir between the seats and wiped her eyes.

❧ ❧ ❧

Back at the hospital Lisa, Alonzo, and Marcus all joked around about who it could have been that shot Alonzo. Marcus started naming off different people from his past that were probably still looking for him after all these years. Lisa joked about Alonzo's crazy ex-girlfriends and they all had a laugh. The doctor strolled back into the room while they were having a good time and said, "Alright Mr. Downing, everything looks fine with your tests. There were no potentially fatal internal injuries. As long as you promise to go home and relax, you'll be alright to leave."

"Cool. That's the best news of the day." Alonzo said, excited about getting out of the hospital.

"Now, if the pain gets too bad, here's a prescription for those pain killers I told you about before," The doctor said, handing him a piece of paper, "Now that you got shot you can probably get you a record label and sell a few million copies."

They all had a laugh as they gather their things and the doctor left. After they get checked out and were heading for the exit doors, Sherise walked in with the girls. She could barely stand to look at Marcus standing there with a smile on his face. She wanted to jump on his face and scratch his eyes out. Her mood had gone from sadness to anger by now and she was ready to attack. It took all she had not to curse him out right there in the hospital lobby. She walked over to the counter and Marcus told her that they were letting Alonzo go home and that everything was alright.

"That's good. I'm ready to go home." Sherise said.

She gave Alonzo a hug and told him she hoped he felt better then turned right around without saying a word to Marcus and went back to the truck. Marcus looked at her strangely but didn't know the full how bad things had gotten. Marcus and the girls walked Alonzo to his truck and he gave his nieces a hug. Marcus hugged him and they said their goodbyes. Lisa jumped into the driver's seat and they pulled out of the parking lot as Marcus walked back to his truck with the girls. He got Angela strapped in and Lasaia jumped in her seat. Marcus jumped into the driver's seat and Sherise was just staring off into space as he pulled out of the parking lot, headed for the interstate.

They made it home around nine o'clock that night. The girls were asleep in the backseat and Marcus brought the truck to a stop in the garage. He had been trying to talk to his wife for the last six hours but she did nothing the whole way home but stare out of her window and ignore him. They climbed out of the truck and got the girls inside. Lasaia woke up but Angela was sound asleep on her father's shoulder. They walked into the house and Sherise said, "Lasaia baby, go upstairs and take your bath and get ready for bed."

Lasaia didn't fight the request; she was too tired to argue. Sherise took Angela from Marcus and went upstairs to get her ready for bed. Marcus went back out to the truck and started getting the bags to bring them in. He got them into the house and decided to leave them in the kitchen until the next day. Marcus rushed to his office to make sure he didn't miss any emails that he needed for work the next day. He only saw one new mail and it was from Lasaia. Marcus didn't feel like dealing with the aggravation, so he logged out of her email account without opening her email. After a few minutes of web surfing he shut his computer down and headed up the stairs.

He saw his little girls asleep in their beds and headed for his room. As he walked through the door he saw Sherise sitting on the bed with some kind of cloth draped across her lap. As he stepped closer, she realized he was in the room and looked up at him. Her eyes were filled with tears and they fell from her cheeks into her lap.

"Baby, what's wrong?" Marcus said, rushing over to her.

After his first two steps, he looked into her lap and realized what she was holding. He stopped where he was and just stood there looking at her.

"What? You don't have anything to say to me?" She said, between her tears.

Marcus just stood there looking down at the shirt he wore the night of his affair.

He was frozen in his spot.

He wanted to tell her how sorry he was.

He wanted to tell her it would never happen again.

And, above all, he wanted her to believe him.

He wanted to say something that would comfort her. But, instead, he just stood there unable to form the words.

"So you're not gonna say anything to me? How could you Marcus? 7 years...7 years we've been married. 7 years of love, 7 years of pain, 7 years of having and raising children...YOUR children. And you throw it all away for what? A bitch you haven't seen in over a decade?" Sherise got loud and Marcus closed the door so she didn't wake up the girls.

"Baby, I..."

"No, I don't wanna hear some fucking excuse, ok? I just want to know why." Sherise yelled through her tears, tossing the shirt at him.

He caught the shirt and walked over to her. Sherise jumped out of the bed and stood across the room from him.

"No, don't come near me."

Marcus didn't say a word and just stood there looking down at his shirt.

"I found that in your closet, hidden away in your suitcase. I didn't think anything of it. I figured you had just messed it up. But, today when I go to that bitch's house, I find all five of the missing buttons in her room. Then our child runs up to me talking about she found her picture. Your picture Marcus…the one she drew for you before you left to go to that damn football game. So how long has this been going on? Did you fuck her then too?" Sherise asked.

"No, I swear. It was only once." Marcus said.

Sherise got weak from her stress and collapsed to her knees.

"Baby!" Marcus said, rushing around the bed to help her.

"NO, don't come near me!" Sherise yelled while on her hands and knees rubbing her stomach and crying. She felt like she was about to throw up.

"I can't believe you. How could you do this to me? To us?" Sherise said, rolling over and sitting down on the floor. She couldn't stop the tears and just sat there like a little girl hugging her knees. Marcus had no idea what to do. Usually he was the one she would run to when she was upset, but she was upset with him this time and there was nothing he could do to help her. He knew this day was coming, but had no way to prepare for it. Sherise sat there crying for a few seconds, then looked up at him and asked, "Was it me? Did I do something wrong?"

"No, baby you're perfect."

"If I'm perfect, why did you do it?"

"I don't know. I just…we were drinking and having fun, next thing I know…"

"Don't you love me?"

"Yes, baby I love you and the girls more then anything else in this world."

"Then why would you do this? Who was there for you when you dad died? That bitch or me? Who was there with you when we didn't have a dime? Living in a tiny apartment, huh? Who gave you two beautiful children? Who has made sacrifice after sacrifice just for you? Me or her?"

"I know baby, I know. You have always been my backbone. I just…I was just stupid. It was a stupid thing to do and will never happen again."

Marcus was able to work his way over to the sobbing Sherise and picked her up off of the floor. She was crying uncontrollably and he stood there holding her in his arms. He slowly rocked back and forth trying to help her calm down. Her sobs slowed down as she pressed her head against his chest.

"That was it right? You didn't do anything else did you?" Sherise asked, calming down a little. Marcus closed his eyes wishing she hadn't asked that. His memory of that night at Alonzo's house jumped into his head and he didn't want to tell her but didn't want to lie to her anymore. Sherise heard the hesitation in him answering and pushed away from him.

"What else did you do?" She asked, backing away from him, holding her stomach with one hand.

"Nothing, I," Marcus took a deep breath and said, "When I went up to Alonzo's for the game. She came over that Saturday and...we made out on the couch...but that's it."

Sherise's tears returned and she quickly walked into the bathroom and shut the door. Of course that night was a lot less terrible then the night he cheated but Sherise didn't know what to believe anymore. That had happened before he cheated and he didn't tell her about that either. Sherise just felt all alone and had no one to run to. He walked over to the door and said, "Baby, I know. I'm sorry, but nothing happened that night. I stopped it. I..."

"It doesn't matter Marcus. You just don't get it." Sherise said, sitting on the floor of the bathroom, her back against the door.

"Baby, please I..."

"Just leave Marcus. I don't want you here."

"Sherise, we can talk about this."

"Just go."

Sherise sat on the floor of her lavatorial fortress and cried. Marcus could have easily broken into the bathroom and cornered her and made her listen, but it wouldn't have done any good, and he knew it. He backed away from the door. In the silence, he could hear her crying on the other side. She felt like he had ripped her heart out of her chest and threw it to the ground. She loved Marcus with all her heart and now the one person she would do anything for had betrayed her.

Marcus silently packed a bag and walked out of the room. He slipped into each of his little girls' rooms and gave each of his sleeping angels a kiss on their forehead. He wasn't sure when he would get to see them again and wanted to look at them. He walked down the stairs and set his bag outside his office. He walked through the door and started packing all of his work things into his laptop bag and briefcase. After he finished, he walked back out of his office, grabbed his bag and headed out to his truck. He took Angela's car seat out of his car and put it in Sherise's and then jumped into his truck. He pulled out of the garage and down the street. Sherise saw him leave from the bathroom window and left the bathroom and jumped into her bed, crying herself to sleep.

❧ ❧ ❧

He drove around Jacksonville for a few hours just thinking about how stupid he was for what he had done. He pulled into the parking lot of a motel and got a room for the night. He went to his room and threw his things in the corner and jumped on the bed. He missed his family already and wished he knew this feeling before he actually had the affair. If he had known it would feel like this, he would have never laid a finger on Lasaia. Marcus lay there for a few minutes trying to think of ways he could possibly fix things when he remembered he had that email from Lasaia. He thought that she must have told Sherise when she was at her house and was emailing him to gloat. He figured this was part of her *Welcome to a Cold day in HELL* email. He rushed to his laptop bag and pulled it out. While the system was loading, he took the phone cord out of the back of the motel room phone and plugged it into his laptop. He signed onto his email account and opened Lasaia's email.

Marcus,

Sherise just left my house all upset. She knows we had sex. I don't know how she found out. One minute we were in my room and I answered the phone, next thing I know she's down stairs screaming about how I fucked her husband. See, I didn't tell her just like I said I wouldn't. But now that she knows, there is nothing stopping us from being together. I love you soooo much and I know we can work things out. I'll give you a call on Monday and tell Alonzo I hope he feels better.

Marcus couldn't believe how insane this woman was. She figured since Sherise knew and she wasn't the one that told her that he would just fall into her arms. Marcus turned off his computer and took a shower before going to bed. For the next three days, Marcus called in to work sick. Even though he didn't have a fever he did feel sick without his wife and family around him. He didn't sleep all that much, he hardly ate, and he wouldn't answer his cell phone. Everyday he would call Sherise's shop and the house a few times a trying to get her to talk to him. He missed her and wanted to make sure she knew how much pain he was in without his family. Sherise never took his calls and would ignore the phone when his name appeared on the Caller ID. She would even erase his message as soon as she heard his voice come through the answering machine speaker. Marcus was completely cut off from his family. Of course, he could have went to Sherise's shop or to the house when he knew she was there but he knew that wouldn't do anything but upset her more and he didn't want to do that.

On the third day of his absence from work, Mike called Marcus's cell phone. This was the first time since Sherise kicked him out that he actually answered. Mike told his friend that Alicia had told him everything the night before.

"Man, I'm sorry." Mike said.

"It's alright man, you don't have anything to be sorry for."

"Yes I do. I'm the one that told you not to tell her. This is kind of my fault."

"Nah, I'm a grown ass man. I'm the one that messed up and should have been man enough to tell my wife I was wrong. My brother told me I needed to tell her, but by that time it was already too late."

"Yeah but…I don't know. If there's anything I can do to help you out, just let me know."

Marcus thought for a moment and said, "Actually, you can…"

Marcus gave Mike a message. He figured if Sherise wouldn't listen to him, maybe she would listen to her friend. Even Alicia was feeling sorry for Marcus, a little. With all the trash she talked about him, she really did like him underneath it all. When Sherise told her what happened she wanted to find him and kick his ass but she knew that the two of them belonged together. She knew how much Sherise loved him and how much he loved her back. She knew they were made for each other. Their bodies just fit together too perfectly for them not be together. Mike took Marcus's message and promised to pass it on to Alicia. Mike was able to talk Marcus into going to work the next day and even got him to move out of the motel and stay with him until things got straightened out. Marcus went to work, but he didn't feel the need to do much work. His family was his main motivation. He constantly went to work looking for ways to make some things happen for his family. Now, he didn't know if he would have them much longer and didn't have the drive he had before. After a few messages between Mike and Alicia, Sherise finally agreed to let him call the house. For a month after that Marcus was able to check on his little girls over the phone.

All during that month Marcus would shower Sherise with flowers, candy and gifts. He would send them to the shop and catch her off guard at home sometimes with a delivery. Every card sounded more pitiful then the last and it started to wear on her. He knew how much she loved flowers and knew she wouldn't turn them down. That was his only chance to actually get a word to her besides through Mike and Alicia. Lasaia would constantly send him emails, but he didn't respond to most of them and the ones he did respond to, he told her he wanted nothing to do with her. Angela's third birthday was quickly approaching and Marcus wanted to see his little girls so bad he was about to explode. On the Friday before her birthday Marcus called the house after he knew the girls would be in bed. They talked for a few minutes about their day but she still refused to talk about *them*. She would only talk about things involving the girls. Marcus gave up on reconciliation and begged Sherise to just let him come to his little girl's birthday party. He just wanted to see them. He told her how much he missed all of them and would make any compromise to see them.

"I promise, I will do whatever you want. If you want me to leave after an hour, I will. If you want me to clean up the whole house after everyone leaves, I will. If you want me to wash your car, I will. Anything. I just want to be there."

Sherise was silent for a few seconds, took a deep breath, then said, "Ok but…"

"Name it."

"You can't spend the night."

"Done."

Marcus heard Sherise start to sniff on the phone. Even though he couldn't see them, he knew the tears were there.

"What's wrong baby?"

"I can't do this."

"Well if you can't handle the party by yourself, I can…"

"No, I mean this…us…I don't like us being like this."

"I know baby, I know. I love you so much but…we just need to talk about some things."

"I know. You really hurt me Marcus."

Marcus was surprised she was actually bringing up her feelings. She had been so cold toward him all this time.

"I know and I wish there was something I could do or tell you to make it all better but there isn't. I messed up. I messed up bad. But, I want you to know that I am truly sorry for hurting you."

"I miss you so much."

Sherise could barely get her words out between her tears.

"I miss you too baby."

"I love you Marcus. And, as much as I want you to be…I can't have you here right now. I just can't."

"I know, and believe me, I understand. But, we can get through this though, if you are willing to give me another chance. I will do whatever it takes to regain your trust."

Sherise couldn't see through her tears at this point.

"I…I need to go." She said, trying to get off the phone before she completely broke down.

"Ok."

Sherise hung up the phone and threw her face into the pillow, crying uncontrollably. After all the time that had passed, the gash in her heart hadn't healed at all.

Twenty-four

The next day Sherise woke the girls up as usual and started getting the house ready for Angela's birthday party. Marcus woke up and got ready to spend time with his family for the first time in over a month. He impatiently sat at Mike's house flipping through channels trying to kill time before he left. Seconds were minutes and minutes, hours. The party was scheduled for 1:00, and he couldn't wait to see them. At 12:15 he couldn't take it any longer and left Mike's house, headed for home. He got to the house at 12:30 and walked through the front door.

"Daddy, Daddy!" Lasaia said when she saw him step through the front door. She ran over to him with Angela a few feet behind her. They both latched onto their father's legs and he knelt down to give them both a big hug. Sherise walked out of the kitchen and saw the girls wrapped around their father. Marcus looked up at her and she looked more beautiful than the day he married her.

"I know you said one, but I couldn't wait to see them."

Sherise looked at her little girls, and how they were clinging to their father, she smiled.

"It's ok. You can help me." Sherise said.

She wasn't showing it, but Sherise wanted to run and latch onto him too. Marcus followed his wife into the kitchen and helped her with the food. After finishing up the decorations, kids and parents began to arrive. Angela's party wasn't as big as Lasaia's but all the kids had a great time. Marcus and Sherise really enjoyed their first day back together, as a family.

Later that night, while Sherise was washing the dishes, Marcus was upstairs getting Angela ready for bed while Lasaia was in the bathtub. He finished with the tired little one's clothes and put her in the bed. He grabbed a book off of her shelf and sat down beside her bed to read her a bedtime story. He had really missed doing that over the last month. Usually, after she fell asleep, he would stop reading but this time he completed the whole story, even though she didn't make it pass page three. He didn't want their time together to end. He wanted it to last all night long.

After finishing the story, he closed the book and put it back on her shelf. He knelt down and gave her a kiss on the forehead before turning off the light and leaving the room. He walked into Lasaia's room and saw her playing with some of her birthday dolls on the floor.

"Ok baby girl, time for bed."

She got up from her spot and carefully put her dolls away. She jumped into her bed and Marcus knelt down next to her.

"Have you been helping your mom around the house?" He asked.

"Yes sir."

"Good, I want you to help her out as much as you can, ok? If she asks you to do something, I want you to do it…for me. Ok?"

"Ok Daddy."

Marcus leaned forward and kissed her on the forehead.

"Goodnight baby." Marcus said, before turning to leave the room.

"Goodnight daddy."

Marcus was about to walk through the doorway when Lasaia said, "Daddy?"

He stopped and looked back at her and said, "Yes sweetie?"

"I'm sorry I was mean to you and made you leave. But you can come back now. I'll be nice again."

Marcus rushed over to his daughter's bedside.

"No, no, no baby girl. It wasn't you. Me and your mother…we're…we're just going through some things right now. But none of that is your fault. Daddy did something very stupid and your mom is very upset with me. Sometimes for grownups it's best for one of them to leave and let the other one calm down before they talk. That way they can think about things before they say something they don't mean. You understand?"

"I think so."

"But you do know that it's not your fault, right?"

"Yeah."

"Ok well that's all you have to understand right now. Just know that your mother and I love you very much and we are going to work things out. We're gonna be a family, again."

"Promise?"

"I promise."
"I miss you daddy."
"I miss you too baby. I miss all of you guys. But daddy is the one that messed up really bad and I have to try and make it up to mommy."
"I'm gonna tell mommy to stop trippin'."
Marcus laughed.
"Will you be here when I wake up?" She asked.
"No baby. But, I promise you I will be here every chance I get, ok?"
"Ok." She said, yawing.
She loved her daddy and missed him not being around.
"You get some sleep now ok."
"Ok. Goodnight daddy."
"Night baby."
Marcus turned off the light and walked out of her room.

He headed down the stairs and found Sherise sitting at the breakfast table, sipping on some coffee.
"You're gonna be up all night with that stuff." Marcus said, jokingly.
He would always make fun of her about drinking coffee late in the evening, then not being able to sleep. Sherise giggled at his joke as he had a seat at the table across from her.
They sat in silence a few seconds.
Neither of them ever expected to be in this situation. Marcus was the first to speak and said, "Look…I know there is nothing I can do, or say, or buy you, or anything to make up for what I did. And I don't blame you for anything that you have done over these past few weeks. I know you're upset and I am sorry about what I did. I don't expect you to just take me back and everything go back to normal. All I want is a chance to prove to you how much I love you and I…I want this to work."
Sherise looked at him and said, "I don't know what to tell you. My mind tells me not to ever trust you again, but my heart can't just get rid of you that easy. I love you Marcus. I have always loved you. From that first day we met in the library…I told Alicia that day that you were going to be my husband. She didn't believe me," she giggled, "Even when you cheated on me the first time, I still loved you. Yes, we were only together for a few weeks back then but it has been 10 years since, and you did it again. And, I find myself still loving you. When I look at this from the outside I say that I wouldn't ever think of keeping a man that cheated on me, but now, I don't know. I can't just end it all and not look back. I think we have more together then that."

"Baby, I know I was wrong and I felt terrible right after I did it. You and the girls mean everything to me. I can't imagine my life without any of you."

Sherise was quiet for a few seconds, then asked, "Did you use protection?"

Marcus didn't want to answer her question but he did.

"No."

"Well how can I believe that you care so much about us and you didn't even try to protect yourself. You don't know how many men she has done this to."

"She was a virgin. That was the whole reason she was after me. I made a promise to her back in high school that I would be her first and we never were able to keep that promise. So she had been waiting all this time for me to keep my promise and I messed up."

"So what happens next time?"

"Next time?"

"Yes. Next time you get caught up in the moment and feel these same urges. What happens then? Do I just forgive you then too?"

"There will not be a next time."

"That's what you said when you did it the first time. So did you mean it then?"

"Yes, of course."

"So why should I believe you now?"

"I don't know. All I know is, the feelings I felt the night you kicked me out and all this time since is a feeling that I do not want to have again. I know you have been just as hurt and I don't want either of us to go through this again. I do understand what you're saying though, and probably would doubt you in the same situation too. All I know is that I will not hurt you and my girls like that again. I don't know what I was thinking. I was blinded by the fact that we ran into each other again and wanted to spend time with her and catch up. But every time we were alone together, either on the phone or in person, she would completely change. She would go from the nice, sweet person you met, to trying to rip my clothes off and asking me when I was going to leave you and get back with her. I won't lie to you, I did feel a lot of old feeling come back when she was around. I thought they were all long gone by now, but they weren't. She was my first actual love, and she brought that out of me. But, that was my fault. I should have never let her do anything to make me break my promise to you just to keep one to her. We had sex, and yes we were drinking and I was not in full grip of reality, and she took my card so I couldn't get back to the hotel...but none of that is an excuse for what I did and I am so sorry."

A confused look jumped onto her face.

"Took your card?"

"Yeah, we were at the little jazz bar thing because she was trying to cheer me up after I lost the account, and I had to go to the bathroom. So, I told her I would be right back. She asked to see the pictures of the girls again, so I gave her my wallet, not thinking anything of it, and went to the bathroom. I come back to my seat, get my wallet, then all of a sudden she is ready to go. We were both too drunk to drive her car and I ended up hailing a cab and I let her take it and was about to get another one. She was about to pull off when she asked if I had any money. I checked my wallet and my card was gone. I figured I had left it in the room and jumped into the cab because I had no idea where I was and didn't have any money. I figured she was just going to take me to the hotel and I could pay her back later, but the next thing I know we are pulling up to her house. We had a few more drinks and talked about old times, and things went too far. I found my card when I was looking through her purse for some money to catch a cab out of there. But still, what she did is no excuse. I still messed up. I should have never got into that cab."

"So y'all didn't plan to go to her house?"

"Nah, I only got in the cab. And, I only got in the cab because I was drunk in a place where I had no idea where I was and didn't have any money."

Sherise sat in silence staring at the floor thinking about what Marcus just told her.

"That bitch." She whispered.

Marcus should have probably shut up right then and let Sherise just blame her, but he had to say something.

"It wasn't just her, I was a part of it."

"I know, and trust me…you're still in trouble. But, she acted like she was my friend while all this was going on. You just fell for her little trick. You didn't know. She was trying to make it happen. And what about her boyfriend? Does he know she cheated on him with you?"

Marcus laughed a little.

"That wasn't her boyfriend. That was a guy she got to pretend to be her boyfriend so you wouldn't shut her out right away. That was the guy that did your hair…umm, damn, what's his name?"

"Rico?"

"Yeah him. That was his boyfriend."

"He was gay?"

"Yeah, we saw them at the jazz bar. They came to the table all hugged up and stuff and talked to Lasaia. He treated me as if it was alright to come into my house and lie to me. I was so drunk that I didn't put everything together until I found that card. She's known them since college."

Sherise stood up, disgusted with what Marcus was telling her. She couldn't believe this woman had went through so much to deceive both of them.

Sherise was ready to fight.

She wanted to call Lasaia and curse her out but Marcus calmed her down.

"Baby, it's ok. We don't have to deal with her anymore. We need to forget her and focus on us."

"Do you actually think she will just let it go like that?"

"She's gonna have to. What's her other choice?"

"I don't think she has all 'em all."

"No, she doesn't. Actually she never did. I think all the abuse and stuff she went through as a child really messed her up. That's why it's important to me to show Angela and Lasaia the same love my dad showed us. I mean he wasn't all hugs and kisses, but he taught us how to treat a woman. And up until now I think I've done a decent job."

"You're alright." Sherise said, giggling.

They talked for a little while longer about the party and about the girls.

Around 10:30 Marcus said, "Well, I better get going. Look...if you have something to do tomorrow, you can bring the girls by Mike's house. I would love to see them."

Marcus got up from this spot at the table and turned to walk to the front door. "I'll just give you a call." He said, walking.

Sherise felt her heart start to sink. She felt like she was losing him all over again.

"Marcus....wait." She said as he made it to the door.

Marcus turned around to see her rushing out of the kitchen and up to him. She placed her hands on his cheeks and pressed her lips against his. Her lips were the sweetest thing Marcus had tasted since the last time they had kissed. Sherise felt like the missing piece of her heart had been replaced with that one kiss. The two of them were formed by God and made for each other. God had created one beautiful soul, split it down the middle and sent it into the tissue of each of their mothers' wombs. For either of them to start a new relationship with someone else would be a certified sin. Sherise couldn't let him leave. They stood there kissing for a few seconds then Marcus said, "I thought you said..." Sherise put her finger over his mouth and said, "I know, and you're still in trouble. And it's time to start making it up to me."

They shared a few more kisses before Marcus picked her up and carried her up the stairs. They spent the rest of the night having the best night of makeup sex ever.

The next morning the two of them woke up and Sherise went downstairs to start their Sunday morning breakfast while Marcus woke up the girls. Lasaia was so happy to see her father's face come into focus when she opened her eyes that morning. She jumped up and hugged him like it was Christmas day. They had their usual Sunday breakfast and all went upstairs to get ready for church. They all got dressed and Sherise walked into the room with Lasaia to make sure she was ready. She saw her daughter's earrings on her dresser and said, "You gonna wear your earrings sweetie?"
Lasaia looked at her and said, "No, I don't want to."
"Why? I thought you liked them." Sherise said.
"Not anymore. They're dirty."
Sherise smiled at her daughter and tossed the expensive earrings into the small waste basket next to her door. Lasaia smiled as if she agreed with her mother's actions and they both walked out of the room. The family climbed into Marcus's truck and left for church. The preacher's sermon this week was on forgiveness. One phrase in particular stuck in Sherise's head
"No matter what someone does, if you are still breathing, forgiveness is an option."
Sherise and Marcus looked at each other throughout the sermon and knew that this one was for them too. They left the church after the service and had a family dinner at a restaurant they let Lasaia pick. They all went home and Sherise and Marcus worked together to get the girls in bed. The two of them had a wonderful evening talking and starting to make up.

The next day Marcus went to work and was in the best mood he had been in over the last two months. He was working in his office when Mike knocked on the door. Marcus motioned through the glass for him to come in and he stepped into the office.
"What's up man, I heard things are getting back to normal between you two." Mike said.
"Yeah, she's still a little upset about everything that happened, but I'm back home. That's a start."
"That's good man. That's real good. So, you heard from the psycho lately?"

"She used to try and call but we got her numbers blocked at the house. All she really does now is send emails."

"Well she'll get tired of that after a while. Looks like the worst is behind you. Just act right at home and Sherise will eventually get pass all that. She'll never forget," he said with a laugh, "but she'll let it go. You do that, and stop listening to me and you'll be alright."

They both laughed as Mike got up to head back to work. Just as they were giving each other a pound Mr. Lockson charged into the room.

"Marcus, I've got smashing news! I just got word that *Perimeter* may not be able to hold up their end of the deal. Which means we may still have a shot at this Coca-Cola deal."

"What?" Mike and Marcus said in unison.

"I know, I know...it's bloody fabulous! Marcus I need you to get your presentation together and email it to me so I can send it up. They will be reviewing us and the other company over the next few days and I want to have our presentation up there as soon as possible."

"Yes sir, I'll do it right now." Marcus said, jumping to his computer.

"And Mike..." Mr. Lockson said.

"Yes sir?" Mike said, excited at what role Mr. Lockson might have for him.

"Leave him alone so he can get to work." Mr. Lockson said, turning to the door. He opened the door wide, turned to the two men in the office and yelled, "Let's make money!"

Mr. Lockson flew out of the office and disappeared into the hall.

"Punk ass British mutha...alright man I'm out." Mike said, giving his friend another pound and left him to his work.

Marcus got his revised presentation off one of the backup disks he had in his laptop bag and emailed it to Mr. Lockson. Before Marcus closed his email account he saw a new email from Lasaia. He decided to open and read it.

~

You don't know who you are dealing with, do you? You can't treat me like this. What do I have to do to show you that we are meant for each other? You have until tomorrow to stop playing games and call me before something really bad happens. I don't want to hear any excuses. If you don't call me by this time tomorrow, your life as you know it will change. Don't believe me? Try me and see.

Marcus checked the time the email was sent and looked at his watch. He had five minutes to decide whether he was going to call or let this *really bad* thing happen. Marcus realized he didn't have any idea who Lasaia could manipulate to hurt him or his family. She definitely had the money to do it. Marcus decided he might need to call her before she did something crazy to him or herself. He closed his office door and dialed her number. The phone rang a few times and was answered, but she didn't say anything.

"Hello?" Marcus said, not sure if the call was disconnected.

"So I have to seriously threaten you to get you to call me?" Lasaia said.

She sounded really frustrated.

"Look, I told you it was over between us. I don't know why I say that because nothing really started. Just one big mistake, that's all it was."

"I am really getting tired of being called a fucking mistake. We have never been a mistake. I know you love me…"

"You're right, I do…but I'm *in* love with my wife. Do you know I didn't see my kids for over a month because of you?"

"Because of me?"

"Yes, because of you."

"I didn't make you fuck me."

"I know, that was my fault. And it will never happen again. Why can't you just go away?"

"Because your mine. Why don't you stop playing these games."

"I'm not playing games. And, I'm not yours. I may have been yours when we were kids but that was a long time ago."

"I'm not letting you go. If I can't have you, she can't either."

"What's that suppose to mean?"

"You'll see." Lasaia said and hung up the phone.

Marcus was so upset that he threw his phone onto the desk. He wanted to reach through the line and choke her. He decided he wasn't going to waste energy on her. He took that threat as if they were like all the others, meaningless. When he got home, he told Sherise about it and she didn't pay it any mind either.

The next day, Marcus left for work and Sherise got the girls off to school and daycare. She drove to the shop and walked through the front door. It was a typical day at *Sherise's*. The hair dryers were buzzing, the television was on Divorce Court, and the women had their usual salon-wide conversation going. Around 2:30 Sherise and Alicia went back into the office to do some paperwork.

"Girl, I'm telling you, you can get that man to buy you the Eiffel Tower right now." Sherise laughed and said, "I'm not gonna take advantage of him like that."

"Shiiiit, I would. I'd have that man trying to make reservations to take me to the moon for dinner." Alicia said, laughing.

"I'm just happy to have him back. He has really tried hard to make up to me these last few weeks and I pretty much ignored him. But I love that man."

"Yeah, that's cause he know his ass was wrong. If I was you, I would've made his ass suffer."

"Well lucky for Marcus, you're not me. And, I think he has suffered enough. He loves the girls and being away from them for over a month had to hurt him."

"Well all I know is I would have made him sweat a little more."

The two of them laughed and talked for a little while longer and finished going over their reports and different invoices. About 20 minutes later, there was a knock on the office door.

"Come in." Sherise said from her chair.

The door opened and they both looked up at the person that stepped through the doorway. It was Lasaia.

Sherise stood up with a disgusted look on her face as Lasaia closed the door behind her.

"What the hell are you doing here?" Sherise asked.

She couldn't believe this woman had the nerve to show up at her place of business.

"I'm not here to fight or cause trouble. I just want to say I'm sorry. I never intended for you to find out. I just…"

Sherise broke in and said, "Wait, wait, wait…You never intended for me to find out? So you just planned on fucking my husband and pretending to be my friend?"

"I know you think I'm evil, but I really do love him. I told you that the first night I met you."

"Yeah, well what do you expect me to do about that? He's my husband. I know the two of you had your little relationship back in high school, but he is my husband now."

"Not for long." Lasaia said, a smug look painted on her face.

"Bitch!" Alicia said standing to her feet.

She had wanted to say something since Lasaia stepped into the room and that last comment sent her over the edge.

"Lele!" Sherise said, throwing her hand up, signaling her to stay out of it.

Sherise walked around her desk and stood in front of the unflinching Lasaia.

"So what…you plan on taking my husband?" Sherise asked, standing eye to eye with her.

"No, I'm not going to take him. He's going to come on his own. He loves me, and I know it. We will be together again."

"Do you really think he would throw away the last 10 years of his life, everything he knows, to start over with you?"

"I know Marcus, and I know he wants to be with me."

"You may have been able to get him drunk, trick him into going to your house…"

"Trick him? I didn't *trick* him. He wanted to go."

"Oh really? Is that why you had to steal his credit card so he wouldn't have any choice but to go with you?"

Lasaia went silent.

"Yeah. He told me. So while you're in here talking all this shit about him wanting you…tell me, when was the last time you saw him?"

Lasaia didn't say a word. She just has a fiery look in her eyes.

"Matter of fact. When was the last time he called you? Doesn't seem like he is chasing you too much does it? So, you fucked my husband…yes you did. Am I mad? As hell. But, I do love him with all my heart and he means more to me then your little 30 minute episode. I think the fact that I lost someone I *thought* was my friend hurt more then what the two of you did."

"I guess you should pick your friends more carefully. Marcus will be mine again."

Sherise got agitated and said, "Oh really? Here…let me show you something."

Sherise raised her left hand, showing Lasaia her large wedding set.

"You see this? This is seven year. 'Til death do us part."

Lasaia gave Sherise a devilish grin and said, "Exactly."

She turned and walked out of the office without saying another word. Sherise stood in her spot in front of the door for a few seconds just staring at the spot where Lasaia's face was a few seconds before. She couldn't believe that this woman just told her to her face that she was going to take her husband.

"That bitch gonna make me kick her ass. You should've let me hit her." Alicia said.

Sherise silently walked back around to her chair and had a seat. They finished doing the last few invoices and Alicia left her to go handle a few of the customers. Sherise sat in her office alone, thinking about the whole situation.

Later that evening, Sherise and Alicia closed up the shop together. The sun was setting and the business day was over. Sherise had just gotten off the phone with Marcus. She wanted to make sure he had remembered to pick up the kids and everything was fine at home. She would usually pick them up and every time she had to work late she would call Marcus to make sure he didn't forget.

"Baby we're fine. I'm cooking, and they're in the living room watching TV." Marcus said.

"Ok, well I'll be home in about an hour. We're just finishing things up now."

"Ok, take your time. We're fine."

"Ok, see you in a bit."

"Ok, love you."

"Love you too."

Sherise hung up the phone and headed back out into the shop. Alicia was letting the last few hairdressers out of the store and locked the door behind them.

"Well girl, I'm gonna take this money to the bank and I'll be right back." Alicia said.

"Ok, I'll wait for you." Sherise said.

Alicia left and Sherise lowered the steel window guards on the outside and locked them. Alicia drove off and Sherise went back into the shop and locked the front door. She had a seat in one of the stylist chairs and watched television while she waited for Alicia to get back. She sat there laughing at an episode of *House of Pain* for a few minutes before she heard a loud shattering crash from the back of the store. Sherise jumped out of her seat and yelled, "Hello?"

There was no answer.

She stood there as fear walked hand in hand with her blood.

"There's someone in here." Sherise yelled, hoping that hearing someone would scare them off.

The store was silent.

She rushed to the front counter and picked up the phone to call the police. As she lifted the receiver to her ear she realized there was no dial tone. Sherise's heart started to beat faster and faster and she quickly walked back into the styling area. She grabbed a metal rat-tail comb from the counter and her small canister of mace from her purse. She slowly started walking toward the back of the store, looking around the corner trying to find out what could have made the noise. She slowly walked into the dim storage room and saw a brick lying in the middle of the floor. She looked at the trail of glass from the window and whispered, "Damn kids."

A relieving sigh came from her mouth and her heart rate started to return to normal. She walked toward the door, her eyes focused on the broken window. The only sound in the room came from the crunch of the glass under her feet. She looked through the broken window and into the empty lot behind the salon. Without warning, she was hit from behind and knocked unconscious. Her body fell to the floor, motionless.

Twenty-five

Sherise slowly started to regain consciousness. She could barely breathe and was still a little disoriented. All she could feel was pain and heat. She touched felt the back of her head and looked at her hand. Her fingers were smeared with blood and she could hardly see. The whole room around her was engulfed in flames. Everything was burning and there was no way for her to escape. Sherise was able to work her way to her hands and knees and looked around. Everything was burning. Even the air she inhaled burned as it entered her lungs. All of her autographed photos from different celebrities that had come there were starting to bubble and melt on the walls. Her counters, her chairs, everything was going up in smoke. It was getting harder for her to see and her breaths seemed to get shorter every time she inhaled. The fire started to close in on Sherise and she could feel the heat start to singe the hairs on her arm. She was completely surrounded by a ring of fire and was still barely conscious. The fire reached the storage room and all of the different chemicals began to explode. The smoke had nowhere to go and began collecting so thick on the ceiling that it reached down to her on the floor. The entire back half of the shop was on fire from the explosions and there was no one around that could hear Sherise's screams for help. Oxygen could barely wrestle its way into her body and she fell to her stomach.

Just as she was about to pass out, she heard the roar of an engine begin to get louder and louder. She looked up and saw the front wall of shop come crashing down and the broken grill of Alicia's Navigator break through the front counter. Sherise couldn't move, but she saw her friend rush over to her, screaming and crying hysterically. Alicia grabbed her, dragged her to the truck and put her across the front seat. Alicia pushed Sherise's nearly lifeless body over the seat and climbed into the driver's seat. She shifted the truck into reverse and slammed her foot down on the gas.

The engine revved up but the truck didn't move. There were bricks lodged under the truck from her crash through the front of the store, which had her back tires off the ground. Flames began to close in around the truck and Alicia started to panic. Sherise just lay on the seat and coughed. She was alive, barely. The flames reached just outside the truck windows and the two of them couldn't open the door to make a run for it now if they wanted to.

"Come on, come on, come on!" Alicia said, slamming her hands against the steering wheel.

The wheels quickly spun around and around kicking up dust from the broken bricks. The spinning moved the dust and one of the wheels finally reached the ground. It let out a loud screech and caused the car to begin to rock back and forth. Alicia could feel the flames through her broken window and kept pressing the gas hoping for a miracle.

Her prayers were answered.

After a few quick skids from the tires, the rocking caused the bricks under the truck to collapse from the pressure and the truck fell to the shop floor. As soon as the tires touch the ground the truck careened out of the shop front and into the parking lot. The whole bottom of the truck was still in flames and Alicia was so scared that she didn't remember to take her foot off the accelerator. She flew through the parking lot backwards until she ran over a curb and hit a fire hydrant. The truck came to a halt and the water from the knocked over hydrant put the flames under the car out.

At that moment, Marcus was sitting on the couch with his girls watching television. They had just finished eating and were relaxing, waiting on Sherise to get home. About 15 minutes later the phone rang and Marcus got up from his spot between his little girls. He walked over to the phone and picked it up.

"Hello?" He said into the receiver.

"Marcus! This is Alicia! You gotta get down here right now!"

Marcus had to take the phone away from his ear because she was yelling so loud. He heard the fire engine sirens and police yelling in the background and was confused about what was going on.

"What…what happened?" He said into the phone.

"The shop…everything is on fire. Sherise was trapped inside and…"

"What, I'll be right there!"

Marcus hung up the phone without letting Alicia finish and rushed to get the girls. He led them to the car and flew out of the garage and down the street.

As Marcus pulled up to the scene, the fire was still burning but the fire department had it under control. He parked on the curb across the street from the salon and jumped out of the truck. He got the girls out and they crossed the street through the stand still traffic. A crowd had gathered and Marcus had to make his way through them. He made it to the front and a policeman stopped him from crossing the yellow tape.

"Hold on sir, you can't…"

Marcus cut the man off and said, "That's my wife's salon. Is she alright?"

The officer lifted the tape and motioned Marcus through. The crowd just watched in amazement as one of their most well known businesses was going up flames. The tower of smoke rose high into the sky as another officer escorted Marcus toward an ambulance.

"Daddy, what happened to Mommy's shop?" Lasaia said, a crack in her voice. She was just now figuring out what was going on.

"I don't know baby. But I'm gonna find out." Marcus said having a sneaking suspicion he already knew who was behind this.

They made it to an ambulance and Alicia was sitting on the bumper as a paramedic treated some burns on her left arm. Alicia looked up and saw Marcus and jumped to her feet. She threw her arms around him and started crying.

"What happened, what's going on?" Marcus asked.

"I don't know. I left to go to the bank and when I got back the whole place was in flames." Alicia said.

"Where is Sherise?" Marcus asked.

"She's over there in that other ambulance." Alicia said, pointing to another emergency vehicle parked a few yards away.

"Can you watch the girls for me?" Marcus asked.

Alicia looked at the paramedic that was working on her arm.

"Yeah, you'll be fine. Just a few first degree burns." The paramedic said.

"Girls stay here with Auntie Lele and I'll be right back." Marcus said to the little ones.

"I wanna see Mommy." Lasaia said, tears forming in her eyes.

She knew that only hurt people were put inside ambulances.

"Baby, I'm gonna check on her and I'll be right back ok? If the doctor says it's ok, then I'll come get you." Marcus said, kneeling down next to her.

She didn't want to go along with it but Lasaia obeyed her father's request and had a seat with Alicia and Angela on the ambulance bumper.

Marcus ran to the second ambulance and looked into the open rear doors. He saw his wife lying on a gurney in the back of the ambulance and started to climb in.

"Sir, sir…You can't come in here." One of the paramedics said walking over to stop Marcus from entering the vehicle.

"That's my wife." Marcus said, pushing the man to the side.

He got to Sherise's feet and saw that she was unconscious.

"Is she alright?" Marcus asked, as the paramedic worked on his wife.

"She's got a few burns, but they aren't too serious, a laceration on the back of her head that kinda has me concerned and she inhaled a lot of smoke. We're gonna take her to the hospital to make sure everything is ok, but she should be fine. Her friend really saved her life."

"Friend? Who?" Marcus asked.

"The woman in the other ambulance. She rammed her truck through the front of the store and pulled her out. If it weren't for her, your wife wouldn't be alive right now. That place went up in a matter of minutes. Even with all the chemicals in there, it shouldn't have burned that fast. If she would have called us and waited on the fire trucks, there's no way we could have gotten here in time.

"She really saved her friend's life."

As the paramedic finished her sentence Sherise started to wake up.

"Marcus?" She whispered, eyes closed.

It was almost as if she could feel him there. Marcus rushed over to her side as the paramedic slid out of the way.

"I'm here baby, I'm here. How are you feeling?" Marcus said, caressing her hand.

"I'm ok. Where are the girls?" Sherise asked, barely able to speak.

"They're with Alicia. They're fine."

Alicia peeked around the corner of the ambulance with two little heads beside her.

"Mommy!!" Lasaia yelled, jumping into the ambulance.

She had tears in her eyes and Alicia said, "I'm sorry but she was crying and…"

"It's ok." Marcus said as he lifted his little girl into his lap.

"Mommy, are you ok?" Lasaia said, her words smothered in tears.

"I'm ok baby." Sherise whispered.

"Mr. Downing we need to get your wife to the hospital." One of the paramedics said.

"Ok, come on girls." Marcus said.

"No, no daddy…I wanna stay with mommy!" Lasaia screamed as Marcus pulled her out of the back of the ambulance.

"No, noooo! Mommiiieeeee!" Lasaia screamed as the ambulance doors closed and they pulled off with the lights flashing.

Lasaia cried uncontrollably, screaming for her mother. Out of nowhere, Mike ran up.

"What happened, what's going on?" Mike said, trying to catch his breath.

Alicia gave her boyfriend a hug while Marcus tried to calm his little girl down. Angela didn't fully understand what was going on, but Lasaia knew that something bad had happened to her mother. Marcus got her to stop crying by promising her that they would go see her mother right away. She just stood next to her father sniffling while Marcus said, "The paramedic told me you saved Sherise from the shop?"

"What?" Mike said, looking at Alicia.

"Yeah, well I couldn't let my girl get burned up and just stand there watching." Alicia said, modestly.

"Why didn't you just unlock the door?" Mike asked.

"I tried but my key wouldn't go in the lock and the metal guards where down so I couldn't just break the window. I freaked and my truck was the only thing I could think of that could get inside." Alicia said.

"Your keys wouldn't work? You sure you had the right key?" Marcus asked.

"I'm positive. I use it everyday. It wouldn't even go in the lock at all." Alicia said pulling out her key and inspecting it. The key looked fine and it would have been hard to mistake that key for any of the others on the ring because it was more twice the size of a regular key.

"Did anything strange or out of the ordinary happen today?" Marcus asked.

"Not really. Everything was pretty much the same as every other day. Except…"

"What?" Marcus asked, anxiously.

Alicia's facial expression changed as her thoughts marched to her mouth.

"Your lil' friend came in earlier talking about how you were gonna be hers again and how you were gonna leave Sherise."

"Lasaia was here?" Marcus said, thinking back to their last conversation.

"I'm not letting you go. If I can't have you, she can't either."

"What's that suppose to mean?"

"You'll see."

Lasaia's words rang in Marcus's ears.

Marcus thought for a few seconds and pulled Mike to the side.

"Bruh, I need you to do something for me."

"Yeah man, whatever you need, anything." Mike answered.

"I need you to take Lasaia and Angela to the hospital so they can see their mother. I need to handle this…tonight."

"Man, what are you gonna do."

Mike could see the anger in Marcus's eyes and didn't want his friend to go out and do anything stupid.

"I'm just gonna handle it." Marcus said, walking off.

"Marcus…! Marcus…!"

Marcus heard his friend's call but just kept walking, one foot in front of the other.

Marcus walked back toward his truck with only one thought on his mind. Before he could make it off the scene, he was stopped by a man in a suit who said, "Sir…sir? Mr. Downing?"

Marcus stopped and turned to the man. The fire had been put out and the firemen were walking through the wreckage making sure there was nothing that would start it back up again. The man walked up to Marcus, introduced himself as a detective and said, "Mr. Downing can I ask you a few questions?"

"Yeah, how did you know who I am?" Marcus asked.

"The officer that let you in to see your wife told me you were here. Now, do you have any idea who may want to kill your wife or her partner Miss Carmichael?" The detective asked.

Marcus knew exactly who he thought was behind the whole thing, but he didn't tell the detective.

"Um no, why do you think someone was trying to kill either of them?" Marcus asked, sounding convincing.

"Several things. I spoke with Miss Carmichael and she told me that she was in the shop with your wife. She said that she left approximately 7:15 p.m. and returned no later then 7:35 and the place was already half burned. She said she ran to the door and looked into the shop and saw your wife crawling around on her hands and knees. She tried to scream to her, but she couldn't hear her. She tried to unlock the door, but her key wouldn't go in. And I got this from one of the firemen," The detective said, showing Marcus a half burned lock, "Now, the funny thing about this is that there are toothpicks broken in the lock, so when she tried to put her key in it wouldn't go. That's number one. Number two is the rate at which the fire was burning. Now, I can't say for sure but from my experience, when a building burns as fast as this one did there is usually arson involved. We'll have to wait for the firemen to finish up and investigate, but I think that there is more to this than just some freak accident." The detective finished.

"I understand but…what can I do to help?" Marcus asked.

"Nothing as of now but if you think of anything that could possibly help us find out what happened here, please let us know." The detective said.

"Sure, anything. Now if you'll excuse me, I need to get to the hospital." Marcus said.

"Certainly, here…take my card." The detective said, pulling a business card from his jacket. Marcus shook hands with the detective and turned away, headed toward his truck. The crowd had broken up and Marcus looked across the parking lot from the shop and saw Alicia's truck on the curve with the toppled fire hydrant. The firemen had redirected the water away from that hydrant so the truck no longer looked like some strange type of sprinkler. He saw how badly damaged the vehicle was. The entire front bumper had been pushed back into the grill and the white truck was now charred on the side from the fire that had burned under it. Marcus owed Alicia a great deal. If it hadn't been for her, Sherise would be in the back of the coroner's truck instead of an ambulance. Marcus had come close to losing her all over again…this time forever. Losing Sherise to a divorce would have hurt him, losing her to death probably would have killed him. He made it to his truck and climbed into the driver's seat. He pulled off of the curve and drove away from the flashing lights and chaos.

He couldn't believe that Lasaia would go to such lengths to get him back. Did she actually think that killing his wife would make him run to her? Was she really capable of something like this? What other reason would she have for being in town and not telling him? Questions flooded his mind as he drove through the streets of Jacksonville. He couldn't believe that his wife almost died just a few short minutes before. He began to get angry all over again. He thought about what Lasaia had done to his family and all the trouble that had been started as a result of him running into her again. Without thinking, he flipped open his phone and dialed Lasaia's cell number. He figured if he could get her to tell him where she was that he could put an end to everything. The phone rang a few times before she answered it.

"Hey baby!" Lasaia said as soon as the call connected.

"Hey, what's going on." Marcus said trying to sound like he really wanted to talk to her. He had to play it cool to get her tell him where she was.

"Nothing, just sitting here, hanging out," Lasaia said, "I bet you can't guess where I am?"

"Where?" Marcus asked, as if he didn't already know.

Lasaia didn't even notice the sudden change in Marcus's attitude toward her. He hadn't called her willingly since before their little episode in Atlanta, but now he was talking to her as if everything was just fine.

"I'm in Jacksonville." She said, bubbling with joy.

"Oh yeah, what are you doing here?" Marcus asked, laying the foundation of the conversation.

"Just passing through, really. Got here earlier today actually, but I've been in this hotel room all day. I'm on my way to Miami for a little vacation…Lord knows I need one." Lasaia said, giggling.

"Oh ok," Marcus said, trying to keep his voice calm, "Look, I'm real sorry about the things I've been saying to you over these last few weeks and the things that went on between. We're not a mistake, never were. I mean, I'm married now, but things won't be the same now that Sherise knows. She says she doesn't want me to leave, but I have an inside source that tells me that she has been meeting with a lawyer and stuff so I think that we are actually on the outs. Even tonight, she was supposed to be letting me see my girls and I haven't heard anything from her since yesterday. If you are willing, and want to let me make it up to you, I would like another shot." Marcus said, lying through his teeth on the phone.

He knew she was just gullible enough to fall for it. She would have taken any deal he offered her. All she wanted was to have the man she loved back with her.

Lasaia was overwhelmed.

She could barely get her words out on the phone.

"Oh, um…yeah, I mean sure…if that's what you want. I would love to give you another chance." She said, flabbergasted.

"Great, I wasn't sure what you would say. I know I have been down right evil to you, but it was all a front. I mean I do love my wife, but it's like you said, I can't fight the fact that I love you too. I can't help but feel that there is something still between us."

"I know. That's what I've been saying."

"I know, I know. So, what are you doing tonight?"

Marcus could almost hear her smile over the phone.

"Nothing."

"Why don't I come by and see you, so we can talk?"

Lasaia could hardly believe her ears. First he called her, then he wanted to get back together with her, now he wanted to come see her. She couldn't help but accept Marcus's offer and told him exactly where she was. He knew how to get there and told her that he would be in her arms in a few minutes. An evil grin briefly jumped across his lips as he sped through the streets in Lasaia's direction.

Twenty-six

Marcus made it to the hotel and pulled into the parking lot. He stepped out of his truck and quickly disappeared through the glass front doors. His tunnel vision was fixed on the elevator. Less than a minute later he was knocking on Lasaia's door. He could hear her footsteps headed toward him. Marcus's instinct was to jump on her as soon as she opened the door but he quickly talked himself out of it. He needed the truth, first.

She opened the door. Marcus flashed a fake smile, hugged her and walked in. She had changed into some *special* clothing just for him. She had on a silk lingerie teddy with a thin matching shawl that draped over her shoulders. The teddy was barely long enough to cover her thighs and if she were to sit down it would not be able to conceal anything below her waist. This was definitely a standing room only teddy.

"Hey what's up?" She said, letting him into her room.

Lasaia didn't half step at all when it came to her living arrangements. Her hotel room was huge. She had a living room area with a big television and a coffee table where she had set up a little bit of champagne and two glasses for them to celebrate. There was a balcony that led outside with a deck overlooking the city below and a huge king-sized plush bed. Nothing as intricate as her room at home but it was still beautiful. Her bathroom had a huge Jacuzzi tub and a gigantic mirror that only a woman would have the capability to make full use of. Marcus didn't care about any of that at this moment. All he wanted was answers. They had a seat on the couch in front of the champagne and Lasaia threw her shawl over her lap to keep from showing everything to him. It didn't really matter, he had seen it all before. But, she was still a lady. Marcus noticed a thin wrapping around Lasaia's right arm, around her bicep. It almost looked like a bandage, but Marcus couldn't tell with out getting caught staring. She poured them some champagne into each of the glasses and they had a toast. She was just as beautiful as always, but Marcus was in no way interested.

"So, what have you been doing since you got here? I know you haven't been sitting in this room all day." Marcus asked, playing his card.

"I went out for a little bit, but not for long. I don't really know much about Jacksonville and got lost pretty easy, so I came back." Lasaia told him.

"So you didn't go anywhere earlier today?" Marcus said, roping her in.

He was getting aggravated with her and he only saw her as more guilty when she didn't admit what he knew was true.

"No. Like I said, I went out for a little while, but I got lost and had to find my way back here. After that I just gave up on going places. Why?" Lasaia said, getting a little uneasy at his line of questioning. Marcus smiled, downed the rest of his drink, and said, "So, why is it that people tell me you went by my wife's shop today?"

Lasaia looked confused. She thought he had come to talk about the two of them and he brought that up.

"Um, yeah, I did stop by there. But I…I just went in." Lasaia said, nervously.

"So you were there. Why did you just lie to me then?"

"Baby what does this have to do with us? I mean…"

"Nothing. It has nothing to do with us. This has everything to do with you trying to kill my wife."

"Kill your wife?"

"Don't play games with me. Did you tell my wife that you were going to get me back and that I was going to leave her?"

"Yeah but…"

"And when they closed down that night did you break in and set her salon on fire?"

Lasaia was silent for a minute and then got up from her spot on the couch. She walked over to the big sliding glass door that led to the balcony and just stared out at the city of Jacksonville.

"I did it for us." She said, her back still toward him.

"So you did do it." He said, standing to his feet, walking toward her.

He truly hoped she would have had nothing to do with it, but he still had to ask. Lasaia turned before he got too close and said, "Yes but, I only did it because I knew that she would only cling to you because I wanted you."

"Because you wanted me? Did it ever occur to you that she might love me?"

"She doesn't love you. Not like I love you. She couldn't possibly have the feelings for you that I have. Don't you realize I will do anything for you?"

Marcus looked at the sincerity in Lasaia's eyes and he knew she meant what she said, but she didn't have a firm grasp on reality. Even though he knew she wanted nothing more then to be with him, that didn't stop him from wanting to grab her around the neck and choke the life out of her for what she did. Marcus couldn't even stand to look at her anymore and turned to leave.

"No baby wait," Lasaia said, grabbing him by the arm, "I'm sorry! I didn't know what to do! Please don't leave me!"

Lasaia started crying and pulling at Marcus trying to stop him from leaving her.

"I'm sorry baby! I didn't know what else to do. Shooting your brother didn't keep you in Atlanta and I…"

She was unable to catch her words before they escaped from her mouth.

Marcus stopped fighting her and turned back.

"What did you just say?" He said, grabbing her by the arm before she could pull back.

"You shot my brother?"

"Yes, I did it to get you to come back to Atlanta. I didn't know how else to get you there. You wouldn't answer my emails, you wouldn't call me…I needed to see you."

"You really are crazy." Marcus said, releasing her.

The look on Lasaia's face changed from tears to anger.

"I am *NOT* crazy. Yeah I shot him, but I didn't even try to kill him. If I wanted him dead I could have easily killed him. And your wife…that bitch is just getting in our way. I wish she were dead."

Marcus grabbed Lasaia by the neck faster than the *Matrix*. He could feel the blood rushing through his fingers as he squeezed. Lasaia tried to break his grasp, but her small hands were unable to break his grip.

"You think you can control my life? I could kill you right now." Marcus said.

Lasaia gagged.

She could feel herself getting weaker. She was able to force out a few words and said, "Well do it then. I'd rather die than not be with you."

Her words caused Marcus to release his grip and she took a few deep breaths. Marcus looked at his old friend and felt nothing for her at all. Lasaia recovered and said, "I knew you couldn't do it. You're weak. You've always been weak. You think this is over? As long as I'm alive you won't be happy."

"As long as I'm not with you, trust me, I'll be happy." Marcus said.

Lasaia was so upset by his words that she slapped him across his cheek. Marcus's eyes grew big and he backhanded her across the jaw. She fell to the floor and looked up at him. Lasaia seemed to lose touch with reality as she looked up at him. Instead of Marcus standing there, she saw her stepfather, Willy. Even as he spoke, his words came out in the voice of Mr. Jones.

"I don't wanna see you ever again. If I see you near my family again, I will kill you myself." Marcus said before turning and walking out of the hotel room.

Lasaia just sat on the floor and watched as he left.

She didn't cry.

She just watched him with an evil look in her eyes.

Marcus made his way down the stairs and out of the hotel. He sped off out of the parking lot, headed for the hospital. About twenty-five minutes later, he was parking his truck and rushing up to Sherise's room. As he opened the door he saw Sherise sitting up in the bed talking to Alicia and Mike. Lasaia and Angela were in bed with their mother, one on each side. They were just happy to see that mommy was ok.

"Heeeey baby." Sherise said as soon as she saw Marcus.

He bent down and kissed his wife on the lips and took the seat next to her bed.

"How are you feeling?" Marcus asked.

The doctor had wrapped her head in a bandage from her head wound, but she seemed to be feeling ok. She could talk a lot easier and her movements were much more fluent.

"I'm fine. A little headache and my arms hurt, but I'm feeling better. Where've you been?" She asked.

For a second, Marcus didn't know what to say. He definitely didn't want to tell her that he was coming from Lasaia's hotel room. He knew she didn't have any idea that Lasaia was behind her store getting burned down and his brother's shooting.

"I know, I'm sorry. I had a flat." He lied

"Bad night for everyone I guess. You ok?" Sherise asked.

Marcus chuckled and said, "You're the one that just got pulled out of a burning building and you're asking me if I'm ok?"

Sherise laughed at him and Marcus looked over at Alicia. She was just sitting there smiling and staring at her friend lying in the bed. She broke her gaze and looked over at Marcus as if she felt his gaze. Marcus couldn't stop looking at Alicia with an admiring glance. He knew that if it hadn't been for her, who he had never really gotten along with, his wife probably wouldn't be alive right now.

"What," Alicia said, confused by his look, "I got a booger or something?"

She wiped her nose.

"Nah, nah," Marcus said, smiling, "Can I talk to you for a minute?"

"Oh lawd, what I do now?" She said, jokingly as she stood up.

The two of them walked out into the hallway. Marcus turned to Alicia after closing the room door and said, "Look, I know we haven't been the best of friends, and I know you probably really hate me now after what happened. You and Sherise have been friends since before the two of us got together and I know you only want the best for her. I want to apologize to you for everything..."

"Aw Marcus you don't have to..." Alicia said, trying to stop him but Marcus cut her off.

"Yes, yes I do. I messed up, and I have to deal with that. But, I want you to know that I do love your friend, my wife, with everything I've got and I want to thank you for not letting her get hurt tonight. If it wasn't for you...I...I don't know. I don't even want to think about it. All I know is that I owe you more then you will ever know and I want us to be able to get along and be friends." Marcus ended his short speech with an extended hand. Alicia looked down at his hand with a blank look on her face then looked back up into his eyes. The silence scared Marcus a little and he began to think that his words had been said in vain. She pushed his hand to the side and opened her arms, giving him a big hug. She had always liked Marcus, she just couldn't show it because she didn't want to let her guard down. Even though his mistake was still fresh in her mind, his words pushed her to the point where she felt she could trust him and let him in. The two of them shared an embrace in the hallway and headed back into the room. Alicia took her seat next to her man and Marcus sat down next to his wife's bed.

"So what were you two out there talking about?" Sherise asked.

"Nothing girl, you so damn nosey." Alicia said as she and Marcus shared a concealing smile. She couldn't let Sherise know she liked him just yet, it was too early.

"Lele!" Sherise said, looking at her little girls.

"Oops." Alicia tried to catch herself but it was too late.

"Oooo Auntie." Lasaia said, wagging her finger.

"I'm sorry baby." Alicia said, as the adults laughed at her being chastised.

The four adults talked for a few minutes about the night's events and Alicia asked Sherise, "So girl, what happened? I left you alone for 20 minutes and you burn the whole place down. I know you ain't closed down the store in a while but dang!" Alicia, Mike and Sherise all laughed as Marcus only let out a low

chuckle. He was the only one that knew exactly what happened, but he didn't know what to say. Whatever it was, he definitely wasn't going to say it here.
"Anyway, after you left I was just sitting there watching TV and I heard a crash in the back. I went to the storage room and there was this brick in the middle of the floor. I went to the window and didn't see anyone but there was some red stuff on the glass. That's the last thing I remember before you pulled me into your truck." Sherise said.
"Well I don't think that was no accident," Alicia said, "I think that bitch was behind this."
"Lele!" Sherise said, reminding her of the little ones again
"Oooo," Lasaia said, looking at Alicia again, "I'm gonna tell your mama, auntie."
"I know baby I'm sorry, but auntie just gets a little emotional sometimes."
They all laughed and a few seconds later the doctor walked in.
"Mrs. Downing, how are you feeling?" The doctor asked.
"I feel a lot better. Thank you."
"Any real bad pains?"
"No...well a little on my arms and I have a headache, but it's not too bad."
"Ok, well that's to be expected. Something interesting though, I finished reviewing a few of your tests and the bump on your head doesn't seem like it was caused by something falling off a shelf. It looks like you were hit with something. The blow was too great for it to have been a box full of shampoo or something like that." The doctor chuckled.
Sherise looked baffled.
"But who could have...I mean who would want to..." Sherise stuttered.
Marcus knew exactly who was behind it all, but he remained silent.
"Well it could have been someone who was trying to rob your store and didn't know you where there." The doctor said.
Marcus sat there wanting to just yell out the name of the culprit, but for some reason his mouth wouldn't open.

Before Sherise was able to ask another question a man and woman entered her hospital room. Marcus recognized the man as the detective that stopped him in the parking lot of Sherise's shop, but didn't recognize the woman. Marcus stood up as the two of them walked over to Sherise's bed.
"Mrs. Downing, Mr. Downing, I am Detective Russo and this is Detective Bodine." the female detective said.
"Excuse me officers," The doctor said, "I need to go check on some more of Mrs. Downing's tests, do you need me?"

"No I don't think so doc, if we do we'll find you." Detective Bodine said.

The doctor left the room and Detective Russo continued.

"We're here because we have a few questions. I'm gonna be straight with you because the first few hours after a crime are crucial and we don't want to waste any time. Your store didn't *accidentally* catch on fire. It was burned down. Granted, the chemicals in the back storeroom did help it along, but we found traces of what is either gasoline or lighter fluid or something all over the floors in the styling area. On top of that, the speed that the building burned and the fact that the fire kept restarting only proves our case further. Now, our question to you would be, do you know of anyone that would want to cause harm to you or Miss Carmichael, that's you correct?" The detective said to Alicia.

"Yes." Alicia sat up in her chair.

"Ok, do either of you know of anyone that would want to cause you any harm?"

"No, not that I know of." Sherise said.

The detective turned to Alicia.

"No, no one." Alicia said.

"Ok, well the reason I ask is that several things point to an arson/attempted homicide. For one, the front door locks had small pieces of wood which look like toothpicks jammed into them and broken off which is why you were unable to get your key into the lock." The detective says to Alicia.

"Then there is the flammable chemical that was all over the place which caused the place to burn at an accelerated rate. There is no way that place could have burned that much in such a small amount of time without something helping it along. And the last thing was that the fire department found a small amount of what looks like blood on the back storage room window. We are sending it to the lab to be sure but we don't want to leave any stone unturned. To us it looks like the assailant broke the window with the brick that you found, then reached into the window and unlocked the door. We believe that they cut themselves in the process of reaching in and that is where the blood came from." The detective said.

Marcus immediately thought back to the small wrapping that he saw on Lasaia's arm.

"I can't believe this. I mean who would…"

Sherise went silent. Her face showed a sudden degree of realization and she looked over at her friend. Alicia saw her expression and said, "You know who I think did it."

"Lele! Stop it!" Sherise sad.

"What?" Detective Bodine asked.

"It's nothing, I mean…I don't wanna accuse someone of something without proof, but…" Sherise took a deep breath and continued, "A friend of my husband did come into my shop out of the blue earlier. Her and my husband grew up together and had a childhood relationship and they ran into each other after like 10 years. She had fallen back in love with him, I guess, and me and her had a real bad falling out." Sherise told them.

"What did she say to you?" Detective Russo asked.

"Nothing really. I mean, she was talking about her and my husband were going to get back together and I don't really remember the full conversation but I do remember the last thing she said." Sherise said.

"And what was that?" The detective asked.

"I had gotten a little agitated and I showed her my wedding ring." Sherise said, lifting her hand. She looked down at her hand and noticed her ring was missing. "My ring! Where is it?" Sherise said, getting upset.

"I'm sure they had to take it when they brought you in. Don't worry, you'll get it back before you leave." Detective Bodine said.

Sherise calmed down and said, "Ok, well I showed her my ring and said, 'You see this…this is 7 years. Til' death do us part.' and then all she said was 'Exactly,' and walked out of my office. I was so mad at the time that I didn't even think about it, but now that you ask, that is the only thing that I can think of that was out of the ordinary today." Sherise finished.

"And what is this old friend's name?" Detective Russo asked.

"Lasaia Lewis." Marcus said, entering the conversation.

"And where can we find this Miss Lewis?"

"I don't know, she lives in Atlanta. I have no idea where she could be staying here." Sherise said.

The detective turned to Marcus.

"Do you know where she is?" She asked.

Marcus knew he should tell her, he knew he should just say the name of the hotel. He knew exactly where she was and what she had done. He knew that his family was more important to him then Lasaia ever was.

"No, I don't." Marcus said.

His heart dropped.

He knew he was wrong.

He knew he could have possibly ended it all with a few words, but he didn't.

"Ok, well we will see if we can locate her." Detective Russo said, pulling a card from her jacket pocket.

"Here's my card, if you come up with any information that you think may be related to this case, no matter how small, please give me a call."

Sherise took the card and handed it to Marcus and said, "Ok I will."

The detectives said their goodbyes and left the room.

Sherise looked over to Alicia and said, "Can the girls stay with you tonight?" Angela had fallen asleep by this time and Lasaia wasn't far behind her.

"Yeah sure, you know they can come with auntie." Alicia said, standing to her feet. She walked over to Angela and picked her up off the bed. As Mike went for Lasaia she started to cry.

"Nooo, I wanna stay with mommy." She said, trying to stay in the bed.

Sherise was able to calm Lasaia down and got her to leave with Alicia. Marcus and his wife spent the night together in the hospital talking. As much as Marcus wanted to tell her, he kept the fact that he knew where Lasaia was and what she had done a secret.

They woke up the next morning and Marcus called in to work so he could spend the day with his wife. For that day, and the next, Alicia would take Lasaia to school and Angela to the daycare and bring them to the hospital to see their mother afterwards. The doctor kept running numerous tests to be on the safe side and all of them kept coming back as her being fine. Marcus would slip away for a few hours each day and go home to work on his projects while Sherise rested.

One day while Marcus was out and Sherise was resting, a nurse came into the room carrying her lunch tray. Sherise was just lying in the bed watching television and the nurse walked over to her. The nurse was a heavy set older black woman and Sherise could tell that she had been a nurse for a very long time. Her whole demeanor was nurturing and Sherise loved to see her coming. She reminded Sherise of her grandmother.

"Heeeey sugah, how you feelin'?" The nurse asked.

Sherise smiled and said, "Fine, how are you?"

"Oh, these ole' bones can't complain. The good Lord let me get up another day and that makes everything alright." She said in her comforting, aged giggle while setting up Sherise's lunch cart.

"Ain't that the truth." Sherise said, sitting up in her bed.

After the nurse set the food tray down on the cart and joined Sherise in blessing her food she said, "I have great news."

Sherise dug into the food and looked up at her and said, "What's that?"

"Well I asked the doctor to let me be the one to tell you because I wanted to give you the news myself, but…"

Sherise was confused at how excited she was and set her fork down.

"What is it?"

"Well I just want you to know that the baby is fine."

Sherise was puzzled.

"What baby?"

"Your baby. I just wanted you to know that all the stuff you went through didn't hurt the lil' one, one bit." She said, rubbing Sherise's stomach.

"I'm pregnant?" Sherise asked.

"You didn't know sweetie?"

"No."

"Oh my lord yes. You're almost two and a half months now."

Sherise was shocked. She had no idea she was pregnant. Maybe those early morning stomach pains really were morning sickness. Sherise's heart rate started to rise and she began to feel short of breath. She began to take quick deep breaths and couldn't seem to get enough air.

"Baby what's wrong?" The nurse said, rushing to her side.

She took Sherise's hand in hers and put her arm around her shoulders. She slowly rocked back and repeatedly told Sherise that everything would be fine. Sherise's breaths started to slow down and she was able to think back. It must have been when Marcus got back from visiting Alonzo. She couldn't believe that there was a baby inside of her all this time and she didn't know it.

"Now, I don't want you to get scared on me now. I saw your other two little girls. They are beautiful and you have done an amazing job with them. They are smart and so nice and I know you can do the same with this one, Ok?" The nurse said, still rocking the nerve-racked Sherise.

"Ok, ok…you're right. It's just a shock. We can do this, right?" Sherise asked

"Sure as shootin' sugah. Now, I gotta get outta here. I'll see you later ok?" The nurse said, getting up from the bed.

As she walked out Sherise began to think of everything that had gone on in her life over the last few months. She thought about the whole scenario…from the time her husband left for Atlanta to the time he told her he had cheated on her, to now, pregnant with their third child. Sherise didn't know what to think. She knew she needed to tell her husband, but she didn't know how she was going to break the news. She was too nervous to finish her lunch and sat in the room rehearsing how she was going to tell Marcus when he got back.

Twenty-seven

Marcus sat in his home office, working on a few of his projects, when his cell phone rang. He picked it up and looked at the display. The phone read *Unknown Number.* He immediately thought the worst. It must have been Lasaia calling him. He didn't know if he should answer it or not. While he was deciding the phone continued to ring. Marcus made his decision a split second before the voice mail picked up. He flipped his phone open and said, "Hello?"

"Hello, Mr. Downing please?" A male voice came through speaker.

"That's me, who am I speaking with?"

"Hello sir, this is Detective Bodine."

"Hey how you doing? Where you able to find out anything?"

"Well yes and no."

"What do you mean?"

"Well, we were able to contact her district police department up in Atlanta, but when they went to the house there was no answer. They are in the process of getting a warrant to search the home, but until we can get that we're pretty much stuck where we are now. Has she tried to contact you or your wife in the last few days?"

"No, I've pretty much been at the hospital with her and there have been no messages here at the house."

"Ok, well that's good I guess. If she is behind this then no contact could mean that she is long gone. But we will still try our best to find and question her. She is the only suspect we have right now and it seems kind of strange that she is no where to be found now that all of this stuff has gone down."

"Yeah, have you guys questioned any of her agency people?"

"Agency people?"

"Yeah, her modeling agency. The one she owns in Atlanta. My brother has a night club there and a few of the women that work for him also go through her for modeling jobs."

"I'm not sure but I will definitely look into it. How can I contact them?"

Marcus gave the detective Alonzo's phone number and number off of Lasaia's business card. He figured between the two he would be able to get in touch with someone that may be able to help. The detective thanked Marcus and told him he would be in touch with him the minute he knew something. Marcus thanked him for his dedication and hung up the phone. He looked at his watch and realized it was later then he thought and he jumped up from his seat to head back to the hospital.

❧ ❧ ❧

At this time, Sherise was still sitting up in the room alone thinking about how she could tell Marcus that she was pregnant, again. So much had gone on with their marriage in the last couple months that she didn't know what this new addition would do to the already stressed situation. She sat there watching a soap opera. Drama was so much more appealing on the screen. A few minutes later, her doctor walked in.

"Mrs. Downing, how are you doing today?" He said, making his way over to her bed.

"A lot better. My head doesn't hurt as much anymore and my arms are better and…"

"How would you like to go home today?"

Sherise's mouth dropped open for a second before it was replaced by a big grin. "Don't play. Can really?"

She had only been in the hospital for a few days, but she had already gotten tired of looking at the same walls, and the bed was no where near as comfortable as the one waiting for her at home.

"Yes you can but…" The doctor started.

"But what?"

"You have to promise that you will relax. No stress, no cleaning, no cooking, not too much walking around, and definitely no lifting."

"You mean I get a prescription to be lazy? I know I can handle that." Sherise said, laughing.

The doctor laughed along with her and said, "Yeah I guess so. I'll send the nurse in to help you collect your things."

The doctor left and Sherise jumped out of the bed and quickly began to gather her things. A few minutes later the nurse came in and helped her change her clothes and pack her things. As they made it downstairs and Sherise was about to call her husband to come pick her up, Marcus walked through the front doors of the hospital. He had a confused look on his face as he walked up to her.

"What are you doing down here?" He asked.

"The doctor said I can go home." Sherise said, the same radiant smile on her lips.

They finished filling out the paper work and Marcus escorted his wife to the truck and the two of them went home.

Later on that afternoon, Alicia brought the girls home and they were ecstatic about having their mother back. They spent the entire afternoon in their parent's bedroom and even had dinner on the bed. Sherise tried to help Marcus get the girls ready for bed, but he made her stay in bed while he tackled the task himself. After he had the girls in bed and got the kitchen cleaned up, he headed upstairs. Marcus had a bad feeling in his heart. He knew the complete story behind everything that had gone on, but hadn't told a soul. He probably could have ended everything if he just would have told the truth about where he was the night of the fire, but he chose to keep quiet. The feeling overwhelmed him and he couldn't take it anymore. He needed to tell someone. After he was sure the girls were asleep, he looked over at Sherise and said, "Baby…"

Sherise slowly turned her head from the television and said, "Yeah?"

"We need to talk."

Sherise heard the sincerity in his voice and was confused.

"What's wrong?"

Marcus took a deep cleansing breath and said, "I know…I know who burned down your shop."

Sherise's eyes grew huge.

"What? Who?" She screamed as she sat up in the bed.

Marcus quieted her down so she didn't wake the girls and said, "It was Lasaia."

"What? And how do you know that?"

"Because I saw her that night."

"What night?"

"The night your shop burned down."

"You went to see her?"

"Yes, but only to find out if she was behind this. When Lele told me she was in the shop earlier that day I just knew she had to have something to do with it."

"And she told you that she did it?"

"Yes. And…" He paused. "And she was the one that shot Alonzo."

The look on Sherise's face changed from anger to confusion.

"What?"

"Yeah, when we were at the hospital and y'all left to get something to eat Alonzo was telling me that he saw her at the club that night. He said he saw her right before he got into the fight. Then when I was in her room she told me that she did that to get me to come back to Atlanta but she didn't expect me to bring you and the girls."

Sherise had a disgusted look on her face.

"And she acted like she was sooo surprised that it happened. That bitch has problems. I mean what did she think you were gonna do when you got there? Run off into the sunset with her?"

"I don't know. But, she admitted everything."

'Wait," Sherise said, thinking back to that night, "If she told you that then, why didn't you say anything to the police detectives when we were in the hospital?"

"I don't know. I…I know I should have but, for some reason I couldn't."

"Well, baby you need to tell the police. If she is out there running around loose, she could really hurt someone. If she was willing to shoot your brother and try to kill me to get to you, there is no telling what she would do to someone else."

"I know, I know. You're right. I just…" Marcus paused and realized his wife was right. "Ok, how bout this. I'll call Detective Bodine tomorrow and tell him everything."

Sherise didn't like him waiting but she agreed to his compromise. The two of them dozed off and quietly slept through the night.

The next day Marcus got ready for work and he and the girls headed out for a usual day as Sherise got some rest at home. Marcus was half way through his day when Mr. Lockson barged into his office.

"Aaaahh haa haaa haaaa!" He exclaimed, walking toward Marcus with his arms open wide. Marcus stood by his desk with a confused look on his face.

"Marcus, my boy! You did it!" Mr. Lockson said, throwing his arms around him.

"Did what?" Marcus asked, confused.

"The Coke account. You did it! They loved it. I mean we do have one more hurdle to jump through. The presentation has to go to the C.E.O. but we are the only company that can offer what they want. This is big Marcus, very very big." Mr. Lockson said, releasing him and walking to the door.

"I'll keep you posted." He said, then took off into the hall.

Marcus stood in his spot for a few seconds wondering why he worked for such a strange boss. He let out a quick chuckle at Mr. Lockson and had a seat to return to work. That brief conversation with his boss could mean big things for Marcus, but he was so preoccupied with everything that was going on in his life that it didn't even matter right now. As he was typing away on the computer his phone rang. He reached across his desk and picked up the receiver.

"This is Marcus."

"Hey baby, what's up?" Sherise's angelic voice came through the phone.

"Heeey, how are you feeling?"

"Fine. Bored. I need to get out of this house."

"Now you promised the doctor that you would take it easy."

"I know, I know…Daddy. How is your day going?"

"Pretty good. Mr. Lockson just came in here and said that we may still get the Coca-Cola deal."

"Really, that's wonderful! When will you know for sure?"

"I have no idea. He came in, told me, hugged me, and took off."

"That's a strange little man."

The two of them laughed.

"So did you call the police yet?"

Marcus swore under his voice.

He knew she would ask that.

"No."

"Why not?"

"I am…I mean I will."

"Marcus this is serious. You really need to call them. I know she hasn't done anything lately but I have a feeling that she is willing to do *anything*. She really needs help."

"Ok. I'll call them now."

"Ok. Call me later."

"Ok baby."

"Bye."

Marcus hung up his phone and thought for a few seconds. As he reached across the desk to pick up the phone again his cell phone came to life.

Twenty-eight

He reached into his jacket pocket and pulled out his phone, answering it.

"Hello?" He said.

"Mr. Downing, this is Detective Bodine." The detective said.

"Hello detective. What's going on?"

"Not too much yet sir. I just got off the phone with your brother. We got some valuable information from him. We have also filed for a warrant to search Miss Lewis' business. Hopefully between the two we will be able to find something that will be valuable to the case. We got a chance to speak with a few of her personal assistants and they haven't seen or heard from her in over a week."

"Well thank you for keeping me posted, actually I was just about to call you anyway because…"

Before Marcus could get his sentence out there was a beep on his phone.

"Can you hold on for me for just a second detective?" Marcus said, realizing he had another call coming in.

"Oh I don't want to interrupt your day. That was pretty much it. I just wanted to let you know where we were with this case. I'll keep you informed."

Before Marcus could stop the detective and tell him everything he hung up the phone. The incoming call began to ring and Marcus answered it, a little frustrated.

"Hello?" He said.

"So you can't call and tell me shit now?" A male voice erupted from the phone. It was Alonzo and he was not happy.

"What?"

"Man some detective just called me and told me that Sherise almost got killed a couple days ago, her shop got burned down, and they think Lasaia might have something to do with it. Man, what the hell is going on?"

"Bruh, shit's crazy right now."

"I figured that. What happened?"

Marcus told Alonzo the whole story of what happened the night Sherise's salon burned down.

"And you couldn't call and tell me? I had to hear it from some detective."

"I'm Sorry man. It's just that ever since Sherise found out about me and Lasaia I…"

"What? You told her?"

"No."

"How did she find out?"

"When we were up there and she went to Lasaia's house, she found baby girl's picture that I had left over there that night."

"Aw hell nah. So, yall breakin' up?"

"No, no, no…I mean she was upset the night she found out, and for about a month afterwards. But, we talked about it and we're going to work it out."

"Oh, well you're a lucky man. Most women would never even think of giving you another chance."

Marcus had no idea how true those words were. The two of them talked for a few more minutes about the case before Alonzo said, "Well alright man. I just wanted to get a chance to curse your ass out for not filling me in about this. Next time man, call me. And, if you guys need anything don't hesitate to hit me up. I'm here if you need me."

Marcus remembered that he needed to tell his brother the truth about what happened the night he got shot.

"Ayo, Zo." Marcus said.

"Sup?"

"I gotta tell you something. But, you have to promise that you won't get mad."

"Alright, what's up?"

"I know who shot you."

"Who?"

"Lasaia did it."

Alonzo burst into a loud laugh.

"No, no, no I'm serious. That night when you saw her in the club, she was there to shoot you. She told me everything."

"The Hell? Are you serious? When did she tell you that?"

"Trust me man. She told me. I wouldn't lie to you about that"

Alonzo was silent for a few seconds then said, "You tell the cops?"

"No. Not yet. I wasn't going to but Sherise thinks I should."

"Nooooo. If you didn't tell them right off, don't tell them nothin' now."

"Why?"

"Obstruction of justice, aiding and abetting, accessory to the crime...take your pick. Do they know that she shot me?"

"No."

"So what are you going to tell them? That you always knew who tried to kill your wife and who shot me? That's a crime bruh. Do they have any evidence that can link her to the shop?"

"Um, yeah. They have some blood that they think is hers."

"Have they called her yet?"

"Yeah, the detective that called me said they are trying to get a search warrant for her house and business."

"Ok good, good. They can get DNA evidence from damn near anything. I say just keep it quiet. Don't tell them nothing else, and when they catch her they can still link her to the blood at the shop. I ain't really worried about them linking her to me 'cause if I see her she might not make it to trial."

"Whatever man. Don't do nothin' stupid. I gotta get back to work."

"Aight man, but I'm tellin' you...don't say nothin'. Just let the cops do they job and keep quiet. Before they have you in the cell next to her." Alonzo said, laughing.

"Anyway fool, Peace."

"Love and soooouuul. Holla."

Marcus hung up his cell phone and put it back into his jacket pocket. He sat and thought about what Alonzo just said. Maybe he was right. If Marcus told them now that he knew everything since that night, they very well could put him in jail. Then he thought about what Sherise said. He thought about how Lasaia really needed to be off the street and in front of a psychiatrist. All kinds of emotions flooded his brain at once and he could barely think. Marcus took a few deep breaths and extended his hand over the phone on his desk. He picked up the receiver and was about to dial the number when he hung the phone up. Marcus couldn't picture himself being taken away from his family again. And, Alonzo was right. As soon as they got the search warrant they would be able to do their DNA tests on anything they find and they will still be able to link her without him saying a word. And even if he did say something, it would be his word against hers. She could just as easily deny seeing him at all. Marcus talked himself out of calling Detective Bodine and went back to work.

He finished out his Friday and headed home to be with his wife. He stopped by a store and picked her up a nice box of chocolates on the way, but forgot them in his truck. Alicia brought the girls over and things reached a small amount of normality in the household.

The next morning Marcus woke up to an empty bed. He walked out of the room and down the stairs. He heard some noises coming from the kitchen and knew that Sherise must be in the kitchen making breakfast.

"What are you doing down here?" Marcus said, entering the kitchen and seeing his wife standing over the stove. Sherise turned around surprised, "Oh, hey. I'm making you guys something to eat."

"Baby you know the doctor said…"

"The doctor said I needed to rest. Not rest in peace."

Marcus chuckled and had a seat at the breakfast table.

"So, what do you want to do today?" Marcus asked.

"I don't have any plans. I guess just hang out. It's not like you're going to let me go anywhere. Uuggh! I feel like I'm on bed rest." Sherise said.

Her eyes got big as she realized what she had just blurted out. She still hadn't told Marcus about her being pregnant. Marcus didn't think anything of her comment and laughed it off. Sherise looked around nervously for a second then rushed over to the refrigerator.

"Aw we never have anything sweet in here." She said, trying to cover up the comment she just made. Her comment caused Marcus to remember his chocolates.

"Oh, I got something for you." Marcus said, jumping up from his spot at the table and rushing to the garage door. Sherise smiled and said, "What is it," before following him to the garage. Marcus made it in between the cars just as Sherise reached the doorway. She looked at him for a second as he just stood there looking at his truck.

He seemed frozen.

He wasn't opening the door.

He wasn't getting her surprise.

He was just standing there.

After a few seconds Sherise's smile turned to a look of concern.

"Baby what is it?" She called to him from the doorway.

Marcus looked back at her and quickly snapped back into reality.

"Huh? Nothing." He said as he quickly opened the rear door to his truck and pulled out her box of chocolates. He turned around and saw his wife standing in the garage with her hands covering her mouth. All four of the tires on his truck had been slashed and the word *Bastard* had been carved all the way down the driver's side.

Tears began to form in Sherise's eyes. She knew this meant that Lasaia was even closer than ever. Somehow she had gotten into their garage during the night without them hearing a thing.

"Baby, baby...it's ok, it's ok." Marcus said, wrapping his arms around her.

Sherise pushed him away.

"How Marcus? How is it ok? She got in here somehow and we didn't hear a thing. The alarm didn't even go off."

"Well, the alarm is only on the house, not the garage."

"I don't care if it's only on the bathrooms, this scares me. What if..."

Sherise paused for a second then turned around and darted into the house. Marcus was confused for a second then he realized that neither of them had checked on the girls since they woke up. He took off after her. By the time Marcus reached the door, Sherise was already out of the kitchen and headed for the staircase. Both of their hearts were pounding as they ran up the stairs. Marcus made it to the top of the steps a few seconds behind his wife and they separate, each of them taking a room. The girls were fine, both of them were asleep in their beds. That didn't take the fear out of Sherise's heart. The two of them slowly left the rooms, letting the girls sleep, and met at the top of the stairs. Sherise's eyes were filled with tears. Marcus threw his arms around her and pulled her against his chest.

"I don't like this Marcus. She is getting way too close. Did you call the police and tell them everything?" Sherise asked.

"No, I didn't." Marcus said.

Sherise pushed him away and walked down the stairs.

"Baby, baby wait." Marcus said, chasing her down the stairs and into the kitchen.

"Baby I couldn't. I..."

"You what? You couldn't protect your family from some crazy woman who is willing to kill to get to you? Why are you protecting her? She obviously isn't stable and needs help. Do you still love her or something?" Sherise asked, removing the meal from the stove and turning to him.

"No, it's not that..."

"Well what is it then, Marcus? Why can't you tell the police what this woman has done?"

Marcus stopped for a second and looked at his wife.

"I was on the phone with Detective Bodine and I was about to tell him everything when Alonzo called."

"And he talked you out of it."

"Well, yeah."

Sherise lets out a frustrated grunt and turned her back. Marcus walked over behind her and placed his hands on her shoulders.

"Baby listen to me. Me and Alonzo were talking and he told me that if I told them now that I could be looking at going to jail for obstruction of justice. And it's true. If I come clean now after they have been looking for her all this time I could be looked at as an accomplice. I thought about it and I couldn't see myself being away from you and the girls again. Detective Bodine said they are getting a search warrant to search Lasaia's house and they will be able to run the DNA test off of something they find in there. They will still get all the evidence they need and I won't have to say anything."

"And what about her shooting Alonzo? Does he know about that?"

"Yeah I told him. He said don't worry about that. He just doesn't want me to go to jail." Marcus rubbed her shoulders and she turned around.

"So what are we suppose to do?" Sherise asked, her eyes searching for some kind of guidance.

"Well I'm gonna call the police and see what they can do about this and after that, all we can do is wait."

Sherise shook her head and said, "No, no…I'm not going to sit around and wait for this woman to go too far. If you don't want to call the police, that's fine, but I don't want the girls here. If that bitch hurts my babies, I will kill her myself."

Marcus had never heard his wife talk this way before, but the look in her eyes told him that she was serious.

"Ok, ok…How about I call Alonzo and see if it would be ok for the girls to come up there."

Sherise wasn't happy, but she accepted his offer. As Marcus gave his wife another hug and told her that he would handle everything, one of their little girls walked into the kitchen.

"Good Morning." Lasaia said, walking through the doorway rubbing her eyes.

"Heeey baby. You hungry?" Sherise said, trying to speak as calmly as possible.

"Mhh Hmmm" Lasaia, said nodding her head.

Marcus disappeared out of the kitchen and grabbed his phone from his office. He dialed Alonzo's number and waited for him to answer.

"What up?" Alonzo said picking up the phone.

"What's goin' on man?"

"Not much. Chillin', you good?"

"Not really. You said call if I need you right?"

"Yeah, what's up? What happened?"

Marcus sat down on the couch and took a deep breath.

"Man I woke up this morning and went out to my truck. This girl slashed all my tires and scratched the word *Bastard* in the side of my truck, in my garage."

"Whaaaaat! Damn. I always knew she was a little off, but that brawd is crazy. How she get in your garage?"

"Man I don't even know, but now Sherise is spooked and doesn't feel safe with the girls here."

"True, I feel that. What you need me to do? You know I got your back."

"Can the girls come up there and stay with you until we get things sorted out here?"

"That's it? Of course. You know my lil' nieces are always welcome here. Hold on."

Marcus heard Alonzo tell Lisa that the girls were coming up to visit. All he heard was Lisa start screaming with joy and clapping. She loved the girls the one time she met them.

"Um yeah man, I think she would love for the girls to come." Alonzo said, joking about her excitement.

"You sure it won't interfere with you guys? I mean I don't know when they'll be able to come back." Marcus said.

"Nah man. It's no problem at all. I don't be at the club nearly as much anymore and if I do need to go somewhere Lisa will be here. We can make it work." Alonzo told him.

"Well ok. I guess it's settled then. I appreciate it brotha."

"No problem man. We'll be down in a couple hours."

"Oh, you ain't gotta come down here. We can bring them there."

"Aw man, it's no problem. I want to bring Lisa down there anyway. Let her see how success runs in the Downing family."

Marcus laughed at his crazy brother and agreed to let him come get the girls. Marcus hung up his phone and saw another little person making their way down the stairs.

"Hey little girl." Marcus said, walking over to Angela.

"Gu Mawnin." She said, giving her daddy a hug as he knelt down.

He picked his little girl up and carried her into the kitchen where Sherise was getting a plate ready for Lasaia.

"Look who I found?" Marcus said, putting the little one down.

Angela rushed over to her mother and gave her a hug around her legs.

"You hungry baby?" Sherise said, looking down at the little face.

Angela nodded her head and rushed over to get in her seat.

"Alonzo said that the girls can come up there for as long as we need." Marcus told his wife.

A look of relief jumped onto her face.

"I've always liked him." Sherise said, sarcastically.

Marcus twisted his lip at her and walked back out of the kitchen. She laughed at her husband and turned to the girls and said, "You guys wanna go visit your uncle Alonzo?" Marcus heard the girls scream, "Yeaaaaa! Uncle Zo, Uncle Zo, Uncle Zo," as he made his way down the hall. He took a seat on the couch in the family room and grabbed the phone off the end table. He dialed the number to the police department and waited for someone to answer.

"Duval county police department." The voice said on the other end of the phone.

"Yes, hi. I need someone sent to my house to write up a vandalism report." Marcus said. "Sure no problem sir, what's your address?"

Marcus gave the woman his name and address and she told him she would send an officer over right away. Marcus hung up the phone and put it on the couch beside him. He took a deep breath and couldn't believe that the hell he put himself in was still raging strong. He thought the worst was long gone, but it was obvious that the extent of Lasaia's damage was yet to be seen.

Twenty-nine

Marcus got up from his seat and walked into the kitchen to have breakfast with his family. As they were cleaning up the dishes and the girls were watching television, there was a knock at the door. Marcus dried his hands and walked to the front door. He looked through the peephole and saw two officers standing on his porch. He quickly opened the door and the officer introduced himself.

"Hello sir. I'm officer Brown, this is officer Townsend. Did you call about some vandalism?"

"Yes sir, come right in." Marcus said, backing up into the house, allowing room for the men to enter. Marcus shook the officers' hands and told them to follow him to the garage. As they passed the family room Lasaia looked up and saw the officers and her little curious mind won't let her sit still. She snuck up behind them and followed far enough behind for her father not to see her. Marcus introduced the officers to Sherise before he led them over to the garage door. Sherise spotted the tailgater as she tried to sneak by her and said, "Little girl, what are you doing?"

Lasaia was startled that her mother caught her in the act and stood up straight as a post.

"Nothin'."

She darted out of the kitchen before Sherise could say another word. Sherise smiled at her little detective and went back to cleaning up the kitchen.

Marcus and the officers walked into the garage and over to his truck.

"Whoa." Officer Brown said, his tone not sounding all that impressed.

"Ok, what information do you need from me?" Marcus asked, trying to get the ball rolling. Officer Townsend made his way around the garage looking for any evidence and examining the damage as Officer Brown started the report.

"Well, we got pretty much all the general information we need. It's Marcus Downing correct?"

"Yes." Marcus said.

"Ok, Well we have the address. All we really need is a list and description of the damage. So let me see here. We have four flat tires…."

"Five Rick. Spare's been slashed too." Officer Townsend said, from the other side of the truck."

"Really?" Marcus said, quickly stepping to the back of his truck.

He looked underneath and sure enough his spare had a gash in it.

"Oookay, five flat tires, and the word *Bastard* scratched along the driver's side. Now were there any items stolen from inside the truck?" Officer Brown asked, scribbling notes onto his report.

"Um, I don't think so. I didn't want to touch anything until you got here." Marcus said.

"Well check out your things and let me know, just in case." The officer said.

Marcus opened the door to his truck and looked around for a few seconds. Everything seemed to be in place. He didn't keep much in his truck anyway, so there wasn't much to take. Marcus was about to close the door and tell the officer everything was fine when he looked at his dashboard. The picture of him and his family was missing. He kept it there so he could look at it everyday to remind him what he was living for, now it was gone. He noticed it as soon as he looked up there because it had been there so long it had almost become a part of the truck. He pulled his head from the driver's door and said, "My picture's missing."

"What picture?" Officer Brown asked.

"I keep a picture of my family on my dashboard and it's missing. That's all they took." Marcus told him.

"You sure it was there?" The officer asked.

"Definitely. I've had it there for like, forever." Marcus said.

The officer looked into the truck and saw that Marcus had a pretty expensive stereo system and looked back at him.

"You're saying that this person passed up all this high tech equipment to take a picture?" The officer asked.

"Can I speak to you for a second?" Marcus said, walking over to the corner of the garage.

He didn't know why he felt he needed privacy from the other officer. He was sure he would just tell his buddy as soon as the got back to their patrol car.

"Off the record, I have a pretty good idea who did this." Marcus said, lowering his voice.

"Yeah?" The officer said.

"I ran into an old girlfriend a few months back. And, I guess things went a little too far. Long story short, she has been doing all kinds of things to disrupt my life and I think this is another one of them." Marcus said, giving the officer a quick rundown.

"I gotcha. Well I'll just write up what we have here and we will do what we can to help you out. Only other thing I can tell you is to call your insurance agency and see if there is something they can do for you. 'Cause unless we can link her to the crime, we can't make her pay." The officer said.

The officers finished up their report and Marcus walked them back to the front door.

"We'll be in contact if we come across anything, but by the looks of things there won't be a quick resolution." Officer Brown said, walking out of the house.

"Thank you officers, I really appreciate you coming by." Marcus said as they left.

Marcus walked back into the house and met up with Sherise as he was getting the girls up from the table. "Take your sister upstairs and I'll be up there to help you guys pack in a minute." Sherise said to Lasaia.

The little ones walked hand in hand up the steps and Sherise walked to her husband and threw her arms around his waist, resting her head on his chest.

"Thank you for calling your brother." She said giving, him a kiss.

She wasn't really scared for the two of them. She knew that they could handle themselves, but she didn't want anything to happen to her babies. Marcus just stood there with his hands on her hips, captured by the look of his wife's eyes. She really was the most beautiful thing in the world to him, he knew it now more then ever. Sherise gave him another kiss and headed up the stairs to get the girls packed for their trip to Uncle Alonzo's. Marcus headed to the family room to get some rest and tried to forget about what had gone on over the last few hours.

After Sherise got the girls dressed and packed, she called for Marcus to help her get the bags downstairs. Marcus got up from his seat on the couch and walked up the stairs. Sherise had packed each of the girls a mammoth-sized suitcase like they were moving out instead of going for a visit.

"What's all this?" Marcus asked, laughing at the size of their luggage.

"It's stuff for the girls. I figured we don't know how long it will be, so I packed enough for anything." Sherise said.

Marcus kissed his wife on the cheek and grabbed the bags. He took them downstairs with Sherise, the girls following closely behind. The four of them spent the next couple hours talking and watching television as they waited for Alonzo and Lisa to make it to town.

Around 3:30 the phone rang and Marcus got up to answer it. He picked up the phone and heard the music in the background before he even got the receiver to his ear.

"Hello?"

The music quieted down.

"What up big bro, we're in Jacksonville. We'll be there in a few minutes."

"Ok we'll be here waiting." Marcus said, hanging up the phone. Marcus walked back into the family room and told Sherise that Alonzo was close by. It wasn't until then that Sherise realized that her little girls were going to be gone soon and she didn't know when she would see them again. Tears began to form in her eyes and Marcus saw how hurt she was. She wanted them to be safe, but at the same time she wished that they could stay. Marcus walked over to the couch and sat down next to her. He put his arm around her shoulder and she lay her head on his shoulder. She didn't want the girls to see how upset she was but it seemed like Lasaia knew before she even turned around. She got up from her spot and walked in front of her mother.

"It's ok mommy, I'll come back." She said.

Sherise was so proud of her little, grown woman.

"I know baby. Mommy's gonna miss you though." Sherise said.

"That's ok. You can call me anytime you want." Lasaia said, as if she had a phone for her to call. Sherise laughed at her little woman and gave her a big hug. Lasaia could always make her mother feel better.

About 15 minutes later Marcus heard a low thumping sound coming from outside. As a few more seconds passed it began to get louder and louder. Marcus knew it had to be Alonzo and his loud music headed down their street. He got up from the couch and headed to the front door. He opened it just as Alonzo's Suburban was pulling into the driveway. The engine powered down and the doors swung open. Alonzo and Lisa jumped out. Lisa walked around the truck and stood next to her man, but she was unable to take her eyes off of Marcus's house. Alonzo had told her that his house was nice, but she didn't expect it to look like this. Alonzo had to guide her by the arm to keep her moving toward the front door.

"What's up man?" Alonzo said, throwing his arms around his brother.

Sherise made her way to the front door and Lisa ran up to her screaming.

"Heeeey girl!" She said, giving Sherise a big hug.

The four of them walked into the house and Lisa said, "Girl, this house is beautiful."

"Well thank you. You guys want something to drink?" Sherise asked.

"No thank you, I still got some Henn in the truck." Alonzo said, joking.

Sherise didn't think his joke was very funny and gave him a crazy look. She didn't like him joking about drinking when he was about to leave with her little girls.

"It was a joke. I'm just playin'." Alonzo said after a few seconds of silence.

Even Lisa had given him a look to let him know this wasn't the time for jokes.

"Come on girl, I'll have some coffee if you got some." Lisa said, breaking the silence.

"Sure." Sherise said smiling at Lisa and the two women walked off to the kitchen.

"Uncle Zooooo!" A little voice screamed from behind them. Alonzo turned around to see Lasaia running up to him. He knelt down and picked up the little girl and held her in his arms.

"There goes my little girl." He said, holding Lasaia, "You gonna come hang out with me and Auntie Lisa?"

"Yeap!" Lasaia said in an excited voice.

Alonzo put her down and she ran back to the family room and tried to grab her bag. As she was struggling to pull the bag that was almost as tall as her, Marcus said, "Little girl stop before that bag fall on you. Y'all ain't leaving right now. Go sit and watch TV until your uncle is ready."

Lasaia released her bag and slowly walked back to her spot in the family room.

"So, let me see your truck. I wanna see what kinda hurtin' she put on you." Alonzo said joking with his big brother.

Marcus was reluctant at first, but he decided to let Alonzo see why he had to make the trip to Jacksonville. The two men walked through the kitchen, passing Sherise and Lisa who were sitting in the kitchen talking up a storm. The two of them seemed like sisters, sitting there just as comfortable with each other, like they had grown up together. The two men walked out into the garage and Marcus showed his brother the damage.

"Daaaayuummmm!"

Alonzo's mouth was open for a good 5 seconds as he walked toward the truck.

"I know, right." Marcus said.

"Man she put you straight to the floor. You *ridin'* on dubs fa' real. Nothin' but dubs." Alonzo said, laughing.

"At least it was in the garage. This shit would be embarrassing just sittin' in the driveway like this. How the hell she get in here anyway?"

"We don't know. We ain't hear nothing. The door was down and the alarm was armed. Some how she got through the garage door and did it. Then, she got inside and stole my family picture that I keep on my dashboard."

"She stole a picture?"

"Yep. The one I kept in my truck."

"All the speakers and system and CD's you got in here and she stole a picture?"

"That's it."

"I knew she was a lil' off. Now I know for sure…that bitch is crazy."

Marcus grabbed the girls' car seats and handed one of them to Alonzo and the two brothers had a laugh about his comment and headed back into the house.

Sherise and Lisa looked up as they walked in.

"You had to see it, huh?" Sherise said, looking at Alonzo.

"Yeah, that's crazy. I see why you want the girls outta here. I don't blame you. If she did anything to one of them y'all would need some bail money for me. That's real!" Alonzo said, trying to sound a little more sensitive this time around.

Sherise smiled.

She felt a little better knowing that Alonzo would be protective of her little ones.

"Well thank you guys so much for taking them up there. I'm not really worried about us; I just don't want anything to happen to my babies." Sherise said.

Lisa put her hand on Sherise's.

"Don't worry about a thing. We'll take care of them like they're ours."

"Ours? Don't be gettin' no funny ideas. This is just temporary." Alonzo said, joking with his woman.

Lisa cut her eyes at him.

"Whatever. You gonna give me a baby pretty soon anyway." Lisa said, her face straight.

"Aw shit. Alright, time to go." Alonzo said, walking out of the kitchen.

He heard laughter follow him out as he made his way toward the living room.

"Thanks again." Sherise said to Lisa.

"Come on girls, we 'bout to ride out."

Alonzo's muffled voice could be heard through the hallway.

"Y'all really about to leave?" Sherise said, surprised that they were leaving so soon. She still hadn't adjusted to the idea that the girls were going to be leaving and expected them to stay a little longer. The three adults walked toward the living room where Alonzo was standing by the suitcases.

"Y'all about to leave already?" Marcus asked.

"Yeah, I need to get back because I have a meeting in the morning at the club. Since I don't get out there as much anymore all the work I used to do at night I have to do in the morning." Alonzo said.

"Aw, let me say good bye to my girls then." Sherise said, tears already building in her eyes. She walked into family room and called the girls over to the couch.

"You be good for Uncle Alonzo and Auntie Lisa, ok?" Sherise said to the little ones.

"Ok." The girls said, nodding their heads.

"You gonna miss me?" Sherise asked.

"Of course mommy." Lasaia said, in her grown little tone.

All of the adults laughed as Marcus and Alonzo grabbed the bags from the doorway.

"Come on girls." Marcus said, signaling them it was time to go. He had to step in because he didn't believe that Sherise would have ever made them get off the couch. She really didn't want them go.

At their father's request the girls jumped up from the couch and headed for the door. Sherise grabbed the car seats from Marcus and Lisa got the other one from Alonzo and everyone walked outside to Alonzo's truck. After the bags were loaded and the girls were strapped in, Sherise gave Lisa and Alonzo a big hug.

"Thank you again." She said.

"No problem sis. I told my big brother he could count on me and I meant that." Alonzo said, slapping Marcus on the shoulder.

"He needs practice with some kids anyway." Lisa piped in.

"Here we go." Alonzo said.

Lisa just stood there smiling. Marcus gave the two of them a hug and they climbed into the truck.

Just as Alonzo started up the truck, Marcus's neighbors pulled into their driveway. Lasaia saw their truck and shouted, "Wait…waaaittt! I have to say bye to my friend." Alonzo looked back at her and put his truck in park. Marcus saw Lasaia struggling with her seatbelt and opened her door. Alonzo rolled down his window and Sherise asked, "What's going on?"

"She said she gotta say bye to her friend." Alonzo said, laughing.

Sherise looked over into their neighbor's yard and saw Bill and his family getting out of their car. Lasaia was finally able to get free from her seatbelt and bolted out of the truck. She made it around the front of the truck and screamed out, "Miiisssiiieee," as she shot across the lawn. Melissa stopped in her tracks and looked over to see her best friend running toward her. A huge smile leaped onto her face and she began to jump up and down anticipating her friend's arrival. "Laaaccciiieee!"

Lasaia made her way right in front of Melissa and said, "Hi Missie"

"Hi Lasaia." Melissa said.

"I wanted to come say bye." Lasaia said.

"Where you goin'?"

"To my uncle's house. He lives in Atlanta."

"When you comin' back?"

"I don't know."

"Well, I'm gonna miss you."

"I'm gonna miss you too."

The two little girls gave each other a big hug and Lasaia ran back to the truck.

"Howdy neighbor." Bill yelled across the yard to Marcus.

"Hey Bill." Marcus yelled back.

Bill and his family headed into their house as Lasaia climbed back into her seat.

"Don't mess up my little girls hearing with all that loud music." Sherise said, joking with Alonzo.

"Don't worry, the ringing only lasts for a couple minutes after you get out." Alonzo said, laughing.

He put his truck in reverse again and started to back out of the driveway. Marcus put his arm around his wife who was on the verge of tears at this point. The girls hadn't even made it down the street yet and she already missed them. When they were around she always wished for a little peace and quiet. Now that they were leaving she wanted nothing more then to walk into the house and have them there. Marcus and Sherise waved as they pulled off. They stood in the driveway until the truck was out of sight. They went back into the house and Sherise made her way upstairs. She claimed she didn't feel well and wanted to take a nap. Her injuries from the fire were healing perfectly, but this new injury to her heart wouldn't be fixed as easily. She wanted someone to pinch her so she could wake up from the nightmare that had become their reality. Marcus made sure she got upstairs and in the bed before heading back downstairs to try and relax a little.

A few hours later Marcus was downstairs watching television and Sherise made her way into the family room.

"Hey baby." Marcus said, as she headed his way.

"Hey." She said, taking a seat next to him. She rested her head on his shoulder and started watching the television without saying another word. She still had the same sad look on her face that she did when the girls left.

"Hold on wait," Marcus said, sitting up, "You hear that?"

Sherise sprang up beside him, looking around for the problem.

"What?" She said, not hearing anything.

"Silence." Marcus said, looking over at her.

"Oh, anyway. I…"

"Shhh. I want to enjoy this while I can." Marcus said, closing his eyes.

Sherise smiled and pushed her husband for making fun of the situation but it was exactly what she needed. She knew that her little girls would be fine and that they would be back as soon as things settled down. Sherise curled up under her husband's arm and felt like she was safe from harm. The two of them spent the rest of the afternoon sitting right in front of the television. They even ordered some Chinese food so neither of them would have to cook.

Thirty

Around 10:30 that night a ring penetrated the atmosphere. Marcus and Sherise had fallen asleep on the couch and he jumped up to answer the phone. He rushed into the kitchen, picked up the phone and said, "Hello?"

"Hey man, we made it." A voice said over the phone.

It was Alonzo letting them know they had made it home safely.

"Oh ok. Where y'all at?" Marcus asked.

"Just pulled into the driveway."

"Good, good. Well Sherise will be happy to hear that. What are the girls doing."

"Aw man, they both out like a light."

"Figured that. They didn't get on your nerves on the way up there did they? I know how they can get on a road trip." Marcus said, laughing.

"Nah, no problems at all. That lil' Lasaia is a trip. And she's smart too. Lisa tried to fool her when we stopped for food. Lasaia wanted McDonalds and we stopped at Wendy's. So, Lisa figured she would take the burger and fries out of the wrapper and give them to her like that, like she wasn't gonna know. She said, 'This ain't McDonald's, you tryin' to fool me.' We just busted out laughin'."

"Yeah, that lil' girl is a mess. Well I ain't gonna hold you up man, I know you need to get some rest. We really appreciate what you guys are doing for us."

"Aw ain't no thang brotha, you know I gotcha back."

"Yeah, I know. Well, we'll give you a call tomorrow. If you need anything, just let us know."

"Alright man. Peace"

"Later."

Marcus hung up the phone and headed back to the family room where he found his wife fast asleep, stretched out on the couch. Marcus walked over and nudged Sherise until she woke up.

"Come on, let's go to bed." He said, helping her to her feet.

"Who was that?" Sherise said, drowsy, as they made their way up the stairs.

"Alonzo. He said that they made it home and were about to take the girls inside."

"Oh, that's good. What are the girls doing?"

"He said they were knocked out."

Sherise was completely silent and was probably using all her energy to make it up the steps. Marcus took his wife upstairs and got her in the bed. Before the sheets got a chance to settle on top of her she was out cold. He looked at her and chuckled, before walking out the room.

Marcus headed back downstairs and turned off the television in the family room. He was about to walk back up the stairs when the day's events flash through his head. Without completely thinking, he walked into his office and grabbed his cell phone off the charger. He walked through the house, toward the garage, dialing Lasaia's number. The phone rang a few times and was picked up just as he entered the garage.

"What do you want?" An attitude filled voice said through the phone.

"What do I want? I want to know what makes you think that you can come into my house, slash my tires and scratch up my truck. That's what I want." Marcus said, getting defensive.

"I guess that's what happens when you think you can treat me any way you want. It didn't have to be like this but this is how you wanted it so..."

"Whoa, whoa, whoa...how I wanted it? I didn't want it to be like this. I told you over and over that I didn't want anything to do with you."

"So, is that why you fucked me? Because you didn't want anything to do with me."

"I keep telling you over and over, that was a mistake. Allowing you to seduce me was a mistake. The two of us together was a mistake."

"STOP SAYING THAAAAAAT!!!" Lasaia screamed through the phone.

Marcus had to take the phone away from his ear because she was yelling so loud.

She was silent for a moment then said, "I loved you. I gave you my heart, and you stepped on it. You think you can just treat me any kind of way and expect me to just move on?"

"So, what do you expect me to do? You are wanted by the police. You are the only suspect in my wife's shop getting burned down. You shot my brother..."

"All for you baby."

"And you expect me to still love you after that?"

"Yes. If you would just follow your heart..."

"Follow my heart? That's what I'm trying to do. My *heart* is with my family. This is where I belong."

"No, no...you don't mean that. You love me, I know you do." Lasaia said, sounding like she was about to cry.

"I can't be with you. I don't wanna be with you. Running into you has been one of the worst things that has ever happened to me."

"Your life? Your LIFE! What about my life? I can't even go home. I can't answer my phone. I can't even talk to my friends. And, that is entirely your fault."

"Well, what did you expect? You can't just hurt and try to kill people to get whatever you want?"

"All I wanted was you."

"Look...why don't you just turn yourself in and get some help?"

"What? So I'm crazy now?"

"No, I'm just saying..."

"Fuck you Marcus! Do you want me to hate you? You don't want me to hate you, because things can get a whole lot worse."

"What? So, I'm supposed to be scared now? You know what? Go ahead and do whatever you're gonna do then, 'cause you ain't gonna drag me through hell with you," Marcus said getting upset, "Crazy bitch."

The words slipped out of his mouth before he was able to stop them.

"WHAT! Oh, I'm a crazy bitch now? Ok, we'll see who's the crazy bitch. Don't forget that I can get to you anytime, anywhere. Kiss your wife goodbye Willy."

Lasaia hung up the phone before Marcus was able to get in a word.

"Willy?" Marcus whispered to himself, looking at his phone

Why did she call me Willy?, Marcus thought to himself.

He walked back into the house and made his way up the stairs. Marcus didn't think anything of Lasaia's threats and took a shower before climbing into the bed with his wife. The two of them slept through the night, peacefully.

Marcus woke up the next morning and started to get ready for work. Sherise woke up and slowly climbed out of the bed. She made her way to a sitting position on the side of the bed and sat there for a few seconds with her head down. Another morning with a stomachache. She was sitting there silently when Marcus walked out of his closet and saw her sitting there.

"You alright babe?" He asked, laying his clothes on the bed. She still hadn't told him that she was pregnant and wasn't ready to tell him now.
"I'm fine. Just a little sore." She said, getting up from the bed. Sherise knew she needed to tell him, she just didn't know how. Marcus continued getting ready for work while Sherise headed downstairs to make something for them to eat. Marcus finished getting his things together and headed down the stairs. Sherise was in the kitchen cooking him a quick meal before he had to leave for work. She made each of them a plate and brought them to the table. After they said a blessing, they dug into the meal. Marcus could tell that something was bothering his wife. She was just sitting there in silence with a sad look on her face.
"You miss the girls that much already?" Marcus asked.
Sherise wasn't thinking about the girls at all. Pregnancy was the only thing that ran through her mind. She couldn't come up with a tactful way to do it so she just figured that the best way would be to just come out with it.
"No, but…I do have something to tell you." Sherise said.
Her heart started beating so hard in her chest that she just knew that Marcus could hear it over the silence.
"What is it baby?" Marcus said, wondering what could be bothering her so much.
"When I was in the hospital and they were about to let me go…they told me that I…"
Sherise's words were interrupted by Marcus's cell phone ringing.
"Oh, hold on baby." Marcus said, reaching into his jacket pocket.
He looked at the display and it read, *Private Number*.
"Oh, maybe this is one of the detectives." Marcus said as he flipped open his phone and stood up from the table.
"Marcus Downing" He said into his phone.
"Marcus my boooy, we did it!" The voice said on the other end.
"Mr. Lockson?" Marcus said, not sure he was talking to his boss.
"Yes my boy. You did it. We got the account. The Coca-Cola deal is ours. I just got word." Mr. Lockson's voice shot through the phone. He was talking so loud that Sherise could hear his voice coming out of the speaker. She didn't pay it any mind though. She put her hands over her face and let out a deep sigh. She didn't know if it was a sigh of relief or a sigh of frustration…probably a little of both. Marcus continued his conversation with Mr. Lockson for a few more seconds then said, "Yes sir…yes sir…Ok…yeah…I'm on my way now…ok…bye."
Marcus closed his phone and turned to his wife.
"We did it baby! We got the account!" Marcus said, excitement I his voice.

"That's great baby, I knew you could do it." Sherise said, getting up from her chair to give him a hug. She was happy for him, but frustrated that her chance to tell him was interrupted.

"Oh, oh baby I'm sorry. You were telling me something. I'm sorry, what did you want to say?"

"Huh? Oh, it was nothing. It can wait. You go ahead and get to work and we'll talk later." Sherise said, having lost her courage to tell him now.

"You sure?" Marcus said, eager to hear what she had to say.

"Yeah, I'm sure. I know you have to go." Sherise said.

Marcus let her go and rushed to his office, cheering himself on the whole way. He reentered the kitchen with his briefcase in hand and walked over to his wife.

"You gonna be ok today? Why don't you call Alicia and see if she wants to come over?" Marcus suggested.

"I'll be fine. You go have a good day. Don't worry about me." Sherise said.

Marcus gave his wife another kiss and headed out the door to the garage. He took one look at his truck before chuckling and jumping into Sherise's car. With the money he just found out he made, he could buy ten trucks. He started the car, pulled out of the driveway, and headed off to work. Marcus made it to the parking deck about 20 minutes later and rushed upstairs to his floor to find out exactly what happened.

The doors of the elevator opened and Marcus walked down the short hallway to his office. Before he could walk through the doorway of his office, Marcus heard a roar of applause erupt from behind him. He turned around to see his co-workers being led by Mr. Lockson headed right for him. Marcus couldn't do anything but smile as they closed in on him. The crowd got right on top of him and Mr. Lockson extended his hand to Marcus. The crowd was so loud that the glass on Marcus's office wall began to shake. Mr. Lockson quieted the crowd down and said, "Let's hear it for the man who just took us worldwide".

The crowd exploded into another round of applause. Marcus was smiling so big his jaws began to hurt. He was on top of the world. Even when he didn't come through before they were behind him, and now that he did follow through they were even more excited. Mr. Lockson quieted the crowd down and the hallway slowly emptied as people return to their work. This deal meant big things for everyone at the company.

Marcus walked into his office with Mr. Lockson following closely behind.

"So when did you find out?" Marcus asked, putting his briefcase on his desk.

"This morning. I got a message from their Chief Marketing Executive or Marketing V.P. or whoever he was. He said that they loved your presentation and that we got the account." Mr. Lockson said.

"So when do we get started?" Marcus asked.

"Well, our lawyers are finalizing the contract now but we take over the first of the year," Mr. Lockson said, standing to his feet, "Good job Marcus, good job."

Just as Mr. Lockson got his words out, Mike popped his head through the office door.

"Sir, you have a call from one of the Coca-Cola executives."

"Right." Mr. Lockson said, headed for the door.

"Marcus, you did good my boy. Take the rest of the day off, you've earned it."

Mr. Lockson walked past Mike and disappeared into the hallway.

Mike waited for his boss to turn a corner and walked into the room.

"My brotha, my brotha." Mike said, walking over to Marcus. The two of them gave each other a pound and a hug.

"Good job brotha, good job. You really came through," Mike said, "So what you gonna do with all that money?"

"Aw man. First thing I'm going to do pay my tithes. I got to give the Big Man his for this one. Then, I'll probably pay off my house." Marcus said.

The two men conversed for a few more minutes when Mike asked, "Man, did you ever hear anything from those detectives about Sherise's shop?"

Marcus let out a quick sigh.

"Man, they're trying to get a warrant to search Lasaia's house up in Atlanta, right now."

"What? So they really do think she had something to do with it. Alicia been talkin' a lotta junk about her. You think she did it?"

"I know she did it."

"How you know that?"

Marcus told his friend the whole story of how he went to see Lasaia and how she told him everything that she had done. He told Mike about what happened to his truck, and how they sent the girls up to Atlanta to stay with Alonzo. He ended his story with how the police still haven't been able to find her anywhere.

"Whoa, so did you try and call her?"

"Yeah, I spoke to her last night."

"Well, what did she say?"

"She still believes that I love her and that we will be together again. I'm telling you, she's off. She threatened me, talking about 'Say goodbye to your wife.'"

"And you don't believe she'll do anything?"

"Nah. I mean, what could she possibly do?"

"She got in your house once. What's stopping her from doing it again. She's probably still in town."

Marcus thought about what his friend just said. Of course, Lasaia didn't keep all of her threats, but she did follow through on a few of them. And those were the ones that had the worst consequences. Marcus picked up the phone to prove to his friend that Lasaia wasn't going to do anything and mostly to reassure himself that his wife was ok. He dialed the number and Sherise picked up the phone.

"Hello?" She said, in her usual energetic voice.

"Hey baby." Marcus said, looking up at Mike with an I-told-you-so look.

"What's going on, everything alright?" Sherise said.

"Yeah baby, everything's fine. Just calling to see how you're doing."

"I'm fine, just got off the phone with the daycare and Lasaia's school to let them know the girls are out of town."

"Oh, ok. What did they say?"

"Nothing, they just said to give them a call when they got back."

"Oh ok. Well you know what, I want you to pick out a nice dress and think about where you want to go out to eat tonight. We got some celebrating to do"

"Really? You're actually gonna let me out the house?" Sherise said, giggling.

"Anyway, you act like I have you handcuffed to the bed or something."

"Hmmm, maybe that can be after dinner. If you handle dinner, I'll handle dessert." Sherise said, flirting.

Marcus laughed and said, "Sounds like a plan to me. I'll see you in a little bit."

"Ok baby. Bye."

Marcus hung up the phone and looked over at his friend.

"See, she's fine."

"Man you just talked to the crazy chic last night. She ain't gonna try nothin' the next day. If I were you, I'd watch my back. If she's willing to shoot your brother, try to kill your wife, and break into your garage to destroy your truck…she's willing to go all out. No holds barred. And, if the police can't find her…that means she has some kind of connections. Trust me; I've dealt with a few crazy muthafuckas before. You'd be surprised at what she's capable of."

Marcus chuckled at his friend and thought he was being overly paranoid. While the two of them sat there talking, Marcus's office phone rang.

“Marcus Downing.” He said into the receiver.
“Mr. Downing, this is Detective Bodine. I’ve got some good news for you.”
Marcus’s face straightened.
More business like.
He hoped the next words out of the detective’s mouth would be, “We got her.”
Maybe then, life could start getting back to normal.

Thirty-one

"Did you find her?" Marcus asked, hoping that his answer would be yes.

"Well, no sir but we did get that search warrant. The Fulton County, along with the Atlanta PD, are on their way to search her home now."

"That's great, is there anything else?"

"Well the only other thing is that we were able to get a legal freeze on her accounts and we found out that she recently withdrew over $250,000 dollars in cash. With that type of money she could be anywhere by now."

"Well I believe that she is still here in Jacksonville."

"What makes you think that?"

"Because I woke up yesterday and all the tires on my truck were slashed. If it wasn't her, I know she had something to do with it."

"Really? Did you file a report?"

"Yes I did."

"Ok well good. I assure you Mr. Downing, wherever she is, we *will* find her."

"Thank you detective."

"No problem. I'll call as soon as I find out something from the Atlanta police department, sir."

"Ok. Thank you for everything detective."

Marcus hung up his phone. Even though Mr. Lockson had given him the rest of the day off he decided to stay and get some work done. He had just won a major account for the company but he still had work to do on some projects that he had been neglecting. He finished out his day and headed home for a romantic night out with his wife.

Marcus walked through the door to his house and everything was silent. Usually he would hear Sherise moving around, or she would hear him and come to greet him, today was different.

"I'm home."

Marcus's voice echoed through the empty house. He waited a few seconds, but got no response.

This was strange.

In all their years of being together, Sherise was never late on greeting her husband when he walked into the house. Marcus's first assumption was that she was probably in the shower and couldn't hear him. He walked up the stairs to the bedroom and found clothes thrown all over the place. Marcus's mind started to race and he immediately thought the worst. The sun began to set through the bedroom window and Marcus tried to think of where his wife could be. All kinds of scenarios ran through his head as he stood there in the bedroom.

Had Lasaia come into his home again and this time kidnap his wife?

No, maybe she's tied up somewhere in the house, hurt, and can't call out to him. Marcus searched every possible place that he thought Sherise's body could fit. He checked every bathtub, every closet, he looked in the kitchen cupboard and even checked inside his truck.

She was nowhere to be found.

He rushed back into the kitchen, from the garage, and grabbed the phone off the wall. He figured that he had to call the police and get them looking for her before Lasaia did something. He pressed the 9, 1, but right before he pressed the last number he heard the front door open and some laughter rush into the house. Marcus looked around the corner and saw Sherise and Alicia walking through the door, shopping bags in their hands. Marcus breathed a deep sigh of relief. At that moment, he realized that this needed to do something to end this now. He couldn't keep going through a panic every time he didn't know where his wife was.

"Hey baby." Sherise said, kissing him on the cheek as she walked into the kitchen. "Hey Marcus." Alicia said to him, following right behind Sherise. Marcus was still standing next to the doorway with the phone in his hand.

"Hey baby, Hey Alicia." Marcus said, hanging up the now buzzing phone.

"Who was that?" Sherise said, grabbing two mugs from the cabinet to pour her and Alicia some coffee.

"Huh? Oh, nobody. Wrong number."

Sherise poured her friend and herself a cup of coffee and said, "Oh baby, guess what?"

"What?" Marcus said, opening the refrigerator and grabbing an apple.

"Alicia called the insurance company that covered the shop today and they are going to pay to replace everything. Isn't that great?"

Marcus was still recovering from his short scare, but popped back into reality and said, "Oh really? Yeah, that's great."

Marcus took a bite of his apple and Sherise looked at him strangely. She had just told him that they wouldn't have to pay to replace a single thing in her shop and all he had to say was, *Yeah…that's great.*

She expected the *money-saving pioneer* to be jumping up and down.

"You ok baby," Sherise asked, "Did something happen at work?"

"No, everything is fine. Work was great. We got the account, remember?" Marcus said.

"Yeah, I remember but I just told you that we don't have to replace anything and you don't even flinch. What's the matter? You look upset." Sherise said, walking over to him.

"Nothing, I'm fine. It's just…when I got here and you weren't here I started to worry." Marcus said.

"Aw, I'm ok baby. Me and Lele just went shopping. I went through all my clothes and couldn't find anything special. Wait until you see what I bought." Sherise said, throwing her arms around Marcus's neck and giving him a kiss.

The two of them stood there kissing for a few seconds until Alicia said, "Oh gawd, you two are nasty." She stood up and grabbed her bag off the floor.

"Sherise girl, I'll holla at you tomorrow. Y'all have a good time."

"Ok girl, call me." Sherise said.

"Alright, bye Marcus."

"Bye." Marcus said as she walked out the door.

The two of them hurried upstairs to start getting ready for their night out.

Marcus got into a nice formal suit and had a seat on the bed. It toke him less then 45 minutes. Fifteen minutes passed and Marcus realized he hadn't seen his wife in over an hour. She had been held up in the bathroom ever since they came upstairs and all he got was an, "I'm almost ready," every five to ten minutes. He had to take a shower in the girls' bathroom because she was taking so long. Finally, after an hour and a half of preparation, Sherise emerged from the bathroom. She was stunning. She had on a beautiful dress that wrapped around her neck and covered her in the front. There was a diamond shaped opening on the chest that showed a little cleavage. The entire back of the dress was out and went all the way down to the small of her back. The bottom of the dress fit snuggly around her hips and thighs, then opened up at the bottom. She looked like a real Nubian princess on her way to a ball. Her makeup and hair were flawless and Marcus realized why he married this woman all over again. Any woman who could have two kids, still look this good, was intelligent and treat him as good as she did had to be much too good for him. It seemed like she walked out of the bathroom in slow motion and he couldn't take his eyes off of her. His fantasy was broken up when she said, "Ok, ok, I'm ready. I just need my shoes." She disappeared into her closet and came out with a pair of sexy, black shoes.

"Ok, I'm ready." She said, looking up at him.

Marcus just smiled and walked over to her. He slowly placed his hand on her cheek and leaned forward as if he was about to kiss her and said, "TIME," while looking at his watch.

"An hour and 45 minutes. I think it's a new record."

Sherise smiled and pushed him away.

"Anyway," She said, "It was worth it though, wasn't it?"

Sherise did a quick spin in front of him and he had to admit that she was gorgeous.

"You look beautiful, baby." He said, giving her a kiss.

The two of them get into her car and left for their night out.

They arrived at the restaurant about 8:30 and were seated right away. The two of them had a wonderful meal, talking and laughing about the day's events. Around 9:15 Sherise got a call on her cell phone. She pulled it from her purse and answered it with a giggling, "Hello?"

"Hi mommy." A little voice said on the other end.

"Heeey baby! How you doing?" Sherise said, excited to hear her daughter's voice.

"Fine. What'cha doin'?" Lasaia asked.

"Me and your daddy are having dinner. What are you doing?"

"Nothin'."

"You having fun with Uncle Alonzo?"

"Yeah, we went to Chucky Cheese."

"You did! Wow, did you have fun?"

"Mmh Hmm, I won a bear."

"You did? Oh, that's great baby."

"Don't tell daddy. I'm gonna surprise him."

Sherise laughed and said, "Ok, I won't. Here, say hi to your daddy."

Sherise extended her arm over the table and handed the phone to Marcus.

"Hey baby girl." Marcus said, placing the phone to his ear.

"Hey daddy."

"What are you guys doing?"
"Nothing, Uncle Alonzo said I could call you before I went to bed."
"Oh ok, where is your sister?"
"She sleep already."
"Oh ok. Are you being good for your uncle?"
"Yes sir."
"That's my girl."
There was a short moment of silence before Lasaia said, "I wanna come home daddy."
Marcus could hear the sadness in his little girl's voice and it made his heart drop.
"I know baby, I want both of her home. But, I promise you that you and your sister will be back as soon as possible, ok?" Marcus said.
"Ok." Lasaia said in a sad but accepting tone.
"You miss us?"
"Yeah."
"We miss you too, both of you. Ok?"
"Ok."
"I love you."
"I love you too daddy."
"Alright, let me talk to your uncle."
"Ok, goodnight daddy."
"Night baby."
Marcus heard Lasaia give Alonzo the phone.
"You ready to go to bed too?" Marcus heard Lisa say in the background.
"Yeah." Lasaia said in a low drowsy voice. Marcus thought to himself that it was never that easy to get that little girl to bed. She must have really been sad.
"What's up Boy?" Alonzo's voice shot through the phone.
"What's going on?" Marcus said.
"Aw nothing much man. Just enjoying your little ones."
Marcus laughed and said, "Yeah, you'll be ready to bring 'em home in a few days. How is Lisa holding up?"
"Oh man, she's lovin' it. You gotta come get them though, before she gets too hooked. Be around here trying to have some of her own."
Marcus laughed and said, "You might as well. I already had my first one when I was your age."
"Yeah, well…I ain't trying to get into all that right now. What you and Sherise gettin' into?"

"We just here at the restaurant."

"Restaurant? Oh, y'all ditched the kids on us and now y'all hittin' the night scene huh?"

Marcus laughed and said, "Nah, nah. I got that account today. We're just out celebrating."

"Account? Oh, the Coca-Cola one?"

"Yeah."

"Oh ok. True, true."

"Yeah, so we came out to celebrate."

"Oh, well man I ain't mean to interrupt nothing. I just promised the little one I would let her call you guys."

"Ain't no problem man, we needed to hear from y'all."

"Ok, well I'll let you get back to your dinner. She'll probably want to call tomorrow anyway."

Alonzo and Marcus shared a laugh.

"Tell Sherise I said hey."

"Alright man, I will."

"Alright peace."

Marcus hung up her phone and looked across the table at Sherise. She was sitting there looking radiant and his eyes latched onto her.

"What?" Sherise said, smiling at her husband.

He hadn't realized that his look had turned into a stare. Marcus reached across the table and put his hand on top of hers and said, "You really look beautiful."

Sherise blushed and said, "Well thank you. You don't look so bad yourself."

"Oh, Alonzo says hi."

"Oh, how are they doing?"

"Good. He's slowed down on the club a little and Lisa is happy about that. He said we gotta come get the girls though."

"Why?"

"He said Lisa's getting too attached and she's gonna want one of her own."

"Hmph. He needs to go ahead and marry that girl."

"I think this is the one. He ain't held onto no girl like he holds onto her."

"She must got that *thi-yow*." Sherise said, laughing.

"So, why is it when a man slows down and decides to stay with one woman, it's because the woman got some good booty? Why can't he just want to settle down?"

"I don't know. But, but that's how I got you."

"Oh really?" Marcus said, laughing.

The two of them had a good laugh and finished their dinner.

They made their way back home and walked through the front door. Marcus typed in his code to disarm the alarm system and the system beeped and disarmed. Sherise began to walk toward the steps when Marcus grabbed her by the arm. He pulled her close and wrapped his arms around her. He looked deep into her beautiful brown eyes and slowly leaned forward, pressing his lips against hers. Their lips seemed to mesh together and become one pair. Sherise let out a low sexy moan. She loved for him to kiss her like that. Their lips separated and she looked up at him and said, "You ready for your dessert?"
Marcus smiled and kissed her again.
"Why don't you go and get some strawberries and whipped cream out of the fridge and meet me upstairs in 2 minutes." Sherise said.
Those words alone caused his penis to get hard, but he tried to play it cool. He stated to walk toward the kitchen as she headed upstairs.
"You want a bowl with that?" He said, joking.
"We won't need a bowl…but you might want to get some new sheets out of the linen closet before you get up here." Sherise said, taking the first few steps. Only one word ran through Marcus's mind after she said that, *Damn*. He knew he was in for it. He rushed to the kitchen and grabbed a large plastic bowl out of the cabinet and filled it with some fresh strawberries from the refrigerator. He rinsed them off, grabbed a small tub of whipped cream and strutted out of the kitchen doing his, *I'm gonna get some* dance. He was ready to get it on. No kids, no waiting for after bedtime, no threat of interruptions, oh, it was on! Marcus made it to the top of the stairs and zeroed in on their room. The door to the bedroom was almost completely closed. The light was on and it seemed to glow through the small crack.
"We didn't have any of the whipped cream in the can baby, so I just grabbed the tub," Marcus said as he pushed the door open with his foot, "But I think that you will…"
Marcus paused in the doorway and stared into the room. He saw his wife standing motionless in the middle of the room. She was standing completely still with her hands at her side. Her eyes and cheeks were filled with tears and she seemed frozen.
"Baby, what's wrong?" Marcus said, walking toward her.
"MARCUS NOOOO!" Sherise yelled as he made it a few feet into the room.
After his second step, Marcus was blindsided. He was hit in the temple and fell to the floor unconscious.

SPLASH

Marcus woke up after having a cup of water thrown on his face. He looked around trying to get his eyes to focus on anything in the room. That blow to the head really had him disoriented. After a few seconds, he was finally able to focus in on his wife's face.

"Baby, baby wake up." Sherise said, trying to shake Marcus awake.

"Get up bitch!" A voice shouted from out of Marcus's view.

He was still laying face down on his stomach and couldn't move. All of a sudden Sherise disappeared from his view. He tried to raise his head up to see where his wife went but his vision went blurry again. All he could see was the outline of a figure towering over him. His eyes began to slowly focus as he heard the figure begin to speak.

"Hello Marcus."

His eyes focused completely as he heard the words.

It was Lasaia.

She was standing there over him dressed in some camouflage pants and a black t-shirt. Somehow she had gotten into their bedroom and was now standing over him. Marcus was finally able to gain complete consciousness and tried to get to his feet but his wrist had been cuffed to the bed rail.

"Aw what's wrong Marcus, you having trouble getting up? It wouldn't be all that interesting if you could just stand up and beat me up now would it?" Lasaia said, kneeling down and putting her hand on his cheek.

"What…what do you want?" Marcus said, struggling to get his words out.

"Oh, now you're concerned with what I want? It's too late for that now. Do you remember what I said the last time we talked?" She asked.

Marcus had no idea what she was talking about. He just lay there in silence.

"No? Well let me remind you. I told you that I could get to you anytime, anywhere. I have very skilled friends that have taught me quite a lot over the last few months. Did you get a chance to say goodbye to your wife?" Lasaia asked.

Marcus looked up at her and said, "If you hurt her…I'll…I'll…"

Lasaia started to laugh.

"You'll what? Kill me? And how do you plan to do that?" Lasaia said, standing to her feet and reaching behind her back. She pulled out a small pistol from her waist and aimed it at Marcus.

"Well if I can't have you, she can't either."

"WAIT!" Sherise said, standing to her feet.

Before she could even take her next breath, Lasaia pulled the trigger.

BANG
Sherise screamed and tried to rush over to her husband. She just knew that this crazy woman had killed him.
"Sit…yo' ass down!" Lasaia said, turning the gun on Sherise.
Sherise stopped a few feet before the barrel of the gun and slowly backed up to her spot on the bed. Marcus moved around trying to find a pain to know where he was hit. He couldn't see it but Lasaia had missed his leg by a few inches. She knelt down next to him and said, "You know Marcus, all this could have been avoided. I wanted to give you everything. But that wasn't good enough for you, was it?" Lasaia said, throwing a small key at him.
"Take the cuffs off." She said, keeping the gun on him.
Marcus grabbed the key and put it into the opening on the lock. The cuffs clicked and loosened as he turned and he was freed from his capture.
"Now, take them off the bed." Lasaia said.
Marcus's heart was beating quickly with anger. He wanted to just rush across the room and jump on Lasaia but he did as she instructed and removed the cuffs from the bed. Lasaia backed over to the corner where Sherise's makeup area was located and rolled the big, plush chair across the floor, into the middle of the room facing the bed.
"Sit." Lasaia said, looking at Marcus, pointing at the chair.
She had lowered her weapon and Marcus saw his opportunity. He started to rush over to her. Before he was able to take more then a few steps Lasaia raised her gun, pointing it right at him.
"Un un unnn. It's not gonna be that easy. Now sit down, like a good little boy." Lasaia said, a look of confidence on her face.
"What you gonna do? Shoot me," Marcus said, taking another step toward her, "I'm the one you want…remember?"
Marcus figured that she wouldn't shoot him and decided to call her bluff. Lasaia looked at him, confused. She didn't expect him to try anything. Marcus took another slow step.
"Stop!" Lasaia said, still pointing the gun at him.
Marcus took another step.
"I'll shoot, I swear it." She said, sounding nervous.
"No you won't. You love me…remember?" Marcus said, his voice calm.
He took another step.
The look on Lasaia's face went from confused to fear. She knew she couldn't shoot the only man that she had ever loved but she knew if she didn't do something quick he would be on top of her and everything would be over.

"Come on, give me the gun." Marcus said, extending his arm, palm open. Lasaia took a step back and had a look on her face like a scared child being approached by a bully. After Marcus took another step he heard a voice from behind him say, "Baby."

It was Sherise.

She didn't want Marcus to try anything and end up getting hurt. Lasaia immediately took a step to the side and aimed the gun at Sherise. Marcus stopped dead in his tracks.

"You know what? You're right. I can't shoot you. But, I *can* shoot her." Lasaia said, confidence returning to her face.

Marcus took a step back as a sign of surrender and said, "Ok, ok...calm down." He still had the cuffs hanging from the thumb of his left hand.

"Good, now sit!" Lasaia said, taking back her control.

Marcus walked to the chair and sat down.

"Put your hands through the back." She demanded.

Marcus reached his hands through the spaces on both sides of the chair as she requested.

"Now, put the cuffs on." Lasaia said.

Marcus hesitated for a few seconds but he put the cuffs on one wrist first, then the second.

"Good boy," Lasaia said, standing behind him, "Now drop the key."

Marcus dropped the small handcuff key and Lasaia walked up behind him and picked it up. She squeezed the cuffs tighter around Marcus's wrist and made sure he couldn't get out. Once she was confident that Marcus couldn't get out she walked around and stood in between him and Sherise.

Sherise was sitting on the bed almost frozen by what was happening to them. The tears and sniffs were the only thing that penetrated the silence of the room for a few seconds. Marcus and Lasaia just stared at each other with a lot of anger in their hearts for one another. Lasaia walked in front of Sherise and said, "Move," signaling her to slide over to the corner of the bed. Sherise was so overwhelmed with fear that she hesitated to move right away after the request. Lasaia switched the gun from her left hand to her right and backhanded Sherise across the face, causing her to fall over on the bed. Marcus jumped to his feet with the chair still cuffed to his back and yelled out, "Hey!"

Lasaia turned to him with the gun pointed at Sherise and said, "You want her dead? 'Cause I can do that! Now sit down!"

Marcus slowly lowered his chair to the floor. Sherise scurried to the corner of the bed, still sobbing and recovering from her attack. Lasaia walked to the other corner and had a seat, crossing her legs.

"Now, we're gonna play a little game," She said, her voice calm, "It's called *Who do you love?*"

"What?" Marcus asked.

"Who do you love?" Lasaia repeated.

"There's only one question. If you get it right, things will be fine. If you get it wrong…"

Lasaia turned to Sherise and aimed the gun right at her forehead, "She loses."

Sherise's heart rate quickened.

"So what…you think that I'm gonna just let you walk outta here after you kill my wife?"

Lasaia looked at him, laughed and said, "No baby, if you get it wrong…only one of us will be walking out of here."

Marcus could see how serious she was. She had come into their home prepared to kill them both and get away with it. Marcus's heart began to beat faster. He knew he needed to make a move, but he still didn't think she had it in her to kill. She was able to shoot Alonzo, but she wasn't trying to kill him.

Marcus didn't know that by now Lasaia had crossed into a totally different reality. The way she saw things, she was the victim. All she wanted out of life was the one man that made her feel like a woman. The one man who brought some stability to her otherwise chaotic young life. Marcus didn't know it, but by him simply keeping his promises to her over the years meant a lot more to her than just coming to a play or not leaving her in a haunted house. Lasaia built her entire young world around this man and would have jumped in front of a bus to save him if she had to. Marcus didn't know about all the times she went home thanking God that she didn't do anything stupid to push him away. He was her rock and when they lost contact, her world fell apart. She was able to pull herself together and continue living but that was only because she was able to convince herself that he would come back, one day. Then, when they reunited, she felt complete again. And, when they made love, she knew that things were right. Her whole mind had shifted to him, nothing else mattered. She walked away from a two hundred and fifty million dollar a year company, to chase a married man, and didn't care. All she ever wanted out of life was Marcus, nothing else. She couldn't cope with losing him again. She was willing to do anything to get him back, and if she couldn't, she had no reason to live.

There she sat, on the corner of the bed, holding her gun, looking at him. Lasaia was a mess. Her hair was all frizzed, she didn't have on any makeup, and even though she was a very beautiful woman, she looked like she hadn't slept in days.

"So, it's game time." Lasaia said.

She raised the gun up and pointed it at Marcus.

She looked into Marcus's eyes and spoke, "It's up to you…Who…do…you…love?"

Thirty-two

Marcus's heart rate began to skyrocket. He didn't think Lasaia had the ability to kill, but he wasn't willing to risk his and Sherise's life on that. He looked over at Sherise who couldn't stop crying. She still couldn't believe what happening to them. Even though she wasn't tied up, she might as well have been, because she was frozen in her spot.

Marcus just looked at both of them. He was sure in his heart what his answer was, but he wasn't completely confident that Lasaia wouldn't fly off the handle, anymore than she already had, after hearing it. He sat there in silence, looking at them for about ten seconds before Lasaia got restless. She pointed the gun at Sherise and said, "Answer!"

Marcus still sat there in silence.

Lasaia put her thumb on the hammer of the gun and pulled it back.

"Ok,ok," Marcus said, seeing it was time to act, "I love…my wife."

Lasaia's eyes grew to the size of pool balls. She couldn't believe that he actually said it again.

"You don't mean that." Lasaia's said, her voice beginning to crack.

He had rejected her again.

"Yes I do. I love my wife. The two of us had something special but, that was years ago. When we were kids you were the most important person in the world to me but that was then. Things are different now. We each went our separate routes. Come on, it doesn't have to be like this." Marcus said, trying to talk Lasaia into giving up.

Lasaia started to break down into tears, just sitting there, looking at him. It had finally hit her that she would never get him back.

Lasaia still had the gun pointed at Sherise, but her eyes were full of tears. "I can't lose you again." She said, through her sobs.

"You will never lose what we had. No one can take that from you." Marcus said, trying to calm her down.

Lasaia lowered the hammer on her gun and slowly placed it in her lap.

She was beaten.

She was confused and had no idea what to do now. She had ended her life to try and join his and now that she saw that wasn't going to happen.

She had nothing to return to.

"But, why...why would you sleep with me if you didn't love me?" She said, tears falling from her eyes.

All these years she had equated sex with love. That was the real reason she had never been with anyone before. The only person that she ever loved was Marcus, and since sex meant love, no one else even got close to being with her.

"I don't know. I'm sorry," Marcus said to the completely broken down Lasaia, "That was my fault. I shouldn't have let things go that far. Don't blame yourself, it was my mistake."

Marcus tried to slide his chair a little closer to Sherise. His wife had stopped her tears and was actually feeling a little bit sorry for the intruder. She really had been through a lot in her life. The abuse she suffered throughout her younger years had really destroyed her inside. She saw things in a totally different light then the two of them and the truth was all crashing down on her right now.

It hurt.

Lasaia let Marcus's words register in her head for a few seconds. She immediately stopped crying and wiped her eyes.

"What did you say?" She asked.

Marcus saw her whole demeanor flip. Something his last few words had returned her to her state of anger. Lasaia got up, walked over behind Marcus and jammed the gun barrel in between his neck and collarbone.

"I told you to stop calling me a mistake, didn't I?" Lasaia said, yelling into his ear while wiping the remaining tears from her face.

"I wasn't calling you a mistake, I was..."

"SHUT UP," Lasaia said, breaking in on his sentence, "You know what? You're right. We were a mistake. I left my whole life behind for you...now I have nothing."

She walked around to face him.

She took a deep breath.

"But that was my mistake. I guess one more wouldn't hurt."

Lasaia extended her hand behind her, pointing the gun at Sherise. She pulled back the hammer back again and Sherise gasped. Lasaia was battling within herself to pull the trigger. Sherise looked at Marcus and mouthed the words, "I love you," then closed her eyes. She had given up and was ready for the blast. Marcus couldn't stand by and let his wife be killed right in front of him. Lasaia's fingers began to squeeze around the trigger.

"NOOO!!" Marcus yelled as he jumped to his feet and charged at Lasaia head first. He knocked her onto the bed right before the gun fired. The bullet barely missed Sherise's head and struck a picture on the wall. Sherise screamed and ducked as Marcus covered Lasaia on the bed with the chair still handcuffed to his back. Lasaia struggled to get Marcus's huge body off of her while still holding onto her gun. She tried to knock Marcus off of her by hitting him in the neck with the butt of the gun. The blows hurt, but the adrenaline flowing through his body caused him to only focus on saving his wife.

Sherise recovered from her shock and saw her husband covering Lasaia on the bed. She quickly rushed over and tried to help her husband overpower her. Lasaia struggled with the two of them and pulled her arms under Marcus to try and push him off of her. During the struggle the gun went off and the three of them stop moving. Sherise stood up and looked at the two motionless bodies lying on the bed. Marcus slowly slid back on his feet and fell back into the chair. Lasaia moved a few seconds later and had a smeared blood stain on her shirt. She got off the bed and checked herself for a gunshot wound. Neither her nor Sherise had been hit. They both looked over to Marcus who was just sitting in the chair with his head down. A small red stain began to get bigger on his white dress shirt.

"Baby!" Sherise yelled, rushing to his side. The stain was growing very quickly and covered almost one fourth of his shirt. Marcus was bleeding badly. He was still breathing, but it was very swallow and if he didn't get help soon he would most likely bleed to death.

"Baby, baby don't leave me." Sherise said, shaking Marcus, trying to snap him out of his daze. Lasaia was just standing there with her hand covering her mouth. This wasn't what she wanted. She never meant to hurt Marcus.

"Move!" Lasaia said, pushing Sherise to the side.

She walked behind him and unlocked the cuffs. His hands fell lifeless from the cuffs as if he was already gone. Sherise was sitting on the floor with her hands over her face crying for her husband. She couldn't believe that he was gone. Marcus's body just sat there motionless, slumped over in the big plush chair. Lasaia started pacing back and forth on the floor next to his body. She didn't know what to do. Her whole plan had gone wrong. She came in there wanting to hear him say that he loved her, now he was sitting dead in a chair. She kept walking back and forth, back and forth, across the floor with her hands over her ears, trying to block out Sherise's cries. She needed to think. After a few minutes, she got aggravated and walked over and grabbed Sherise by the hair.

"GET UP!" Lasaia yelled, pulling her up.

Sherise struggled to her feet and Lasaia jammed the gun against her neck, still holding her by the hair.

"Look at what you caused," Lasaia said, turning Sherise's head toward her husband, "If it wasn't for you, this would have never happened."

Lasaia pushed Sherise across the room and pointed the gun at her.

"It's all your fault. You didn't deserve him." She said, walking toward Sherise.

With every step Lasaia took toward her, Sherise took a step back.

"He was mine, and you took him from me!" Lasaia said, tears falling from her eyes too.

Even though she was the one to shoot Marcus, destroy their bond, and basically cause all the trouble, she still refused to accept responsibility. Sherise backed up all the way to the wall and looked for somewhere to go. She saw Marcus's open closet door and slid down the wall toward it. Lasaia kept walking towards her yelling. Sherise made a dash for the closet and tried to close the door before Lasaia could get to her but Lasaia was able to get her foot in the crack before she got the door all the way closed. The two of them struggled with the door, one trying to push her way in, the other trying to push the door closed. Lasaia squeezed the gun through the crack in the door.

BANG *BANG* *BANG*

Sherise ducked down behind the door trying to avoid being hit by the wild shots. After the shots stopped Sherise noticed that Lasaia was no longer trying to break into the closet. Her arm had disappeared from the crack in the door and the door was no longer being pushed in. Sherise was so scared that she just sat there against the door crying. She didn't know if Lasaia had ran off, but was too scared to open the door to find out.

On the other side of the door, Marcus had gotten up from the chair and grabbed Lasaia from behind. He struggled with her, but his wound had greatly reduced his strength. He threw her on the bed and the impact caused the gun to fly from her hand and into the headboard. Lasaia flipped over and tried to go for her weapon, but Marcus grabbed her by the leg and pulled her back right before she got to it. He climbed on top of her and wrapped his hands around her neck. Marcus began to squeeze and Lasaia started to gasp for air. He squeezed, tighter and tighter, letting out all his anger for this woman who was trying to ruin his life. Lasaia's face began to turn a different shade as she gagged, slapping at his arms, trying to get him to let go.

Before she passed out, she balled up her fist and punched him in his gunshot wound. The blow sent an electric shock of pain through his body. Marcus lost his strength and fell down on top of her. Lasaia was able to roll him over onto the bed and climbed on top of him. She punched him in his wound again and said, "So you were gonna kill me?"

She gave his wound one more strike and Marcus let out a loud scream. She reached for a black sheath strapped to her hip and pulled out a double-edged throwing knife. She pressed it against Marcus's neck as he was trying to recover from the blows to his abdomen. She pressed the knife so hard that it caused a drop of blood to trickle down the side of his throat.

"I'm sorry baby. But this is how it has to be." Lasaia said, raising the knife with one hand preparing to stab him in the chest.

BANG

Marcus felt what seemed like water spray onto his face. He looked up at Lasaia who was still frozen with the knife poised over him. She slowly fell to the side and rolled over, onto the bed. Marcus raised his head up and looked around to see what happened. He saw Sherise, standing in the doorway of his closet, his gun in her hand. Tears were running from her eyes, as she stood there, frozen. Marcus pushed Lasaia's legs off him and made it to his feet. He grabbed the knife from Lasaia's hand and her gun from the bed before rushing over to his wife. She couldn't even look at him. All she did was stand there looking at Lasaia lying motionless on the bed and cry. She had never done anything like that to anyone, but she would have done it all over again if she had to in order to save him.

"It's ok baby. It's over." Marcus whispered into her ear.

She threw her arms around him and this time she believed him. Marcus walked over and grabbed the phone and called the police.

A few days later, Marcus was sitting in his hospital bed watching television. He had lost a lot of blood that night and the doctors wanted to make sure everything was alright before letting him go home.

Knock knock knock
"Heeeey baby." Sherise said, walking through the door.
"Hey." Marcus said, looking at her.
"How you feeling?"
"Better. They still won't let me leave, though."
"Well that's ok. You'll be out of here soon. I have a surprise for you, though."
"What?"
Sherise searched through her purse and pulled out a small bag of pork rinds. Marcus's face lit up like a kid at a surprise birthday party. She passed him the bag and he ripped it open. After throwing the first one in his mouth all Sherise heard was a long "Mmmm." He looked over at her and said, "See, I knew there was a reason I married you."
Sherise laughed and said, "Well, I thought you might like that."
She took the seat next to his bed and said, "Baby, I have something I need to tell you."
Marcus was still enjoying his treat and didn't take his eyes off the bag.
"What's that babe?" He said, throwing another chip into his mouth.
"I…"
The door opening disrupted Sherise's sentence. It was Marcus's doctor. He walked over to the bed and said, "Mr. Downing, how are you feeling? How are you Mrs. Downing?"
"Fine." Sherise said, before the doctor turned back to her husband.
"I'm good. No complaints. Can I go home today?" Marcus said.
The doctor chuckled.
"We'll see about that. I don't want you leaving until I know you'll be ok. We've been keeping track of your progress over the past few days and things are looking pretty good. You should be out of here soon. Your wife tells me that you needed the time off anyway."
Marcus laughed and said, "Ok doc, sounds good."
The two of them shook hands and the doctor left the room. Sherise turned back to her husband and said, "Ok, baby. This is gonna be a shock but…"
The hospital door opened with a knock again. The two of them saw Detective Bodine's head peek around the edge.
"Mr. Downing," The detective, said walking into the room, "How you feeling sir?"
"Mrs. Downing." He said, shaking Sherise's hand.
"I'm fine. Getting better." Marcus said.

"Good to hear. I just wanted to stop in and let you know how much we have found out on your case."

"Found out? What do you mean?" Marcus asked.

"Well we were able to link Miss Lewis to several of the things that have been going on in your life." Detective Bodine said.

Marcus put down his bag of chips and sat up a little in the bed.

"Really? Like what?" He asked.

"Well, first and foremost we were able to search her house and find out a few things. She had old pictures of the two of you thrown everywhere. It was like she was building some kind of shrine to you or something. We were able to run a DNA test on that substance we found on the broken window in your wife's shop and matched it perfectly to a hair sample we found in her bedroom."

"So she really did burn down my shop?" Sherise asked.

"Yes ma'am. We were also able to link the gun she had the night she attacked you guys to the one used in your brother's shooting in Atlanta. And, we found the picture that you reported taken from your truck in a hotel room that was under an alias she was using. The desk clerk at the hotel recognized Miss Lewis from the news reports and called us over. After we got in the room we found the fake I.D. and your picture."

The detective handed Marcus the wallet-sized photo. Marcus looked at the picture and saw that Sherise's face had been scratched out.

"This links her to the vandalism of your truck."

Marcus took a deep breath as the detective continued.

"Now, we were also able to arrest a Mr. Tony Willard, I'm not sure if you know him." The detective said pulling out a mug shot of Tony.

"That's the guy she brought to my house and said was her boyfriend. She said his name was Greg." Sherise said, looking at the picture.

"Well it's not. His name is Tony Willard, ex-Navy Seal. Dishonorably discharged after it was found out that he was part of a ring of people who were selling weapons to gangs out in California. He made a deal and only did a year for squealing on his partners. That was about 6 years ago. But he has knowledge of a lot of different things and we think he was assisting Miss Lewis and made her the fake I.D."

Sherise handed the picture back to the detective as Marcus said, "So, I guess my only question is, how she got into our house?"

"Oh ok, let me show you." Detective Bodine said, reaching into his jacket pocket.

He pulled out a small black device, about the size of a small remote control, with about 20 buttons.

"What's that?" Sherise asked.

"It's a transmitter of some kind. I've never seen anything like it. It can program itself to different electrical devices. Watch..."

The detective turned and pointed the device at the television and pressed the top button. The light on the transmitter flashed a few times and beeped. After the beep, the detective pressed another button and the channels on the television began to change.

"What the..." Marcus said, amazed.

"Yeah I know. It has some kind of smart chip in it or something. It can change channels, disarm car alarms; unlock electric doors, change traffic signals, and a range of other things. Of course, one of them being opening garage doors. We think she got it from overseas somewhere. I have never seen one before. This is what she used to get into your garage to vandalize your truck. We also think this is what she used to get in the house the night she attacked you. We know she came through the garage, but we have no idea how she disarmed the house system. We contacted the alarm company and they didn't show any suspicious activity between the time you guys went out until the time you got back. Do you know of a time when she could have possibly overheard your code or got it off a piece of paper or something?" The detective asked.

Marcus and Sherise looked at each other and tried to think of a time when she could have possibly stolen that kind of information. Sherise was at a loss, she had very little contact with her and had no idea where she got it.

Marcus was lost too.

"No, I mean she did come to the house a few times and stayed over one night but,"

The memories of that night flew back into Marcus's brain and he went silent. The night the silent alarm went off at the house and she was there. She could have easily picked up the phone in the kitchen where she was and listened to him give the code to the security representative.

"What baby?" Sherise said, bringing Marcus out of trance.

"I think I know when she got it." Marcus said.

The told Sherise and the detective his theory.

"That would have to be it then, but all that is irrelevant. They have her back in Atlanta now. She's going to face charges both there and here. But you don't have to worry about that. You two need to focus on getting your lives back together." Detective Bodine said.

"Thanks detective." Marcus said, shaking his hand.

"Well if you two will excuse me, I have plenty of paperwork to do." The detective said, turning to leave. Sherise got up and followed him to the door.

"Thanks again." She said, as he was about to leave.

"Not a problem." The detective said, turning back to her. He paused for a second and said, "You are a very lucky woman. I was in your situation about 15 years ago."

"What do you mean?" Sherise asked.

"My wife's ex-boyfriend came back and told me she was his and that I better back off or else. I didn't and he kidnapped and killed her. That's what made me join the force. That's why I was so passionate about your case. I didn't get a second chance. You do. Promise me you won't take it for granted."

Sherise could feel tears forming in her eyes for the detective.

"I promise." She said, looking him in the eyes.

She wanted to say something to make him feel better but she didn't know what to say. He saw the appreciation in her eyes, smiled and shook her hand before walking off down the hospital hallway. Sherise closed the hospital room door, locked it and moved a chair in front of it before turning back to her husband.

"Now, no more interruptions." She said, taking her spot next to her man.

"Well, just one more," Marcus said, "I want to ask you something."

"What?" Sherise said.

"How did you know I had a gun in my closet?"

Sherise giggled for a second and said, "I've known you had that thing since for ever. I just didn't know how to bring it up because I knew you were going to be like, 'Well what you doin' in my closet?'. But I've always known it was there."

Marcus laughed at the fact that he thought he could actually hide something from his wife. They stopped laughing and Sherise looked at him and said, "Ok. My turn."

"Ok. Your turn."

Sherise took another deep breath and said, "I'm…I'm…"

Marcus broke in and said, "Here, let me help you. I'm, pregnant."

A look of shock jumped onto Sherise's face.

"You knew?"

"Of course. Let's not forget, I know you too. That, and you haven't bought any of your *products* in the last few months. And you haven't had a drink in a few months either."

Sherise giggled for a second at her husband's deductive reasoning.

"And you're not mad?" Sherise asked.

"Mad? For what? I'll have three hundred kids as long as I can raise them with you." Sherise smiled and stood up to give her husband a hug.

"I love you so much baby." She whispered in his ear.

"I love you too." He said, squeezing his wife in his arms.

His wound hurt a little during their embrace but he refused to let her go.

Marcus spent the next few days in the hospital and finally got to go home. He spent the next couple weeks at home recovering from the whole ordeal. His company won the Coca-Cola account and they were on their way to becoming a worldwide name in the advertising business. The following year Sherise gave birth to a beautiful 6 pound 10 ounce bouncing baby boy. After finding a new location, *Sherise's* was back in business, and more popular than ever. Their lives got back on track and they began living in a safe state of mind again.

While Marcus and Sherise were putting the pieces of their life back together, Lasaia went through her trials and was sentenced to 15 years in a mental health facility. Marcus spent a majority of his time at home everyday making sure that Sherise and the kids knew how much he loved them. While they were celebrating Christmas, Lasaia was going through therapy. While they were bringing in the New Year, Lasaia was fighting off nurses who were trying to give her large amounts of medication.

One particular Sunday afternoon around 12:30, Marcus and his family were sitting in church listening to the preacher speak about *mistakes and moving on.* Sherise and Marcus could once again relate to this particular sermon. The two of them had been through so much over the last year that they really needed to hear an encouraging word.

⁂

At that exact moment, Lasaia's nurse was bringing her some food. She had looked in on her earlier, but she was still in the bed and decided not to wake her. She made her way to Lasaia's door and peeked in through the small square window. She saw her still in the bed covered completely up by her sheets. All she could see was her hair sticking out from under the cover.

"Oh no baby, you gotta get up sometime." The old heavy-set black woman said, parking her food cart outside the door. She reached for her key ring and unlocked the door.

"Wake up sweetie, it's time to eat." The nurse said, shuffling across the floor toward Lasaia's bed.

"You can't sleep the whole day away. You need to…"

The nurses pulled the sheets back and screamed.

"DOCTOR!!!"

She ran from the room and down the hospital hallway. There in the bed was the body of Officer Harden. She had been strangled and thrown in the bed. Her uniform and keys had been replaced with Lasaia's clothes. Officer Harden was notorious for leaving work early without telling anyone so her disappearance the night before came as no shock to her co-workers, but finding her body in Lasaia's bed did. Lasaia had killed the woman and escaped into the night without anyone batting an eyelash.

As the nurse ran screaming from the hospital room, a woman across town placed a bag onto the check-in counter at Hartsfield-Jackson International Airport.

"Hi, how can I help you today?" The clerk asked.

"Yes, I have a reservation." The woman said, handing the clerk a confirmation print out. The clerk pulled up the reservation and said, "Ok, here we go. I'll just need to see your I.D."

The woman pulled out her wallet and showed the clerk an identification card.

"Ok, here you are," he said, handing her the boarding pass, "Your flight is due to arrive in Jacksonville at 2:30."

"Ok, great. Thank you." The woman said, taking the pass and reaching for her one piece of luggage.

The clerk saw the ring on her finger and had to comment.

"That ring is beautiful."

"Thank you. My husband gave this to me years ago. I'm on my way home to him right now. I haven't seen him in a while."

"Well, have a nice flight Mrs. Downing." The clerk said, as she left the counter.

"Thanks again." She said, smiling.

She disappeared through the security checkpoints and blended into the crowd of passengers rushing to get on their flights.

You should always be careful what you tell someone you will do whenever you make…

Promises…

Yeah Real Lovin'

Every time the phone rings
A smile grazes my lips
See…
I know you ring
And…
I linger on each and every one of your words
And…
I even heard Heaven giggle when you spoke
Got me feeling like the dawn
Refreshed and filled with blessings
Yes I say to your invitation
Inviting me to your love
And…
I remember how you first spoke my name
My heart beat an irregular pace
Placed my faith in your arms and there I rested
Guess this is some kind of jones
See…
Because Brotha…
I've loved you before we existed
Yeah…
Before there was light
Planned our first U and I verse before this mankind
Yeah…
Birthing your first manchild
And I know I couldn't have imagined this…so it has to be real
I feel something more than destiny

And…
This feeling won't let me rest
See…
You bring out the best in me
Things about me I've never seen
Or…
Couldn't recognize
Like my eyes being opened and sight is mine for the first time
Yeah…
I'm digging you like that
Digging you like wayward slaves and you're my tunnel to freedom
Yeah…
Digging you like irrigation ditches
Waiting for your rain to come
Yeah…
Deep and profound
See…
I've found more than just a friend
And…
Excuse me but I'm not trying to let it end
I want everyday to be a new beginning for us
Even though us…
Isn't a reality
That's just a formality
See…
I'm working on that
Yeah…
Working…and I don't mind sweating
Letting this permeate my very being
And…
I breathe you
(Inhale)
Oooh what you do to me

All metaphysical
No concerns with what's between my knees
Superceding a need for acceptance
See…
You…you are all I need
Yeah…
My merriment
My nutritional supplement
Because you're my food for thought
Curbing this hunger
Rendering me full and content
Spent the better part of my life praying for you
And…
Who knew I'd find you with just one phone call
All my prayers answered
And…
I've somehow put into words what things unseen seem to speak
Yeah…
Whispers of mutual mellowness
And…
I guess this is some kind of jones
See…
Because Brotha I've loved you before we existed
And…
I know I couldn't have imagined this
So it has to be…
It has to be…
Real

By Tonaka K. Gary

978-0-595-41853-
0-595-41853-8

Printed in the United States
63703LVS00003B/34-36